He watched her lips move . . .

They were lovely, plump and ripe and strawberry hued. But he wouldn't kiss her. Wouldn't trust her. Never again.

"Tell me, Princess," he said and, loosening one wrist, caressed her cheek. "Is your every word a trick?"

"You'd best get used to it, Dancer, if you hope to survive here."

"And what about this?" Lifting his hand, he pressed his palm against her chest. Her heart hammered frantically against his fingertips. "Your pulse is racing. Is that a trick too?"

"No, I really have a heart," she said, but her voice was breathless.

He laughed. "Do you?" he asked, and kissed her. He pushed away, breathing hard, but her eyes remained closed. Her lips opened, and he moaned as he leaned in.

But in that same instant, he felt the blade against his belly. He froze. Her eyes were wide open now, her lips drawn into a hard line.

"Leave it be," she said, gritting her teeth, "or you'll not be rising from that bed for a good long time."

Other **AVON ROMANCES**

THE BEAUTY AND THE SPY *by Gayle Callen*
CHEROKEE WARRIORS: THE CAPTIVE *by Genell Dellin*
DARK WARRIOR *by Donna Fletcher*
HER SCANDALOUS AFFAIR *by Candice Hern*
MASQUERADING THE MARQUESS *by Anne Mallory*
MUST HAVE BEEN THE MOONLIGHT *by Melody Thomas*
WHAT AN EARL WANTS *by Shirley Karr*

Coming Soon

IN THE NIGHT *by Kathryn Smith*
STEALING SOPHIE *by Sarah Gabriel*

And Don't Miss These
ROMANTIC TREASURES
from Avon Books

DUKE OF SIN *by Adele Ashworth*
MY OWN PRIVATE HERO *by Julianne MacLean*
SIN AND SENSIBILITY *by Suzanne Enoch*

LOIS GREIMAN

SEDUCING A PRINCESS

AVON BOOKS

An Imprint of HarperCollinsPublishers

This is a work of fiction. Names, characters, places, and incidents are products of the author's imagination or are used fictitiously and are not to be construed as real. Any resemblance to actual events, locales, organizations, or persons, living or dead, is entirely coincidental.

AVON BOOKS
An Imprint of HarperCollins*Publishers*
10 East 53rd Street
New York, New York 10022-5299

First Avon Books paperback printing: January 2005

Avon Trademark Reg. U.S. Pat. Off. and in Other Countries, Marca Registrada, Hecho en U.S.A.
HarperCollins® is a registered trademark of HarperCollins Publishers Inc.

Printed in the U.S.A.

10 9 8 7 6 5 4 3 2 1

To Carol Holmes,
kind friend, loyal supporter,
and fabulous publicist.
Thanks for everything.

Chapter 1

In the year of our Lord 1819

William Enton, third baron of Landow, detested weddings. They were tedious shams, filled with foolish hope and soppy sentiment—like attending hell in top hat and tails.

Taking another sip of champagne punch, he wished quite fervently that he were home alone with a bottle of Scotch, quietly drinking himself into oblivion. But it wasn't a common occurrence for the queen of Sedonia to host a wedding. Nor was it every day that the viscount of Newburn wed. Will had little choice but to attend the festivities; thus he gazed across the immense width of Malkan Palace's grand hall and managed not to glare.

Festooned with dried flowers wrapped in bright ribbon, the arched, stone chamber was crowded with elegant gentry and bustling servants, liquored biscuits, baked custards, and spirits. But it was the laughter that kept Will from the stupor for which he fervently longed. It was the pure, unmitigated joy.

God save him.

"Will." Nicol's voice brought him from his watery

cups, where he had hoped to remain until well past dawn. " 'Tis good of you to come."

"Not a'tall." Reaching out with his free hand, William clasped the viscount's palm in his own. They had been friends since boyhood—the impoverished son of a drunken baron and the shabbily elegant heir of Landow—sharing their adolescent wisdom and what dark secrets they dared voice. "I wouldn't have missed it."

Nicol said nothing, but there was something in his eyes that spoke of perceived lies. He was changed since meeting his young bride—open and honest and obscenely happy.

" 'Tis the event of the season," continued William, addressing the doubt in his old friend's eyes. "The fifth viscount of Newburn wedding a virtual unknown. Think of the scandal." He emptied his cup and wondered dimly why he wasn't far drunker. But perhaps one had to expect some sobriety after long years of excess.

"Hardly unknown," Nicol countered. "Sparrow is the youngest daughter of Lord Elsworth."

"Sparrow," Will said, and motioned to a passing steward. The server was there in a moment, one white-gloved hand clasped behind his back as he refilled the empty cup. " 'Tis an unusual name."

"She's an unusual woman."

"And Lord Elsworth. I don't believe I've heard of him."

Nicol laughed, but he was often laughing these days. Not like the viscount of old—cleverly cutting, carefully controlled—but more like a ridiculously elated bridegroom on his wedding day.

Dammit! They must have stronger libations than this watery punch.

"They're Irish," Nicol said, but he was already skimming the crowd, searching for the woman he had married only hours before, as if he couldn't quite bear to spend a moment without her near. As if the very sight of her gave him new life. Something ached in Will's gut even before Nicol's search ended. Even before his eyes lit and his expression softened. That something twisted like a blade in Will's innards.

"You're a fortunate man," he said, and wondered if it was true. Oh yes, the maid called Sparrow was bright and bonny and obviously in love. But did love bring happiness or pain? He had no way of knowing.

Damn, he was morose, he thought, and drank again, though he knew he shouldn't. He should be attentive and clever and charming. But what the hell difference did it make? Nicol's attention was already firmly gripped by that shimmery enigma he called his bride.

Had Will been a different sort of man, he might have been fascinated by his friend's sudden union. As it was, he merely felt tired, battered, and maybe bitter. He supposed he was bitter. But it made no difference. He would parry, he would feign, he would hide away any unwanted spark of emotion behind bland expressions and witty conversation as any true nobleman would do. "She is quite lovely," he said. "Indeed, in a certain light she looks very much like our young queen." Except for her hair color and the lively lilt of life in Sparrow's eyes, they could have very nearly been one and the same.

"Do you think so?" Nicol asked, and pulling his gaze from his bride, smiled again.

"Aye, she could be Her Majesty's twin." Will paused, drank, wondered idly. "Or her impostor," he suggested, and the viscount laughed as if the world was naught but a jest set forth for his entertainment.

"Ahh well," Nicol said, admitting nothing. "The peerage is wont to interbreed. Who knows how the Elsworths and the Rocheneaus might be related on some distant branch of their family trees?"

"I could find out," said Will dryly, but Nicol only laughed again.

"It would do you no good, old chap."

"Are you saying she is truly of noble blood or that I could never prove she's some penniless waif you convinced to impersonate our princess for a time?"

Nicol's teeth shone wickedly white against his dusky features. "I am saying she is more noble than any woman ever I've met, and she is not penniless. Indeed . . ." He found her again and seemed to lose his train of thought for a moment. "She is quite accomplished."

Actual interest percolated in Will's tired soul for a moment. "At what? If I may be so bold?"

Nicol shifted his gaze back to Will's, but his eyes still sparked. "Let me just say that at our first meeting I felt a need to invest in her interests."

"Which were?"

"At the time?" He seemed to be looking back, remembering fondly. "Herself."

"And your investment?"

A smile tugged at the viscount's mouth. "My watch . . . though I was somewhat . . . unconscious when I donated it to her cause."

Feelings sharpened like flint in Will's gut. "She's a thief?" Perhaps his tone was a bit harsher than he'd hoped, for Nicol's expression darkened perceptibly.

"As was Jack," he said, "yet I believe you developed a fondness for him."

And his damned cup was empty again. He glanced about, searching for solace.

"Do you know where he is?" Nicol asked.

"Jack?" Damn the stewards. They were never close at

hand when a drink was most desperately needed. "I suspect he returned from whence he came before you and Her Majesty demanded that I save him from the overly zealous guards."

"We didn't demand, Will," Nicol countered quietly. "There was no need."

Will scowled at the lack of drink while he searched for some clever argument, but none came readily to mind, so he trained his gaze on Nicol and turned his thoughts aside. It mattered little to him that even a ragged scrap of a boy had preferred the streets to the cold comfort of his home. " 'Twas a strangely uncharacteristic gesture from a woman of royal blood, I might add," he said. "I've oft wondered what moved our young queen to do such a ridiculous thing. A Rocheneau siding with a street waif. 'Tis unheard of."

"Perhaps she has more heart than you realize."

Will remained silent for a moment, assessing the other's meaning. "As does your bride?" he guessed.

"Aye," Nicol admitted, and, turning his gaze, found hers. Their eyes met with a velvety stroke of contented longing. "As does my bride."

Will glanced away and tightened his grip on the cup. "Well then," he said, and managed to raise the empty vessel for a belated toast. "I wish you much happiness."

"Do you?" Sincerity echoed in Nicol's voice—and him a damned viscount. What the devil had the girl done to him?

"Of course," Will said.

"But none for yourself."

Escape, shut down, employ the shields, hide the emotions. It was as simple as blinking. "Don't be ridiculous," Will said, and curved his lips into what some might call a smile. "I wish far more happiness for myself."

"Then you should grant yourself forgiveness."

Will's head felt far too clear. Flippancy was needed here. Lacking copious amounts of alcohol and dark solitude, it was the best he could do. "I forgive all," he said. "Even your damnably slow stewards. Can't they see I'm drier than dirt?"

"She would forgive you," Nicol said.

Will kept himself from blanching. "I've no idea what you speak of."

"I speak of your wife's death."

The words fell hard and dark into the room. Will felt the blood drain from his face and glanced again at his empty cup. "If you'll excuse me, Cole—" he began and turned away, but the viscount caught his arm.

"It's been two years, Will. It's past. Let it be. The blame is not yours to bear," he said, and in that moment the months of denial and careful avoidance slipped away like storm-swept clouds. But there was no silver lining. Only more layers of bubbling darkness as far as the eye could see, blocking the sun, choking his life, for his failings had not begun with Elli's death. Indeed, they stretched back as far as he could remember. Back to a fragile girl with a wan smile and haunted eyes. He nearly closed his eyes to the memories, but it would do no good, for they tore at him liked rusty knives.

"It was an accident," Nicol said. "Nothing more. You are not to blame."

But he was, for his wife and his sister and . . . dear God, he'd almost forgotten his own son. What kind of man would forget the death of his only child? "And what about Michael, Cole?" he asked, his tone carefully bland, though his soul was roiling. "Was I blameless in his death also?"

"It was an accident."

"And the highwaymen who stopped their carriage, are

they blameless too?" he gritted, and pulled his arm from the other's grasp. "Is that how it is in your rosy world?"

Nicol's expression darkened, but his tone was even. "In my world, in my wife's world, people forgive themselves for their faults, whether imagined or real. They forgive themselves and move on."

"And where might I move on to?" His voice sounded despicably raspy to his own ears.

Despite the hubbub, silence seemed to settle around them like gritty fog.

"She would not have wanted you to suffer so, William," Nicol said. "She would have wanted you to be happy. As she was. Happy and full of life."

He spoke of Elli, of course, for little Caroline had never been happy. Joy had always been suspect at Landow. Atrocities, however . . . He turned his mind restlessly back to his late wife. It was so much easier to think of *her* death, and what did that say of him? "Yes." His fingers ached as he gripped the cup. "It was like her to try to outrun the brigands. So like her. Full of life, unlike her husband, aye?"

"Will—"

"Unlike her husband, who was far too busy to escort her to her sister's estate."

"You had no way to foresee the future. You cannot blame yourself for—"

But Will interrupted him with a laugh, for Nicol was hideously wrong, and yet his laughter almost seemed heartfelt, but that only attested to his noble bearing.

"Do my ears deceive me?"

Will turned to see Cask shoulder his way through the crowd. Robert Stanley, the amiable baron of Bentor, was tall and paunchy, with a round nose that owned his face. Just now it was as red as a summer tomato. The lucky bastard was drunk. "Or did our William actually laugh?"

No one spoke. Discomfort echoed around them.

"Ahhh," said Cask, looking sheepish. "My mistake."

"Forgive me," Nicol said, his expression somber, his gaze steady on William's. "I did not mean to open old wounds."

But the wounds had been open for years. Weeping, painful sores that refused to heal. " 'Tis nothing," Will said, forcefully lightening his tone.

"In truth, 'tis I who should apologize. I fear I have been entirely too fervent. Perhaps I've imbibed a bit too much punch."

"Too much? There's no such thing," tsked Cask, who had earned his nickname through obvious means.

Nicol held Will's gaze for a moment longer, then gave a single nod. "My thanks again for coming," he said. " 'Tis good to see you, Cask, but if you'll excuse me, I go to find my bride."

For a moment William almost reached out, almost stopped him, almost voiced some kind of blathered explanation. But if a man was bastard enough to ruin another's wedding day, surely he was too much the bastard to attempt to mend the chasm he'd caused.

"The newly wed," Cask said, and shook his head as he watched Nicol disappear into the crowd. "The soppy fools always think they have a right to spread their happiness."

Will tried to push past the caustic emotions, yet even intoxicated, Cask seemed to feel the residual tension. But then the man was no fool. Despite his excesses, he was an honored member of the House of Lords. "It's a damned shame," Cask continued. "I've always said so."

Spying a passing server, Will snagged a bottle from his tray, filling his own mug before seeing to his friend's. "What's that?"

The baron of Bentor sighed. "Elli's death."

Will drank deeply and searched for something to say. But witticisms were in short supply. And wine. There wasn't nearly enough wine. He filled his cup again and drank.

"She was a fine lady."

Still no clever rejoinders. Surely it would not be too difficult to agree, to concur, to murmur some sort of idiotic response. After all, she *was* a fine lady.

"Always gay," Cask said, and he was very nearly correct. Despite her husband's blistering failings, Elisabeth had managed the simplest and most dificult of feats. She had been happy. Regardless of him. Or had he only imagined it? Had he refused to see her discontent? Had he refused to admit her sadness, just as he had refused to admit that the route she took to her sister's house was far out of the usual path. Where had she been going? And why? Had there been another man? A better man? Was she glad to be gone? Was even death preferable to life at Landow Manor, where the ghosts whispered like chill drafts from every nook and cranny?

Will drank again, hoping for the blessed insensibility Cask had already achieved. But that easy condition eluded him, so he must, as long custom suggested, fall back on empty blather.

"Her Majesty has given Nicol quite a marvelous party," he observed, but Cask didn't seem to notice. He was still shaking his head.

"Cole was right. You must cease blaming yourself."

Will tried to look through him, to gaze into nothing as he had learned to do, but the damnable laughter distracted him. How much longer until he was unconscious?

"It wasn't your fault," Cask continued, as if he could somehow make it better. As if he understood. But he did not. No one did. But they had no way of knowing he had been a failure long before Elli's death. "She was an independent thinker. To know her you might have almost thought her silly." Cask grinned sloppily. " 'Member the time she dismantled your father's pistol. Damned near blew her own head off."

Oblivion was painfully distant, for Will did remember. She'd been so young then. His parents had adamantly rejected the idea of their union. Perhaps that alone would have been enough to convince him to pledge his troth, but there had been more. She was bright and lively, the antithesis of everything he'd known. His mother had reminded them both that the daughter of a bankrupt squire was quite beneath them. His father had threatened to disown him, but what could they do? Will was the only remaining heir. Edward, robust and commanding, had taken a commission and died at sea. Caroline had quietly succumbed to a fever. She would have married more wisely, or so his mother had said. But Will knew better. She would have dutifully married whom their father commanded, if indeed, she had been allowed to marry at all.

So Will had chosen his own bride, for he had seen the disastrous results of arranged marriages among the peerage. Unfortunately, one could not easily outmaneuver one's own dark heritage. It was in his blood. Like a poison in his veins.

Cask sighed. "Smart as a whip, our Elli. Everyone knew it."

She was that. Inquisitive and clever and quick. But life was strange, and it had turned out that clever and quick wasn't what Will had wanted after all. Despite what he'd told himself all his life, it seemed he wanted a woman like his mother. Lady Edwina. Cold and remote and calculating. Or, at least, that was what he deserved. For he surely hadn't deserved Elli, and she hadn't deserved him. Indeed, she hadn't needed him, not to make her happy, not to make her complete. She was that and more without him.

"Even the old king mourned her loss," Cask said.

Everyone did. Even himself. Didn't he?

"Are you quite well, Will?"

"What?" William asked, then smoothed his face into a semblance of cheer. "Yes, certainly." He lifted his cup in a sort of toast. "But not quite as well as you, aye?"

Cask scowled for a second, then took the bottle and tipped it toward William's cup. "That's because you're far behind, old man. Drink up."

"I intend to."

"Cheers."

"Aye, cheers," Will repeated.

"Ahh, there's Riven," Cask said. "I've promised to speak to him. You'll excuse me?"

"Certainly." And gladly. Will needed no help getting drunk. He was, after all, a man of some experience. In fact, he would see to it immediately, he thought, and emptied the bottle. But memories stormed through his mind like winter clouds.

Elli's laughter. Caroline's sadness. And his own frozen inability to *do*. Caroline had needed so much. Elli had needed so little. Yet he had somehow failed them both.

Everyone missed her. Even the old king, Cask had said. But . . . Will gazed into the empty bottle. His mind twisted muzzily. When had Elisabeth met Sedonia's late king? She'd shown little interest in politics. Which was strange, perhaps, considering the bright enthusiasm she had felt for other things. Science for instance. She had been startlingly well educated for a woman. Lady Edwina had fervently disapproved, but all things botanical had intrigued Elli, and Will could hardly complain, for her interests kept her well involved, so little was expected of him. It had not taken him long to realize he could never give her what she needed. Could never be the kind of man she deserved. Far better that she lock herself away in her musty little cell and fiddle with things in which he took no interest. Herbs and flowers and formulas and suppositions of all sorts.

Yes, Elli was missed because of her effervescence, but she was respected for her mind. Lord Thorndale himself had once asked her to perform some sort of experiment for the crown, but she had refused his request.

It was strange then that Thorndale had come to Landow to deliver his condolences after her death. Strange, Will thought, and frowned into his empty cup. After all, they hadn't really known each other. Had they? But Cask implied that even the old king had mourned. Of course that was ridiculous. Cask was drunk. Although Will remembered seeing a parchment with the king's own seal in Elli's study. True to his cool, noble nature, he hadn't inquired about it, and she hadn't seen fit to explain. But he wondered now. What had she been working on those last few days in her study? Those days when she'd barely slept? Had she discovered something that excited her, or had she simply found isolation preferable to his own dark company?

When the servants had gone through her chambers, they had found no documents they thought significant, though Mrs. Angler had mentioned that the place was "upturned." But Will had assumed it was simply Elisabeth's usual manner. She had never been a tidy person, tending to storm through life. In the confines of her own study, she was all but buried behind her material, her plants, her experiments, her data. The leather-bound books she kept for each procedure had been strewn about her work space. All but the blue one he'd given her for Christmas. That one had never been found, but she was prone to losing things.

She never walked when she could stride. She didn't discuss when she could argue. And he saw little reason to argue back. When she declared her intentions to take the baby to visit her sister one late-December night, he'd made no objections. Neither had he offered to accompany them. She was well able to care for both of them.

And the fire that had consumed her carriage—it was a beacon to the end of her life. Fitting for the exuberance of her existence. She had ordered her driver to flee the highwaymen who had tried to stop them. The hostler had done so and taken a corner too quickly. She and Michael had been thrown out. The lantern had burst, sending hot oil onto the seats, which had been tossed about during the commotion.

There was no mystery there, he thought, and toddled across the floor in search of more libations. But his mind was spinning now, for a thousand details gnawed at the part of his brain that still breathed through the drunken stupor.

The thieves had pursued her. So why hadn't they stolen her rings or the pearl necklace he had given her at their wedding? The necklace that had remained about her throat even at her funeral.

Ahh there. More wine. Finally. Will poured the drink himself, wondering at the coolness of it as it sloshed over his fingers.

Her skin had felt just as cool when he'd first seen her limp body. As cool and pale as the pearls the brigands had left behind.

Cask had suggested that they must have been frightened off before they could finish their looting, but something was amiss with that theory.

His mind tilted, suggesting a thousand shadows. Thieves. Murderers. Fire. Darkness.

How had she known the king?

He stumbled into a tall man with a cane. "Cask!" he said, barely recognizing his own voice. "Where's Cask?"

"Lord Enton," said the elderly gentleman. "Are you quite well?"

"I need to speak to Cask."

"The baron of Bentor?"

"Where is he?" Will snarled.

The tall man's face swam before Will's eyes, and he stumbled.

"You'd best rest a bit before—"

"Where?" he asked again, but someone else spoke.

"I believe I saw him in the garden with a young lady."

"Lady?" Had Cask been with Elisabeth? He'd always admired her. Had she told him about their troubles? Had she told the king? Did they discuss her experiments, her interests? Had another become the confidant he should have been—had yearned to be?

A door opened, and suddenly he was outside. The air felt cool against his face. Refreshing. Reviving. But off to the right a shadow slipped into darkness. Brigands! Thieves! Highwaymen! They were all around him. And they knew things! Secrets to which he was not privy. Why had they accosted his wife? Why had they left the necklace? Where had she been going? And what of the blue leather book? Yes, she oft lost things, but in his heart he knew she would never misplace her data. Where was it?

The thieves knew.

Off in the darkness he heard a hiss of laughter.

"Damn you!" he growled, and tottered in that direction, but just as he turned the corner, a shadow slipped out the gate. "Where are you going?" he yelled. From his left a trio watched him in silence, but he ignored them, for he almost held the secrets in his hand.

Laughter came again, that niggling wisp of humor at his expense, then he was running. Once through the palace gates, he stumbled to a halt. For a moment he remained silent, listening, watching. His exhalation curled like dragon's breath into the chill darkness.

And then, far off, the laughter again.

Bile churned in his gut. Rage roiled in his soul. Revenge! That was what he needed. No more of this cool civility. No more spineless silence. It had gotten him nowhere thus far. Nowhere but alone and miserable.

"Revenge!" he snarled, and stumbled into the night.

Chapter 2

The air outside Malkan Palace was cold, but the baron of Landow felt hot, invigorated, invincible. He was no longer the dolt. No longer the ineffective fool. This night he was a man.

The road tilted beneath Will's feet, and he stumbled, falling to his knees, but in a moment he was up again. "I'll know the truth!" he yelled, and the sound of his own voice, powerful in the darkness, drove him on. He laughed. Freedom, knowledge, action. They were his.

Off to his right a chaise longue paralleled his moonlit course. The staccato clop of the horses' hooves echoed against the cobblestones. The liveried driver took one glance at him and laid the whip to the matched bays.

Fear. It emanated from the elegant hostler, and he should be afraid, for the Lord of Landow was no longer a foolish fop, an impotent leftover stifled by his own nobility. He was vengeance. He was power. Out to learn the truth and demand retribution. But not here. Not in this neighborhood, where his contemporaries hid their sins behind noble titles and posh pretensions.

He stumbled onward. Manors gave way to shops. Shops to ragged cottages. Fatigue crept up his legs. Or perhaps it was the cold that slowed him. But he would not quit.

17

Off to his right, something rustled in the shadows. He stumbled past. He was William Enton, baron of Landow, and nobody's fool.

"Nobody's fool," he said out loud.

A dog growled, all but shapeless in the darkness.

"I'll have my answers!" he shouted. The words fell into the night like a stone in a fetid pool, brewing in silence. But he cared not. He was not afraid of silence, for he had lived it all his life, trapped in his own cowering web. "I'll have answers."

And then, from the darkness someone responded. "But what is it you'll have answers to, guv'ner?"

Will started, his body stiff and slow, his mind reeling. "Who are you?"

"Me?" A small man stepped from shadows into shadows. "They calls me Nome. And how 'bout you, guv'ner. What's your name?"

Will straightened, wobbling a little with the effort. The street was as dark as hell. Not a lantern shone, not a flicker of light gleamed from the fickle moon. "I'll ask the questions," he said.

" 'Ear that?" asked Nome, and even inebriated, Will could hear the grin in his voice. " 'E says 'e'll be askin' the questions."

"That don't seem very polite." Another man stepped out of the darkness, but where Nome was small and lean, the newcomer was broad, hulking behind his mate like a looming gargoyle, his sleeves too short and his gigantic hands bare.

"Now, you mustn't be jumpin' to conclusions, Frank," crooned the smaller of the two. "The gentleman 'ere 'as questions."

"Course 'e does," Frank said, and the two chuckled together.

"What's your question, my lord?"

Will's mind was spinning like a child's top. Like Michael's top. The one Elisabeth had bought him for Christmas. But Michael had been dead for months now, as had his mother, killed by highwaymen.

"You're thieves," he hissed. Happy—no, *thrilled* to have someone to blame.

"Us? No," argued Nome. "We're naught but honest—"

"Oh come now," argued another, and suddenly there were three shadows in the darkness. "You might just as well tell the gentleman the truth, Nome. He deserves that much. They are thieves," said the newcomer. "And murderers."

"What you doing 'ere, Vic?" Nome's tone turned low and gritty, heavy with malice.

"The same as you, I suspect—wondering what such a fine gentleman is doing in this particular part of town?"

"Who are you?" Will asked, for the voice of the newcomer was neither coarse nor common, but similar to his own.

"Are we exchanging niceties this evening?"

"Get lost," Nome said, stepping forward. " 'Fore you find yourself in more trouble than your dear old da can buy you out of."

"I would love to oblige, but I fear I'm a bit short of gambling money this night," Vic argued, "and it occurred to me that this fine gentleman may wish to contribute to the cause."

"You're a thief?" Will rasped, and Vic laughed.

"Consider me your favorite charity."

"I ain't jestin', Vic, back off 'fore Frank 'ere gets 'is back up."

The big man lumbered forward, but in that moment a pistol appeared in the gentleman's hand. Even in the darkness, Will could see the silvery gleam of the short-cropped barrel.

"I know you're a fool, Frank, but if you don't wish to be a dead fool, you'll stay put."

" 'Ey." Nome stepped back a pace, hands uplifted. "I don't want no trouble 'ere."

"Then take your idiot friend and find other prey."

"Idiot." Frank's voice rumbled in the darkness. "I ain't no idiot."

Vic chuckled. "Keep telling yourself that, Frankie. Now, sir, if you'd hand over your purse, I'd be much obliged."

"You're a thief," Will repeated.

"An investor," Vic argued, his tone going hard as he stepped forward. "Now give over your valuables."

Will reached inside his coat, but in that instant a dozen hard memories struck him. Terror and sorrow and raging regret. And suddenly he was charging.

A gun exploded. Fire burned his chest. He staggered. Someone cursed. Another screamed, high-pitched and truncated. The muted sound of shuffling feet filled Will's senses. He dropped to his knees. In the swirling darkness he could see two men locked in each other's arms. They waltzed slowly together, their heads close, their bodies swaying. He heard music, far away and haunting, then, like an open grave, the earth rose up to greet him.

"Get up!"

Will opened his eyes. Fresh snow had fallen. Even in the darkness, the whiteness was startling, and beautiful. In his mind a few soft strains of a Viennese waltz still lingered. Had he been dancing? He turned his head slightly. Snow settled on his cheek, cool and tentative against his skin. He gazed into the ebon sky. Silvery flakes floated down like sparkling manna. His breath curled into the air like frosted angel wings, but he felt strangely warm. Where was he? Who was he, he wondered.

Will. The name drifted down like the snowflakes, but nothing else troubled his flickering mind, no memories, no explanations. But it hardly mattered. He was content. Restful, lazy, and—

"Get up!" The voice came again, and Will scowled, still watching the enchanted flight of the snowflakes. Sleep called mistily. His eyes fluttered closed.

"They're coming. Get out of here 'afore it's too late." Someone grabbed his arm, shaking madly, awakening the pain.

It roared through him like an ogre, shattering his apathy.

He struggled to sit. His head throbbed violently. "Where am I?"

"The watch is coming!"

"The watch." He touched a shaky hand to his forehead. It thrummed with shattering pain. "Who are you?"

"Hurry!" A young man leaned close. " 'Less you want to end up like your friend there."

"Friend?" Will glanced down. His coat was gone, as were his shoes. He turned slowly, bewildered and groggy and there, not five yards away, a body lay crumpled on the dark, scattered snow. Blood! He could smell it now. Could sense it. He scrambled to his feet, bracing himself against the shock as he would against a gale. "Who is that?" he rasped.

Running footsteps sounded in the darkness. The boy jerked around, then swiveled back. The whites of his eyes gleamed. "Stay if you like," he rasped, "but I'm gone."

And with that he turned and sprinted into the night. It

was then that Will saw the blood on his hands. Panic struck him like a blow. What had happened? Who was he?

Music. Pain. Thieves. The watch was coming!

Mind spinning, he stumbled after the boy.

"Halt! You there! Halt!" Footsteps pounded after him. A bullet whined overhead. He was running flat out now, his feet numb against the frozen earth as he raced down an alley. Another shot. Something struck him, nearly knocking him to his knees, but there was no additional pain, only need, only desperation. He stumbled around a corner, but in that instant hands reached out and yanked him down. He tried to fight his way free, but weakness conspired against him. He was already on the ground. No. In the ground. A grave? Was he dead?

"Lie still," someone hissed, and he felt the cold bite of steel against his neck. A gun? He had seen one only hours before. He remembered a blast and jerked at the vivid jolt of memory. "Don't say a word."

He didn't. Couldn't, for he knew nothing. But no, that wasn't true. He knew he wanted to live. Suddenly and certainly. He held his breath and trembled. Foot beats battered past, nearly atop him. He started, cringing away from the galloping watch, but a hand covered his mouth, blocking any sound. The footfalls rushed away. The cold steel eased away from his neck. The hand slipped from his mouth, and the boy crept out from behind him, crouching on the earth above. Where were they? Not a grave, but some kind of hole beside a tumbledown cottage. Will shuttered again, grappling for reality.

"Who are you?" he asked, but the boy was already retreating.

"You'd best get gone afore they come back."

He tried to think, to focus, but the world spun in a hazy circle. Brigands, watchmen, thieves, gentlemen. Fire, dancing, death, music. It all roiled together. He stumbled to his feet, his head throbbing madly. "Who am I?"

"You're dead is what you are if'n the watch finds you."

"Dead?" A woman's face appeared in his garbled mind. Pale and cold and stiff. He winced at the sight, though he didn't recognize it. "Dead?"

"I gotta be goin'," the boy rasped, and spun away.

"No. Wait." Will grappled at his sleeve. "Where am I?"

"This here's Darktowne," he said, "but some folks call it hell."

Pain again, sharp enough to double him over. The world spun slowly around him. "How'd I get here?"

"The usual way, I suspect."

Will straightened. Pain tore through him, throbbing in his chest, dancing in his cranium, threatening to tear his skull asunder. "I don't . . . I didn't—"

"They're comin' back," the boy hissed, and, yanking his sleeve from Will's grasp, sprinted away.

Will glanced behind him. Someone shouted. Pain melded with confusion and pounded in his brain. Survive. He must survive. That's all he knew. There was nothing he could do but follow the boy. He stumbled forward. The earth threatened to swallow him up again, but he lurched on. Something lay across the floor of the alley. Will tripped. Someone cursed, but he was already careening onward. A dog leapt from a doorway, snarling at the end of its chain. Will reeled away. Seeing the alleyway that opened to his left, he staggered in that direction. Up ahead, the boy whipped around a corner and out of sight. He tried to yell after him. No sound came, but he was already running.

Frantic voices garbled behind him.

Another shot rang out. If the pain increased, Will couldn't tell it. But his legs pumped faster. His lungs burned. The alley opened into a street. Nowhere to hide! He charged to the right and stopped, searching wildly. A tilted shay, a fetid pond. But there. A door. He lurched toward it. His fingers fumbled at the latch, fighting to obey the commands of his scrambled brain. But the door refused to open. Someone shouted again. He turned. Didn't want to die. Not now. The footfalls pounded as if they galloped through his very brain.

The pond. Dark and still. It was his only hope. Without another thought, he raced toward it and leapt. The water hit him like the blow of an icy mallet, stunning him on contact. It swallowed his body in aching cold, covered his head. He couldn't see. Couldn't breathe. Must survive. Must hide. But panic was tearing at his lungs like wicked talons. He resurfaced with a start, gasping and frozen.

Men were shouting.

"Where'd he go?"

"Gone."

"Both of 'em?"

"There was only one."

Three watchmen milled about not forty feet from the water's edge. A bit of clarity slipped back into Will's shocky brain. He shivered violently and forced himself back into the hopeless depths. Blackness swelled over his head. Death crept in, cold and ugly, breathing on his neck.

"God's nuts, man, get off me, you're heavy as a bloody gilt."

Will's teeth chattered. He was lying half in the water, his muscles frozen, his hands curled uselessly against the stiff mud. The boy extracted himself from the pond, dripping as he went. Snow melted beneath the rivulet from his body.

"Get up if you're gonna come."

It was almost impossible for Will to follow the boy with his eyes. "Where y' goin'?" Almost impossible to speak.

"The Den. You comin'?"

Perhaps he tried, but it was difficult to be certain, for another spasm shook him, draining any remaining strength. "Can't."

The boy shrugged and turned away.

Will tried to draw his knees toward his chest. Muscles screamed with muted pain. He tried to clasp his legs, to curl into a ball, but his arms refused to move.

"You just gonna die? That what you want?" The young man had returned, shuffling his feet and dripping on Will's back. "You gonna just give up?"

Will barely managed to turn his head, to stare into the boy's face. It was long and drawn, full of angst and life and feeling. Had *he* ever been so alive?

"That's what they want, you know." He jerked his head toward the alley. "You give up, they win."

Who were they?

"Y' gotta fight."

"Why?" He wasn't certain if he said the word out loud. Music was playing again, drowning reality.

"Cuz otherwise you're dead, and you don't get no more chances. That what you want?"

Perhaps he managed to shake his head. Perhaps he forced himself to his feet, or perhaps the boy dragged him up. He couldn't be certain. But after that there was nothing but pain—the staggering first steps that shattered every muscle, the trumpeting sounds that rattled his head, half-seen terrors as he stumbled through the night. And finally, when he knew he could go no farther, when every fiber in him screamed for relief, the movements ceased. His head spun, and his legs buckled.

He had nothing left. He was no one. Vague images of faces entered his consciousness like old ghosts and disappeared completely. Nothing but blackness remained, too deep even for hopelessness.

Chapter 3

"**I** say we cut 'is throat and 'ave done with it."

Will awoke with foggy uncertainty, as if he hadn't quite been asleep, and would never quite awaken. The world around him seemed surreal, swirling with dark, heavy mist and hardly worth the effort of opening his eyes.

"How surprising," drawled a voice. It wasn't one Will recognized, but the tone was familiar, almost bored, but not quite so. Did his own voice sound similar? "You haven't wished to kill anyone for days, Mr. Oxford."

"Well, this un's ripe for it, I'd say."

"That ain't true. 'E ain't done you no 'arm, Ox." The woman who spoke was nearby. In fact, Will could feel a hand on his brow and wondered vaguely if it were hers.

"You ain't done me no 'arm either," crooned Oxford. His voice was low, with something of an Irish lilt beneath the grainy surface. "So that don't mean much does it, missy?"

There was a moment of silence, then, " 'E ain't done nothing, Master Poke. There's no reason ta see 'im dead."

Will lay absolutely still. He was stretched out on his back, and he was injured. That much he knew, but little else, though fragments of memories floated just out of reach, and senses, once fully loaded, niggled at his nerve endings like small fishes at a bobbing hook. The room smelled of tobacco smoke and other things. Mildew maybe.

"Little Gem," said the man with the cultured voice, "I've not known you to be so concerned with another's pain. Perhaps your time at Westheath changed you."

"Changed me? Course not." The tension in her voice had cranked up a notch. "It didn't change me none. I'm the same as I always was, only quicker with me hands."

"Was there someone there whom you grew to cherish? MacTavish perhaps?"

MacTavish. Did Will recognize the name? But there were so many other factors to consider. There was something in the man's voice. A threat wrapped in velvet. Who was he? He could identify none of the voices, but perhaps he'd be able to say the same for his own. The thought made him want to speak, to sit up, to examine himself, though he knew suddenly how he would look. Tall and lean, with shabby brown hair and a jaded expression. His clothes were unkempt. He remembered someone laughing as she told him so. Was he a pauper, then, like the others here?

"You know I'd never fall for no foppish gent. Except . . ." There was the flirtatious edge of teasing in the girl's tone. But there was caution in equal measure. "Except you of course, Master Poke."

Poke. Will searched his memory, but the name drew not a spark of recognition. The man was laughing now, a dry sound that fell like darkness into the room. "Young Gem, still as nimble with her wits as she is with her fingers, despite her infatuation. But what of you, my lady?"

Will could hear him turn away, could feel the mood change ever so slightly. "I've yet to hear your opinion."

" 'Tis because I have none." The woman's voice was smooth, almost singsong, though not quite cultured.

"Truly? None a'tall."

"Is there a reason I should care if he lives or dies?" she asked, and the shock of those words said with such unconcern seemed strangely surreal.

"Our little Gem seems to think so."

"Then perhaps you should spare him." There was a shrug in her voice. "For her."

The Den! For no apparent reason the memory of a young man's face snapped suddenly into Will's mind. The lad had saved him from the watch and brought him here. To the Den, he'd said. But what was . . . Was this the proverbial den of thieves? Emotions flared in Will's soul, but for the life of him he couldn't identify them. Anger perhaps. Or fear. Yes, fear would be appropriate, for regardless of his disorientation it was clear that he had good reason to be afraid. They were discussing his future survival as one might debate rearranging the parlor furniture. But perhaps this was how he spent his days, fencing terror like a master swordsman.

"Might you find him attractive?" The gentleman almost purred the words, and perhaps there was still the hint of a threat, prompting the woman's delay.

Will waited for a denial. Instead, footsteps rapped across the floor toward him, the stride slow and cadenced until he could feel the woman's gaze on him and was tempted to open his eyes. But his survival instincts were strong. That much was apparent, though memory told him nothing.

"Attractive?" She was close now. Close enough to

touch. He was sure of that, and for one ragged instant he wondered if he should grab her, pull her against his body, and hold her hostage against the others. But the thought left him as soon as it came, for he knew too little of the situation. Regardless of his combat abilities, the odds were greatly against him. "Yes," she said. "He is rather attractive in a shabby sort of way. A bit gaunt, of course, but handsome nevertheless."

The room went absolutely silent. Not a soul spoke. The tension was cranked as tight as a phaeton spring, but suddenly Poke laughed.

"My Princess." His footfalls followed the woman's, striding up to Will's side. The smell of sweet tobacco grew stronger. "Always so honest."

"Not always."

"Perhaps not," he said, and laughed again. "But always bold."

"No boldness necessary," she said, daring to disagree yet again. "There is little reason to be untrue, since I'm certain you are not threatened by his ilk."

"Are you? And why is that?"

The room went silent. "Because you are the master," she said.

The answer seemed to please him, for there was a smile in his voice when next he spoke. "But who is he, do you suppose?"

"Him?" Her voice was soft, dismissive. "He looks very much like nobody to me."

"Then 'ow'd 'e get them trousers?" Oxford asked.

"Perhaps the same place you got yours," she said. "From the last man he stabbed in the back."

Oxford made some indistinguishable sound, but Poke ignored him. "So you believe he's a thief, my love?"

"Peter found him in Tayside. Why would a man be

there in the small hours of the night if he could afford to be elsewhere?"

"But remember, my love, I could be elsewhere."

"But once again," she said, "you are Poke. And he is not."

"So you think he is one of our own," he said, and seated himself on the mattress. Will could feel the heat of his body against his thigh. Could smell the cheroot. Mahogany blend. His favorite, he thought, and felt again the spur of surprise as wispy memories swirled through his mind with sleepy slowness.

"Certainly," she said.

"And what else do your fair instincts tell you, my lady?"

Reaching down, she picked up Will's hand in both of hers. He nearly started at the touch, but instincts warned him to remain still. Her skin felt cool and smooth against his. "He's had some education, but he's fallen on hard times."

"How can you tell?"

"His hands are not sufficiently callused for hard labor. But the nails are dirty, the cuticles rough."

"Still a ladies' maid at heart?" Poke asked.

"I was never a maid," she countered. "Not at heart."

He chuckled again. "So he is an educated man. Perhaps a clerk or a merchant who could no longer hold his job?"

A clerk? No. Surely not.

"Perhaps."

"Or possibly a gambler."

He waited, but she didn't respond.

"What say you, my lady? Is our shabby guest a gambling man?"

"I would not know."

"Then what do you know, my love?"

She was silent for a moment. Once again, he could feel her gaze on his face for a prolonged moment, then she spoke. "I know he's awake."

Shock speared through Will, almost prompting him to open his eyes.

"Truly?" There was surprise in Poke's voice for the first time. "He's conscious?"

"Yes."

"And not entering into the conversation?"

"Not as of yet."

"That seems rather ill-mannered, wouldn't you say?"

"Some thieves are."

"Present company excluded of course."

She said nothing.

"Sir, are you awake?" Poke asked, and nudged Will's hip with an elbow.

Possibilities stormed through Will's battered mind. What now? Admit the sham or remain as he was?

"Well," said Poke, "either you are entirely wrong, or our damaged guest is being duplicitous. Which do you think it is, Princess?"

"I am certain you shall find out."

Laughter again, but there was a raw edge of excitement to it now. "You're right, of course. But how?"

The room went absolutely silent.

"What of this plan? If you are correct and our friend opens his eyes in the next few seconds I shall allow you to keep the entirety of what you brought in today. But if you are wrong . . ." He rose to his feet. Evil crowded in, as palpable as a chill wind. "Then you shall wear the brand of my cheroot upon your palm."

The shock of his words hit Will's mind like a blow, stunning on impact.

"No!" Gem rasped.

"You have something to say, Gemini?"

"You can't . . ." She paused. "You don't want to ruin 'er hands, Master Poke. She won't be no good to us that way."

"Ahh, a fine point, lass. Where would you like to bear the brand, my lady?"

Silence, as deep as the night, then, "You decide." Her voice was quiet, eerily devoid of emotion.

Poke laughed. "Cool as chilled wine, aren't you, love."

She made no response, or perhaps her words were drowned in the tumultuous whirring of Will's mind. What now? What would he have done in the past?

"Your arm then," Poke said. "Just above . . ." The kiss was audible. "There. Where the skin is as soft as a baby boy's. Are you ready?"

"Hell's gates!" Gem hissed, and slapped Will's face. It jarred his system like the splash of ice water. But he had to think. To survive. "Wake up."

"I say," Poke crooned, "our Gem has become decidedly maternal. I shall count to three. One . . ."

Maybe if he lunged for the door! But where was the door?

"Two . . ."

Were they armed? How many were there? And what of himself? Was he hero or villain or—

"Thr—"

Will snapped upright, grabbing Poke's wrist. Pain shot like icy arrows through his chest, clogging his breathing, stopping his heart. But he didn't let go. Couldn't.

Their gazes met and clashed. Poke's eyes were large and limpid, his hair dark, his side whiskers curled. His lips were wide and bright, his face handsome enough to be pretty.

"Good Christ." His voice registered little surprise as

he held his slim cigar steady. "You were right again, Princess."

She didn't respond, and Poke laughed. "I should have known you would not have risked your lovely flesh," he said, but his gaze never left Will's. "And, of course . . ." He smiled. "Neither would I. Welcome to our humble home, good sir."

Uncertainty boiled in Will's mind. Had she been at risk? Was he? Who . . . But in that moment he flipped his gaze toward the woman who stood beside him and his thoughts froze. For she *was* a princess.

Regally tall and as trim as a willow, she wore her hair pinned atop her head. Only a few flaxen tendrils wisped down to her squared shoulders, and her expression was as imperious as a queen's, but it was her eyes that stopped his breath. They were blue, but not a hue that made one think of sunny days and posies. They were a silvery, haunting blue, wide and slanted, reminding him of an Oriental cat he'd once seen.

"Fascinating, isn't she?"

It took several seconds for Poke's words to saturate Will's floundering senses. He pulled his gaze from the woman's with a conscious effort and turned his scowl on her master.

"It's time," Poke said, his expression affable, his tone the same.

Will scowled, doing his best to marshal senses too long languishing in the dark. "Time?"

"To loose my arm before I have Mr. Oxford here remove it for you."

William glanced at his own hand. It seemed strangely disembodied, as if it belonged to another, but he moved it, doing so slowly, buying time, assimilating facts. "Where am I?"

"Where do you wish to be?"

Memories flashed like fireflies through his mind, flittering and elusive. Music. Dancing. Emotion, hot as a poker. He had come here for a reason. What it was he couldn't recall, and the swirling thoughts made his head pound like a Celtic war drum. But he dare not falter now.

"I was looking for the Den," he said.

"The Den." Poke sat back down, his hip settling against Will's thigh again. The position seemed odd, stirring a host of uncomfortable feelings in Will's gut, but he remained as he was. "And why would you wish to be there?"

He was tempted to scan the faces of the people who surrounded him, to search for clues, but he kept his gaze steady on Poke. They were thieves. He was certain of that much. And thieves had . . . what? What had they done? Was he one of them? "I'm told they know talent there," he said.

Poke raised his heavy brows. He had a mole above the left corner of his lips. His skin was clear and very pale. "Talent?"

"Aye," Will said and his voice sounded casual, easy. Was that who he was then? A thief, accustomed to dealing with thieves?

He let himself skim the faces around him finally. The girl called Gem was young, not past her sixteenth birthday, her hair red, her eyes green, her face foxy and pert. Oxford was short and broad, built like a bad-tempered terrier, or perhaps like the beast for which he was named. Life. It teemed around him. "I've got several," he said and, feeling a surge of trilling energy, gave Gem a wink, which seemed to surprise her almost as much as it did himself. But he was still alive, God damn it. Alive, despite the odds. "Talents, that is."

"Do you now?" Poke asked.

"What are they?" The lady's voice was cool in the stillness of the room.

He shifted his gaze back to hers, while his mind scrambled for solid footing. What indeed? Was he a pickpocket? He had no idea, but surely they would ask for a demonstration if he claimed such a talent. So what was he? A thug? A highwayman? The thought flared in his mind, causing an eruption of uncertainty.

Princess raised a single brow at him, still waiting for an answer, but his head was filled with flashing memories and tattered scraps of nothing.

He forced himself to relax. Where there was life, there was hope. Wasn't there?

"Your talents?" Poke said.

He turned his attention to the Den's master. "I'm an exceptional dancer," he said.

The room was quiet for a prolonged moment, then Poke laughed, but the willowy woman's expression remained absolutely unchanged, as if her face were carved from purest marble.

"I fear we don't have a great many grand balls here in Darktowne," she said.

He met her gaze straight on and smiled. The expression felt strangely out of place, but he held on to it. "How do you slip into the parties of the wealthy then, Princess, if you don't know how to dance?"

"I don't," she said. "I slip into their purses and out. Quick as that."

"My lady is an exemplary pickpocket," Poke admitted. "Little Gemini is an excellent thief, and Mr. Oxford . . . Well, Oxford's methods are a bit less artistic. And you . . ." He paused. "You dance?"

"When the queen's orchestra takes up residence in

Tayside we may well need him," Princess said. "But until then he'd be nothing but trouble to us."

Poke tilted his head, but didn't turn his gaze away. "Are you suggesting we kill him?"

Will's heart bumped hard in his chest, but he dare not show fear, or even surprise, so he held Poke's gaze for several seconds before turning his attention casually back to the Den's cool lady. Her eyes never flickered. Silence stretched out for an eternity.

"Someone will surely be looking for him, and dead bodies tend to cause unforeseen problems." She exhaled as if disappointed with her own conclusion. "Thus it would be best to return him from whence he came."

"And what is to keep him from returning here on the morrow?" Poke asked. "With a troop of Her Majesty's brave men close behind." There was sarcasm in his tone. Sarcasm and hatred, deeply ingrained and tightly leashed. Princess ignored both.

"We shall cover his eyes," she said. "He'll not remember his path here."

"He doesn't look particularly daft."

"Not daft," she said, though her tone suggested that she didn't quite agree. "Addled."

Poke looked surprised and mildly interested. "How so?"

Reaching out, she touched the side of Will's skull. He winced at the contact. "He has sustained a head wound," she said.

"Hmmm. Is she right, good sir? Are your wits scrambled? Do you remember how you came to visit us here at the Den?"

"It was dark," Will admitted. "And I was in something of a rush, but . . ." He shrugged. The movement sent crisp shards of pain sprinting like darts through his cranium, but he remembered enough to know that some deep emotion had driven him toward the Den, some burning desire. And though he couldn't remember what that desire had been, he would stay on pain of death. "My sense of direction is nearly as well developed as my dancing ability," he said.

"So perhaps Mr. Oxford was correct," Poke deduced. "Perhaps we have little choice but to kill you."

"What do you remember?" Princess asked, but as Will's mind scrambled for an answer, not a color or a fragrance or a scrap of music could be recalled.

She turned to Poke. "His mind is wiped clean," she said. " 'Tis not uncommon with such blows to the—"

"Slate," Will said and knew she was right. His mind was wiped as clean as a child's writing tablet. Except for his name he could remember nothing. And if he hoped to survive he'd best keep that bit of information to himself.

Every eye was trained on him.

"What's that?" Poke asked.

And Will's mind repeated the word rather frantically in his throbbing head. *What?* "Slate. 'Tis my name," he said.

"Slate," Poke drawled, his eyes predatory. "Tell me, is that your surname or your Christian name?"

He forced a shrug. " 'Tis simply what the ladies call me—in London." What the devil was he talking about? But at least he hadn't mentioned Malkan Palace. The thought zipped through his mind. What did he know of Sedonia's royal palace? Who the devil was he? A spy? A mercenary? A trained assassin?

"London. And what do you do there, Mr. Slate?"

How the hell should he know? He couldn't even remember his hat size. "I dance," he said, and Poke laughed again.

"The waltz or the *contredanse?*"

"Whichever will gain me access to the *ton*'s soirees the quickest."

"But how do you secure an invitation?"

Slate—it was as good a name as any, so he gave a shrug and a tilt of the head as if his methods were his alone. He was Slate, clever and accomplished.

"Ahh, a man of mystery," Poke said.

Will smiled.

"If you are so successful, why aren't you in London even now?" Princess asked.

Will shifted his gaze to hers again, hoping naught but confidence showed in his eyes. And why shouldn't it? He had probably been in a score of situations just as deadly and come out unscathed. "I thought my welcome was wearing a bit thin in Londontown."

"The same might be said here."

He laughed and wondered at the unfamiliar sound of it. "Perhaps 'tis not your decision whether I stay or go . . . Princess."

"And perhaps it is . . . Dancer. In truth—"

But her words were interrupted by Poke's laughter. He rose to his feet. "How very entertaining," he said, and gazed almost fondly down at Will. "It isn't every day we have a guest who can raise my lady's hackles, is it, Gemini?"

The girl shook her head. Her hair was the color of a chestnut horse, long, gleaming and loose about her shoulders. Her skin was milky white, her mouth as soft as a baby's, but her eyes showed caution and a worldly experience far beyond her tender years. "You gonna let 'im stay then?"

"Would that make you happy, lass?"

She scowled a little, cautious to the end. " 'E'll be needin' time to mend afore 'e leaves."

Poke watched her with careful interest. "And when he leaves us where do you think he shall go?"

The girl shrugged.

"So you've not met him before?"

"Me?" She sounded genuinely surprised, and Will supposed she was, for though he searched the far banks of his misty memory, there was nothing about her that seemed familiar. Nothing about any of them . . . except, perhaps, the princess's regal bearing. "Course not. When would I 'ave met 'im?"

" 'Tis difficult to guess," he said, and pulled his gaze from hers.

"Well then. 'Tis nearly dark. Time to return to work."

"But what about Slate 'ere?" asked Gem.

Poke raised a brow as he turned his attention back to Will, then he smiled, slow and sly. "My lady shall see to him." He shifted his gaze to hers. "Any objections, love?"

"Certainly not," she said. "So long as you do not care whether he lives or dies."

Chapter 4

The room emptied quickly. Poke closed the door behind him, leaving Will alone with the woman called Princess. He glanced at her, then shifted his gaze to the window. Light was indeed fading, and now that the drama had come to an end, he felt kitten weak and in dire need of a drink.

"Nearly dark," he murmured. "How long have I been here?"

"It has been two days since Peter brought you in."

He wasn't certain if he was surprised. "I've been unconscious that entire time?"

"Have you?"

He turned to look at her. Her upswept coiffure left her neck all but bare. It was long and smooth, as elegant as a swan's above the worn shabbiness of her gown. An interesting contrast. "Tell me, Princess, were you hoping to get me killed?"

She watched him carefully, her linked fingers relaxed against the gray fabric of her skirt. "If I wanted you dead, Dancer, you would have ceased breathing sometime ago."

"You have such power with Poke, do you?"

She narrowed her eyes slightly as if mildly curious. "Who are you?"

"I believe we discussed my name at some length." He felt battered and tired. Weak beyond words, but damned if he weren't still alive. And he would accomplish his mission. Once he remembered what it was.

"I don't believe I've ever known a Slate before," she said.

"And I've not met another named Princess."

She tilted her regal head at him. "Think of it as a title rather than a name."

"Ahhh, as in *the* princess."

"Just so."

She was a sleek, perfectly sculpted column of ice, but he had been wrong. Her gown was not gray, but a faded powder blue. Outdated and worn, it hugged her slender form from shoulders to hips. Above the bodice, her breasts shone as pale and smooth as snowy hillocks. Her waist was narrow, her belly flat, and when she walked, she moved with an elegant, feline grace.

"And where is your kingdom, Princess?" he asked.

She lifted her hands, palms up as she glanced about. "Can't you tell? You are in the midst of it."

He eased back, trying to lie down with a modicum of grace, but pain conspired against him, stabbing deep, and he fell against the mattress like an axed cockerel, squeezing his eyes shut against the ripping agony.

Waves of pain wracked him, but he grappled through the darkness to the surface, finally opening his eyes to find her staring at him as if he were some strange new specimen. It almost made him laugh. Weakness, he was certain, was not a trait she would admire. Perhaps not even one she could comprehend.

"And tell me, Princess," he rasped finally, gritting his teeth and struggling to roll onto his side before he passed out like a misty-headed debutante. "Is Poke your prince?"

"Lie still," she ordered, and, reaching down, moved to reposition his pillow. He fought to raise his head while she waited impatiently and finally shoved the goose-down under his ear.

Stifling a moan, he braced himself against the impact of that slight motion and peered up at a cockeyed angle. "I'm certain I shall be fine without your tender ministrations," he said, when finally able to draw a breath.

She tilted a glance at him, perhaps reminding him that he could not quite lift his head.

He tried a one-shouldered shrug. It hurt like the devil, ripping pain through his entire being. "I can see it distresses you to see me in such anguish."

Her eyes sparkled and for an instant he thought she might smile, but she did not. "Young Peter went to a good deal of trouble to get you here," she said, and, reaching down, tugged the blanket higher on his chest. "We thought you were dead when first you collapsed on our doorstep, but Gemini found a pulse, and the bullet." She stood back, studying him. "It was lodged against a rib. Took her half the night to dig it out." His head felt light. "There was a good deal of blood." And his stomach felt queasy. But certainly even the fiercest warrior felt the same now and again. "You would have thought we'd been butchering pigs in the parlor."

He was going to vomit, he thought, but suddenly she laughed, and he realized that was her intent.

"Who are you really, Dancer?" she asked. "Where are you from?"

He had no way of knowing, but it made little difference, for only a fool would tell her the truth. But then the question remained ... was he a fool? "Have you ever been to Burnbury, Princess?"

"Yes, as a matter of fact, I have," she said, and watched him with curious closeness.

He gave her a smile. "Then I'm from elsewhere."

She canted her head in concession, but when she spoke her tone was painfully earnest. "You don't belong here."

"What makes you think so?" he asked, and tried to turn on his side again, but she stopped him with a hand on his arm.

"Cease your wriggling before you do yourself even greater damage."

Her hand felt warm against his biceps, and he realized for the first time that he wore no shirt, only a tattered bandage that crossed his chest at an oblique angle. He lifted his gaze from her hand to her face. Her Majesty had nothing on this woman, he thought, and realized with a breath-stopping jolt that he knew the queen of Sedonia, had known her for some time. He knew her because he was ... who? Her guard? Her lover? Her hired assassin? Had she sent him here on some secret, royal mission?

"Are you about to swoon?" she asked.

He hustled his mind back to the present. He would wait, would bide his time. The memories were coming, and when they were complete he would fulfill Her Majesty's command and return to her side. "Don't look so hopeful," he said, and forced his muscles to relax one by one. "Men don't swoon."

"But what of *you*?" she asked.

He would have laughed had he had the strength. As it was, he barely managed to speak. "You're dreadfully skeptical, lass, for a princess."

"And tell me, Dancer, have you known many?"

Memories crowded in again, pressing on his head, but he forced them back. Closed the door. Waited. "Dozens," he said. "Or perhaps they only said they were princesses in an attempt to gain my favors."

She gave him a sliver of a smile. "If you can manage to sit up," she said finally, "I shall find you a bite to eat."

His stomach felt queasy, and his mind unsteady, but he knew what he needed. Knew beyond a shadow of a doubt. "I could use a drink."

She stared at him. "Ahh," she said finally. "So you don't swoon, but you pass out."

He shrugged as if conceding, though in truth he couldn't remember. Perhaps he'd been drunk when he'd come here. But what man of action didn't enjoy a drink now and again? "Entirely different," he said, and she nodded.

"It matters naught to me. I believe Poke has a bit of Scotch in his chambers. I shall fetch you some."

Struggling against the light-headed pain, he managed to sit up, then glanced around the room. Perhaps at one time it had been an elegant parlor of sorts, for it was large, with a high ceiling and arched doorways. But now it was nearly empty and hopelessly dingy, containing a few ratty pieces of furniture and a large stone fireplace. He lay on a divan of sorts. A crack ran diagonally across the wall opposite him, and a yellow stain covered a good portion of the ceiling.

Where was that drink? His chest hurt like hell. Glancing down, he saw with some surprise that blood had seeped into the drab bandage, and his hands were shaking.

Footsteps sounded in the hall, and he looked up eagerly as she entered the room. She carried several things, but the mug was all that mattered. It seemed to take her forever to cross the floor, but finally she was there. He curled his fingers around the cup. His hands shook in earnest now, but he managed to bear the Scotch to his lips, to drink deeply. His nerves eased immediately, and he tilted his head back, appreciating the warmth in his belly.

It wasn't until then that he realized she was watching him.

"What does it cost you to feed that habit?" she asked.

"I take it you don't approve of drinking spirits." He felt more himself already. Whoever that was.

"As I've said, it matters little to me either way. I was just curious what you've given up for it."

Tattered memories flashed through his brain. A funeral. He'd been drunk when they'd put her in the ground. But who was she? And how many times before that had he been just as inebriated? Memories of loss, of pain, sparked through him. He'd lost much. Is that what had driven him to his present occupation? Perhaps he had nothing else to lose. But in the back of his mind a tiny, disembodied voice taunted him. He still had his life. And if he wished to keep it that way, he'd best be careful with the Scotch, for despite his formidable abilities, he would need all his wits about him to survive the Den. Yes, for now he would put the drink aside. Just one more sip then. He took it. Warmth and comfort eased into his system. He kept his palms wrapped around the cup, but why should he not?

She was still watching him. He could sense her gaze on his face and looked up, feeling irritable. "You seem strangely judgmental," he said, "for a thief."

"Not at all," she argued. She was not a woman who agreed easily. "The bottle is nearly full. Would you like me to fetch it?"

He snorted derisively. "I'm certain this will be plenty," he said, but when next he glanced into the cup, he realized it was already empty. Something like panic burbled in his gut.

"Are you all right?"

He raised his gaze to hers, calming his nerves. The queen's man could surely not be so easily unnerved. "I've been shot in the chest," he said, and felt marginally better for the explanation.

"Ahhh. And so I should pity you?"

He gritted his teeth. His stomach roiled. "Did you know that some consider women to be the gentler sex?"

"Do they?"

" 'Tis a widely accepted theory." His legs shook, and he spasmed.

If she noticed she made no sign. "Maybe things are different here than in . . . somewhere else."

He stared at her askance, trying to follow the conversation.

"Somewhere else," she explained. "Where you come from. Are you quite well?"

"Certainly. I'm . . ." But suddenly his stomach was being ripped apart. "No," he growled and leaning over the edge of the bed, spewed out the contents of his stomach. Spasms wracked him. He calmed, shivered, and spasmed again. It took him several moments to realize she had thrust a wooden bowl beneath his head. Rolling carefully back onto the mattress, he concentrated on breathing. Every fiber ached as if he'd been beaten.

Her face swam into view. His own felt hot, his mind the same, hot and heavy and barely coherent. "You poisoned me," he accused and she laughed. The sound seemed loud and strangely musical in the closeness of the room.

"Don't be daft, Dancer. You've poisoned yourself," she said, then there was nothing but blackness.

"You feelin' any better?"

Will looked about. Lucidity wavered in. Gem sat at his bedside, her wide eyes round and innocent, probably deceptively so.

"What day is it?" His voice was hoarse and broken.

"Don't know. You need to eat somethin'."

He croaked a sound.

"You want somethin' to drink?"

He managed a nod.

"I think Master Poke's got some Scotch. I'll fetch—"

But his guts twisted threateningly at the thought. "Something easier on my stomach maybe."

"Sure. Master Poke may be a—" She stopped, pursing her lips and glancing toward the door as if expecting a ghost at any moment. "We eat good 'ere at the Den. We got beer."

"So you're still alive." Princess stood in the doorway.

Will's stomach roiled at the sight of her. Anger flickered through him. She was probably the person he was supposed to bring to justice, he thought, and hoped quite passionately that she was. "Disappointed?"

She laughed. "Not a'tall," she said. "I'm looking forward to seeing you dance."

He scowled, but she was already gone.

"Want some beer?"

His chest ached like hell and his head felt fuzzy, light and hot and disoriented. Spirits would steady him, but his stomach crunched at the thought. "Water," he said. "Just water."

"You don't drink no alcohol?"

His stomach cramped. His muscles twitched with pain, keeping him silent for a moment.

"I knowed a bloke once." Her voice was soft and her expression dreamy, strangely out of place in this den of thieves. "He didn't drink nothin' but cider."

Will tried to relax, though his body felt tight, his mind fidgety and irritable. "A past lover, Gem?"

"What?" She pulled herself from her reverie with a visible start. "Oh. No. 'E weren't no lover. Just . . ." She paused and dropped her eyes. "You want some cider?"

"Can't give Vic's killer cider," said a voice from the doorway.

Will glanced up, startled. A young man stood there. He was tall and lean, with a long angular face and eyes that sparked with mischief.

"What you talkin' about?" Gem asked.

"Yes, Mr. Bald." Poke entered the room, running a slow hand over the lad's shoulder as he passed by. "What are you talking about?"

"Him," said the boy, and easing away from the doorjamb, strode jauntily across the scarred floor. "He killed Vic."

Holy hell. So he was an assassin! But who was Vic and why had he killed him?

The room went silent. Princess appeared in the doorway again and stopped to watch. The women's gazes met and parted.

"Perhaps you should start at the beginning of this tale," Poke said, and seated himself not far from the lone window. A bit of horsehair stuffing poked through a hole in the chair's arm, but despite the state of the furniture, Poke looked as elegant as a princeling.

"I went down to Fairberry Square," Peter said, his

voice rife with excitement. "Thought I'd see what was hatchin'. Sometimes there's soldiers there."

"I thought I told you to stay away from the soliders, Peter," Princess said.

The lad grinned, letting his gaze stray to her. "You needn't worry. They think they're safe from rubbish like me. But you can distract 'em easy as kittens. There was a time—"

"Perhaps you should stick to the story, lad," Poke suggested.

He nodded and pulled his gaze from Princess. "Like I says, I was down to Fairberry Square, talking to a maid or two when some lordy blokes come strollin' up. They was dressed all proper. One of them had a bulge just there." He pointed to his own ribs. "Now me, I thought, here's a likely-looking piece of work, but before I could figure how best to relieve him of that unsightly bump I heard what they was sayin'."

He paused again and took a bite of the apple he held in one angular hand.

"Are you going to share the conversation with us?"

The lad grinned around his mouthful. "They said Lord Rambert was dead. Now that didn't mean nothing to me, but then the other one asks how it happened." He took another bite. Expectation shone in Poke's eyes, but it was surely not so sharp as the burning impatience that seared Will. "And the second bloke said, he was knifed to death . . . in Darktowne . . . by the old mill."

"And that's where you found our friend, Mr. Slate," Poke surmised.

Will's guts coiled up tight. A knife. Good Christ! He'd killed someone with a knife.

"Yeah, that's where he was, right as rain. Lyin' there in

the snow with a ten-inch blade lyin' between him and another bloke. Only I didn't know the dead bloke was Vic."

Will's stomach twisted and his hands shook.

"Lord Victor Rambert," Poke crooned, and smiled eerily as he turned his gaze toward Will. "Would you like to expound on the situation, Mr. Slate?"

Emotions erupted in the silent room, but for the life of him, he couldn't guess what they were. Who the devil was Victor Rambert and why had he needed to die?

"Mr. Slate?"

Will shrugged, fighting for normalcy, for memory. Should he deny it? Admit it? Boast? It was impossible to guess, for the world was a gray haze of uncertainty. "There's little enough to tell," he said, his ridiculous words sounding vague to his own ears.

"Little enough!" Peter jerked forward as if on puppet strings. "Tell us how you done it. Vic was the meanest son of a bitch . . . Begging your pardon, Princess . . . in all of Skilan. Maybe in all of Sedonia."

So Peter wouldn't mourn his passing, but what of Poke? If Slate were to offend the master of the Den, there was little hope he'd escape with his life. In fact, he was entirely uncertain he'd make it to the door, deadly assassin or not.

"We wait with bated breath," Poke said.

Will considered shrugging again in an attempt to appear casual, but the reminder of pain dissuaded him. "It was dark," he said instead.

"But you knew who he was?"

"His name didn't matter a great deal to me at the time."

"He had a gun," Peter reminded them, gazing around at the audience. "Slate here only had a knife."

"So 'e's dead?" Gem's voice was soft, her face pale.

"Dead as a stone," Peter said. "And he was stabbed in the chest. Not in the back like some might." Not a soul spoke.

"Well," said Poke finally, "I believe this calls for a drink. Princess, will you bring us a drop of the good whisky?"

She disappeared without a word.

Will watched her go. Felt his stomach cramp. He shouldn't drink it, he thought, but when she handed him the glass, he took it, watched his fingers curl around the smooth surface, watched the amber liquid slosh gently.

It trembled slightly as he brought it toward his lips.

"A toast," Poke said, interrupting the moment. Will steadied his breathing. "To Mr. Slate's survival." They all raised their glasses. The lovely fluid sloshed gently to and fro. His throat felt painfully dry. "And to Lord Rambert's death."

They drank. Slate bore his glass to his lips with greedy haste. It felt like heaven on his tongue. He closed his eyes to the lovely burn and reminded himself to drink slowly.

"So our guest does gift us with multiple talents," Poke said, swirling the whisky in his glass. Will watched the movement. "He is not only a dancer." He smiled when he said it. "But he is a killer as well."

William said nothing. Two-thirds of the whisky remained in his glass. He took another sip, remembering to savor. He'd only have this one, for he dared not become intoxicated. Not in this company.

"Did he come at you, Slate?" Peter asked. "Or was it you what found him?"

The whisky called to him. "It's not something I care to talk about," he said, and took another careful sip.

"Not talk about it," Peter said, and laughed.

"Ahh," sighed Poke. " 'Tis just as I thought. Our Mr. Slate is a man of mystery. Or perhaps . . ." He watched Will carefully, reminding him not to empty his glass immediately as his body begged him to do. "Could it be that we have a man of morals in our midst?"

His hands felt steadier and his head clearer, but his stomach was cramping up again. Perhaps Gem had been right. Maybe he should have eaten something first, but the whisky was so smooth, so lovely and golden in the glass.

"Which are you, Mr. Slate?"

Will tightened his hand on the smooth crystal and hardened his muscles against the pain in his gut. "I am . . ." His stomach knotted up hard, pitching him forward. He fought down the agony, gritting his teeth against it.

"My apologies," Poke said. "I didn't realize you were averse to strong drink."

"I . . ." he began again, but in that moment his stomach revolted, violently rejecting the offensive alcohol. He shivered, hacked, and shivered again. When next he glanced up through burning eyes, the room's occupants were staring at him with various expressions of disgust.

"Well," said Poke. "It looks as if our conquering hero is not yet quite mended. We'd best leave him to his rest."

The room emptied as if he were a leper. He dropped his head against the wall, drained and sick. Aye, he might well be a hero, but he was most certainly a drunkard.

Chapter 5

"**S**late. Master Slate. Wake up."

William did so groggily, opening his eyes and wondering for a hazy moment who Slate was. But memories came rampaging back in, bombarding him with information that seemed to rip through his body and trample his mind.

"You gotta eat something, luv."

Gem was back at his bedside. He'd wondered a dozen times why she bothered. After all, she was a thief, and he was nothing to her. He remembered seeing her in the misty days and nights just past. She had repeatedly brought him water, and though his stomach had rebelled at the idea, he'd managed to keep it down. Now she sat with a bowl on her lap. Steam curled dreamily into the air, and the smell of cooked onions filled the room. Surprisingly, his stomach didn't churn at the scent.

"I brought you some broth."

What he wanted was a drink, but the memory alone was enough to make his gut twist. His hands trembled as he tried to sit up.

"'Ere then," Gem said, and setting the bowl hastily aside, hurried to assist him. The process was almost bearable.

"There you go," she said, pulling the blankets up to his waist. "Feeling better?"

If better was being flailed from the inside out, then yes, he was feeling quite grand.

"You got some color in your cheeks today."

He drew a careful breath and dared turn his head to look at her. "What color is that?"

She stared at him for a moment, then laughed. "Well, they ain't gray no more."

"Ahhh." He carefully rested his head against the wall behind him. "Is that good?"

She was silent so long that he finally turned back toward her, though the effort cost him dear. Her baby's mouth was pursed, her eyes wide and strangely limpid.

"I thought we was going to lose you there for a while."

Were there tears in her eyes? His mind bobbled at the thought, for he seemed strangely certain suddenly that in the entirety of his life, no one had ever cried for him. But perhaps that was the way of gladiators and warriors.

"But things is lookin' up now," she added. He tried to think of something to say, but no witticisms came to his battered mind. "Come along now, you gotta eat."

What about his mother? Surely there had been one. And surely she had cared.

"Luv," Gem said.

He glanced at her. "I'm not sure I can."

"You gotta," she said, and there was such feeling in her tone, such intensity that he couldn't help but ask why.

She drew a deep breath. "Cuz otherwise you'll die." There had been several hours during which he'd been certain death was undesirable. Now, with his hands shaking and his body screaming, he wasn't quite sure.

"And . . ." His mind was attempting to solve this puz-

zle, to work out the mystery of this place. These people.
"You'd care?"

"Course I'd care."

"Why?"

She stared at him an instant, then lowered her gaze to
the bowl she'd retrieved from the floor. "I ummm . . ."
She paused, glanced up, then flickered her gaze down
again. "Vic . . ." She cleared her throat. "Lord Rambert
weren't no friend of mine."

He wanted to ask why, but it was none of his concern,
and, if the truth be told, he could see the answer in her
eyes. In fact, the feelings there were so raw and intense
that he had to look away.

"I'm sorry," he said.

"Sorry?" She looked up quickly, blinking. "What for?"

"That you . . ." He paused, wanting to tell her that this
shouldn't be her life. That she should be elsewhere, somewhere safe and pampered and loved. But what did he
know of love? Or any of those other things? "I'm sorry
you suffered at his hands."

"Well . . ." She put on a smile. It wobbled a bit at the
corners, but it was an honest expression, and for a moment he couldn't help but wonder how many of those he
had seen in the years before he'd become Slate. " 'E won't
be 'urtin' nobody no more, will 'e?"

There was such gratitude in her expression, such kindness that it was a struggle not to look away. "Why are
you here, Gem?"

She glanced up with the spoon halfway to his mouth
and the bowl propped beneath it. "Cuz this is where I
live," she said, and urged him to eat. He did so with some
misgivings, but the broth tasted delectable, beefy and
soothing.

"Why?" he asked.

She shrugged and gave him another spoonful. "It gets damned cold on the streets."

"Surely you have other options."

"Like which?" She brought the spoon up again and he watched her as he took it. She had a sharp little face, with eyeteeth that slanted in and hair that glowed like a flame. Devil's hair, his mother had called it.

The idea stopped him cold, for his mother was there, in his mind—a woman of noble birth, well dressed, perfectly coifed and cold as death. Which meant that he was what?

A gentleman?

"You feelin' sickly again?"

He marshaled his senses, calmed his nerves. "There must be scores of men begging for your hand," he said, and when he glanced up, he couldn't help but believe it, and that truth stunned him, for she was a thief. But his mother had been a lady, and he knew in the depths of his questionable soul that there had not been a droplet of kindness in her. And perhaps that was what had driven him to his present life. But what the hell kind of life was that?

"Not 'ardly," she said, but there was something in her eyes, a misty hopelessness that drew his thoughts from himself. She was so young, so wounded, and despite what he might have endured, it was a Sunday in the park compared to her life. He knew that without question.

"One man then?" he guessed.

Her gaze skipped to his and her hand stopped midway to his mouth. "What makes y' say so?"

"Because you're kind," he said. "And tough. Pretty."

Her eyes dropped again. "Maybe once upon a time there was a fella who woulda wanted me, but—"

"You two flirtin'?" Oxford stood in the doorway. He was shorter and broader than Will remembered, but all memories were hazy at best these days.

"What you doin' 'ere?" Gem asked. "Poke says you was supposed to be in Wayfield."

The Irishman took a step into the room. Tension crowded in with him. "I thought maybe our friend 'ere might be sidlin' up to me lassie, so I 'urried on back. That ain't 'appenin', is it?"

Will watched him carefully. He had seen evil before, that much he knew, but it was rarely so openly revealed. So blatantly flaunted. Amongst the gentry it was usually hidden behind preening smiles and perfect toilets.

"I ain't yours, Ox," Gem said. "And you better get gone afore the master gets back."

"Poke . . ." Oxford said, and snarled a smile as he stepped closer, "ain't my master."

Gemini looked pale, but her back was stiff and her hands steady. Steadier than Will's, certainly.

"What about you?" Ox asked, staring at William in open challenge. " 'E your master?"

Dammit to hell! Maybe he'd been as fierce as a poked lion in the past, but he felt as weak as a bunny just now, hardly ready for a battle with this ogre. "What do you want, Oxford?" he asked, and his voice was surprisingly level. Impressively steady. Like a warrior's. Like a hero wounded in battle.

"What do I want?" snorted the Irishman, and stepped closer still. "I'm wondering what *you* want."

"I'd like to eat my broth in peace." And that was the truth if ever he'd spoken it.

"And to fuck the girl 'ere!" the other snarled. The words were startlingly sharp, and in that moment Will realized the Ox had been drinking. He could smell it on the man's breath and, despite everything, the scent was intoxicating, scrambling his wits, tilting his insides.

"Is that the way of it?" rasped Oxford. The smell of whisky was almost overpowering, but Will steadied himself as best he could, remembering to focus on the business at hand. The business of living. It took a hell of a lot of concentration these days. Had it always?

"You'd best find a bed and sleep it off, Oxford," he said, and hoped his tone conveyed bored self-assurance. The cocky words of an armored gladiator instead of the sniveling whine of a foppish fool.

But the Irishman laughed "Oh I'm planning on finding a bed," he said, and, reaching out, yanked Gem to her feet.

The soup bowl flew into the air, then landed, spinning crazily on its side. Gem gasped and tried to jerk away, but Ox held her tight. Her expression was defiant, but she couldn't control the horrific dread in her eyes. Dread he'd seen before, though he didn't know where. Revulsion twisted Will's gut, but there was nothing he could do. This was the life she'd chosen after all. The life of a thief. And Oxford had a knife. Will could see the handle protruding past the belt of his greasy trousers. He could see the knife and remember fresh, startling pain with shocking, breathtaking clarity. The smell of blood. The taste of terror.

Oxford looked into William's eyes, and there he saw the horrific truth, for he laughed as he yanked the girl to his side.

She struck him with a fist to his chest, and he backhanded her across the face. She staggered away, still held by her wrist.

"Ox!" Will said, startling himself. The single word fell

like poison into the room, and Will's stomach roiled with dark premonition.

The world went silent. Ox turned slowly. "Aye, laddie?" he said, and pulled his knife from his pants. It gleamed in the firelight but no more brightly than his eyes, which glowed like a rabid wolf's. Half-human he looked. Savage and wild and capable of anything.

Death yawned in William's face. Death and pain and lingering agony, and for what? A thief? Fear gnawed at him. Ox grinned. Evil shone dark and deadly in his eyes.

"Come on then, lovey. 'E ain't gonna bother us none," growled the Irishman, and jerked Gem forward. She whimpered, and it was that sound, that tiny whisper of fear, that galvanized Will's resolve.

"Let her go, Ox." For a moment William truly didn't realize the words came from him, for it would be so much more practical to turn away, to remain in the darkness of his own mind, but he could see the imprint of Oxford's knuckles against the paleness of Gem's cheek. And suddenly he knew—he was not the kind of man to let the innocent suffer. Not when there was something he could do to prevent it.

"What'd you say?" The Irishman seemed surprised to hear him speak.

Will drew a deep breath, steadying his nerves. So even heros felt fear. That much was clear. "I told you to let her go."

Oxford squared off, still holding Gem's wrist. "And tell me, me bonny lad," he said, and smiled again. Death shown in his eyes. "Why might I be doin' that?"

Fear was a glacial block in Will's gut, slowing his motions, gumming his thoughts. His muscles screamed. At any moment, the Irishman was going to charge, and there was little he could do in his present state. Except maybe pray, if he remembered how. He tried that immediately, a garbled, incoherent thought to a God he hoped would favor boldness, no matter how idiotic. "Because Lord Rambert's dead." The words seemed to come of their own accord.

Oxford snorted. "Who the fuck is . . ." But he stopped, and his eyes narrowed.

Will remained absolutely still, letting the silence soak into the room, and praying like hell it would drown his terror. "I believe you may have called him Vic."

The Irishman scowled. " 'E's dead?"

"Yes."

Oxford shrugged, but there was caution in his eyes now. "And what's that got to do with you, bonny boy?"

"I'm sure you're not as daft as you look, Oxford." He said the words with a stiff grin, though he would have sworn he had no wish to die. "It would almost have to be true. So I'll let you work it out in your own mind. We were in Tayside. I was wounded. Vic was killed. That tell you anything, Ox?"

The Irishman snorted, then shuffled his feet as if to turn away, but he didn't. Instead, he kept his narrowed eyes steady on his adversary. "You sayin' you killed 'im?"

William watched him for a moment, saw the fear spark in his eyes, saw the caution overtake the bravado, and for a moment he almost felt whole, almost felt human. Indeed, his hands were all but steady, and he smiled.

Ox shifted his feet about again. "You're a fuckin' liar."

Will managed a shrug. Pain shot like slivers toward his heart, but he held on tight to the grin. Held on tight to the other's gaze.

"Let the lass go," he said finally, and his voice was low and even, though his muscles were cramped tight with gnawing tension.

For a moment, Will was certain Ox would refuse, was certain he would lunge. Could already feel the pain of his strike against the burning ache of his chest.

But instead he snorted and shoved Gem aside. "Don't 'ave time for a skinny wench like 'er nohow," he said, and, turning like a stiff-legged mongrel, stalked off.

The room fell into absolute silence. From some distant part of the house, a door slammed. Will's body went limp. In fact, he let his head drop back against the wall behind him and hoped to heaven he wouldn't be sick again. After all, it might undermine his role as conquering hero.

Footsteps pattered across the hardwood as Gem hurried to gather up the bowl from where it spilled onto the floor. "I'm ummm . . ." she began, and Will turned to glance at her. She straightened, searching for words. "Y' didn't 'ave to do that," she said. "I can fend for myself."

Better than he could. He was now quite certain of that, and yet something had flared in his chest. Something hot and wild and irresistible. Like life itself.

"Still, I'm . . ." The word "grateful" seemed to quiver on her baby's lips, but it didn't quite come. "I'll fetch more broth," she said, and, turning, hustled from the room.

And he was going to piss in his pants. Fucking hell! His bladder felt weak and his stomach queasy, and he wondered vaguely if he could make it to the window before spewing his guts onto the street. Or perhaps, while he was at the window, he might just throw himself out before the facts were revealed to one and all, for he knew the truth now. Oh yes, he knew. He'd been in a drunken stupor when he'd been accosted by the two thugs who had left Rambert dead on the street.

"Should I fetch your bowl?"

He raised his eyes with some difficulty. Princess stood in the doorway, her brows slightly raised as she stared at him. Will held his palms flat against the coverlet lest she see them shake. "What bowl is that?"

She smiled a little, and though she still looked like royalty, there was something of the imp there now, the glimmer of a small girl who knew his innermost secrets. "You look rather green."

He leaned his head back again since he had little choice, but continued to watch her as she walked across the floor toward him. Her russet gown was a bit short for her regal height, but the lines of it were smooth and graceful and somehow managed to make it look as if she were gliding instead of walking.

Gem entered the room with a steaming bowl, and Princess turned toward her. The women's eyes met. Not a word was spoken for a moment, then, "You'd best put a cold cloth on that cheek," Princess said.

Gem's gaze dropped. "It'll be fine."

A flicker of something feral snarled in the woman's eyes, but in an instant it was gone, replaced by her usual cool demeanor. "Aren't you working the fights tonight?"

"Soon as it gets dark."

The princess nodded. "The gulls don't like to see their doves bruised. Go get some rest."

The girl was silent but glanced toward Will.

"You needn't worry on his account, Gemini. I'm not planning to strangle him."

" 'E needs to get something in 'is stomach."

"Then he should eat."

The girl almost seemed to blush as her gaze flickered toward the floor. " 'E ain't strong enough to feed 'isself."

Princess glanced at him again, raising a single brow as she did so. He gave her an innocent stare.

"Very well," she said, turning back. "I shall feed the weakling myself then."

Gem skimmed her dubious gaze from Princess to Will, then, seeming to decide he was safe enough in the other's hands, she nodded finally. "I think I'll lie down then if it ain't no trouble."

Princess made no comment as she took the bowl from the girl's hand and made her way across the floor to take the seat abandoned by Gem.

The room fell silent, and she let it, for she had no wish to speak with him. He didn't belong there, and the sooner he was gone the better. For him, for herself. She kept her gaze on the bowl a moment longer, then glanced up, making certain her expression was superior. Dismissive. "Are you certain you wouldn't rather have a drink?"

He almost seemed to shiver at the thought. So he was a drunkard. But what else was he? Wounded, certainly. He was pierced and battered and abused. And yet that abuse hadn't caused the pain she saw in his eyes. It was something deeper, darker, worse. And so she would not look. Could not afford to.

"Perhaps just the broth this day," he said. His voice was deep, quiet, melodious.

She tightened her hand on the spoon and shrugged as she dipped it into the soup. He opened his mouth obligingly. She could feel his gaze on her face, but refused to glance up, for there were secrets in his eyes. Secrets and pain she had no wish to see.

"I thought you wanted me gone," he said.

And she did. Immediately. Before it was too late. But she merely raised a brow and forced herself to meet his eyes, to see the pain and not care. "Surely a quick recovery will hasten your exodus," she said. "And even a clever fellow like you might find it difficult to heal if you starve to death first."

"Gem was about to feed me."

And perhaps she should have allowed that. But Gemini seemed so fragile these days, and the bruises on her cheek . . . She forced her mind away and shrugged dismissively.

"I saw Oxford leave," she said, keeping her tone steady, her eyes the same.

He watched her. Perhaps he was a killer. Perhaps he was a thief. But in the depths of his eyes, beneath the cynicism, beneath the cleverness, she saw the wounded child. "And?"

She dropped her gaze, though she knew she was a fool. "Gem has enough troubles without defending you."

He said nothing for a moment, then, "My apologies."

She snapped her gaze back to his. Perhaps she had expected anger, or wounded male ego, but there was neither. Sincerity and regret shone like candlelight in the depths of his amber eyes.

She jerked hers away. She should mock him, sneer. "He's dangerous," she said, and wished to hell she hadn't spoken, hadn't walked in, hadn't realized he'd risked his life for a thieving street waif he'd met only days before.

"Truly?"

She glanced up, stunned. "You don't think so?"

He smiled. Though she couldn't seem to pull her gaze from his, she was sure of it, for there was something barely remembered in the deep recesses of his eyes. Was it humor? Was he laughing at her?

"I think I wet my breeches," he said.

Surprise shook her. It was as dangerous as caring. "You were scared?" she asked, and kept her voice steady as she dipped the spoon back into the broth.

"I'm not daft," he said. "Not completely anyway."

"Then why did you do it?"

"Do what?"

She tightened her jaw, resisting the effort to insist that he leave, now, immediately. "Why did you risk your life for Gem?" she asked.

There was a pause as she watched the spoon dip back into the bowl, as she felt his gaze burn her face.

"I've no idea," he said finally.

"Do you always do things for no reason?" she asked, and braced to meet his too expressive eyes once again. They struck her like a blow.

"Yes. I believe I do," he murmured, and for a moment she couldn't quite seem to breathe.

"Why are you here?" she asked, and desperately hoped her tone was level, uncaring.

"Same reason as you, I would guess."

"You're in love with the thieves' master?" Her voice was marvelously flippant.

His was the same. But did a muscle tic in his jaw? "Love is it, Princess?"

She shrugged. "Close enough," she said, and fed him again. His eyes were steady now. And blessedly blank. She almost sighed with relief. "Don't make me tell Poke who you are," she murmured.

She felt his surprise, but was there fear, too? If so, she couldn't hear it in his voice. "I believe I've already told him."

Anger washed through her. "Oh yes," she said. "Slate, wasn't it? Master dancer and occasional murderer?"

"Murderer?" His eyes narrowed. "I was led to believe—"

"Princess!" Poke's voice pierced the stillness like a bullet, but she almost managed not to wince, and when she turned with careful slowness, he was already standing in the doorway.

"You'll not guess who's back," he said, making his way across the room.

"Then you'd best tell me," she said.

He turned his attention to her with a sly smile. Fear skittered up her spine.

"Isn't this lovely?" he crooned, and, slipping his arm about her waist, drew her in for a kiss. It was difficult to breathe, impossible to speak. "I see you've been tending our guest."

She hammered down the panic and turned her eyes to his. "He shouldn't be here," she said, and Poke smiled as he released her.

"He hasn't been bothering you, has he, my love?"

She could feel both men's gazes on her. One cold and predatory, one dark and questioning. She dared meet neither, for she must keep her wits. Must be cautious.

"Yes," she said. "He has."

Silence dropped like a stone into the room. She clasped her hands and raised chin. "He does nothing all day but eat our food."

It was quiet for a moment longer, then Poke laughed. "So impatient, my love. The man is wounded."

Relief flooded her, but she dare not show it. Regal disdain was far safer. "And so he is of little use to us."

"But soon you will teach us your value, aye, Mr. Slate?"

"As soon as I am—" the other began, but in that moment his eyes shifted toward the doorway.

And there, illumined by the flickering firelight, stood Nim, his wheat-toned hair disheveled, his face smudged. He was safe. He was whole, after many long weeks. She opened her mouth to whisper his name, but Slate spoke first.

"Jack!" he rasped, and silence fell like poison into the room.

Chapter 6

Will stared, dumbstruck and confused. The boy's name was Jack. That much he remembered. But nothing else, and with that knowledge came a baffling barrage of raw emotions—frustration, bitterness, and blinding hope that made his head throb with the aching need to remember.

"You know each other?" Poke's question shattered Will's scrambling thoughts, bringing them to an absolute halt.

He sat perfectly still, not daring to breathe. For the truth was there. Almost within reach in the dark recesses of his battered mind.

He was in the Den. In Darktowne. In Sedonia. But he did not belong there.

Memories sifted slowly in, like dust motes in a slanted shaft of sunlight. Faces, names, colors, emotions. His father's glower. His sister's quiet voice. The sculpted garden where he'd first kissed his wife-to-be.

It was true. All of it. And yet it seemed ultimately surreal in the light of the past few days. He was neither a respected spy nor a fearless assassin. He was William Enton, third baron of Landow, and a drunken fool who'd not accomplished a valuable service in the entirety of his life.

71

He was the weakling son of a vicious lady and a soulless lord. A man so flawed that he could not even convince a tattered street waif named Jack to remain under his protection.

The truth pierced him like a knife, sending his mind spinning.

But was it the truth? Or was the truth what you made it? He had saved Gem from the Ox. Had saved her despite his wounds. So perhaps . . . He shifted his gaze back to Jack's narrowed eyes and saw William Enton reflected in all his cowardly weakness. If the lad spilled the truth, Will would surely be lucky to live out the day. *That* was the truth.

But the boy remained absolutely silent, neither loosing the tale of their acquaintance nor denying any existed. Will's mind spun, trying to assimilate the facts, but memories were bombarding him with ferocious intensity. His wife's funeral, his sister's sadness, his ward's escape. How many people had he failed from behind the cushy comfort of his title?

"Nim," Princess said, "you didn't tell me you danced."

It took Will several resounding heartbeats to realize she was addressing the boy. Several more to draw his attention back to the business of survival.

"Or perhaps our guest here wasn't dancing when you met him. Pray, does he have some other skills that would assist us here in the Den? Something besides eating our food?"

Tension lay like lethal toxins in the room, but Princess looked completely removed from it. Above it. And why wouldn't she be? She cared not whether he lived or died. So if he hoped to survive the day, he'd best think of something soon.

"I believe we first met in Wayfield," Will said, finally

managing to speak over the hard thrum of his heart. "I was swindling a baron from Lexington at the time."

Jack's gaze remained steady on Will's, though he spoke to Poke. " 'E weren't in Wayfield," he said, and stepped farther inside. Dread crowded in with him. Poke appeared nonplussed, but he always wore a deadly smug expression, making it impossible to guess his thoughts. And he stood between Will and the door—unfettered by wounds or cringing cowardice.

Will turned his gaze to Princess, but her perfect features betrayed nothing. No help there. No help, and Poke was watching him like a raptor. Waiting to tear him apart.

" 'E were at the docks," Jack said.

Will breathlessly skimmed his gaze back to the boy.

"The docks?" Poke repeated.

"Aye." The lad nodded as he took a swig from the mug he held in one hand. " 'E was tryin' to relieve some overdressed gent of 'is snuff can."

"I thought you said you were not a pickpocket, Mr. Slate."

He'd been attending Nicol's wedding when the madness had taken him, when he'd stumbled, drunk and bitter, into Darktowne. The memories struck him with sudden viciousness, scattering his thoughts like suncured chaff.

"That's the truth and no mistake," said Jack, shifting his gaze from Will and pacing to the fire where he warmed his hands. " 'E ain't. Never saw such a bungled job. If'n I 'adn't come along at just that second, 'e'd a been buggered fer certain."

Will tried to keep up, to marshal his thoughts. In fact, he forced a smile, though it felt ghoulish and green.

True, he had taken the boy into his own home, had fed

and clothed him. But if the weak-kneed baron of Landow had had his way, he would have let the guards take the boy and spared himself the inconvenience. Only a royal order had convinced him to assist the lad. And now here they were, their positions twisted about.

"I owe you, Nim," he said, though he would have sworn himself incapable of speaking, no matter how true the words.

"Aye." Jack's expression was absolutely sober. Far too somber for a lad of twelve. But maybe he was thirteen now. Maybe another birthday had come and gone without note. The boy looked lean and tired and savvy. But spirit gleamed in his eyes. There was no mistaking that. "That y' do." He turned his gaze to Poke. "What's 'e doin' 'ere?"

"As it turns out, Mr. Slate here killed Lord Rambert."

The lad swore, and his face went pale as his gaze spurted to Will's.

"You killed Vic?"

A thousand explanations welled up inside Will. The boy was a thief, a scoundrel, far beneath his own lofty station. So why did he feel a burning need to explain himself, to seek forgiveness. How had it come to this? "There was a fight," Will said, and forced himself to shrug.

"I don't believe it." All eyes turned to Princess. Will had almost forgotten the danger from that front. Had almost forgotten her rabid animosity. "Why does he sit here day after day if he can lift a snuffbox?"

" 'E can't," said Jack, and drank again. "They'd a 'ad him strung up to the nearest yardarm if'n I 'adn't distracted the gent."

"And pray how did you manage that?" Poke asked.

"I lifted a pocket from a nearby soldier and galloped through the crowd with 'im breathing down me neck. Thought 'e 'ad me for a moment, but I skimmed between two boatmen and nipped away." He glanced at Will again. Not a glimmer of a lie showed in his eyes. "Didn't think I'd see *you* again. Not 'ere anyways."

"That's because he doesn't belong here," Princess said.

"So quick to judge," Poke chided, and slipped his arm about her waist. "How do we know whether or not he can shoulder his weight when we've barely given him a chance to wake up. And let us remember . . ." He eased his fingers beneath her jaw, tilting her head up. She met his eyes with easy bravado. "He did kill Vic. Surely we owe him for that if for nothing else, aye, my lady?"

She made no comment, but eyed him coolly.

"Now . . ." He kissed the corner of her mouth. Something curled up tight in Will's gut. "I want you to promise you'll be nice to our guest."

"He doesn't need—"

"Hush," Poke said, and slipped a finger over her lips. Will clenched the top blanket. "Promise me you'll tend to Mr. Slate."

"I—"

Poke smiled and shushed her as he leaned closer. "Promise me," he said, and Will waited for her to spill her doubts, to end his life, but when she spoke her words were innocuous.

"I believe he can care for himself. At least so far as eating is concerned."

"Ahhh, but we want him to feel welcome, don't we?"

She didn't answer.

"I'll tell you what, if you take care of him yourself—with your own clever hands." He skimmed his fingers down her arm and lifted her hand in his own. "I'll give you something special."

"Gem would be better suited to tend him."

Poke chuckled. "No maternal instincts, Princess?"

"None that I've noticed thus far."

He laughed. "Then perhaps you'll tend him because he's so very forceful. After all, Lord Rambert was not easily bested."

She merely stared, and he laughed again.

"Then you'll do it because I insist."

She canted her head in apparent concession.

"Good," Poke said, then kissed her neck where the hair was swept away from the delicate curl of her ear. "But I think I'll give you that something special just the same," he whispered and grinned. "Good night, Mr. Slate."

Will was never certain whether he responded. But in a moment the couple was gone, leaving the room in utter silence. He eased his hands open, forcing himself to breathe. From across the room, he could feel Jack's gaze on him and brought himself jerkily back to the present.

"Thank you," he murmured, but the boy shook his head.

"Leave 'er alone." His eyes were narrowed, his lips pursed. "She don't need no trouble from you."

"I was runnin' to beat hell," Peter said. "And they was right on my heels. Like a tail on a donkey's ass."

Gem glanced up from where she was stitching a scrap of lace over a rent in the bodice of a well-worn gown. It seemed a strangely domestic scene, with the two of them seated in front of the fire. A young, pretty couple, her mending, him spinning a yarn. They'd been there for some time, allowing William to listen as he dozed. Recovery took a tremendous amount of effort, especially when worn memories kept crowding his senses.

"I warned you not to work Overstreet afore mid-afternoon," Gem said. "The watch likes to bet on the cocks there."

"Aye, there was a slew of 'em," Peter admitted. "Fat buggers they was, too. Wouldn't a thought they could get off their arses to save their own mums."

"Looks can be deceiving." Gem portrayed the wisdom of all mending women. Age, it seemed, had no bearing on the matter.

"Ain't it the truth. They can run like racehorses if'n you lift their purse."

"You shouldn't go down there till later," she repeated.

"P'raps, but if I didn't, I wouldn't have got this, now would I?"

Will couldn't see what the lad produced, but his acquisition was impressive enough to make young Gem gasp.

"Rubies! Saints nuts, Pete! Does Poke know 'bout this?"

The room went silent, and the air felt heavy. "I been thinkin'," Peter said, his voice barely a whisper. "Maybe you should have it."

"What? No! Peter! You're talkin' crazy. That must be worth a good fortune."

"It's a pretty thing all right," he said. "But it don't shine near so bright as a jewel like you, Gemini."

"Peter—"

"You could take it," he repeated. His voice was still soft, but there was excitement in it now, passion. "Go back to Teleere."

"There ain't nothin' for me in Teleere," she said, but had there been a pause before her rejoinder, a heartbeat of consideration?

"There's nothing for you here, Gem. Go back. P'raps if you talk to him—"

Footsteps sounded in the hallway.

"Put that away! Put it away!" Gem hissed.

Apparently he did so, though Will couldn't tell for certain. The footfalls crossed the ratty rug and stopped beside his mattress.

"Are you awake?" Princess's voice was quiet but brooked no nonsense.

He opened his eyes slowly, tried to sit up, and stifled a groan with manly discipline.

She scowled down at him, apparently unimpressed. "It's time to change your bandages."

From the far side of the room, Peter and Gem murmured something and departed together. Keeping Poke's share of the spoils couldn't be healthy, but neither was continued association with him. Will scowled, almost wanting to call them back, to warn them. But who was he to interfere? He was naught but a concussed drunkard with a faulty memory and a poor chance of surviving the day.

"Is something amiss?"

He turned his scowl on her. "I'm wounded," he reminded her.

"And cross."

"My apologies," he said, "if I'm unable to match your own stellar jocularity."

She gave him a look that spoke volumes. A sailor would have been hard-pressed to curse as eloquently. "Perhaps you need a drink," she said, and he would have been unsurprised if she had batted her eyelashes in conjunction.

He snorted, refusing to allow her to see the tremble in

his hands. "Tell me, Princess, am I such a threat that you would be rid of me at any cost?"

Her expression of faux shock was priceless, but in the same instant, she pulled the pillow out from beneath him. His head struck the cushion below with a reverberating thud. "You wound me," she said.

He gritted his teeth against the resounding pain. "I've dreamt of it."

"And after all I've done for you." Seating herself beside him on the mattress, she gripped his arm. He managed to sit up with some assistance and immediately wished he hadn't, for she was already yanking at the knot that held his bandage on his chest. "But I suppose I cannot expect gratitude from the likes of you."

He scoffed, but her hands were already brushing his chest. They felt cool and smooth against his flesh, and regardless of her hasty ministrations, something stirred inside him. Something hot and hard and dangerous, but he kept his breathing steady, his attitude remote.

"Your gentle concern touches my heart."

Her eyes met his. A smooth brow raised. "I'm so glad you've noticed."

Her fingers brushed his nipple. His body jerked, remembering feelings long forgotten and best left alone.

He fought for control, but she was breathtakingly close, and he couldn't help but stare. She was life itself, no matter how she tried to hide the fact behind bored expressions and toneless statements. "Of course it would be more touching still if Poke didn't have to bribe you to tend me."

Her gaze spurted to his and suddenly all flippancy was gone, replaced by steely sobriety. "Stay out of it, Dancer."

"Out of what?"

She tugged the cloth away from his chest. Perhaps there was some pain, but she was touching him again, scrambling his feelings. Surely he couldn't be attracted to this woman. He knew nothing about her, except that she wanted him dead, and although that should be enough, it had been forever since he'd been touched by a woman. Of course he'd be moved. It had nothing to do with her. She was a thief, for God's sake. But her hands felt like magic against his skin, her fingers nimble and light as she washed his wound.

"Do you hear me?"

"What?" he asked, feeling lost and foolish and strangely disoriented.

"Who are you?" she hissed, but her lips were achingly pretty, bright and mobile and tempting. He leaned toward them.

Her lips parted, then she pressed her cloth against his wound.

Pain flashed like lightning in his chest. He hissed through his teeth and found her eyes. "What the devil are you doing?"

"Who are you?" she repeated.

But he'd found his wits. "Vic's killer," he said, though he knew it was a lie. There had been two thieves there in the darkness with him that night. One of them had killed Vic. It didn't matter which one, just as long as they didn't show up to contest his story.

She stared at him for several seconds, then breathed a laugh. "It doesn't matter who you are," she said. "Not to Poke."

She was so close, so breathtakingly lovely that he found he wanted nothing more than to make her stay. "And who is Poke? Truly?" he asked.

Her eyes flitted to his. "No one to fool with," she warned.

He forced a casual shrug. "Then 'tis a good thing I've no intention of fooling with him."

Their gazes flashed and melded.

"You're far out of your depth, Dancer."

And being pulled deeper still, but he dare not admit it.

"Am I?" he asked.

"Aye. You've no idea what you've stumbled into," she said, and pulled her attention back to his wound.

"Then why don't you tell me, Princess?"

She pursed her lips as she smoothed some noxious ointment over his injury. The movement of her fingers against his flesh felt ridiculously erotic, but in a moment her gaze flickered to his again.

"Perhaps he seems harmless to you, Dancer. Perhaps to a man of your—"

"Harmless!" He caught her wrist, unable to bear another intoxicating second of her skin against his. "What the hell are you talking about? He was going to burn you!"

She scowled directly into his eyes as if she didn't remember, as if the glory of being with the master sucked such thoughts from her head.

"Your arm," he reminded her, turning her wrist so that the delicate underside showed. It looked hopelessly fragile, enticingly smooth. He pulled his gaze from it with an effort. "What kind of an animal would do that to someone as . . ." Don't say it. Don't. ". . . breathtaking as you."

The words fell like darkness into the room. He'd known better than to loose them, of course, but they were free now, and he couldn't seem to regret them, or to keep from stroking her skin. It was as soft as he had imagined. He smoothed his knuckles along her forearm and down her wrist where her tendons were taut and sharp. Her hand was narrow, her fingers long and delicate. He eased them open and felt her shiver. He imagined them against the heat of his flesh and couldn't help but kiss her there in the center of her palm.

"Quit that!" she hissed, and snatched her hand away.

He barely managed to catch her elbow. "You're too good for him," he rasped, but she yanked her arm free and turned away. Hope went with her, spilling him back into the darkness. "William," he added, and waited for her to turn back, waited for her eyes to meet his with a jolt. "My given name is William."

Chapter 7

William. She stared at him, knowing she should leave, knowing she should back away and never return. But he'd trusted her with his name. And it suited him. He would be called Will by those who loved him. Willie, when he was child, before the world had wounded him. Before the sorrow came to live in his eyes.

"My apologies." His voice was soft now, quiet and deep, a poet's voice. "'Tis just . . . I cannot understand. Why would a woman like you tolerate such abuse?"

"A woman like me?" She should not speak, should not return to his bedside, and yet she did, slowly, warily. "And what sort of woman might that be, Dancer?"

Emotion burned in his eyes. Passion just muted by caution.

She sank onto the cushion beside him, letting her hip graze his. Did he catch his breath at the contact? Did his eyes darken and his muscles contract? "What kind of woman am I?"

He lifted his gaze to hers, but it was the caution that spoke. "I wish I knew."

"I was certain Vic's killer knew everything."

"Were you?" He reached for her hand, and though she knew better than to allow his touch, she did so. His skin was dark against hers, his fingers warm and strong.

"No," she said, ignoring the flash of feeling that spurred up her arm. "I'm lying."

"About everything?" he asked, and smoothed his thumb along her knuckles. Disconcerting feelings shimmered across her skin.

She forced a shrug. "Everything I can think of."

His expression remained sober, but there was something in his eyes, a hint of laughter, a trace of momentary happiness. And it captivated her, not only because she was certain it was a rare thing, but because she knew, somehow, that few others would recognize it, would see beyond the shield he showed the world.

"Don't tell me your name's not really Princess," he said.

"I believe I explained that before."

"Ahh, yes, I am to think of it as a title."

"Exactly."

"And your given name?"

He asked flippantly, but there was interest in his eyes, and the truth could do no harm. Many knew her Christian name. She drew a slow breath and let it out just as carefully. "My mother named me Shandria," she said. "I was born in England, some distance from Bradford."

"Shandria," he repeated, sounding surprised, as he turned her hand and skimmed his thumb across her wrist.

She stifled a shiver, calmed her breathing. " 'Twas my grandmother's name," she said. "And what of you? Why William?"

He shrugged. "Perhaps they thought Slate too graceless."

"They were considering the name Slate for their . . ."

She paused a moment, watching him and guessing. "Heir?"

"*Heir!*" He laughed, but the sound was not quite right. "You make me sound like nobility."

"Do I?"

Loosing her hand, he skimmed his fingers up her arm, sending frenzied shimmers in all directions. "I'm flattered that you think so highly of me," he said.

"I didn't say I think well of the nobility."

"Ahh." He sighed as if deeply disappointed. "Then it's just as well I am known as naught but Slate."

"By the ladies in London," she said.

"Of course."

"And what are you doing here in Darktowne, William?"

He lowered a brow as if disconcerted that she had chosen this one time to call him by his given name. "Just trying to make my way in the world, lass."

"Surely it would be safer in your . . ." She shrugged. "Manor house."

His lips lifted roguishly at one corner, as if amused by her foolish guess, and for once she could not read his eyes. "Believe this, sweet Shandria," he said. "If there were somewhere safe for me, I would be there now."

"So you are penniless?" she asked, and, for just an instant, allowed her fingers to brush his.

A muscle jumped in his dark bristled jaw, but his tone was light when he spoke. "I am not quite so inept as Nim implied."

How did he know Nimble Jack? And what were his plans? Thievery, as he suggested? Thrills? Or were his motives more sinister, something she could not see in his eyes. Had he come for revenge? She felt her heart contract. Had Nim done something to bring this man into their midst? "I would suppose not," she said, and leaned forward a bit so that her breasts nearly touched his chest. "Not if you were able to kill Lord Rambert."

"He was just a man," he said, and, reaching slowly up, brushed a strand of hair from her face.

She let her eyes fall closed. "No," she whispered.

"No?"

She opened her eyes, finding his immediately. "He was an animal."

"Did he . . ." His tone was taut suddenly, his eyes turbulent, as if he cared, as if he could not bear to see her hurt. But she dare not let that sway her. Weakness was death. Hers and others'. "Did he touch you?"

"It doesn't matter now." She dropped her gaze again and smoothed her thumb along his. "I'll not have to worry about him again." She made certain her smile was tremulous when she lifted it to him. "And I have you to thank," she said, and leaned closer still.

His breathing seemed shallow, but his eyes were as deep as forever. "You needn't thank me," he said.

"But I want to," she countered, and, moving closer, kissed the corner of his mouth. Feelings sizzled through her like lightning, but it was nothing, just the thrill of her duplicitous scheme. "And I think . . . perhaps . . ." Lifting her hand, she touched his jaw with her fingertips. "Maybe you could be rid of Poke."

"Poke!" He started back against his pillow, the single word breathy.

"Hush," she warned, letting her eyes go wide and shifting them toward the door. "You must be careful." She touched his jaw again. "He's nobody's fool."

"But . . . you're lovers," he said.

She breathed a laugh as though he must surely understand her reasons. "He's a powerful man."

"He forces you?" His voice was rife with rage, and for
a moment she almost quailed. But she must not.

"There are all kinds of force," she murmured. "All
kinds of power. At first . . ." She glanced at his lips. They
were full and slightly parted. "I thought you had none.
But I see now that I was wrong. If you killed Vic . . ." She
shrugged. It was not difficult to appear nervous. "You
could do the same to Poke." Her breast touched the bare
skin of his chest, burning on contact. "He's dangerous,
Will. More so than you know. And devious. No one is
safe from him."

The muscles of his chest flexed beneath her breasts.
"Then why do you stay?"

"Why?" She breathed a careful laugh. "Where would I
go that he could not find me?"

"Surely if you went back to England . . ." he said, "or
even—"

"You don't understand," she hissed. "He is powerful
beyond your imagination. And wealthy."

"Then why does he remain here?"

"He has plans," she murmured. "And Darktowne
amuses him. We all amuse him. Perhaps that's the true
reason. I can't say for certain, but this I know—people
will suffer every day that he lives. Gem . . ." She winced,
though she had not meant to. "She acts as if she's invincible, but underneath . . ." She tightened her hand in his
blanket. "She's just a child, Will, with a child's dreams.
A child's . . ." Her voice broke. What a marvelous ac-
tress she was.

"He would harm Gem?" His voice was low and deep,
poet turned warrior, and for a moment she was over-

whelmed by his feral protectiveness for a girl he barely
knew.

"Who are you?" she whispered, but continued before
he could respond. "Can you be so naive? Aye, he would
harm Gem. He would harm anyone." She slid her hand
onto his chest. His heart thrummed hard and heavy
against her palm. His skin was warm, his eyes intense,
and for an instant she wanted nothing more than to tell
him the truth. To bare her soul. But fools did not survive
in Darktowne. "Perhaps you were sent to us for a reason."

Silence sat between them, pulsing in rhythm with his
heart, then she kissed him. His lips were firm, his touch a
promise as he reached up to cup her face. But she did not
believe in promises. She drew slowly back, holding his
gaze.

"What do you want me to do?" he rasped.

She drew in a sharp, quiet breath, as though she
couldn't quite believe he had asked and leaned eagerly
against his chest. "If I obtain a weapon, could you use
it?"

Something flared in his eyes. "Guns—"

"No," she whispered, and glanced furtively toward the
door. "It must be done quietly."

"Why—"

"If Ox hears . . ." She shifted her gaze, then settled it
restlessly back on his. "If any of them hear, we'll—"

"Any of who?"

"You don't think he controls Darktowne alone. He's
got men stationed everywhere. We're surrounded by his
hirelings. Protected, he says. But who protects us from
them? From him? Do you think you can simply walk into
the Den?" She shook her head and dropped her attention
to his chest. His wound was healing, but he would for-

ever bear the scar. She brushed his skin with her fingertips and watched his nipples tighten, his muscles dance. "Strong as you are . . . brave as you are . . ." she said, lifting her gaze imploringly to his eyes. "You were only allowed entrance because Peter brought you."

"The house is guarded?"

She laughed, but the sound was soft and breathy. "All of Darktowne is guarded. But I can get us out . . . if Poke falls."

"Where would you wish to go?"

"It matters not. I shall find a job," she whispered, and found that, despite her duplicity, the idea was dreamlike in its beauty, enticing and seductive. But she was not easily seduced. Not anymore. She smiled wistfully and found her equilibrium. "My mother didn't raise me to be a thief. I simply . . ." She closed her eyes and opened them slowly. "But she didn't raise me to endanger another either." Drawing back slightly, she kept her gaze on his. "My apologies," she said, and shook her head as she straightened further. "You're not the sort to take another's life. Not that sort a'tall." Bending down one last time, she kissed his lips. "I'm sorry, Dancer. I'll not—"

"Get me a knife." The words seemed to be torn from him.

She froze. "What?"

"He'll not harm you again," he vowed.

"You'll kill him?" she whispered. She was stretched across his body, hip to hip, breast to chest.

"Aye, lass," he murmured. "I will."

She moved closer. He closed his eyes to the caress.

"You fool!" she hissed.

He snapped his gaze to hers, but she was already on her feet, enraged and shaken and terrified. Aye, she had tried to trap him so that she might use his own words against him, but a part of her had hoped it could not be done, that he would not be so foolish.

"You can't best Poke!" she snarled, and curled her fist into his blanket as she drew herself close. "If he knew your plans . . . if he even suspected . . . he'd butcher you like a bloody shoat. He'd eat you alive."

"So this was all an act?" he asked, and the little boy was gone from his eyes, replaced by jaded amusement. "It was all a game?"

She laughed, feeling dirty and old. "You make it too easy to call it a game, *William.*"

"Then you plan to tell Poke."

She snorted and turned away, but he was out of bed in an instant and spinning her toward him. She scrambled to escape, but he pressed her up against the wall, pinning her with his body, and she stilled, shushing the panic. He held a wrist in each hand, and one of her legs was propped between his. She could feel the hard length of his erection against her thigh.

He closed his eyes, breathing hard, and she wondered for a moment if he would faint. But determination won out. He dragged his eyes open, though his head listed slightly to the left. "Will you tell him?" he asked, tightening his grip on her arms.

"Will you leave the boy be?" she hissed.

"What?" His knees buckled, almost spilling him to the floor, but he managed to stay erect. "What the devil are you talking about?"

She tried to jerk her arms away, but he held tight, wrestling them back up the wall. "How did you know his name?" she rasped.

He frowned as if trying to remain lucid, to follow her line of thought. Did that mean that his appearance in

Darktowne had nothing to do with Jack? Or was he such an exquisite liar? And what of the swirling emotions in his eyes? Did they lie, too? She would have sworn it was not so, but she had judged men wrong before and could not afford to do so again. "Like the lad said, we'd met before."

"In Berrywood. I remember," she said, and watched him.

"That's right," he said, and not a hint of a lie showed in his eyes.

"Where you were swindling a gent," she whispered.

He watched her lips move, and leaned slowly nearer. But only a fool would be tempted. Only a fool, regardless of his shabby beauty, his wounded eyes, his . . .

His lips touched hers. Desire whispered through her like billowing mist, drowning her in silvery shadows. She allowed one moment of pleasure, one heart pounding instant of titillation, then, "But Jack said you were at the docks," she murmured.

He drew back with careful precision, his eyes steady on hers. "Tell me, Princess," he said and loosing one wrist, caressed her cheek. "Is your every word a trick?"

"You'd best get used to it, Dancer, if you hope to survive here."

"And what about this?" Lifting his hand, he pressed his palm against her chest. Her heart hammered frantically against his fingertips. "Your pulse is racing. Is that a trick, too?"

"No, I really have a heart," she said, and he laughed.

"Do you?" he asked, and kissed her again.

Desire swirled through her like windswept clouds, but she would not play the fool. She turned her head and struggled to control her breathing. "Promise me, you'll not bother Jack," she murmured.

He scowled at her. She could feel the intensity of his gaze. "Why? What is he to you?"

"He's a boy," she said, skimming her eyes to his. "An innocent—"

"Innocent!" he scoffed, and tightened his grip when she tried to pull away. "He's no more innocent than you are, Princess. In fact you're quite similar in . . ." His eyes narrowed. "Is that it, then? Is he your son?"

The thought was strange, but almost soothing. Almost kindly. She could imagine the boy as an infant, soft and peaceful in her arms. Had she borne him, she would have been able to protect him, to—

"Yours and Poke's?" he asked.

The dream disintegrated, leaving naught but a bitter taste behind. "Leave him be," she said. "He can do you no harm?"

His lips twitched. "But perhaps he already has."

She held her breath. "Did he steal from you?"

The world was absolutely silent, then he laughed. "From me? Of course not. I'm naught but a thief myself, remember? But perhaps he's stolen from others. Others who are looking for him. Who will pay handsomely for—"

She hadn't planned to threaten him physically. But she always had a knife hidden in her skirts, and suddenly it was in her hand and pressed up against his groin.

She watched him jerk at the brief prick of pain.

"Princess," he said, "there's seems to be a blade pressed into a rather sensitive part of my anatomy."

She gritted her teeth and pressed harder. He tensed. "Leave him be," she warned. "He's been hurt enough."

"Pardon me for saying so," he said, "but speaking of another's pain at this particular moment seems rather . . . ridiculous."

"Promise me," she rasped. "And I'll not tell Poke you plan to kill him."

"I didn't say—"

"Make the vow," she ordered, and gave the knife a careful twist.

He didn't even flinch. "Is he yours?" he asked.

She clenched her teeth and tightened her grip on the knife.

"Is he?" he asked, and moved closer.

She could answer or drive the blade home. "No," she gritted, "he's not."

His eyes narrowed as he watched her. "Why would the ice princess care about some ragtag lad with no hope of a future?" She almost dropped the knife, almost slipped to the floor, but she kept herself perfectly still. "There's hope," she whispered, and found she could say no more.

Silence whispered into the room.

"Because you'll keep him safe," he said.

She exhaled slowly, forcing herself to relax, to find her cool persona, to pull back from the precipice.

"You can't harm Poke," she reminded him. "But I can hurt you."

His lips curled. "That I believe."

"Then believe this," she said. "If you so much as touch the boy, I'll tell Poke you're a spy."

His eyes widened as if shocked by such a ridiculous notion, then he laughed. "Tell me, Princess, why would I be here if I were a spy?"

She shook her head at his naïveté. "So you still underestimate him. He is everywhere. Has his fingers in a thousand pies. Every government from here to France wants to know his plans."

"Is that pride I hear in your voice, lass?"

She felt sick suddenly, weak and shaken, when he was

the one who was wounded. "It's truth, Dancer," she said. "I don't know why you're here. I don't know what you want, but I suggest you go back to where you came from, before it's too late."

Chapter 8

He was healing. There was no doubt about that. His hands were all but steady and he could manage to make it unassisted to the privy, which was a huge improvement over the humiliation of the week past. More than a week by his calculations, and he felt certain his calculations were fairly accurate, for though he was still weak, his mind felt unusually clear, his perceptions startlingly sharp.

It was almost frightening how crystalline things seemed when undulled by the haze of liquor. Not that he wouldn't kill to find that haze again, not that he didn't yearn for it with the very marrow of his bones, but now, after days of abstinence, he realized the lunacy of drinking in his current situation. Although the noble acquaintances of his past may have been less than trustworthy, at least they weren't likely to put a knife between his shoulder blades if he turned his back. He glanced around the room. The same couldn't be said here.

Including himself, seven people sat around the dinner table. It was the first time he'd been asked to join in a meal. Indeed, it was the first time he realized there was a meal. But he had already learned that this was so much more than a simple dinner. It was the time when the thieves presented their loot. The time when Poke meted out humiliation or compliments, depending on the circumstances, or his mood. The tension was like the tide, pulling Will in, roiling him under.

"Two oranges and a bouquet of wilted posies," Poke said now. "I'm disappointed, Nim."

"Sorry, sir," said Jack. The boy had grown since his time at Landow Manor. He was taller, but no broader. His face was thin, his cheeks hollow and though he had almost certainly not continued to learn to read, it was clear he had learned other things, for he could act as if William was not even in the same room, as if they had not shared the remote comfort of another world. "I'll do better tomorrow, if'n I get a decent meal."

Poke tsked like a disappointed father. "As you well know, that's not my decision," he said, "though the others have not done a far sight better." He glanced at the women, who sat side by side. Gem had produced a small wooden box with a broken hasp and Princess had donated a tattered bag of vegetables.

"So, Mister Bald," Poke said as he poured a bit of whisky into a glass, "I hope your night was more successful."

Peter sat down across the table from Will. Tall and angular, he looked lean and chagrined. " 'Fraid the pickin's was slim, Master Poke. No one about much what with the cold and the rain."

Poke cocked his head. "If you let a bit of precipitation stop you, Mr. Bald, you may be dreadfully hungry by spring."

"Well, I did get this," Peter admitted.

He moved his arm and presumably something fell into his hand, because young Jack gasped.

There was a moment of silence, then, "Ahhh, Mr. Bald," said Poke, reaching across the table. "Very good."

So he had decided to hand over the prize he'd offered Gem. Relief mixed with regret and sluiced through Will in equal amounts, but in that instant Peter handed over his treasure—a pillbox made of porcelain. It was no bigger than a copper but even from this distance, William could tell its quality. It was gilded with gold and boasted an exquisite cameo on its lid.

"And pray, lad, where did you obtain this little jewel?" Poke asked.

"A lady in Uphill. She was givin' her maid a sore scoldin'. Poor wee lass was barely the size of a butterfly." He grinned. "I figured it was only fittin' if she lost a bit of somethin'."

Poke smiled with predatory pleasure. "Mister Bald, as masterful at righting wrongs as he is at filching treasures."

Peter rubbed his hands together. "Looks like I'll be divvying up the meal tonight."

"What 'bout me?" Oxford had been absolutely silent so far, but when William glanced his way, the man's excitement was clear. His body was tense, and his eyes glowed with some emotion Will could not quite identify.

"Ahh, Mr. Oxford," Poke said, leaning back in his chair and steepling his fingers. "Have you a gift to contribute to our happy family?"

Oxford's sharp eyes skittered sideways and back. "Could be I got me a little somethin'."

"Well . . ." Poke lifted his hands palm up. "Don't keep us in suspense. What is it?"

Oxford licked his lips. "Just this," he said, and dangled a strand of pearls over the table.

Gem gasped. Peter swore. Princess remained absolutely

still, frozen in place. Perhaps she saw what William saw—a streak of blood, marring the perfect, gleaming orbs.

His stomach roiled.

"Mr. Oxford, that is truly lovely," Poke cooed. His tone was impressed as he reached for the necklace. But Oxford curled it back into his grimy fist and pulled his lips away from his teeth in the facsimile of a smile.

Poke settled slowly back into his chair. Silence sifted into the room. "Decided to go your own way, have you, Mr. Oxford?" His voice was soft, his lips smiling. Not a soul moved. Not a breath was drawn.

Ox swallowed. " 'Course not," he rasped. "But this little trinket wasn't got easy." There was blood on his hand, smeared with the dirt that caked his knuckles and nails. "And I just wants ta make sure I gets what's comin' ta me."

Poke lifted an elegant hand, indicating the table in front of him. "As you well know, the spoils go to the night's victor. The entire meal is yours if you like. Or you can distribute it as—"

"I want the Princess," Ox growled.

The room went deadly silent. Will snapped his gaze to hers, but nothing showed in her eyes. Not fear, not anger, nothing.

"What's that?" Poke asked, canting his head as if he hadn't quite heard.

Oxford leered at his coveted prize, then spurted his gaze back to Poke. "I want 'er," he said.

Poke laughed. "Granted, there's not much flesh to her, but still, I fear you could never finish her off in one meal."

Oxford licked his lips. Jack's face was as white as death.

"I want 'er for the night."

"Well, Mr. Oxford, as you know . . ." Poke smiled. "Princess is my lady. I hardly think it would be seemly to share—"

"Master Poke!" Gem interrupted, her tone sharp, her eyes ungodly large. "Ya only said food. We only choose the food for the night. You can't—"

"Stay the 'ell outta this!" Oxford growled, leaning across the table and baring his dark-stained teeth. "It ain't your turn tonight, missy."

"Master—" Gem tried again, but Poke shushed her.

"Hush now," he crooned, and gave Oxford a whisper of a smile. "I fear young Gemini is correct, Mr. Oxford. In the past the victor chose only the meal."

"I don't want the meal."

"Well . . ." Poke turned up his palms and glanced around the table with a sheepish grin. "That would surely leave more for the rest of us. What say you, my young cubs?"

Jack's hungry eyes were as wide as his plate. Peter's were narrowed, and Gem's knuckles were white atop the table's rough grain.

"No response? Then I suspect—"

"This ain't right." Peter's voice was low. Gone was the good-natured lad. In his place was a young man, teetering dangerously on the edge of explosion.

"Not right?" Poke said and blinked as though confused. "Are you saying this is morally wrong, Mr. Bald, or that you want our princess for yourself?"

Peter's face reddened. He flickered his gaze to Princess and back. "It should be her choice."

Poke laughed. "The spoils don't choose. Isn't that correct, Princess?"

Something sparked in her eyes, but she said nothing. William's throat ached with the tension. Beneath the table, he loosened his fists and remained perfectly still.

"I fear it is my unhappy decision to make, and I shall have to say . . ." Poke sighed as he scowled at the faces around him. "Oxford brought in a lovely prize. He deserves to choose his reward."

Peter jerked to his feet. "Over my dead body."

Poke smiled. "If needs be, Mr. Bald," he said, and reached languidly into his jacket.

Peter stepped back and froze, his eyes wide with terror, but Poke only pulled out a cheroot and inhaled the scent. Oxford laughed as he rose to his feet. His chair grated against the floor and his footsteps rapped sharp and hollow as he paced around the table toward his prize.

"I am sorry, my dear," Poke said, and shrugged as he struck a match and touched it to his cigar. "I shall save you some supper."

She rose to her feet. Her gaze was steady on Poke, as though the Irishman weren't directly behind her. As though he weren't nearly touching her. His breath on her neck. His hand—

Fuck it to hell!

"Oxford!" William found himself standing, though he didn't remember rising.

The Irishman flitted his narrow eyes sideways. "This ain't got nothin' to do with you, Mr. Fancy Trousers."

He was right. So right. Holy hell! He was way over his head. He was a baron, for God's sake. Wounded. Addled. Trapped. And she was a . . .

"Touch her, and I'll kill you," Will said.

The entire world went silent, then Oxford laughed, low and evil and happy.

"You?" He curled his lips away from his teeth. "You couldn't kill a snake."

Will's mind was issuing a low, steady warning—sit down, shut up. Sit down. Shut up.

But he pushed back his chair. It scraped loud and jarring in the heavy silence. "Luckily," he said, "I only have to kill you."

Oxford faced him, then slowly pulled a knife. " 'Ave at it," he said.

Will's legs felt weak. This wasn't his way. This wasn't him. He was a coward. A sniveling titled bastard who let others suffer rather than disturb his comfort.

"I 'ate ta kill twice in one day," Ox rasped, "but a man's gotta do what 'e's gotta do."

"Funny thing," Will murmured. "It seems I just heard that recently." All eyes were on him. Sweat beaded at the back of his neck. "Who was it . . . Ah, yes, that's what Lord Rambert said."

"What's that?" Ox asked, turning his head slightly.

"Vic," William explained and just managed to force himself away from the table. Far better to hide under it. Crawl away. Flee. "He said much the same thing. Just before . . ." He shrugged. Pain ripped through his shoulders and chest. Dammit all. He didn't want to die. Not now. "But he was better armed than you."

Oxford chuckled, but he skimmed the others as if looking for allies. "You're a lying shit."

"He ain't," Peter said. "Vic had him a gun in his hand when the watch found him."

"Well, he shoulda used it then, eh?"

" 'E did," Gem whispered. "Twice. I took out the bullets meself."

And the wounds burned like hell. Damn! He was going to pass out. Will took a step forward. "Take the meal, Ox," he advised. "It'll be healthier."

Ox shuffled his feet and glanced about, but in the same second, he lunged.

Terror screamed through Will. Death! Pain! He reached out wildly, trying to block the charge. A chair crashed into Oxford's face. The Irishman staggered backward and dropped to the floor like a dazed cow.

William stared down at his hands. The remains of a slat-backed chair dangled from his fingers. He lifted his gaze to Oxford, who lurched drunkenly to his feet.

Dammit all! He was going to charge again! He was going to—

"You'll pay!" hissed the Irishman, and, wiping his bloodied mouth, staggered from the room.

Silence fell like nightfall, then someone clapped.

It took an eternity for Will to realize the applause came from Poke. "Excellent," he cheered, taking the cheroot from his mouth. "Such drama. I couldn't see better on a London stage."

Will realized a bit belatedly that he had arrived at Shandria's chair. Their gazes met.

"Are you well?" His voice sounded oddly normal.

"Yes, my dear," cooed Poke, "are you quite well?"

Anger stabbed through Will's system like poisonous needles. He turned and took a stiff step toward the Den's master. But in that instant he felt something cold and sharp against his neck.

He scowled, turning his gaze downward.

Princess stared up at him, her cool eyes inches from his. In her hand was a knife, and its point rested against his jugular.

Sanity floated in like wispy clouds. What the hell had he just done? And why? If he was reading her sentiments correctly, and he thought he was, she didn't want his help. He should have figured that out earlier, because it would just be embarrassing to die now, on her blade. He'd just fought the villain for her. His mind felt muzzy, his hands unsteady. And damn, if he retched he was going to be a laughingstock.

So he smiled into her eyes. "My apologies," he said. "I didn't realize you were attracted to him."

It almost seemed that her hand shook, but it didn't matter, for the point stayed exactly where it was, and he had no doubt in his mind she would send the tip home. Dammit! He hated blood.

"No one fights my battles, Dancer," she said.

"Even you?"

She smiled. There was not the least bit of joy in the expression. "I do what I will when I will," she said. "And it has naught to do with the likes of you."

For a moment he went insane. He knew it, because for one tattered second he actually considered yanking her up against him. Considered ignoring the knife and kissing her.

"I'll keep that in mind," he said instead.

She nodded and drew the blade away from his throat. "You do that," she suggested, "and you may live out the night."

The room fell silent.

"Oh, bravo!" Poke was clapping again, but louder now and with immense enthusiasm. "I've never seen a livelier performance. Excellent. Just excellent. Well . . ." Rubbing his hands together, he reached for a bowl of turnips. "There's nothing like the threat of death to stimulate one's appetite. Let's eat."

Princess drifted into her chair.

As for Will, it was all he could do to reach his room before he silently expelled the contents of his stomach into the privy bowl.

Chapter 9

***

Shandria carried the scarred, wooden tray as if it were a crown. Her slippered feet were silent against the floor, and her expression was absolutely serene.

Frustration growled like a demon in Will's churning gut. He'd had a full day to ruminate on the scene with Ox. A full day to grind his teeth and swear to God he'd never do something so idiotic again. But then he would see her face in his mind, and his thoughts tangled like fishing lines. Even now, remembering the feel of her knife against his throat, knowing the lunacy of trying to save her, he couldn't help wanting, aching, to do just that. The idea made him as cranky as a cat in a bag.

"I already ate," he said, and, sitting up, swung his feet to the floor. Once again, pain skittered through his torso and down his legs, but pain was his friend, making him remember, helping him focus.

She tilted a glance at him. "Unaided?" she asked as if hugely impressed. "Congratulations are certainly in order then."

"Tell me, Princess," he said, gritting his teeth against the screeching agony. "Do you hate everyone, or is it just me?"

" 'Tis everyone. But you especially," she said, and, placing the tray on the chair beside the bed, slowly lifted a four-inch razor from the wooden surface.

He resisted the temptation to pass out and eyed the blade with what he hoped was casual disdain. But it might have been wide-eyed panic. "What are you planning to do with that?"

She smiled. "Surely the man who killed Vic isn't afraid of a harmless lass like meself," she said, employing an innocent brogue entirely at odds with her demeanor.

He watched her narrowly. She knew he hadn't killed Vic. He was certain of that much, though he couldn't guess how she'd come to that conclusion, and that knowledge grated at his frazzled nerves. But she was watching him, her brows raised, and he jolted himself back to the present.

"Not afraid," he scoffed, and hoped his voice didn't quiver. "I'd simply prefer not to die with my throat cut."

"Really?" she said, and, glancing down, stepped up close beside his shoulder. Her arm inadvertently brushed his bare skin, causing gooseflesh to course up his spine. Fear or desire—he didn't know—but one was as despicable as the other.

"How *would* you like to die, Dancer?" she asked, and set the sharp edge of the blade against his neck.

"Old," he said.

She chuckled and scraped the blade upward.

Wincing at the scratch of discomfort, he shifted his gaze up to hers. "If you plan to decapitate me, you could, at least, use a bit of soap."

She paused, saying nothing for several moments, and he glanced up. Her hair was loose this morning and hung in gentle waves about her face, making her look young and strangely vulnerable.

"Gem said you'd already washed." Did he hear nervousness in her voice? Uncertainty? From the Den's noble lady? The idea intrigued him, and he scowled, glancing sideways as an idea struck him.

"Are you afraid you'll have to bathe me, Princess?"

She tilted the razor slightly so that he felt the blade clearly against his skin. "Do I seem afraid, Dancer?"

She had a point.

"Soap," he said. "And a little water. For shaving."

She scowled and eased the razor away a fraction of an inch as she looked at the bowl that remained on the tray. Apparently she hadn't been the one who had filled it with soapy water.

"Shall I assume you don't shave Poke or that he enjoys being scraped to death?"

Lifting the tray, she set it beside his hip and seated herself on the chair. Once there, she plucked the grainy bar from the water. "Assume whatever you like."

Her voice was cool, and there was something about that insouciance that made his hackles rise. He watched her hands as they dunked the soap into the water and rubbed, then dunked and rubbed again.

"Are you going to put that on my face or worry it to death?"

Her eyes came up. Anger was evident, but there was something more, a spark of uncertainty that fascinated him.

"For a man dependent on the good graces of others, you are quite an irritating man, Dancer."

"Oh, and whose good graces are those?"

"Master Poke, of course." She said the name almost dreamily as she smoothed the soap onto his cheek. Her hand felt warm and gentle as it skimmed his beard. "'Twas he who took you in. Saved your life."

Poke *had* taken him in, and Poke could destroy him just as easily. Will would be a fool to cross him.

"He would have let the Irishman have you," he gritted.

She stopped the razor halfway to his face, caught his gaze, then silently scraped the blade up his cheek.

Every emotion was hidden carefully away again. She was like glass, as cool and hard as marble. But two could play that game. He was the baron of Landow for God's sake. Reserve was his stock-in-trade. Lack of emotion was—"Dammit all!" he snarled. "Is that what you wanted? To bed the Ox?"

She touched the blade to his throat. For a moment he thought he felt her hand bobble, but her eyes remained absolutely steady as she swathed the blade upward again.

" 'Tis none of your concern who I bed, Dancer."

She was right. He would stay out of her affairs before Poke took offense. His own survival was everything. Nothing else mattered. Surely not hers. He didn't care who she lay with.

"But you prefer Poke." He almost gritted his teeth against the words, but they were already out, spilled like poison into the room.

"Who would not?" she said, and sighed dramatically.

His fist shook against his thigh. "So it's true. You love him."

She watched his eyes in silence for a moment, then she laughed.

The muscles in his arms and chest cranked up tight. "Something amuses you?"

She touched his lower lip with her damp fingertips. The razor eased upward, over his clenched jaw. "Aye, Dancer," she said. " 'Tis your naïveté."

"Oh?" His stomach knotted up hard and fast. "And how, pray tell, am I naive?"

"Do you truly think that only those in love share a

bed?" She smiled into his eyes. "Share their bodies."

Unwanted images stormed through his mind. Images of her, naked, with another.

"You're right," he agreed, and carefully splayed his fingers against his thigh, trying desperately to disavow the tension, to refuse the deadly emotions. "Why not spread your legs for every madman—"

She whipped the knife downward. It skimmed his blanket and sank, reverberating, into the wooden tray. "Cease!"

His heart pounded in his chest, and the hairs along his arms stood upright.

"What is it you think, Dancer?" she snarled, and, gripping his bandage in her fist, dragged them together, face-to-face. "Might you believe this is some fine game we play for your amusement?"

Anger and frustration swirled like blind bats in his mind, but he steadied his nerves, marshaled his senses. "Believe this," he said. "I am not so easily amused."

"Then why are you here?"

An image of Elli flashed through his mind. He had come to learn the truth about her death. To unravel the mysteries. To seek vengeance. But so much had happened since he'd staggered from Malkan Palace. He'd learned much—about himself. About the world. But so little about the enigma called Princess, for she kept her secrets close, and he must do the same. "Is it so difficult to believe that I am what I say I am?"

She laughed, low and quiet. "I am poor," she said. "Not demented."

He lowered his gaze to the razor. It had sliced a swath through his blanket and still vibrated busily in the wooden tray. "Perhaps you can be both," he said.

She scowled. "Use your head. Or lose it. There is no other choice. Not here. You're not in your grand house anymore."

So she still believed he was wealthy, and yet she did not trust him. No more than she trusted Poke, or the devil himself. "Tell me," he said, holding her gaze, "what is it you think you know about me?"

She stared at him for an eternity. "I think you're a fool if you believe you can best Poke," she whispered finally. "And I've no wish to die because of that foolishness."

What did that mean? Did she know he'd come for revenge? Had she known about Elli's flight from the highwaymen? Did she know why they'd left his wife's jewelry after running her aground? And worse still, had Princess somehow had a hand in Elli's death? His stomach knotted painfully. "But you've no objections to others' deaths. Is that the way of it, lass?"

She lifted her chin slightly. "That's right, Dancer. Feel free to get yourself killed. Challenge Ox. Cross Poke. Drink yourself to death if you like."

But he'd barely had more than a toothful of spirits since he'd arrived in Darktowne. He scowled at her. Memories buzzed like hornets in his head. Conversations, circumstances. She'd tried to be rid of him from the first. To convince Poke to throw him out in the cold, to keep him away from Jack, to poison him with whisky.

And each act had kept him safe, kept him quiet, kept him sober. He shook his head, trying to clear his mind.

"Are you . . ." He scowled against the baffling thought. ". . . protecting me?"

She stared at him, her eyes earnest; and then she laughed.

"And I thought you were slow of wit, Dancer. Silly me.

It looks as if you've worked it all out. I'm your guardian angel," she hissed, and turned away, but he caught her arm. And in that instant she yanked the knife from the board and held it like a spear.

"Let me go, or I'll kill you myself."

"So!" Poke stepped into the room.

William jerked as if stabbed. Princess turned slowly, razor in hand.

Poke raised his brows, glancing from the impromptu weapon to William to his lady. "Ahhh," he chuckled, "my two scrappers. I don't believe I've thanked you properly for your performance last night, Mr. Slate."

Will tried to clear his head, to function, to think, but it took several seconds to remember the name he'd given himself. Longer still to remember he absolutely could not pull the girl down beside him just so he could feel her heart beat against his, to ask her again if she felt something for him. He absolutely could not do that, for even if Poke didn't kill him, she very probably would.

"So I thank you now," Poke continued. "It was immensely entertaining."

Will shrugged. Maybe his tension dissipated one small whit. Maybe not. If he couldn't pull the girl to him, surely he could take her knife and vow to send Poke to hell if he ever touched her again. "I owed you," he said, and that was the devil's own truth.

Poke laughed. "Yes, you did that. Indeed, you owe me still. And so . . ." He rubbed his hands together with brisk happiness. "I've a bit of a task for you."

Premonition rumbled in Will's gut. He kept his face absolutely immobile, hoping wildly that the traitorous emotions were hidden. "A task?"

"Might you be familiar with Pentmore Hall?"

Pentmore Hall. He'd heard of the estate though he'd never visited the property himself. Nor had he met Lord Ives face-to-face. "No, I don't believe I am," he said.

Poke watched him with bright, predatory eyes, but finally he shrugged leisurely. "Well, no matter. I'm certain you'll find your way. Ives is hosting a bit of entertainment, I believe. The place should be quite lively. A clever chap like you shall have no trouble lifting a few trinkets. Aye?"

Holy hell! Nerves tightened up like leather thongs, constricting his lungs, squeezing his heart. "I fear young Nim was correct," Will said. "I'm not exceptionally clever at picking pockets."

"Ahh, but not to worry. There will be no pockets that require picking. 'Tis quite a different sort of larceny I propose."

"I would like to be of assistance," Will said, "but I fear I'm not yet up to my usual form. Perhaps you should send another."

Poke watched him narrowly. "Had I not seen you with Ox just last eve, I might think you frightened, Mr. Slate."

Will canted his head, hoping to appear casual, though his movements felt leaden and slow. "I would hate to disappoint you with my current ineptitude."

"Ahh," Poke said. Crossing the floor, he smoothed the back of his fingers up Princess's cheek. "And I do so hate to be disappointed."

The tendons in Will's wrist twitched, but he kept his body perfectly still. "Why Pentmore's?"

"There's a trinket there I covet," Poke said, and skimmed a finger along Princess's collarbone as if imagining some sensational jewel resting there. "Several actually. I believe you'll find them in a small, wooden chest in his library."

He kept his gaze resolutely pinned on Poke's face, not allowing himself to watch the progress of his hand against his lady's satiny skin. Not acknowledging the hot swell of emotions that accompanied it. "If he's hosting a party, won't his wife be wearing the jewels?"

Poke turned his eyes toward Will. "He no longer has a wife, Mr. Slate," he said, and smiled. "Some men lose their beloveds in the most inconvenient ways."

Anger and fear sluiced through Will's system like a poisonous tonic. Did Poke know of Elli's death? Had he caused it? Had he known Will's identity from the very beginning?

"What say you, Mr. Slate? Can you get it for me?"

Will shoved the shattering thoughts away. Tamped the panic back into darkness. "I fear I'll need a bit of time."

"Time? For what?"

To leave. To disappear before his very life was forfeit. He should never have come here, he thought, but he could remember the feel of Shandria's hand against his skin, the brush of her lips against his. "I fear my talent is quite different from Oxford's or even Peter's. I do not lean quite so heavily toward sleight of hand as sleight of eye."

"Whatever do you mean?" Poke asked.

"I misguide my victim, misdirect them. Thus I'll need some time to determine how best to retrieve the chest so as not to disappoint you."

"Well certainly then," Poke said, and smiled. "Take your time, so long as I have the baubles by tomorrow morning."

Will felt his hands tremble, but he kept them flat against the blankets.

"If you succeed," Poke began, "you are welcome to remain in our cozy little den as long as you like, but if you fail . . ." He shrugged and brushed Princess's ear absently with his knuckles. "Someone will have to pay for your shortcomings," he said, and tucking her hand under his arm, escorted her from the room. The razor, Will noticed, was still in her fist.

Pentmore Hall was lit up like Michaelmas. It stood atop a hill surrounded by a wrought-iron fence and sweeping acres of frosty lawn.

William blew into his hands, then rubbed them together, but there was little hope of warming up. The temperature had dropped with the sun. His breath curled into the black night like ghostly dreams.

From across the frozen turf, an echo of laughter found his ears. He shivered against the effects and wondered if he had received an invitation to this particular party. He often ignored the engraved cards that lay piled in a tray on the marble table in his vestibule. But he wondered now if his old friends thought about him. Did they assume he was dead? Did they think he had drunk himself into a stupor and made some foolishly fatal mistake? Were they surprised? Did they care that he was cold? That he was tired? That he was wounded?

"Drink yourself to death if you like."

Princess's words echoed in his memory. He had very nearly made a foolishly fatal mistake. Indeed, he had nearly made several, even when sober. What would have happened had he been drunk? What lethal truths would he have spilled? He scowled at the thought, remembering his stomach's reaction to the spirits Princess had given him. Had his illness saved him from his own foolishness? Might that have been her intent despite her words to the contrary? He shook his head and paced silently along the fence. Back in his own world, he had dozens of friends, scores of associates. He'd been inebriated with most of them. Scores of times with the baron called Cask, and not once had Will been poisoned. But neither had the jovial baron asked him to change his self-destructive ways.

He nearly laughed at the thought. Obviously he was losing his mind, for she had surely not hoped to save him from himself. Far more likely she'd planned to get rid of him for all and good. Turning, Will paced back along the black metal fence. The wind found his face, biting on contact, gnawing at his fragile resolve.

There was no reason he couldn't return home. No reason except . . . Princess's face blew mistily into his mind. Her silvery eyes were watching him, and her lips were slightly bowed, as if hiding a thousand secrets.

Footsteps from behind brought him out of his trance. Was someone following him? He turned, stilling his breath and waiting. Not a whisper of sound disturbed the night. He searched the trees behind him. Darkness and billowing fog conspired against him. But if he could not see, surely the same could be said of any who might have tried to follow him . . . unless the other had the senses of a beast.

Oxford's squat image flickered in his mind. Will braced himself against a shiver. If he was quiet, if he was careful, he could return home. Forget all this, get himself a drink. But it would be different now, for he had learned much, realized, in fact, that he had been killing himself by slow increments. He'd dulled his senses and lived in shameful darkness for a score of years, but he would not do so again. One drink. That's all he'd have, for he no longer wished to die. Thus, he'd return to Landow Manor and change his ways, become a new man.

"Surely you would be safer in your manor house."

Her words seemed to echo from the darkness around

him. What did she know of Landow Manor? What did
she know of him? And how did she know it? Had she
somehow been involved in Elli's death? Memories flickered in his mind. Laughter, sadness, whispered words—
but each image was of a silvery-eyed princess and not of
the wife he'd failed.

Gritting his teeth against the guilt, Will grasped the
iron bars of the fence and levered himself over. Pain
ripped up his chest, gnawing hungrily. Every muscle
jerked tight when he dropped to the ground on the far
side and he paused for a moment, letting the agony sub-
side to a dull growl before making his way quietly across
the crisp grasses.

A hum of noise issued from Pentmore Hall. Will eased
into the shrubbery, careful of every footfall until he
stopped but a few yards from the towering manse. He
waited there, letting his heart settle, letting his hands
steady and closing his eyes against the lunacy of his present actions. It seemed to take forever for the bump of his
heart to slow. The rumble of noise separated itself into
individual voices, some near, some distant.

Opening his eyes, he grasped a fir bough and peered
between the ever-fresh branches. A pair of gentlemen
stood on the stone walkway, one tall and one stocky.
They stood shadowed and illumined by the beveled
lantern that hung from a curved iron rod, and smoke
from their cheroots danced over their heads. The scent
was sweet and strangely nostalgic, causing the ache in his
chest to intensify.

"Aye," said the taller of the two men, "she's young,
but 'tis said she's got some starch to her."

"And a good thing, too," said the stocky fellow and
leaned toward his companion. " 'Tis said there's a traitor

in the palace, one who's spilling Sedonian secrets to those who shouldn't hear them."

"Aye, well, she's got Laird MacTavish at her side now."

"That she has," agreed the squat nobleman, and puffed on his cheroot. "And 'tis just that that worries me." He removed his cigar and squinted through the smoke. "Good Christ—he's a pirate."

"Was, at any rate," agreed the other, "but he cleaned up the isle, didn't he? Perhaps he can do the same for Sedonia."

"Or perhaps the old lord's nephew will put a knife through his chest and claim everything MacTavish calls his own. Which would include our young queen and the very soil on which we stand."

"Wheaton has neither the manpower nor the wealth to best MacTavish. As you said, he's a pirate at heart. It'll take more than a disinherited weasel like Wheaton to beat him down."

The political conversation droned on as they turned and made their way inside. Will pulled his attention away to scan the area. A wreath hung on the heavy timber of the front door, holly berries, as red as blood, snuggled in the greenery. From inside a woman laughed. William raised his gaze up the rough stone exterior. A candle flickered in every window, haloed by a fat dollop of golden light. Laughter wafted from the house again, sounding content and cozy, unaware of the masses that huddled behind the cold, iron fences. Unaware, or at least uncaring, about the scared, hungry populace. Unappreciative of the wondrous comforts found behind closed doors.

Will curled his fingers into his palms. They no longer

felt cold. Indeed, they were hot and stiff, too numb to climb to one of those golden windows. He skimmed the length of the house. The back door was probably open, but even if he did succeed in entering there, what then? He was dressed in little more than rags. Peter had found him a pair of shoes. They were two sizes too big. His trousers had once been high-grade wool, but were frayed and dusty now. And his shirt. There was no disguising the shirt, even with the coat Gem had given him. It was three inches short at the wrists and bore a hole in the back that made him doubt if the former owner had died of natural causes.

Memories of Landow's coffers filled his mind. Not for many years had he cared about the state of his garments, and yet every article of clothing he possessed was preferable to what he now wore.

What the hell was he doing here? He should go home. The thought of Landow Manor filled him with a sharp yearning. Warmth, security, light—they could all be his. Had been, in fact, and yet he hadn't known it, not for as long as he could recall.

"Go back to where you came from, before it's too late."

But too late for what? He scowled at the mansion that loomed overhead, but a flicker of motion caught his eye. Someone was racing toward him. He jerked back, but the truth registered in a moment. He'd not been discovered in his piney bower. It was naught but a young couple searching for a few minutes alone, giggling as they fled the house and made for the bushes. The lad's old-fashioned top hat was tilted at a precarious angle and the girl's eyes gleamed with mischief as they raced across the cobbled walkway and into the nearby shrubbery.

Will could hear their breathy whispers in the darkness.

"James!" Her tone was aghast, but there was teasing heavily laced with the shock. "I must insist that you cease."

"I can't."

She giggled again. "If my father finds out—"

"I'm not about to tell him."

They were silent for a moment, presumably kissing before the girl spoke again. "You're mad."

"I'm randy."

"Harriet says you're always randy . . . and hard."

"Julia." The boy's voice was a growl. "Do that again, and I'll not be responsible for my actions."

"Oh . . ." There was a moment of silence. "And what might those actions be?"

He groaned. "Come to my carriage."

"Someone would see us."

"They'll not recognize us in the dark."

"In that hat?" she scoffed.

"I adore this hat," he said, as if mightily wounded. "What's wrong with it?"

"The buckle shines like a beacon. You look like a bloody pilgrim."

"As it happens, the pilgrims were excellent lovers."

She snorted. "You're intoxicated, James Crogen."

" 'Tis not true. I'm but mad with longing. I must—"

"Shh," she hissed.

Voices sounded from the lawn, deep and male. A trio of gentlemen passed by, close enough to smell the hot buttered rum they carried in steaming cups.

Giggles issued from the bushes. Will tensed, but the gents kept walking, oblivious to the fornication about to take place nearby.

"James! What would—" But the words stopped, and she sighed. "Pilgrims do have lovely hands."

"Aye," he whispered, "and other things that are love-lier still."

"James Crogen, whatever are you suggesting?"

"I think you know." His voice was rife with frustration.

"We'll freeze."

"Freeze! The devil, I'm burning up. Feel this."

She sighed, and he groaned.

"Julia, please. I'll keep you warm, I swear it. Just a moment." There was the sound of madly rustling clothing. "Lie on my coat."

"James—"

The sentence was cut short.

"My God, you're beautiful." Clothes rustled again.

She gasped. "Harriet was right. You're far bigger than Timmy."

"Touch me like that again, and I swear I'll explode."

"Like that?"

He growled something Will couldn't quite understand. But the meaning was clear enough.

"You know we shouldn't."

"I know no such thing. I'm dying, Julia."

"Really?" Will could hear her kiss him. "Will it stay hard even after you're dead?"

"Julia!" He sounded honestly scandalized.

She giggled, and he groaned.

"Save me," he whispered.

There was a moment of indecision, then, "If you take off that ridiculous hat."

In a heartbeat, Will heard the thing sail through the air and land not ten inches from the bush behind which he hid.

An idea struck him like flint. A decent hat and coat could cover a host of fashion sins. Even he knew that much. Staring into the darkness, he made certain he was not being watched, then reached out to snatch up the hat. His heart was pounding, though probably not so hard as the nearby couple's. He could hear their heavy breathing as he stepped out of the bushes.

"Oh, God, Julia! Oh God!"

The boy was quick. Will would give him that, but a little honest fear of God wouldn't hurt either of them. They shouldn't take the Lord's name in vain anyway, he thought, and almost smiled as he spoke.

"Julia!"

A rasped hiss sounded from the bushes.

"Julia, where the devil are you?" He rustled his hand around in the brushes some ten yards from where they lay hidden. "By God, Mr. Crogen, if you're out there with my daughter, there'll be hell to pay."

There was a whisper of noise. Bushes rustled, then the hustle of beating feet could be heard.

William glanced about. No one was in sight as he made his way through the shrubbery. A black shape lay upon the ground. Picking up the coat, he brushed it off, shed his own tattered garment, and pulled on the new. It still bore the heat of young love—or lust as the case may be. It was a bit tight across the shoulders, and the sleeves were too short, but he'd never been known as a natty dresser. Still, he realized as he buttoned up the tailcoat, he would need a cravat of some sort. Pulling his shirt out of his pants, he tore a strip off the bottom. In the flickering light it was impossible to tell just how filthy it was, but he had no other options, so he tied it sloppily around his neck, tore the buckle from the aged hat, and tilted it onto his head.

"Julia?" A man's voice sounded from the back door. "Where the devil have you gotten off to now?" A dark form strode around the corner of the house and stopped at the sight of William. "Who are you?" His tone was filled with the harshness of too much liquor and an elevated opinion of his own importance. Will had heard it a thousand times and wondered vaguely if his own voice had sounded the same.

"Lord Ives," he said, chancing a shot in the dark. "I am Sir Benjamin Bowery. I don't believe we've ever met." He extended his hand and forced himself to breathe.

The portly fellow took his palm in his own. "I don't remember inviting you," he said, but his tone had mellowed a bit.

"Your daughter asked me to come."

The man swore with some fervor. "Where is she?"

"Julia?"

"Where the devil has she got off to?"

"I believe I saw her strolling in the garden with a young—" he began, but Pentmore was already gone, rolling away like a steam engine.

William watched him go, then turned toward the looming house. It leered at him. This was madness. Insanity. He didn't know how to find the library. He couldn't identify the bloody chest if it fell into his lap, and he had no idea what to do with it if it did.

"Nobody fights my battles."

But no one had fought his sister's either, and she was long dead. He remembered how she had looked to the skinny boy who had peered into her casket—hollow, fragile, and eternally sad. Ancient demons cackled in his soul. Failure loomed like ancient gargoyles.

The back door opened. Light blasted out like the fires of hell. His stomach twisted as three dark shapes emerged and tottered down the walkway, nearly ricocheting off Will as they went, but none so much as turned his way. Despite everything, he was one of them. And yet he was not. Not tonight, for he was Slate—bold, clever, strong.

If he could just control his stomach until the jewels were in his hands.

Chapter 10

No one stopped him. No butler, no mistress, no armed guard. Will's shoes rapped on the marble floor of the foyer. He had forgotten the opulence of the snobbish upper crust. Already, after only a few days of hunger, their world, *his* world, seemed painfully decadent, or perhaps it always had.

"Good evening." An elderly man gave him a nod and went back to his conversation. William kept walking. The library. Where would it be? Off to his left, voices hummed and laughter twittered, rising above the general hubbub. A couple passed him. The woman glanced at his face. Her eyes widened. She squeezed closer to her partner, and they hurried past. William didn't take time to look back, but he could hear her whisper to her companion and wondered at the reason. Perhaps his "stock" was soiled, or his hat wasn't tilted at the proper angle. It was impossible to guess with the noble class. Any of a thousand fashion faux pas could set things against him. Then again, it could be that Shandria had all but butchered him during shaving, and the nick near his jugular was bleeding again.

A door stood open on his right. Two women sat drinking tea and talking. He bobbed his head and moved quickly past. A drawing room, a parlor, a gaming room, but no library. Stairs loomed ahead, wide mahogany steps that wound upward like a snaring coil. A gentleman turned toward Will, but he pivoted away in unison, reaching for a drink from a nearby server as he did so, then there was nothing to do but mount the stairs.

A foursome descended, talking amongst themselves. Will gave them a nod and turned right at the top of the stairs. Rooms spread out in both directions. A nursery, a solar, more rooms, unidentified but unimportant, for the library loomed at the end of the hall. He could see the scholarly rows of books through the open doorway. His heart lurched. Not a single candle shone inside the room. But he didn't look right or left. Instead, he hurried inside, sidestepped, and abruptly stopped. From the hallway he heard someone laugh. Footsteps echoed off to the left. His breath came in shallow rasps, but no one stopped him, no one questioned him. He waited until the thrumming in his chest had retreated a bit, then casually took a candle from the hallway and moved back into the shadowy recesses of the room. Still no one accosted him. He closed the door, certain someone would burst in at any moment, but seconds ticked away until there was nothing he could do but move forward. Search.

The desk door squeaked as he opened it, but it was clear in a moment that the chest wasn't there. He moved on. Drawers. Endless shelves of books. Nothing. And then the cabinets. He rummaged through the first with bated breath, closed it, and moved on. But the second didn't open.

Closing his eyes, he tried to think where he would keep the key for such a cabinet, but a quick search in the obvious places yielded nothing.

Footsteps echoed on the stairs. Men's voices ascended.

Premonition screamed through him. He was out of luck. Out of time.

Turning toward the cabinet, he grasped a handle and yanked it toward him. Wood moaned and splintered. Inside a small chest occupied the very center of a shelf.

Voices sounded from the hallway. He snatched the box to his chest and scanned the room, but there was nowhere to run. Nowhere to hide.

". . . thought I heard something," a voice said.

Panicked, Will shut the cabinet. Cramming the chest under his borrowed coat, he crushed it between his arm and his ribs and snatched a book from the shelves.

The door opened. Lord Ives and a companion stood in the hallway. Both men stared in some surprise.

"My lord," Will said, and nodded with prim precision. "I hope you don't mind that I borrowed a book. I've a bit of a headache, and the noise was beginning to wear on me."

Ives scowled as if trying to see the cabinet behind, but Will's position blocked that possibility. Didn't it? Sweat trickled down his spine, but he stared blandly at his host.

"Did you find your bonny daughter, my lord?"

The man's scowl deepened. "I'm certain she just stepped out for a bit of air."

"Julia's gone missing?" his companion asked.

William glanced at the fellow, noticing for the first time that he was considerably younger than the girl's father, though a bit puffier about the belt. He had a large, bowed nose and cheeks flushed with emotion or wine or a potent combination of the two.

Will shrugged. The chest slipped a little inside his borrowed coat. "We were all young once, I suppose."

"You know Julia?" the boy asked.

"We met just briefly," Will said. "I am new to Sedonia,

and she thought it would be a kindness to invite me here."

Ives's brows lowered another degree.

"I'm sorry," said the younger man, stepping forward and offering his hand. "I don't believe we've met. I am Timothy Tyron, the viscount of Bisburn."

Heart thumping, Will squeezed his right elbow tightly against the chest, set the book on the desk, and extended his hand.

"Julia's betrothed," Timmy added.

Will jerked slightly and in that instant a number of things happened. Ives strained to see behind him, the chest shifted, and Will's borrowed coat gaped open.

Both men's gazes dropped. Will drew his hand back and looked down, and though the chest was not visible, his shirt was. It was smeared with blood and a host of other unnamable substances visible even in that flickering light.

Ives's scowl was a glare now. Tyron's eyes were hooded.

"What did you say your name was, sir?"

Will's mind spun. What now? What the hell now?

"There you are," said a woman from the doorway. All eyes turned in that direction.

And she was there. Princess Shandria, dressed in a teal gown that was gathered at the high waistline and showed a wealth of snowy cleavage. Her hair was piled atop her head, and her smile was bewitching. But why the devil was she there?

"I cannot leave him alone for an instant," she said, addressing the gentlemen and gliding inside. "*Mon dieu*, he has such an aversion to crowds. I blame it on Mama. She doted on him so, you see. He never learned to interact with his contemporaries."

The men were staring at her as if she were an apparition.

"I'm sorry," she said, and laughed. The sound was as light and high as silvery bells. She extended a gloved hand. "I am being quite rude. I am Lady Winifred."

The scowl was gone from Ives's face as he bowed over her hand.

" 'Tis a pleasure to meet you, my lady."

"The pleasure is all mine," she said, and gently tugged her fingers from the old man's grip only to be seized by Timothy, who pressed a kiss to her knuckles.

She smiled, but turned her gaze to Will. Her eyes snapped with urgency. Reality snagged his tottering mind. Self-preservation followed. Escape. Now! He stepped toward the door.

". . . so very nice of you to invite us," she was saying as she eased her hand from Tyron's and pressed it, splay fingered to her bosom. The flesh was bare there, pale and high where her breasts were mounded above her bodice. "But we must away."

"So soon?" Timothy asked.

"I fear so," she said, and stepped into the hallway. William went with her. She settled her hand on his arm and turned gaily to the men behind. "But I shan't forget either your beautiful home or your wondrous hospitality."

"Surely you could stay a bit longer," Ives said. "I could show you about."

"If I but could," she countered, and tightened her hand like a claw around Will's biceps. "Mayhap some other time."

"Tomorrow, perhaps."

"Perhaps."

They were almost to the stairs, but the men were following them like a pair of hounds.

"I will make certain to tell Julia I met you," said the lad.

She hesitated not a moment. "Oh do," she said. The mahogany stairs echoed under their heels.

A woman's gasp sounded from upstairs.

William swore under his breath and hustled onto the carpet. His legs felt stiff and his chest tight.

"Are you completely insane?" she rasped, her lips barely moving.

"Shut up and hurry—" he began.

"My chest! My jewels!" someone gasped.

They didn't delay another moment, but lurched for the door.

Footsteps thudded above. The latch stuck beneath Will's fumbling fingers, then they were outside, scrambling down the stairs, and galloping into the darkness.

"Stop them!" someone yelled, but they didn't turn back. "Thieves!"

There were several seconds of bewildered silence, then men thundered after them. Will and Princess hurtled down the driveway, between carriages. Horses snorted and shied away.

"Halt!" someone shouted.

Lurching toward the dark shape of a landau, Will jerked off the brake, grabbed the reins, and swatted the team's haunches. The bays gathered their strength and sprang into action even as Will dragged Princess into the shrubbery. Branches burned his face. Shouts sounded from every direction. A hack pounded past, its rider bent furiously over its straining neck. From the bushes beside them, a couple stumbled onto the road.

"This way." Princess's whisper was little more than a

hiss in the darkness. He followed as silently as he could, slipping through the garden. But suddenly the shrubbery disappeared, and he stumbled onto the road, into the open, unprotected and alone.

Hoofbeats thundered toward him through the darkness, then a hand reached out and yanked him backward. A pair of riders galloped past, nearly atop him.

"Come!" someone hissed, though he didn't know who. But options were limited. Life was short. He stumbled after a dark shadow and through an open doorway. It took him a moment to realize they were inside a carriage house, but there was no time to question. Someone snagged his sleeve and dragged him into a dark enclosure. A stall? A—

"Get down," a voice ordered. He did so, crouching in the shadows, and there he recognized his newest companion.

"Jack!" he rasped.

"Hush!" Princess ordered. Her eyes were wide and rimmed with white.

"The carriage was empty." The voice outside was close and breathless. "They must have jumped out before we stopped it."

Someone swore.

"Have you searched the gardens?"

"I fear they're long gone, my—"

"Then what the devil are you standing about for? Go find them!"

Voices agreed and argued. Footsteps rushed away. Inside the carriage house the trio waited in silence, huddled together in the darkness, and finally, after what seemed an eternity, the world outside went quiet but for an occasional, distant snatch of dialogue.

William exhaled and carefully turned his back to the

wall. His chest burned like a Yule log, and his legs felt weak.

"What the devil are you doing here?" he asked, turning to Jack.

The lad met his glare straight on. "Saving your arse, looks like," he said.

"Why—" he began, but the boy interrupted him.

"You all right, Princess?"

"Dancer's right," she said, her voice a thin whisper in the darkness. "You shouldn't have come."

The boy scowled and shook his head. " 'E don't 'ave no idea what 'e's doin'."

Will could feel her gaze on him. "That much is clear enough, lad," she agreed. "Still, 'tis too dangerous here."

The boy straightened slightly. "Why are you 'ere then?"

"Find anything?" A man's voice sounded close outside.

Will's breath froze in his throat.

The answer was distant and negative. Noises faded reluctantly into the night.

"You'd best get back to the Den, Nim," Princess murmured, "before they make an organized search."

"What 'bout you?" the boy asked.

Even in the darkness, Will could see her eyes soften. "Don't worry on my account," she said, and, reaching out, brushed a lock of tumbled hair from his brow. "I'll be well enough. You just—"

" 'E ain't gonna be any use to ya," the boy said, and jerked a nod toward Will.

"Not everyone can have the skills of Nimble Jack," she agreed.

"True 'nuf," said the boy and grinned, his teeth flashing in the darkness. "But 'e don't 'ave no skills a'tall."

She laughed, low and quiet. Perhaps Will should have

been insulted, but there was joy on her face, despite the danger, despite the hardships . . . and life was getting shorter every second.

"I can dance," he countered.

She turned toward him with a look of surprise, and he held out his hands. "Want to try?"

They stared at him in numb silence, then, " 'E's off 'is nut," Jack said.

She pulled her gaze away with an obvious effort.

"It'll be safer if we leave one at a time," she whispered, addressing the boy.

"You're stayin' with 'im then?"

"Worry about yourself, lad," she murmured. "He'll reach the Den safe enough."

The boy stared as if he might object, but finally he nodded once and slipped like a ragged shadow into the night.

The carriage house went quiet. The stall where they hid was long and narrow, barely five feet across and heavily bedded in oat straw that shone gold even in the darkness. They'd hunkered down under the manger and would be all but invisible from three sides.

Voices sounded, but there were no shouts, no reason to believe Jack had encountered any trouble.

"So you came to look after me?" Will's voice was quiet to his own ears, for there was no reason to speak up. She sat less than eighteen inches away, with her knees pulled up to her lovely bosom and her eyes bright in the darkness.

She didn't look at him, but kept scanning the world outside their fragrant sanctuary. "Things are quieting down," she whispered. "You should be able to slip out unnoticed, unless you're completely inept."

He watched her. Her face was a pale oval against the

rough timber at her back. "So I was right," he mused, seeing past her tough demeanor. "You've been protecting me all the while."

Slipping out from beneath the manger, she rose easily to her feet. "There's a back door. Go now."

"Why?" he asked, and stood up beside her.

"I don't know!" she hissed, turning abruptly toward him. "Perhaps so you don't get shot once it's light enough for them to find you."

"Why did you come?" he asked, and stepped up close. She didn't move away, though it was entirely possible she couldn't, for her back was against the wall, literally and figuratively. "So you could guard my back?"

She snorted. "Believe this," she said. "I'd call them down on you as soon as breathe."

"Then why didn't you?"

"Jack seems to have developed a fondness for you." Her eyes snapped with anger.

"So you came on his behalf."

She glanced fretfully out the door. "I feared he might attempt to help you."

"I had no idea you knew him so well."

"And I had no idea you knew him at all."

"Life is full of mysteries."

"They say death is the ultimate one. Do you plan to stay and find out?"

He ignored her gibe. "So you only came to make sure the boy was safe?"

She raised an inquisitive brow. "Why else, Dancer?"

" 'Tis what I ask myself. At the first you tried to be rid of me. Was it because you detested me or because you protected me?"

"I detested you," she said. "Same as now."

"And why is that?"

She looked back at him. There was something hypnotic about her gaze, as if she could stun with nothing but her eyes. "You're weak," she said simply.

"So it's weakness you detest?"

"Weakness," she said, "will get you killed."

He smiled in the darkness and moved a step closer. "I'm not dead yet," he breathed.

She turned toward him. Their faces were inches apart, her eyes snapping. "Through no fault of yours."

"No. The fault is entirely yours. I merely wonder why," he said, reaching up and brushing his knuckles across her cheek.

For a moment, he thought she trembled, but in an instant she'd stepped away.

"Lay a hand on me again, Dancer, and I'll have to kill you," she said, but her voice was strangely breathy.

He watched her lips move. "I don't think you would."

"Whyever not?" she asked, as though truly fascinated, and he shrugged.

"It seems like a good deal of bother," he said, turning his hand slightly and lightly grasping her fingers in his, "for a weakling such as myself."

"You're daft."

"All the more reason to wonder," he said, and leaned closer.

She tightened her grip in warning.

"No hands," he whispered, and kissed her.

Her lips were soft and yielding beneath his. Her fingers trembled against his chest. He shifted closer, unable to bear any distance between them. His erection brushed her abdomen. She moaned, and it was that noise, that tiny whisper of passion that ripped hot excitement into every part of his being.

Need roared through him. He dragged her up against

him and realized her hands were no longer passive, but were squeezing his buttocks, pulling him closer with frenzied heat.

He groaned and, dropping his head, kissed the soft flesh of her bosom.

But in that instant she jerked out of his grasp, breathing hard and looking terrified. "I told you not to touch me!"

He stared as his body screamed in frustration. "But you were just—"

"Get out of here," she said. "Go back where you came from."

"I came from the Den."

"Damn you!" she snarled. "Why do you wish to die?"

Memories rushed in like a dark tide. But everything had changed. "I don't," he said. "Not anymore."

"Then you shouldn't be here."

"But you're doing such a grand job of protecting me."

"I'm not protecting you."

"Then why did you come?" he asked, and though he knew better than to ask, he could not help himself. "Do you . . . Might you have feelings for me?"

"Feelings!" She laughed, low and raspy. "Why would I have feeling for a man with naught but tortured eyes and foolish . . ." She paused, breathing hard.

He waited, breathless. "Foolish what, lass."

"Foolish . . ." She scowled, glancing nervously toward the door. "Foolish notions. Trying to save others." Her gaze flickered back, haunted and mercurial. "When you can't even save yourself."

He dared a careful step closer, watching her, thinking. "Gem would have saved herself."

She winced at the memory, as if it hurt her. "Ox is an animal," she whispered.

Dear God, she was beautiful, and he wanted her with an intensity that ached, but there was something to be learned here, something to figure out. "Is that why you came then, Princess? Do you think you owe me?"

"Hardly!" She laughed. The sound was breathy.

"Then why?"

She lifted her perfect chin with a jolt. "I came for the chest."

"The—"

"The chest," she hissed, and pointed to where it lay nearly hidden beneath the manger.

He glanced in that direction. "Why—"

"Because Poke wants it," she said, leaning in. "Perhaps you think me foolish enough to let you gain his trust, his gratitude. But I am not."

He felt battered, uncertain. "You came to find the chest?" he repeated, peering at her and trying, against all likely odds, to calm himself. He'd never liked emotions, wasn't comfortable with them. And he detested passion. It made fools of men, and worse. Far worse. He was the cool baron of Landow—never rash or reckless or foolhardy. Indeed, it had been half an eternity since he had been aroused to this degree, and now it seemed unlikely that his member would ever retract. It ached, in fact. "Because you want to give it to Poke yourself."

"Yes."

He tried again to calm himself, but he was throbbing. "Because you detest me."

"Yes."

He grabbed her arm and stepped up close before she could escape again. Her breast brushed his chest. She gasped, and he gritted his teeth against the contact. "Forgive me," he said, and kissed her.

Her knees seemed to buckle, but he had already

wrapped his arm around her back and drawn her up tight
against his chest. She moaned in his embrace, and he
drew back, breathing hard and eyeing her in the darkness.

"But it doesn't seem as if you detest me," he murmured.

"You imagine things," she whispered, and shifted out
of his grasp.

He dropped his gaze to her breasts, pale in the silent
darkness. "More than you know."

She moved back a step, as if fearful he might pounce.

"So you feel nothing when I kiss you?" he asked.

She remained silent, eyes wide.

"And you feel nothing," he said again, "when I kiss
you?"

"Nothing at all," she rasped, and pivoting about, rushed
away.

Will watched her go, watched the night swallow her
up, felt his body drain of energy. Exhaling heavily, he let
himself sink against the thick timbers behind him.

So it had finally happened. He'd completely lost his
mind. What the devil was he doing? Pretending to be
what he was not. Stealing! And if that wasn't enough, he
was now forcing his attentions on a woman who had no
interest in him. He tightened his fist against the golden
straw. The baron of Landow had never been so crass. Of
course, the baron had never cared enough to be crass.

But wasn't that better? Wasn't the self-imposed apathy
preferable to this terrible torture of feeling?

An image of Princess appeared in his mind, her eyes
snapping, her body atremble.

No. Apathy was not better. Not anymore. He chose
life. And yet . . . He drew a slow breath. She felt nothing

for him. In fact, she'd risked her life to keep him from ac-
quiring the very thing he'd risked his to obtain.

But . . . He glanced toward the manger, spied the chest
nestled in the straw, and smiled into the darkness. Apparently, she'd forgotten her reasons for coming.

Chapter 11

❧

Shandria huddled in the fetid darkness. The air was chill. Her breath curled like ghostly images over her head, but it was not foolish apparitions that she feared. It was the denizens of Darktowne. True, most of them knew she was Poke's companion and let her pass unmolested. But she was still a good way from the Den, and there was a stranger on the streets. She watched him from the layered shadows of a tumbledown ale house. He was a giant of a man, his rumbling voice barely audible in the darkness.

"I've no quarrels with ye, lads," he said.

"Don't you now?" Someone chuckled. She thought it might be Frank. A pistol gleamed in his hand. Poke's guards were numerous and well armed. "Do you hear that, Brandy? The brute 'ere says he ain't got no quarrels with us."

" 'Tis good to hear," snorted the other, and stepped away from an unsteady inn. Watery moonlight shone dully on the cutting edge of his curved sword. "But Poke may 'ave a quarrel with 'im."

"Poke." The stranger turned slightly, following Brandy's movements. "Is he your master then?"

"I ain't got no master, Brute. I do what I will when I will."

"Mayhap you can help me then." His tone was deadly calm. "I'm looking for someone."

"Someone?"

"A lass," he rumbled, and the others chortled.

"Yeah, ain't we all."

"Her hair is chestnut hue. A wee mite of a thing, no more than six-and-ten years."

Frank chuckled. "You like your whores young, old man?"

Silence slipped into the night for a moment, then, "She's no whore," rumbled the stranger.

"Then you come to the wrong place. Cuz that's all that lives 'ere. Ain't that right, Frank?"

"Aye," said the other, "though 'is description sounds like Poke's little strumpet."

The giant turned and, even in the darkness, Shandria could sense his tension. "Where would I find her?" he asked.

"Well now, there's the funny thing," Brandy said, and raised his sword. "You wouldn't."

The stranger turned slightly. "Think now," he warned, his tone steady as the earth. "Don't be doing something you'll regret, lad."

"Cocky bastard!" hissed Frank, and raised the gun.

Shandria tried to scream, tried to warn him. But everything happened in an instant. Brandy leapt forward, hacking wildly. The giant grunted. A gun exploded. Then there was silence, and only one man left standing.

Shandria gasped and the giant turned as if listening. She pressed her knuckles to her mouth, stifling any noise and shrinking deeper into the shadows. But he didn't search for her. Instead, he wobbled slightly, as if wounded, then turned and headed north, toward the Den.

Who was he? What did he want? Slipping from her hiding place, Shandria hurried down a rutted street, then ducked into a narrow alley. It smelled of dead fish and worse, but she had no time to consider such things. A giant had come. A giant searching for a young girl with red hair. Gem. But why? What had she done? She was just a child. But perhaps he wasn't an enemy. Perhaps he'd come to save her.

Shandria's heart bumped in her chest. Maybe there was hope for one of them. Maybe. But the giant hadn't yet reached the Den, and it would be all but impossible for him to battle his way through Poke's labyrinth of guards. Impossible for him to reach Gemini alive.

Unless he had help.

The journey back to the Den chilled Will's bones and tortured his muscles. Even with the coat he'd confiscated, the damp chill seeped in like old ghosts, haunting and raw.

The back alleys were as dark as sin. Furtive noises sounded from a dozen creepy sources. His fingers felt cramped and numb against the smooth frozen wood of the chest, but he trudged along, his mind wandering jerkily. What had he just stolen? Jewels? Coin? Or was it perhaps something entirely different?

Princess said Poke had his fingers in a hundred different pies. That he was involved in politics. Perhaps he should check the contents. Perhaps he should learn what it was Poke wanted so badly, but the chest was locked and Poke, with his lazy eyes and unreadable expressions, would surely know if someone had tampered with his prize. Then again, there was no reason he truly had to return to the Den. Maybe Princess was right. Maybe Poke was involved in politics, and the contents of this chest was something the crown should see. But William already knew he would not force the lock, would not risk the chance of making Poke more suspicious of him.

Perhaps Poke was pivotal in some international scheme. Shandria had suggested as much. Maybe she was right. Perhaps Poke was as omnipotent as a demigod, or perhaps her words were just the sentiments of a woman in the inescapable bonds of love.

Pain coiled in his stomach. Did she love Poke and detest Will? Perhaps. Who could say? The Den's master must seem all-powerful to one in her position, while the man she called Dancer would appear to be nothing more than a hapless oaf. One who couldn't even manage to perform a simple theft unaided.

So she had helped him. Why? Did she pity him? Desire him? Despise him? The questions haunted him. Someone chuckled from the anonymity of the shadows. Will hunched his back against the eerie feelings and hurried on, but even the ever-present danger of Darktowne could not quite keep his mind from clattering back to the silver-eyed woman.

It was impossible to see past the mercurial coolness of her gaze. Impossible to divine her thoughts. But when had he ever cared to do such a thing? He'd spent most of his life keeping others out.

And now he found, inexplicably, foolishly, that he wanted to let someone in. To understand. To be understood.

And the amusing part was that she wanted nothing of the sort.

Wealth and power. Apparently that's what she desired. And Poke possessed both. He had dozens of guards, or so she'd said. Was it true?

As William drew closer to the Den, he slowed his pace, watching the shadows from the corner of his eyes and wondering where those men might be hidden, but no one stopped him. Indeed, no one so much as asked his intentions.

It was nearly dawn when he stumbled down the last alley toward his destination. Tension lay tight between his shoulders, for there was no guessing what his reception might be. Perhaps, in fact, Princess had told Poke of Will's inability to seize the chest himself. Perhaps he was no longer welcome in that questionable refuge. And what of Jack? What was his role in this drama? And why had he appeared at Pentmore? Perhaps the lad, too, had hoped to steal the chest himself. Or perhaps . . . Perhaps, against all odds, the boy worried for Will's safety. It was impossible to guess, for his world had turned upside down and everything was as it had never been before.

A moan issued from the shadows and a voice rose, gravelly and unsteady. "Who goes there?"

William turned warily, searching the darkness, and a man lurched forward, knife in hand.

"Who the devil goes there?" he snarled again, but in an instant the fellow dropped his back against the nearest wall and slid with weary lethargy to a seated position. The bloody blade wobbled.

Will waited, breath held.

"I'll kill 'er for this." His words were muddled, his head beginning to list toward his tilted shoulder.

Something cranked up in Will's gut. Fear and suspicion ground up with something more. "Kill who?" he asked.

"She's already dead," the man slurred, and drooped sideways.

"Who are you going to kill?" Will asked, premonition

pumping into his system as he took two rapid steps toward the downed man.

"Already dead," he repeated. "She just don't know it." The weapon dropped from his hand, and he slumped sideways, sliding regretfully against the moldering wall behind him.

Will strode forward, but the other was already dead. He knew it without question, though he didn't know how. And suddenly silvery eyes glimmered like twin beacons in his mind. He turned without thought; and then he was running, racing down the alley and up the stairs to the foreboding sanctuary.

The front door stood open. Will stumbled to a halt. Caution returned with a jolt. Voices sounded from within, one low and smooth, one gritty and tight with excitement.

Oxford.

William made his way up the stairs. His movements were slow and wary, his heart heavy as molten lead in his chest, but he forced himself to step inside. Even through the doorway of the shabby entry he could see that the parlor was crowded with people; but they didn't notice him, for they were busy with another—a stranger who stood in the center of the ring, barely visible past those who surrounded him.

" 'E's a spy." It was Oxford's voice again, as subilant as a snake's. "Come to learn our secrets."

Will's heart clenched tight in his chest. Were they talking about him? His steps hitched.

"We don't know that." Gem's words were cropped short, wound up tight. The fear was palpable.

"No." Poke's voice was typically calm. Will could see his face past the shoulder of a man he failed to recognize. His smile was serene, but there was something in his eyes, an eager brightness as he turned with predatory premonition to find Will through the doorway. "We don't. Yet another mystery, aye, Mister Slate."

A half dozen faces turned toward him. There was nothing for it but to enter the room, to creep in with careful strides, though he hoped to God he looked casual. Meeting Poke's gaze took all the strength he could muster, but the other only smiled.

"Look," Poke said and nodded sideways. "We are blessed with yet another guest."

William glanced to his right, and there, near the center of the room was a bear of a man. He stood well over six feet and was as broad as sundown. He wore a Highlander's dark kilt belted over a rough tunic and little else but for laced boots that barely contained the muscles that strained like living roots from his thighs and calves.

Blood was matted in his hair and dripped in darkening hues down his temple. There was a gash in his right forearm from which blood dropped in rhythmic cadence. The knife in Oxford's hand was the same ruddy hue. He grinned as he shifted the blade and circled the giant.

A curse echoed unbidden from Will's lips.

Poke raised a brow. "Might you know our large intruder, Mister Slate?"

"No." Honesty came quickly if a bit gutturally to his lips. "We've not met."

"Then he did not come on your behalf?"

Nausea cranked at Will's stomach. "No? Why would he?"

"Why indeed? And however did he get past my faithful guards?" Poke smiled as he paced. Oxford growled as he did the same. Opposite him were two others, men Will had never met, but they looked to be the same ilk as Oxford—quick, hard, and cruel to the bone.

"Will you answer?" Poke asked, but the giant merely stared, his eyes expressionless as they followed the other about the room.

"I don't think . . ." Gem darted her eyes back and forth. "I don't believe 'e can talk."

"Truly? A mute?" Poke mused. "Perhaps he's had his tongue removed. A barbaric tradition from times past, I know, but sometimes 'tis still done, is it not, Mr. Oxford?"

The Irishman licked his lips and almost giggled. "Aye, sometimes it is."

"Are you missing your tongue, Goliath?"

The giant didn't answer, but watched Poke with narrow, solemn eyes.

"Why are you here?"

He said nothing.

" 'E can't talk," Gem rasped. " 'E's daft. I'm sure of it."

Poke smiled. "Daft enough to slip past my guards? That I doubt. But even if that were the case, why would he go to such trouble? What is your business here, Goliath?"

Still no sound came from the man at the center of the room. But he turned slightly, following Poke's movement, and with that motion Oxford and his cohorts tensed like dodging terriers. It was then that Will realized that one held a club of sorts while the other carried a long, wicked blade. It was curved like a scimitar and etched with foreign letters.

Strange how every detail seemed sharp and significant to Will's bombarded senses. Strange, when life hung by a thread. He could sense death crowding in, could feel it like the cold. But it would not be quick, and it would not be painless. Oxford circled his prey, eyes gleaming.

Bile burned Will's throat. "Perhaps he has no business here," he said, and found himself barely able to force out the words. "Perhaps he simply stumbled into our midst."

"As you did?" Poke asked.

Shut up now. Before it's too late. "Yes," he said, "much the same."

Poke canted his head. "You're certain you've not met him before?"

The giant's gaze met his and held, but it was impossible to read anything there. Perhaps Gem was right. Perhaps he was daft. Perhaps he was a deaf mute. But he was also a mountain of a man, bulging with muscle and potential danger.

"I would remember," Will said, and Poke laughed.

"Yes, he would stick in your memory, would he not, young Gemini?"

Her eyes were as wide as eternity, her face pasty white. "Aye, Master Poke, I surely wouldn't forgot a bloke like 'im 'ad I met 'im before."

He smiled at her. "You look worried, lass."

Her lips trembled. "I don't wanna see no one get 'urt."

"No." He touched her cheek with gentle fingertips. "The softness of a woman, but it's a harsh world, my dear. We cannot let anyone breach our fair fortress, can we?"

"'E ain't breached nothin'," she breathed, her eyes flickering from the master to the giant like a cornered hare. "'E just stumbled in."

"That's not what Mr. Oxford thinks."

"Devil take ye!" gritted the Irishman, and lunging forward, thrust his blade into the Highlander's side.

The man grunted and spun about, but Ox was already out of reach and grinning. Blood soaked the back of the giant's tunic and sank like a dark flood into his plaid.

"Is that right?" Poke's voice was perfectly steady, as if he were discussing the price of tea over crumpets and not watching a man slowly lose his life's blood. "Are you a spy, Mister Goliath?"

He didn't answer, but turned, watching Poke again with steady eyes.

"Who sent you?"

The silence was as heavy as death, the quiet only broken by Oxford's raspy breathing.

"Reticence will do you no good," Poke said, his voice almost sorrowful now. "Indeed, if you spill the truth I may well let you live, but if you do not . . ." He raised his hands, palms up, and Oxford leapt in again.

Gem screamed. The Irishman jumped back, and the giant dropped heavily to his knees, one arm dangling.

"No!" Gem had grabbed Poke's hand and fallen to her own knees. "Please. 'E don't know nothin'."

Poke placed a well-manicured hand on her flame bright head. "How would you know that, Gemini?"

"Look at 'im," she pleaded. " 'E's a dolt. Surely 'e is, elsewise 'e would defend 'isself."

Poke shook his head sadly. "So young," he said. "So sweet and naive. We do not know what he knows and what he does not. Therefore, I must find out, in order to protect my little cubs." He slipped a hand under her jaw. "In order to protect you, sweet Gemini."

" 'E don't know nothing," she repeated, still grasping his fingers. "I'm sure of it. 'E's bad 'urt already. Take 'im away. Dump 'im somewheres else. 'E won't come back."

Poke seemed to consider her words but finally shook his head again, slowly, as if the decision pained him. "I fear I cannot. Not without learning the truth, Mr. Oxford."

"No!" Gem pleaded.

"I've got the chest," William rasped, and though he couldn't have said what he hoped to accomplish, he yanked the box out from under his coat.

"Ahhh." Poke shifted his attention toward Will. "Well done, Mr. Slate. I am impressed indeed."

"Let him go," Will said, his heart beating heavy and hard as if he'd been climbing and could not quite draw enough breath. "And I'll not demand a share."

Poke raised a brow. "Demand?"

Hatred, raw and acidic, brewed in Will's system, and that, too, was new. Hate, like love, demanded energy. Far better to draw back and let the world slide dizzily by. But it refused to do so and raucously crowded his senses.

"Ask," he corrected. "Let the Highlander be, and I'll ask for nothing from the chest."

"Tell me, Mr. Slate, do you know what's in it?"

He was glad now that he hadn't opened it, for almost it seemed that this man could read his thoughts, could see through his fragile bravado to his trembling soul. "I can only assume it's of some value."

Poke laughed. "Aye, it is that, and you'd trade your share for this man you've not met?"

"I'm a thief," William said, and shifted his gaze to Ox. "Not an animal."

"Did you hear that, Mr. Oxford?" Poke asked.

"You callin' me an animal?" The words were growled.

"Certainly not." Caution warred with vengeance in Will's gut and lost. " 'Tis said animals need a reason to kill."

"I got me a reason," Ox said, and, circling the downed giant, approached Will, knife ready. "I got me plenty of reason."

Poke chuckled fondly, then turned his attention back to the Scotsman. "I shall ask once again," he said. "Why have you come?"

Silence echoed like a death knell in the room.

Poke shrugged and turned his palms up as if they were washed clean, as if he had no choice in the matter. "Gentlemen," he said.

"No!" Will rasped, and stepped forward, but Ox lunged toward him, knife upthrust. Will parried with the chest. The blade slashed across it.

Something exploded. The world froze.

Will turned like a wooden marionette.

"Stop it!" Gem stood, feet braced wide, gun smoking. Her knuckles were white and her hands shook like poplar leaves as they gripped the weapon. "Stop it."

The giant lay on his face, unmoving, his life's blood seeping sedately into the floorboards.

"Why, Gemini," Poke said, his tone amused, "you took my pistol."

"I'll kill 'em." Her voice trembled, but her hands looked steadier now, and sharp color rode high on her cheeks. "I'll kill the next man what moves."

Poke smiled. "What if it's the giant?"

She pursed her lips. "Don't mock me, Master Poke," she said. "I ain't in the mood."

He canted his head as if studying an interesting new species. "And what mood are you in, wee Gemini?"

"I know they ain't of much value to you," she said, "but you tell Ox and 'is cronies to back off, or I swear I'll kill 'em all."

"There are three to your one, lass."

The gun wobbled. "Then I better get started."

Not a soul breathed, then Poke chuckled and shook his head. "Ahh, Mr. Slate, look what you've done." His eyes were bright when he turned to Will. "Ever since your arrival the women have been wild with passion." His grin was still in place. "However did you manage it? I must learn your trick."

"She can't get us all," Ox rasped, shifting his knife to his left hand. "And I can do 'er first."

"Mr. Oxford." Poke's tone was almost sorrowful, his expression disapproving as if he scolded a wayward schoolboy. "We do not kill women here in the Den."

Ox growled something unintelligible.

"No," Poke said, and smiled beauteously at the girl. "And neither do we stifle their passion. Very well." He nodded once with paternal kindness. "I leave him in your gentle hands, young Gemini."

She glanced toward the body on the floor but didn't move, as if frozen in place, as if terrified to hope.

"Tell me you don't mistrust me, lass."

Her gaze flickered, and he sighed. "Go," he said, and, reaching out, took the gun from her hand. "I'll not forestall you."

She released the pistol and stumbled toward the giant.

"What about 'im?" Oxford's voice was raspy as he yanked his gaze from the Scotsman to Will.

"What indeed?" Poke mused.

" 'E's trouble."

"Aren't we all?"

" 'E ain't one of us."

"Perhaps not, but it appears as if he has accomplished his mission."

Will watched him carefully. Past Poke's shoulder, he saw that the Highlander had not yet moved. His stomach clenched.

"Perhaps I misjudged you," Poke was saying. "I confess, I expected you to fail."

Will tried to focus on the matter at hand, at the slippery task of survival. "Did I disappoint you?" he asked.

"Not at all. Indeed, I am delighted."

"Then perhaps you should call off your hounds."

Poke laughed, sounding surprised. "First an animal, then a hound, Mr. Oxford. If I did not know better, I would think our Mr. Slate dislikes you."

Oxford snarled a smile. His teeth were stained and his gums red. "Want to 'ave us a go, Mister Fancy Trousers?"

"I believe we already did that," Will said, his tone remarkably steady. "Or would you have assistance this time?"

Ox stepped closer, his eyes darting sideways. "I don't need me no 'elp for the likes o' you."

Will's knees all but buckled. They were about to give out—along with his stomach, and he was going to pitch forward into his own vomit—seconds before he was hacked to pieces by this rabid mob. "That didn't appear to be the case last time," he intoned.

"Fuck—" Ox began, raising his blade, but Poke held up a hand.

"Cease," he said. "I've had quite enough entertainment for one day."

"I'll cut your bloody 'eart—"

"Quit," Poke said. His voice was deathly quiet. Yet somehow it shivered through the room. Not a soul moved. He smiled. "That's better. Now, Mr. Slate, will you adjourn to my office with me?"

Will shifted his gaze to the downed Scotsman.

"I'm certain Gemini can take care of our reticent guest."

"Yeah," said one of Oxford's companions. "And we'll 'elp."

Poke turned his sleepy eyes toward the man with the club. He was lanky and bowed, with an Adam's apple that jumped like a nervous tree frog. "The interrogation is over, Mr. Black. You will allow our guest to rest now."

"Yeah," he said and chuckled as he tapped his club against his palm. "I'll let 'im rest . . . in peace."

Poke laughed. "Very good, Mr. Black. Very good," he said, then raised the pistol and pulled the trigger.

The gun exploded. Gem screamed. Ox swore, and Black stared in wide-eyed disbelief. A neat circle of red marked his forehead, but the wall behind was not so tidy. Brains and blood were spattered across the cracked plaster like curdled milk from broken crockery. He made a gurgling sound in his throat. His club fell to the floor, and he lifted his hand, fingers bent like claws, and fell forward, toppling stiff-legged onto his face.

Poke turned to Will and lifted an elegant hand. "After you," he said.

But William couldn't move, couldn't breathe. A glob of fatty brain matter slid languidly down the wall to the floor.

"Mr. Slate," Poke said, tilting his head slightly, "you look a bit green. Is your stomach still bothering you?"

He was going to be sick. His hands felt clammy and his throat tight.

"Perhaps you'd best give me the chest and get yourself some air."

William turned numbly toward Poke. The gun was still in his hand, the smile still on his face.

"Mr. Slate?" he said, reaching out.

There was nothing Will could do but surrender the chest and stumble toward the door.

Chapter 12

❦❦❦

"**H**e's dead." She croaked the words into the darkness like a lost child, knowing she should be silent, knowing she dare not care. "I killed him."

"Hush. Hush now." Peter's voice was quiet, too, but not devastated, not mourning, not broken like a child's. "Else someone will hear you."

She knew he was right, knew she must be cautious. Emotion was weakness. Weakness was death. It was as simple as that. But . . .

"He'd done me no harm," she whispered. Indeed, she had barely ever seen the man called Dag. He was but one of Poke's guards—the numberless, faceless army that surrounded the Den, keeping her in as effectively as they kept others out. But she'd crushed his skull. Struck him with a scrap of timber before he could do the same to the stranger. She shivered. What had she become? A murderer. And for what? She'd never even met the giant. Didn't even know his name.

And perhaps Dag had only been doing his job. Perhaps he had a family to feed. The idea clawed at her chest, scraping her heart. She lifted her eyes to Peter, finding his face in the darkness. "Did he . . . did he have children? Do you know?" she whispered, but Peter snorted.

"Dag? Naw. None that was human nohow. God's bones, Princess, he was a bastard and worse. He would of killed you quick as a snap. You know that."

"But he didn't," she whispered. "I'm still alive, and he's lying back there with his skull—"

Peter grasped her arms, shaking her. "That's cuz he was set on killing the other bloke, the giant. It's not as if he was on his way to chapel, Princess."

"I just . . ." She scowled at her hands. The darkness hid all manner of evil, but she knew her fingers were stained. She knew it, whether she could see it or not. She could feel it on her skin, on her damaged soul. Her stomach twisted. "The Scotsman," she whispered, remembering foggily. "I don't know him. I don't . . . Perhaps he's worse than Dag. Perhaps—"

"It don't matter," Peter hissed. "It don't. You did what you did. What you thought was right. We just gotta keep it quiet now. Can you do that?"

Her hands were shaking. She stared at them. They never shook. Fear was fatal. Weakness was death. "So much blood," she whispered.

"Princess!" Someone rushed at her from the darkness. She jumped, disoriented and terrified. But it was only a boy. How long would he live? No hope. She jerked at the memory of Slate's words. "Princess, you 'urt?" the lad rasped, but his words made no sense to her fluttering mind.

Death was all around her, smothering her. Killing her.

"Get away," she said, staring at boy, staring but not really seeing. "Go."

"What's the matter with 'er?" His eyes were round, his narrow body all but invisible in the heavy darkness.

"Nothing," Peter said, "there ain't nothing' wrong. She's just scared."

"Scared," the boy breathed.

She drew a slow, deep breath. Reality eased in a careful inch. It was Nim. Nimble Jack. The boy with the earnest eyes and the quick smile. The boy with no hope.

"Princess don't never get scared," he murmured.

"Get out," she whispered, and gripped his jacket in fingers gone numb with cold and regret. "Go back, Nim."

She could see him scowl in the darkness, could feel his confusion. "Back where?"

She pulled him close, and whispered, softer still, "Back where there's hope."

He leaned away, his eyes wider than ever, his voice raspy. "I don't know what you're talkin' about. This 'ere's me 'ome."

She tightened her grip. Her bloodstained fingers ached. "I can see the difference in you," she whispered. "I felt it when you came back to us. Where were you?"

"I told you, I was in prison. But I escaped."

"Do you want to die?" She pulled him closer still. The whites of his eyes gleamed in the darkness as he strained away. "Is that what you want? What you think you deserve?"

"Let go," Peter said, his voice quiet. "Let go now, love. You're scarin' him."

She realized in foggy dismay that her nails were digging like talons into the boy's tattered jacket. She eased up a bit, and he pulled away and stepped beyond her reach.

"P'raps you should go, Nim," Peter said.

The boy backed up a pace. "She gonna be all right?"

"Sure. Sure she is. Just, don't tell nobody 'bout this."

The boy shook his head, turned, and disappeared into the darkness. Like a wraith, like a ghost, like someone who had never been.

He would be dead soon. Dead and gone. Tears stung her eyes. "Don't let it happen, Peter."

"Don't let what happen?" He was holding her arms, whether to soothe her or restrain her, she couldn't say.

"Don't let them kill him."

"No." He moved closer and slipped an arm around her shoulders. His body felt warm against hers. " 'Course not."

She shivered in his embrace. "So much death."

"Dag woulda killed the other bloke," Peter said. "And you. He woulda killed you, if it come to that. You did what needed doin'."

What needed doing. She had no idea what that was. Perhaps once she had. Perhaps once life had made some sense. But no more. "Blood." She held her hands out again, searching for the stains. "Pain." She winced. "Fire." She shivered again, feeling cold and hot in vicious cycles. "Death. And why?" She lifted her eyes to search for answers in his face. But there were none. Only sadness, only worry. Only . . .

"Peter." Reaching up, she touched his cheek. "Are you crying?"

"No." He cleared his throat, but her palm was wet when she drew it away. "I'm just . . . sorry is all."

"Sorry?" she whispered.

"A lady like you . . ." He shrugged and eased away, dropping his arm from about her shoulders. "You should be dressed in fine clothes and fed proper, not . . ." He dropped his voice. "Not whorin' for Poke."

Lucidity returned like falling snowflakes, lighting cautiously in her mind. She drew a breath. "How old are you, Peter?"

He shrugged. "Near eight-and-ten I suspect."

She smiled wistfully. Had she ever been so young, she wondered, and doubted it. For she felt ancient, old and beaten and weary to the bone. "It's not too late for you," she murmured.

"For me to what?"

"To get out. Make a life. Maybe have a family." Images, warm and happy slipped into her mind.

"Me?" He laughed. "Who'd marry me? I'm a—"

"You're kind," she said, and slipped her hand onto his cheek again. "Do you know how uncommon that is? True kindness?"

"*You're* kind," he countered, but she shook her head.

"Perhaps once."

Reaching down, he drew her fingers into the warmth of his. "You could leave him, Princess. You could get away. Sail—"

But she covered his mouth with her fingers, hushing him before she weakened completely, before she fell from the sky forever. "You cannot worry about me, Peter. You must get out."

His eyes were wide and earnest, but finally he lifted her hand and kissed her palm. "And leave you here cryin'?" he asked, and grinned.

"I'm not . . ." she began, but he touched her cheek and she felt the tears smear across her face.

"We can't have no one see you like this. Our princess in tears."

She shook her head, weak and fuzzy. "I'm sorry."

"For what?" His eyes were soft, his voice the same. "For savin' the big bloke's life?"

She exhaled carefully, grappling for strength. "For being weak."

He laughed. "You ain't weak."

She shuddered. Another tear slipped down her cheek, burning with heat and silent regret. "Then I'm sorry for taking a life."

"You did what you had—" He stopped, his eyes lifting. "What is it?"

"I think I heard something."

"What—"

"Who's there?" queried a voice from the darkness.

She opened her mouth, but Peter placed a finger to his lips. "Stay," he whispered. Dropping his hand, Peter sauntered into the night.

"It's me," he said, his voice jovial. "And who might you be?"

"What the 'ell you doin' out 'ere?" The voice was deep, gruff with suspicion and self-supposed superiority.

"I'm 'avin' me a smoke," Peter said. "Or would be if I could find a damned match. You got one?"

"I thought I 'eard voices."

Peter laughed. "I been known to talk to meself in lieu of a cigar. You want one?"

The guard was silent a moment, then grunted, seeming to find Peter harmless. "Why you 'ere?"

"I was just headin' back to the Den. Want to come along?" He laughed. "Keep me safe?" His tone was marvelously casual.

From her place against the unforgiving wall, Shandria saw the brilliant flare of a match. It set the two faces in sharp relief for a moment, then yanked them back into darkness.

"You 'ear about Dag?" asked the guard.

She could smell the pungent scent of tobacco.

"What about 'im?"

"'E's dead. Someone killed 'im. Clubbed 'im 'ard enough to scramble 'is brains."

"No!" Peter said, and turned back toward the Den. The guard followed.

Their voices faded into the darkness. Shandria closed

her eyes. Quiet settled in, frightening and soothing at the same time.

"Why'd you do it?"

She stifled a scream and tried to scramble away, but her back struck the wall, and she cringed. The advancing shape stopped some yards away, watching her in silence, giving her time, giving her breathing space. She calmed herself with desperate speed.

"Dancer." She grappled for control when she recognized him, but her mind clattered wildly on. How much had he heard? How much had he guessed? "Do you make a habit of sneaking about in the dark?"

"Doesn't everyone?" he asked, and watched her in the ensuing silence. She struggled to read his mood, but she could barely guess her own.

"What are you doing here?" she asked, and found that despite everything, her voice was steady. What did that say of her?

He advanced another step. "I thought I'd ask the same of you," he said. "You missed all the excitement."

She locked her knees. "Excitement?"

"We had a visitor at the Den."

"Did you?" She controlled her breathing with an effort and lifted her chin slightly, fighting for control.

He still watched her, unmoving, not speaking, as if gauging her every word. "A Highlander by the looks of him. Giant of a man."

She forced a laugh. It sounded maniacal in the gritty darkness of the alley. "I didn't think you the type to make giants out of shadows, Dancer."

"Who was he?"

"How would I . . ." she began, but the weight of his words crashed in, nearly sending her to her knees. "*Was?*" She felt her legs tremble and splayed her hands against the cracked plaster behind her. It bit into her fingers, and she pushed harder, revived by the bite of pain.

"Oxford and his cronies had already gotten to him before I arrived," he said.

Her head felt light, her stomach knotted. She had been sure when she'd first seen the Scotsman that he was just passing through, a lost vagabond whom she would never again lay eyes on. She had been certain she could remain hidden in the shadows, watching, but then Dag had appeared and she had been forced to do something.

"What was he to you?"

She shook her head, trying to think, to maintain, to survive. "I don't know what—"

"God damn it!" he snarled, and lurched forward.

She forced herself to straighten against the wall, to remain where she was, but inside she was curling into herself, sobbing hopelessly, begging for mercy.

His fingers snatched her arms. "I know." His words were softer now. "I heard your conversation with Peter."

Dear God! Oh dear God! He would tell Poke, then it would all be over. But not quickly. Not easily, and long before she could right the wrongs that surrounded her. And yet it was not in her simply to crumble. She could not, no matter how much she longed to. "Did you?" she asked and met his eyes as she drew a slow breath. It seemed to burn her lungs. "So you're a thief *and* an eavesdropper, Dancer?"

His face was close to hers. "Why did you try to save him?"

"I didn't—"

"Why?" he growled, and tightened his grip painfully on her arms.

She closed her eyes, fighting with everything she had, but it wasn't enough. "Is he dead?" she whispered.

"Why would you care?"

"I wouldn't. I—"

He shook her again.

She squeezed her eyes shut and held back the tears. "I don't know him. I swear it," she whispered.

The night went silent. His hands loosened on her arms. "Then why did you kill the guard?"

"The giant, he seemed . . ." Not harmless. Hardly that. "He seemed a good man."

"And the guard was not."

She didn't attempt to stifle her chuckle. "He worked for Poke."

He watched her. "As do you," he intoned. "Indeed, you share his bed."

She stared at him as pain blistered through her heart, but what did she care what he thought? Who was he to judge her? Who was he at all? "Yes," she said, her voice finally steady. "That I do."

She waited for his recrimination, but he said nothing. The silence bore down on her. His eyes were sharp in the darkness. He wore his soul there, deep within, but just visible if one knew what to look for. She glanced away, not wanting to see.

"Why?" he asked.

"So many questions, Dancer. I can't hardly keep track—"

"Why do you stay with him?"

"Do you not think him attractive?" she asked, and pulled her arms from his grip.

He said nothing. Silence stretched into eternity. She shifted her gaze back to his.

"You hide in the darkness," he said, his voice as quiet as the night, "and cry over a man you don't care about; but when Poke threatens you, you shed not a single tear."

Quiet again, eating away at her. "You don't even ask for mercy. Why?"

She tried to turn away, but his eyes held her captive and horrid honesty knocked insistently at her mind. "What good do you think it would do me, Dancer? Do you think he would set me free? Kiss away the pain?" She shuddered.

He scowled, watching her, too closely, too damned close.

"What good does it do to cry here?" he asked.

She raised her chin, struggling madly. "None," she admitted. "None at all. So if you'll excuse me . . ."

"Where are you going?"

She smiled. It was a miracle she could make it happen. "To my lover, of course."

He grabbed her arm again, hard and fast. She glanced down, and her heart beat like mad against her ribs. "Don't go," he said.

She didn't close her eyes. Didn't melt. Didn't weaken. "Whyever not?"

His eyes smote hers. "Why?" His fingers bit into her flesh. "A man is dead."

"Many men are dead."

"Did you know the one called Black?"

Black was dead. She knew it, felt it in his words. More death. She could smell it. Could taste it. It strangled her. "Who killed him?"

"You're not surprised he's dead."

Her heart was tearing, ripping in two. "Did the giant . . ."

"Poke killed him."

"Oh." Relief rushed through her, and in some corner of her mind she knew that was twisted and strange. But she had taken Dag's life to save another's. And if that other was a murderer . . .

"Your lover has killed a man, splattered his brains against the wall like so much . . ." He ran out of words, out of breath. She could hear him struggling for control. He shook his head. Even in the darkness, she could see the agony in his eyes. She turned away from it, shielding her heart. "And you're not even surprised? Not even—"

"You think I don't know what he's capable of?" she hissed, jerking back. "You think I don't know?" Her hands were shaking. She pressed them against her skirt. "He's not what you think he is."

"Then what is he?"

She shook her head, feeling crazed and frenetic, drowning in terrified uncertainty. "He's a ghost," she whispered. "A magician. He can make you believe lies and doubt the truth."

"I believe he's a thief and a murderer."

She laughed and shook her head. "A thief? Oh no, not Poke. He has others to do that. Hundreds of others."

"I think you overestimate him."

"Then you think wrong," she whispered, leaning close. "If it is stolen in Sedonia, there will come a time when he will hold it in his hands, no matter how much blood is spilled to place it there."

"Then where does he keep the goods?"

She stared at him, her throat tight. "Don't do it," she murmured. "Don't even let it cross your mind."

"Do what?"

"He'll know," she said, and felt her throat contract with the need to retch.

"He's not God," he said, and touched his fingers to her cheek. Warmth spread through her like the lap of a golden fire. Comfort. Hope. Strength. It was there in his hand, but death was there, too.

"God?" she said, and pulled resolutely away. "There is no God in Darktowne."

"Lass." His tone was nearly silent, his eyes entrancing. "You don't need to stay—"

A noise sounded from the alley. Her heart lurched. "Leave," she hissed. "Go, before it's your brains on the wall."

He remained exactly as he was, watching her, drilling into her thoughts.

"And what of you?" he whispered. "What of your safety?"

She slanted her gaze rapidly to the right. Someone was near! Maybe within hearing. Her heart knotted up hard, but she turned back to him. "Don't be a fool. He'll not hurt me."

His fingers dug into her arms, and he laughed, low and harsh. "Because you're his princess."

"No," she said, and yanked from his grasp. "Because I'm his property."

Chapter 13

William roamed the streets of Skilan, but it seemed as if he had never seen them before, and perhaps he had not, for he had different eyes now, different clothes, a different mind.

He was sober, and never had he regretted that more deeply. Reality was a terrible beast to face without the comfort of a drink. A muffled roar rose from the Blue Fox. He had never been inside that particular pub. It would be safe to go in. His hands shook as he held the thought at bay. But why should he not imbibe? He wouldn't be recognized. And he had a few coins. He could buy a glass of wine, just enough to slake his thirst.

He paused at the door. One drink. Just one. He needed it, ached for it. Surely one glass would do him no harm. But dark honesty crept sneakily into his subconscious. One drink was not what he wanted, what he longed for. Oblivion was what he cherished—the sweet unconcern of inebriation. He scraped his knuckles across his mouth, knowing without a doubt that intoxication would get him killed, would leave her alone—with Poke.

He swore viciously, gritted his teeth against the punch of temptation and moved on, his stride stilted, his body stiff, for the truth was undeniable. The memory of his roiling stomach no longer kept him from drinking. It was the memory of the face of a woman who, by her own admission, belonged to another. A woman who had no feelings for him.

And yet she had saved him. Repeatedly. Didn't that suggest some sort of emotion? But no. She had killed Dag, had crushed his skull in an attempt to keep a stranger safe. If she had feelings, it was for the populace at large and not any particular to himself. But maybe she had lied. Maybe the giant was no stranger. After all, she had cried. The street seemed to go silent at the memory. In his mind's eye he could see her in Peter's arms, all her icy strength melting away as she surrendered to the boy. Not sexually. But so much more importantly—emotionally. She had cried. And Peter had done the same. Is that why she allowed the lad to touch her, because she found something in him she could not receive from others? Was it honest emotion that she longed for?

God knew Poke had no soul. But perhaps Will's soul was gone as well. When was the last time he had cried? Not in years certainly. Not even at his family's funeral.

Anger tore at him, burning inside, and he turned rapidly back toward the pub, determined to do away with this mind-numbing sobriety, but images of his son's tiny face flared up in his mind.

No, he had not cried at the boy's passing as he had not rejoiced at his birth. What did that say of him? Why had he failed to live? Why had he spent all those years in a dull haze? And why had they died instead of him?

Questions tormented him. But he had no answers. Only gnawing uncertainty. But he would learn.

"*He makes lies seem like truth.*" It had seemed that Elisabeth had died because of her own decisions. But what was the truth?

"If it is stolen in Sedonia, there will come a time when he will hold it in his hands," at least according to Shandria. But nothing had been stolen from her carriage. Unless she had taken her leather journal with her. Unless the highwaymen were not out to gain jewels and coin, but had something more specific, more scientific, in mind.

Will shook his head. What could she have been working on that would have been worth her life? The theory was crazy. But it was the only theory he had. Thus, he had little choice but to pursue it, for he had vowed at Nicol's wedding to learn the truth. And in order to do so he must remain at the Den. Of that much, he was certain. And he could not remain there unless he had something to show for his efforts. He glanced down the street. There was an inn some way along the rutted thoroughfare. His stomach crunched with hunger. There would be food there and families with enough funds to pay their way. Perhaps he could steal some coin. His heart cranked up in time with his stomach, and he strolled past. Courage. The courage it must take to steal was incredible. He had not considered it before. Indeed, he had always thought it a coward's life.

A carriage passed him, carried by a smart four-in-hand that strutted like peacocks. The occupants watched him through the small square windows. Well fed and impeccably groomed, they stared as though he were so much rubbish on the street. He glanced down at his own shabby attire and nearly laughed. Except for the coat and hat he had taken from the lusty boy, his costume was despicable. What would he have thought if he had seen such a person on his way to the pub? Would he have condemned him as slovenly and contemptible or would he have seen more, looked deeper?

But wasn't that why he had dulled his senses? So that he wouldn't have to look at all.

Up ahead a stable appeared on his right. The shingle above the tall door was barely visible in the waning light, but the aroma was enough to announce it as an equine establishment, and the warm scents called to him. Avoiding the crackled ice of a half-frozen puddle, he crossed the rutted street and paused in the doorway. Inside, a cock-hipped piebald snorted contentedly from its stall, then returned to munching oats from a badly cribbed manger. The place smelled of well-cured hay and leather oil, of horses and wealth. Of home, though he had never felt it fill his senses like this.

A harness hung from a nearby peg, its buckles shining in the last rays of the setting sun. Will touched a line, feeling the suppleness of it and letting his mind slide back to the past. Yes, there had been pain. There had been loneliness and loss, but there had been laughter, too. Feasts, fine clothes, and soft beds. Why had he never noticed? he wondered, but rapid, pounding hoofbeats drew his attention back toward the door.

Two gentlemen galloped in, laughing as they came.

The younger man was lanky and loose-limbed. His striped waistcoat was well fitted, his stock undone. Flushed with youth and Scotch, he'd thrown his coat over his gelding's whithers. It flared dramatically over his skinny thigh as they bumped to a halt.

"You there," called the older of the two. He glanced down, top hat askew over his apple red nose as he sawed his steed to an openmouthed halt. He held a silver flask in his right hand, and his voice was slurred. "Steady my animal."

Will stared at the flask, and every question seemed to

be answered there. His very hands shook with the need for that ancient, intoxicating wisdom.

"Are you daft?" snarled the gentleman. "I said hold the beast while I dismount."

Will reached out to grasp the stallion's reins. Its burnished, liver chestnut hide shone in the failing rays of sun, and it rolled its eyes as its rider swung a fat leg over the cantle. But his energy could not be stilled, and he pranced grandly, swinging rhythmically in place.

"Damn it all!" Jostled against the pommel on his descent, the rider bumbled to the hard-packed clay of the aisle, then steadied his stance and his flask. "What kind of demmed hostler are you? He 'bout made a eunuch of me."

The younger man grinned as he toppled from his gray. "Can't have that. The ladies at Grayson's would be sorely put out, and that would be bad indeed." Taking a drink from his own flask, he tipped it slyly toward his companion. "Since we've already worn out the Bryerly lassies, aye, Percy?"

The inebriated fellow snorted, seeming unimpressed by his companion's wit and keeping his scowl trained on Will. "What's your name, boy?"

Boy. Will stared. What an intresting phenomenon. Had he been so arrogant, so rude, so god-awful, grindingly irritating?

"Good Christ, we've got a sharp tack here," snorted Percy and leaned in closer to speak in slow, spitting syllables. "What the fuck's your bloody name?"

"I'm called Slate," he said, meeting the other's eyes and feeling a strange stir of earthy superiority.

"Are you now?" Percy asked, and stepped back to watch Will narrowly, as if assessing the even answer.

"Well, they call me Lord Perceval of Dalkirk Manor. Can you get your mouth 'round that, boy?"

Will said nothing, and the gentleman laughed. "Thought as much. I hope he's better with horses than he is at speaking, aye, Douglas?"

Douglas took a long draught from his own flask. "Bound to be," he managed, and slapped his gelding's reins into Will's hand.

"Have them tacked and ready upon our return, or there'll be hell to pay."

"Hell from your wife if we're late," Douglas chortled, and drank again.

Percy ignored him and narrowed his eyes as if to punctuate his message. "This stallion's worth more than you'll make in a lifetime, laddie, so look lively."

What did one make in a lifetime as a thief?

Percy thumped him on the chest with a blocky index finger. "You listening to me, boy?"

William turned his gaze from the handsome stallion to the bloated master. "Aye, my lord," he said, and almost smiled. A clear head, he realized, was a dangerous thing. "I am."

"Good," said the other, and, turning unsteadily, marched from the stable. The younger man gamboled after like an unsteady satyr until the two were out of sight.

Reaching up, Will straightened the stallion's forelock. The animal was tall and gallant, far too good for the likes of the man who rode him. But perhaps that was generally the case. And perhaps it was time to right one wrong in the world.

Glancing toward the back of the stable, Will came to a foolishly sensible decision. Taking the redingote from the gelding's neck, he pulled it on, buttoned it to the neck, and swung onto the chestnut. The seat felt as natural as breathing. The stallion pranced, the gelding followed, and the piebald munched distractedly as they left the solace of the stable. Snowflakes drifted languidly from an ebon sky, lighting delicately on the horses' manes.

It wasn't more than a ten-minute ride to the next livery. A flame burned in the square-paned lantern that hung beside the gray stone building.

Will dismounted as a gnarled old man shambled outside, gray cloth cap pulled low over bushy eyebrows. He scrunched his face as he studied the horses, showing a lack of teeth but a keen mind. "A handsome pair of steeds you have there, my lord. You'll be wantin' them put up for the night?"

"*Non*," William said in his best French, and laid a regretful hand on the stallion's elegant neck. "I sail for home with the morning tide. I fear I must sell them."

The Den was quiet when Will stepped through the door. Morning had only just risen over the eastern horizon. Not a soul intercepted him as he made his way through the echoing foyer and into the parlor.

Gem sat beside the bed where the giant lay. She lifted her gaze as Will stepped inside. Dark rings accented her evergreen eyes, and her sharp, vixen's face looked gaunt and pale.

"You should sleep," Will said, but Gem scowled and shifted her gaze back to her ward.

" 'E's going to need something to eat soon as 'e wakes up." She fussed with the blanket that covered him. He made not the slightest movement. Indeed, if he was breathing, Will could not tell it. "Big bloke like this . . ." She cleared her throat. Her hands shook.

Will stepped up close. Her patient's face was as pale as hers now that it was washed clean of the blood that had soaked his hair. If he wasn't dead, he soon would be, Will thought, but he would not say the words out loud. Was that mercy or weakness?

"Get some rest, Gem," he said, but she was already shaking her head. " 'E wouldn't rest. Not if it was me. 'E'd . . ." She paused abruptly and spurted her gaze to Will's, eyes wide and feral.

He shifted his own to the door and back, but they were alone. "He'd what?"

She said nothing.

"What would he do?"

She tightened her hand in his blanket and cleared her throat. "Well there's no tellin' really, is there? I'm just . . ." Her usually bright mouth was pale and pursed. "I'm pretendin' is what I'm doin'. Thinkin' girlish things," she said, but a single tear dripped down her cheek. "Spinning tales in me head."

From the far side of the house, a noise scraped the morning silence. Poke? Ox? It hardly mattered. Both were deadly, feeding on the emotions of others.

"Pretendin'," she said again, her voice dreamy.

"Well quit." Will's tone was firmer than he would have believed he could make it, and though his muscles quaked, he reached out and shook her. "Unless you want to see him dead, you'll keep your thoughts to yourself."

" 'E—"

"Quiet," he ordered, and leaned closer. "Listen to me. I don't know who he is. He could be your own father for all I know, but you must stick to your story. And stick fast. You don't know him. You've no special feelings for him. He's just a daft fool who stumbled into the Den, much as I did. Do you hear me?"

Her lips parted as if to protest, but she nodded.

He drew a careful breath. "Does anyone else know you were here all night?"

"Don't think so."

He nodded, then, reaching into his pocket, he drew out a silver buckle. Footsteps sounded in the hall, heading their way.

He shoved the buckle into her hand and closed her fingers over it. "You got it off a fancy sop in Berrywood. You hear?"

"Aye," she said, and bobbed her understanding. "Passed out cold, 'e was, with 'is wine bottle beside 'im— 1810." A glimpse of her old spirit shone in her lightning-quick eyes. "'Twas a damned fine year."

William almost laughed.

Gratitude scampered across her foxy features, then she hid the trinket away quick as lightning. "I won't forget," she said softly. "And neither will 'e, once 'e comes to."

Will glanced at her patient. Not a flicker of awareness shone there, not a breath of hope. But perhaps the lass called Gemini was accustomed to hopelessness and hoped anyway.

Chapter 14

"My apologies for cutting our entertainment short. I fear I am not feeling quite up to snuff," Poke said.

Shandria inclined her head. The adoring companion. As if she were disappointed but accepting. And indeed she was. For even watching blood shed was preferable to this—time alone with the man who called himself her master.

"Do you forgive me, Princess?" he asked, and with one hand on the bedchamber door, reached up to stroke her cheek.

"Of course," she said, and remembered not to shudder, not to shrink away.

He smiled. Perhaps he was a handsome man. She could no longer tell, for she knew the state of his soul. Or the absence of one.

"You've never much cared for the fights, have you, love?" he asked, turning the latch and ushering her inside.

She set the glowing candle on the cluttered commode. "I prefer . . ." she began, but in that instant she knew something was different. What? Senses honed for danger screamed a warning. She scanned the room with lightning furtiveness. There. A wispy trail of smoke lifting lazily from a candlestick near the bed.

Someone had been in the chamber only moments before. Which meant—Dear God, he was still there. Somewhere. She was sure of it.

"Is something amiss, love?" Poke asked, and tossed his coat aside.

She turned her back to the candle, trying desperately to do so slowly, casually. "'Tis nothing," she said and though she managed to keep from skimming the room again, she saw that the armoire was open. A hundred glimmering items shone from the shelves. Someone had breached Poke's sanctuary, had dared gaze upon the loot he reveled in keeping for his own. Where was he now?

"You're distracted this evening," he said. Loosening his stock, he tossed it on the discarded jacket.

"Not at all," she said, and prayed her voice was steadier than her hands.

"It's not our guest, is it?"

William. He was in the room. She knew it suddenly. Knew it as certainly as she knew her own name.

Her heart contracted, but she slipped out of her shoes and turned, allowing herself one quick glance around the room before placing the slippers by the bedstead. "What guest might that be?"

Poke laughed as he crossed the floor and dipped his head to kiss her neck. Her skin quivered at his touch, but she didn't move.

"It is true," he said. "We are suddenly inundated with strangers. But I doubt you'll need to concern yourself with the one."

Fear speared through her like an icicle to the heart. "Which one?"

Poke's brows raised with slow precision. "Does it matter?"

She shrugged, just managing to breathe, to keep her head. He must be under the bed. Draped in scarlet curtains, it was the only structure large enough to hide an intruder. "I merely wondered. You know how Gem is these days, nursing every wounded sparrow."

"Yes," Poke said, and sighed. "It will be difficult for her. But life is hard at times. She may as well learn that now as soon as late."

She almost laughed out loud at the absurdity of his words. As though Gem hadn't suffered enough! Maybe it would have been better to let the giant die in the street rather than let the girl watch his slow demise. Shandria's stomach clenched. "You're so certain the Scotsman will die?" she asked.

Poke eased a few tendrils of wispy hair from her cheek, then slipped around behind her and reached for the clasps that held her gown in place. The hairs on her neck stood erect, waiting. "Quite certain."

She closed her eyes, breathing carefully. "Why not let him go?" she asked. "He can't harm you."

She could feel his gaze on her face and forced herself to remain as she was. Poke could smell fear. Indeed, he fed on it.

"Ahh, Princess," he said finally, and sighed. "You wound me with your suspicions. I did not mean to imply that I planned to murder the poor fellow. I merely meant I doubt he'll survive his current wounds."

All lies. "And if he does?"

His hands moved lower, loosing the long line of buttons down her back. "Why the interest, my love?"

"He seems harmless."

"So our Mr. Slate does not?"

Could he see them? Was he witnessing her humiliation?

"I am told he killed Vic," she said.

"Yes," Poke agreed, then fell silent.

Had he noticed the open armoire? Could he see under the bed? Shandria flitted her gaze to the floor beneath the four-poster again, but there was nothing to be seen there.

"Curious, isn't it," Poke said, and kissed her neck. She shifted her gaze to his face and saw that he, too, was staring at the bed. Her heart boomed like a cannon in her chest. She couldn't bear to witness another death. She wouldn't survive it. If Will was found, she would do what it took to save him. And damn her duties. "Our Mr. Slate looks so bland . . . innocuous even. But you have to wonder. Is he, perhaps, some dark and dangerous villain?" He faked a shudder. "Come now. Admit it. You must wonder. After all, he's a handsome chap, don't you think?" he asked, and turned his gaze back to hers, as though he didn't know they were being watched, as though he weren't, even now, anticipating a kill.

Maybe he didn't know. He was only human—not the devil himself, thus she must distract him. She must. Reaching up, she pulled a pair of pins from her hair. It fell free, spilling around her shoulders. Poke reached up, slipping his hand into it, letting it slide between his fingers.

"Princess?"

She tried to remember his question, but she'd forgotten his words. Panic stormed through her.

He raised a brow at her. "Do you think our Mr. Slate handsome?"

She forced a shrug. "He's not you," she said simply.

"Ahhh." Poke sighed and, lifting his hands from between their bodies, slid the sleeves from her arms. "So flattering to know you think of no one else." The gown fell to the floor. The air felt cold against her exposed skin, but she kept from covering herself, even when he turned her to face him.

" 'Twas a lucky day indeed when I first met you."

He skimmed his knuckles along the frilly edge of her chemise. Gooseflesh followed in his wake. "Don't you agree, Princess?"

"Certainly."

"And you've been faithful to me?" His gaze settled on hers as he slipped his fingers around her throat. "Body and soul?"

Terror ripped through her, but she remained as she was, vulnerable and sick. "I'm no fool," she said, and he smiled.

"No love, that you are not," he agreed, and, opening his hand, skimmed his splayed fingers down her body. "Indeed, you are quite intelligent. And discerning." His eyes darkened. "Not like MacTavish's late bitch." His breathing had become labored suddenly. She waited for the rage, the slavering jealousy. But he stifled his emotions and cupped her breast with trembling fingers. "There's a new bride now though, isn't there? A *true* princess." His gaze raked her. She swallowed hard, trying to breathe through the terror. "What of this one?" His words were hissed, barely discernible, as if he spoke to someone else. "I'm told she's enamored. Of course I've not had her yet. But she'll not refuse me."

He tightened his grip, and despite herself, Shandria winced.

"Ohhh, my apologies," Poke crooned and loosened his grip. "I didn't mean to hurt you. After all, you're not like the others."

Who were the others? she wondered frantically. *Had they survived?*

"Are you?" A wild light gleamed in his eyes.

"No," she said, barely able to force out the word. "I am not."

"Good. Good." He sighed and backed away. Sanity, or a clever facsimile returned to his eyes. "Disrobe for me, love."

Bile burned like poison in her stomach, but she would not refuse him, and he knew it. Bending, he kissed her lips and sauntered across the room, where he lowered himself to a chair.

She snapped her glance toward the bed again. Could he see beneath the bed from that vantage point? Could he— But no. She wouldn't consider it, wouldn't let the thought into her mind, for nothing was safe from him. Not even her thoughts.

Poke settled back in his chair, his eyes half-closed, his full lips lifted in the parody of a smile. Her heart trembled as she untied her chemise, but her hands were steady. Her gaze the same. He met it with lazy anticipation, then watched as her clothing fell to the floor. His eyes gleamed like a rabid wolf's, but she would not quail. She would not.

"Your stockings," Poke said, and she bent to loose her garters and roll the sheer fabric down.

He was smiling when she straightened. Her stomach tightened with dread.

"Come remove my shoes, love," he said, and unbuttoned his shirt.

She crossed the floor like one in a trance, then bent and tugged off his shoes. He stroked her breasts as she straightened.

"Now my trousers." He stood, and for a moment, for

one weak second, she was sure she couldn't do it, couldn't bear to touch him, but she did.

Loosing the buttons, she pushed his trousers down. He was flaccid. But that didn't mean she was safe. Stepping out of the garment, he kissed her neck. Her lungs ached. She remembered to breathe.

"Princess." He drew back, finding her eyes with his. "Are you nervous?"

She was going to be sick. "Should I be?" she asked.

The room went silent, then he laughed. "My lady, as regal as a queen. As loyal as a slave." He slipped his hand lower, down the midsection of her body. His fingers slid like a serpent into her private hair.

"And all mine," he whispered.

She stifled a shiver. Her reprieve was over. Hell had come, she thought, but in that instant he stepped away.

"Good night, my love," he said, and, tossing his shirt aside, strode naked to the bed.

Shandria held her breath, waiting hopelessly, but he did not pull the pistol from beneath the pillow, did not laugh as he admitted he knew the truth. There were no screams of rage. Instead, he sighed as he pulled the blankets over his pale body.

She stood frozen in place. He glanced at her as if curious, and she forced herself to turn. Pacing to the nearby trunk, she opened it with clammy hands. The hinges moaned. She drew out a nightrail like one in a trance. The fabric sighed over her hair, drawing her marginally back to reality.

All was well. He didn't know of the intruder. But eventually he would. Eventually there would be blood.

Fear clawed at her guts. She dare not cross him. She glanced toward the candle Will had left behind, but the frail wisp of smoke was long gone. Maybe she'd been wrong. Maybe she was imagining, she thought, but she knew better.

She had no choice.

"I shall fetch you a tonic," she said. "For your ailment."

Poke propped himself on one elbow, watching her with sloe eyes. "How thoughtful of you," he cooed. "But tell me, Princess, is it loyalty or fear that makes you the perfect companion?"

She could find no words. Fear had left her numb.

"Or do you stay in the hopes of protecting your friends?"

She found her tongue and her demeanor with icy desperation. "I have no friends," she said.

"Not even in this room?"

Terror flashed through her. Dear Jesus! He *did* know. Her mind scrambled, searching wildly for an explanation, an apology, a weapon. But in a moment she recognized his tone.

It was pouty. Teasing. She felt weak with relief. Sick with the tight remains of panic.

"Not even in this room," she said, and he laughed.

Turning on wooden legs, she lifted the candle from the commode and exited.

It only took her a moment to find the bottle of his favorite Scotch. Her hand shook as she tipped it into a glass, then she delayed, praying hard. But in the end she pulled a tiny cloth bag from behind the flour in the kitchen. Glancing breathlessly about, she added a pinch to the drink, replaced the bag, and forced herself back to the bedchamber. The flickering candlelight wavered across the floor like a ghost leading her to her doom.

Poke sat up as he took the glass from her hand. His chest was narrow and sprinkled with dark hair. "Thank you, my love," he said, and took a sip.

She watched him, forgetting to breathe, neglecting to move, and he raised his brows.

"You seem strangely tense this night," he said, and smiled before he took another sip. "If I didn't know better, I would think you were trying to poison me."

Jerking herself back to reality, Shandria casually cupped the fragile flame and blew the world into darkness.

"No comment?" Poke asked.

"If you were gone . . ." She forced her tone to be fluid and level. "Who would take your place?"

Poke laughed and set the glass aside. "My Princess," he said. "Pragmatic till the last. Sleep well, love."

It was almost impossible to keep from collapsing like an abandoned doll of rags. Almost impossible to force her legs to carry her to the far side of the bed.

But she did so and finally lay, staring into the darkness, and praying.

Chapter 15

The world was quiet. Shandria liked the darkness, liked the night, for she could hide there. When no one was looking she could be a child. Unmasked. Herself. She was not afraid of who she was, only of what she might become. But she put that thought behind her now.

The day had gone well enough. She had been left alone for most of it. When evening had fallen she had traveled to Fairberry in search of game. She was not particularly adept at sleight of hand, but she could sneak into a house as quiet as a mole. Thus, she was returning to the Den with a silver-capped walking stick and a pair of ivory earbobs. Poke would be pleased.

Her stomach cramped. Her steps slowed. Yes, Poke would be pleased but it was impossible to guess what that would mean. He was unpredictable, but so were serpents.

"My thanks."

She jumped, clutching her hands and shoving her back up against a nearby wall. But no one lunged toward her. No one threatened. Indeed, no one spoke, but she managed to make out the intruder's face even in the darkness.

"Mr. Slate." She made certain her tone was level. "You again."

He stepped closer. He was not a giant of a man, but evil came in many sizes and was oft impossible to identify immediately. Had she misjudged him? she wondered, but she didn't retreat.

"For helping me," he explained, and took hold of her arm.

"I've no idea what you speak of." She tilted her head and scowled as if trying to see his expression in the darkness. "Perhaps you're confusing me with Gem."

"You knew," he said, his eyes gleaming with bright intensity in the darkness.

Her heart lurched, but she held her ground. "I do so hate to be the one to tell you," she said. "But I fear you may have lost your mind."

He gritted his teeth as if wanting to shake her. "Are you trying to say Poke always sleeps so soundly?"

Dear God, she'd guessed right! He had sneaked into Poke's bedchamber. He had hidden beneath the bed, and sometime during the night, he had managed to creep back out. She had almost convinced herself that she had imagined the entire episode. Had certainly hoped as much. But in the small hours of the morning she had heard a faint rustle of noise. Had heard and hadn't dared to do so much as glance up, lest she disturb Poke's slumber. Her stomach churned at the thought of the consequences just avoided. Damn him! Did he know nothing of pain, nothing of death? she wondered, but she gritted a smile. " 'Tis difficult to say. Whyever do you ask?"

"You gave him a potion." He bored her eyes with his own, but an eternity of uncertainty was there, an ocean of roiling confusion. Even in the darkness she could see that much. "You knew."

"Knew what?" she rasped, and yanked her arm from

his grip even as she skimmed the darkness, searching. There were spies. Everywhere. Always.

A host of emotions flashed across his face, but finally he shook his head. "Tell me, Princess, how can he keep himself from you?" His voice was low and entrancing. But he did not reach out, did not touch her.

And yet she was falling, losing her footing, slipping into the abyss of his earnestness. "I don't know what you speak of," she repeated, but her voice was weak and trembled dangerously. Could he hear it warble? Could he feel her frailty?

"You lie," he said, and in that moment she knew he sensed her weakness, for he did the unthinkable; he told the truth. "You knew I was in your chamber. You knew, and you protected me."

"You're insane," she whispered, and desperately wondered if it were true.

They were face-to-face, so close she could feel the warmth of his breath on her cheek. The world slowed. Their gazes met and melded. And then he kissed her, not with wild heat or frenzied lust, but with slow, deadly tenderness.

He pulled away, his eyes finding hers again. "Why?" he whispered. "Is it because . . . Might you feel something for me?"

Her knees felt weak, and her hands trembled, but fools died bloody, and their friends died with them. "No," she said. "Nothing."

His face was absolutely solemn, his eyes steady and somber in the aching silence, but finally he spoke. "Then I'll consider it a compliment," he said. "For at least you're not repulsed. Not as you are with Poke."

How did he know? She was so careful. Ever vigilant

not to let her emotions show. Her heart fluttered frantically, but she kept her expression stoic, her hands steady. "Feel free to flatter yourself, Dancer. I only ask that you try not to get me killed with your self-indulgence," she said, and stepped away unsteadily. For a moment she was certain he would pull her back, would, at least, follow her, but he did not. So she strode away, her steps steady and even until she was certain she had left him behind, until she could match her footsteps with the pace of her racing heart.

What was happening to her? She dare not feel. She rushed toward the Den. With any luck, Poke would be gone, and she would be alone, insulated by the others' fear of him.

Except for the fire that burned in the parlor, the house was dark when she stepped inside. Quiet as a wraith, she closed the door behind her. Caution was her salvation. Fear kept her alive. But the thieves who shared her world were gone, all but Gem, who guarded her patient with hollow-eyed persistence. Why? Why the tenacity? Why the caring? she wondered, but she dare not ask, for if she did not know, she could not tell.

Slipping silently into the hallway, Shandria headed for the bedchamber, but a noise snagged her attention. It was no more than a quiet moan of sound, but senses sharpened by fear could not be fooled.

"You're awake," Gem breathed, and in the hall, Shandria let her eyes fall closed. The Scotsman lived, but for how long?

"I worried." The girl's voice broke. "Thought you'd forgot 'bout me."

So she'd been right. They knew each other from the past. Shandria's heart fisted. Had he come to take Gem away? Had he come to save her? Some warm unbidden emotion smoked through her, but it was drowned in survival instincts. Regardless of his size, regardless of his fortitude, he could not best Poke. Not now. She stepped into the doorway to tell them that, to warn them, but the sight of his face stopped her.

His nose had been broken, his lips split. An angry gash ran from his high-boned cheek into his hairline, but it was not his wounds that stopped her breath. It was his eyes.

They were as steady as the earth, as deep as the sea as they settled on Gemini's face.

Silence spilled like ink into the room. He reached toward her, then paused and curled his battered fist into the blanket.

His throat constricted and his lips moved, but there was no sound except for a tortured croak.

Gem pulled her gaze from his, fumbled with a nearby cup, and bore it hastily to his lips. He drank, deep and long, but his gaze never for a moment slipped from her face. The cup bobbled as she set it aside, then he shifted as if attempting to rise.

"No!" Her hand looked fragile and pale against his chest as he struggled to push himself to a sitting position, but she held him down. "Don't. Don't move."

His eyes bored into hers, his throat contracted, and he winced as he spoke, but his voice were audible. "Why?" he rasped.

Gem's eyes were bright. Too bright, but she held on, pretending not to hear as she fiddled with the blanket that covered his massive chest. "You've been sore 'urt," she said, shifting her eyes restlessly away. "But you're on the mend. Big bloke like you. It'd take a good deal more—"

He grabbed her wrist. Their gazes met with a snap, his

narrowed and angry, hers round and terrified. "Why're ye here?" His voice was gruff, but his hand shook with violent tremors.

Her face contorted, but she brought it back under control and tilted her head at him. "You gotta rest, Viking," she said.

He growled something inaudible, but his head had already dropped back against the pillow, as if that exertion was too much for his straining muscles. His eyes fell closed.

Gem's lips parted. Her fingers crunched the blanket against his chest. "Viking?"

"Not safe," he murmured deliriously.

She closed her eyes as if in prayer, and her lips twitched with emotion, but suddenly he was sitting upright, his eyes like blazing coals.

"Leave!" he ordered, and grabbed her arm. "Leave now."

Her face contorted, but she shook her head. "No. I ain't goin'."

For a moment neither moved, and then he dropped back against his pillow, his skin as pale as death.

Gem leaned over him, terror in her eyes, but he spoke again, proving his determination.

"You'd stay?" His words were gritty and labored. "Just to spite me?"

A tiny whimper slipped from her lips, but she set her jaw. "That's right, old man. I ain't leavin' 'ere."

He whispered something, but his words were drowned in his raspy breathing, then his hand slipped from her wrist and onto the mattress.

Terror, sharp and bright and horrible, filled Gem's eyes. "Viking! Viking!"

His eyes opened, slow and heavy.

She loosened her clawed fingers in the tattered blanket. "I ain't goin'," she said. "Not 'less you make me."

Anger flared in his eyes, and for a moment it almost seemed as though he would rise. His broken body trembled with the effort, and then, like a huge child too long aplay, he fell back against the pillow and did not move.

It wasn't until that evening that Shandria saw Gem again. She took her place by the table quietly, her eyes shadowed, her face pale.

"Leavin' the corpse in peace?" Ox asked.

The girl gave him a muted glare but said nothing as she glanced toward Poke.

He smiled fondly. "Your large friend hasn't awakened yet, Gemini?"

She was silent for the slightest moment, then, "Just once, for a short time."

"Truly? Perhaps your vigilance is not wasted then."

"She's lyin'," Ox scoffed. "You ask me, the ugly bastard's already dead, in his 'ead, leastways."

" 'E ain't dead!" Gem's voice was strident, but she caught control in an instant and steadied herself. " 'E spoke."

"Did he?" Poke asked, seeming pleased, as if he weren't to blame for the man's condition. As if he'd had nothing to do with the mangled face, the pool of blood. An actor on his favorite stage. "What did he say?"

Shandria held her breath, but she needn't have worried, for Gem's survival was founded on far more than blind luck. " 'E wanted water."

"He said as much?"

She lowered her eyes as if hiding the true extent of his debilitation. Poke wasn't the only actor in the room. Indeed, the Den was full of them. "I knew what 'e wanted."

"Ahh," Poke said, and smiled again, though the expression was gently pitying this time. "So you're not certain if his mind is clear."

She delayed for several seconds. "I'm afraid 'e may be addled, Master Poke."

"Ohhh." The other sighed as if deeply disappointed. "I am so sorry, Gemini. I know how you've taken to him."

"Aye," Ox said. " 'Tis a terrible shame. I bet 'e was brilliant afore."

"Compared to you any road," Gem hissed.

"Shut yer trap!" snarled Ox.

"Hush now, my little cubs," Poke soothed. "I've some business to discuss."

The room went quiet as all eyes shifted to Poke. The man called Slate watched from a nearby chair. Who was he? Shandria dared not glance his way, but she knew how he would look. Shabbily elegant, almost relaxed, as if he'd spent each day of his life in circumstances just as deadly, just as macabre, and was not moved a whit. But there was something wrong. Something she couldn't quite decipher. Something sad in the depths of his amber eyes.

"I'm afraid profits have been a bit short of late," Poke said. "What with two new mouths to feed, it seems more money is going out than coming in. Thus I've decided to set certain tasks for each of you. Of course, I shall assist. In fact, I fear I'll have to leave you for a time again soon to see to some distant business, but until then we must all bear down. I expect profits to double."

"But Master . . ." Gem's voice was strained. "If I could 'ave but a few more days, I'm sure the big bloke will be on 'is feet and—"

"Aye," interrupted the Ox. "I'm sure of it. If she prods a stick up 'is arse and props 'im in the corner."

"Shut your filthy—"

"Quiet!" Poke said, then softened his tone. "I'm sorry, Gemini. Truly I am, but you must admit, I've been more than generous, letting you tend him these past days."

"But 'e's almost—"

He raised a hand in gentle admonishment. "The truth is this, lass, I'm worried for you. I fear you are becoming too attached. But for the buckle you gave me some nights past, you've contributed naught to our little family. No." He shook his head sadly. "I must insist that you return to work and let our guest fend for himself."

She nodded, and he smiled.

"I want you and Nim working the docks together. Fetching as you are, you'll have no trouble distracting the gentlemen so that the lad can lift a few purses. Am I right, young Jack?"

The boy nodded solemnly. Shandria's gut twisted. The docks were always dangerous. Picking pockets made them deadly.

"Ox, I want you to spend some time round about the gambling hells."

"Glad to do it," said the Irishman.

"But try not to kill anyone."

"I'll do me best," Ox said, "but sometimes there's naught else for it."

Poke shook his head and chuckled as if humoring a wayward child. "Peter, get to the market when the maids are making their purchases. That handsome face of yours is bound to garner you some coin."

"And some titties if you play your cards right," Ox added.

Poke ignored him. "And you, Mr. Slate," he said. Turning slightly, he stared at the Den's newest denizen. "How would you like to spend your days, I wonder?"

Slate shrugged. "I'm at your disposal."

"Yes, you are. Princess," he said, twisting toward her as if suddenly inspired. He smiled, but his eyes were too alive, too eager. Trouble was brewing, boiling up a storm that could destroy them all. "I believe you and Mr. Slate should join forces since you work so well together."

He knew! Somehow he'd found out that she had saved Slate at Pentmore Hall. Her mind screamed, but she forced herself to remain still, to stay quiet. There was nothing worse than a panicked denial. Think, she insisted, but Ox was already on his feet.

"Why you puttin' them two together? Princess and me, we're a fit."

Poke pulled his gaze slowly from her to the Ox. "You think so?" he asked. "Mr. Slate, come here and stand by my lady."

He rose slowly from his chair, crossing the distance casually to stand beside her. Her skin tingled where their arms touched. Poke smiled and shook his head with paternal pride. "Such a handsome couple, don't you think, Mr. Oxford."

"I think 'e's a pasty-faced fop."

Poke laughed. "A pasty-faced fop who killed Vic."

Oxford narrowed his eyes. "Maybe."

"You doubt?"

"Aye, I don't think 'e's got the stones."

"Truly?" Poke asked and laughed. "And what of you, Princess? Do you think our Mr. Slate here has stones?"

She didn't glance toward him. Her mind was racing madly, but she kept her gaze on Poke's, desperately showing no expression. "As you know," she said, "I prefer to work alone."

"I was under the impression that you were growing fond of our guest here."

"No," she said. "You weren't."

He raised his brows, eyes sparkling. Had she gone too far? Crossed that fine, lethal line? "Are you saying I'm a liar?"

"I am saying you're no fool."

The house went silent, and Poke laughed. "My princess. So diplomatic. But what of you, Mr. Slate? How do you feel about working with my beloved?"

He glanced at her. She could feel his gaze on her face, could feel the heat of his attention, the pull of his warm, enigmatic allure. "Certainly," he said. " 'Twould be a rare pleasure."

Something sparked in Poke's eyes. Something deadly, but he smoothed it away. "It's decided then," he crooned. "We've a match."

Chapter 16

It all seemed ultimately surreal to Will. He sat with his hands folded in his lap, his head swaying to the rhythm of the rented carriage. He had recognized the driver's face, and though he didn't know the hostler's name, he was certainly one of Poke's men.

But it was Shandria that fascinated Will. Shandria who stole his breath. She was quite fashionably dressed, her gown mint green, her hooded, emerald cloak lined with silver fox. Only her shoes were out-of-date. Just visible past the hem of her narrow skirt, they were boxy and scuffed, strongly resembling the color of dirt. And for reasons unknown, the state of her footwear made him irrationally angry.

"So . . ." He watched her profile as she looked out the window. "The all-powerful Poke couldn't afford a decent pair of slippers?"

"Damn you!" She jerked from the window, her eyes snapping. Gone was the icy princess. Emotion flashed like lightning in her face, stunning him for a moment. She was always beautiful, but now . . . when she lowered her shields and showed the stoked fire within, it was all he could do to keep his hands to himself, to steady his mind. What the devil had happened to the cool baron who shunned passion and scoffed at sentiment?

"Are you trying to get me killed?" she asked, her voice quieter as she struggled for control. Her nostrils flared, but she wrested her features back under submission, and he found that despite his noble heritage, he immediately missed the fire that had snapped in her eyes, though he failed to understand the reason.

"It's not my foremost goal," he said.

"Then why . . ." She paused as if struggling, then continued. "Why would you tell him you wish to work with me?"

So that was it, he thought, and shrugged. "Sometimes the truth is as good as a lie."

Anger again, sharp and bright on her porcelain features.

He smiled. "But if you remember," he added, "I didn't actually say I—"

"I know what you said, and I know how he interrupted it," she snapped.

"Can I help it if I enjoy your charming company?"

"Damn you!"

Honest emotion. How had he lived so long without seeing it on her face? "I could hardly lie to your lord and master."

She leaned forward. "You've lied every moment since you've arrived," she snarled. "Why now would you—"

"Ever see yourself in a mirror, Princess?"

She narrowed her eyes at him. Her hair was piled in tight ringlets atop her head, making her eyes look all the more feline, her face all the more exotic. He had seen beauty before, certainly, but there was so much more here. Grace and hardship and intellect, melded with countless unearthed secrets.

He stared at her in silence, drinking her in. "Tell me," he said finally. "Do you think him daft?"

She said nothing, and he continued.

"Do you think him deluded enough to believe I'm unmoved by the sight of you?"

Uncertainty flickered warily across her elfin features. He smiled, steeping in the pleasure of making her uncertain. God knew he had been off-balance since the first moment he'd seen her face.

"Believe me, love, I'm no saint."

She settled back against her seat and folded her hands primly in her lap. Emotion had been overwhelmed, whipped into submission. Control was back in vogue. "My mistake then."

He raised his hands, palms up. "A common one."

"And so easily made. So tell me, Dancer, if not a saint, who are you?"

"I shall make you a bargain," he said. "You answer my question, and I shall answer yours."

"No."

He canted his head. "No, you won't answer mine, or—"

"No," she corrected. "I won't lie with you."

He couldn't help but laugh, for though she had guessed the question wrong, she had certainly divined his poorly camouflaged desire. Still, he longed for understanding even more desperately.

"Why didn't you tell Poke I was in his chambers?" he asked.

For a moment he thought she'd deny any knowledge again, but finally she glanced out the window and spoke as if she were talking to the snow-covered rooftops. "How is it that you've survived so long, Dancer? Sometimes I lie awake at night wondering."

" 'Tis good to know you think of me at all."

"Have you no sense whatsoever?" she asked, and glanced at him as though she sincerely wanted to know.

"I've sense enough to admit I want to spend time with you."

Anger lit her face again, but she tamped it down in an instant. "He would have killed you," she said. "Right there. Right then."

"If he had found me beneath his bed."

"Yes."

"So you protected me." Joy. It was the only way to describe the feelings that spurted through him. Unbridled, burgeoning happiness. But he carefully tucked the feelings away for later dissection. That was one of the many problems with being sober. It left so bloody much time to think. "By drugging him."

She rasped an inarticulate denial. "I did not—"

"Because you couldn't bear to see me hurt."

She fell silent, her face flushed, her expression somber. "You, Sir Dancer," she said finally, "are deluded."

"You're saying I'm wrong."

She breathed a laugh. "You think I would risk my life for you? A man I've just met and care nothing about?"

When she said it that way, it almost made him doubt. "I was surprised, too," he said.

She gave him a wry glance from beneath lush lashes. "I learned long ago to worry about myself and none other."

"Truly? Is that why you traveled halfway across Sedonia to Pentmore Hall?"

"As I told you before, I hoped to steal the chest."

"You've a terrible memory then, lass. For you left it lying in the straw."

A glimmer of frustration flitted across her face, but she settled against her seat and shrugged, setting aside any hint of emotion. "Believe what you will. But my concern is for myself."

"So you've no feelings . . . even for the boy called Nim?"

Her mouth, lush and tilted and cherry blossom pink, twitched the slightest amount. "What is he to you?"

He shook his head. "You've only answered the one question, love," he said, "and that one not very convincingly. Still, I'm a generous man and shall answer one for you. Which is it?"

She stared at him for one long moment. "Why are you here?"

Their gazes struck and held. A thousand reasons to lie scuttled through his mind. "I came to find answers."

"To what?"

"Questions." He exhaled carefully and wondered with lightning quickness what it would have been like if he had met her under other circumstances. If he had first seen her at some posh ball at court. If she had glanced coyly at him from under the brim of a stylish bonnet. If he had watched her over a sterling cup of champagne. Would he still see the exploding life in her? Would he still realize her exquisite value, or would he have been numb, even to her?

"You don't plan to tell me what those questions are?"

"Not unless you explain why you drugged Poke."

She turned away to stare out the window again. "So you think me a monster."

Her profile was that of an angel, sculpted, golden, alluring. "I wish I could," he said.

She turned back, her bottomless eyes glimmering.

" 'Twould be safer," he explained. "But when I look into your face . . ." He laughed at himself, for it was so tempting to spill the awful truth. Infatuation was rarely a pretty thing. But on a man of his jaded vintage, it looked decidedly silly. He shrugged. "Life was easier when I was drunk."

She said nothing.

"But you knew that, didn't you?" he asked, watching her, studying her. There would come a time when she was gone, and he would be alone in the numbing darkness. "Didn't you?" he asked again.

She watched him a moment, then turned again to silently study the wintry countryside roll past, as if she were an elegant lady of quality, well above the need to answer his bothersome questions. And perhaps she was. He was hardly one to judge. His sister had been considered the epitome of fine breeding, a great lady in the making, genteel, refined, retiring. Not one to cause a stir, not even to protect her own life. Was that what a lady would do? Or would she fight? Would she use every scrap of wit and strength at her disposal?

"You knew I was a sot," he said.

She shook her head. "How would I know?"

"Are you saying you poison everyone's drink at the Den?"

Her brows rose in surprise, but whether it was real or fake, he couldn't tell. "Are you accusing me of attempted murder?"

"No," he said, and was somewhat surprised to hear himself say it out loud. "I'm accusing you of saving my life."

She smiled. "Back to the angel of mercy theory, are we?"

Did she know that she looked like an angel, that sitting by her felt ethereal and hallowed?

She cocked up one brow at his reticence.

"Some men blather on when they're inebriated," he said.

Her eyes were as steady as stone, but the quirk of her mouth questioned his meaning. "Do they?"

He nodded. "That could get a man killed in a place like the Den."

"If he had secrets to hold."

"Yes."

"Are you trying to tell me something, Dancer?"

It was strange, really, for he found that he wanted to tell her everything, to reach into his past and pull forth all the scalding sins that had accumulated there. But he'd been trained at birth to be a nobleman, and she . . . She had been taught to guard herself. So he took a deep breath and leaned back into the plush cushion of the seat behind him. Resting his arms across the top, he examined her in silence. And then he saw the fear. It was hidden, but it was visible if one looked closely enough. She was afraid. Of him. Of the consequences of knowing too much. His secrets were as dangerous to her as to him, and in that moment he truly believed he would die if he hurt her. "No," he said. "I've nothing to tell you. I'm simply trying to be mysterious."

A glimmer of a smile flickered across her face, and he saw with an inexplicable mix of joy and sadness that she was willing to play along. To pretend he was not what he was. "Truly?"

"Yes. Are you intrigued?"

"Ever so much."

"Good, then we're even."

She tilted her small, regal head the tiniest degree. "I'm intriguing?"

He forced himself to refrain from laughing at the absurdity of the understatement. "A thief who carries herself like a princess and acts like a personal bodyguard. Yes, some might find that rather fascinating."

Her face was somber now. "And you?"

"I think you know how I feel." Far too well.

Their gazes held, but she pulled hers abruptly away to glance out the window again. "We've almost arrived."

His stomach twisted. For a few priceless moments he'd almost forgotten the reality of their surreal existence.

"Shandria."

She glanced back at him, but there was caution in her face again, and he mourned the loss of that abbreviated moment of trust. "I was thinking we might call a truce."

She settled back slightly. "Are we at war, Dancer?"

"Yes." He nodded. "I think we are. But perhaps we could put it aside. Just this once. For today. No battle."

She studied her gloved hands. "I've heard it said that life is a battle," she said, and when she glanced up, he saw that there was a world of hurt in her face, a limitless edge of pain held neatly behind her careful mask.

"Perhaps it doesn't have to be."

"Maybe not for you."

Silence tumbled in, and though he tried to keep quiet, he found he could not.

"You could leave him. Go—"

"Quit." She lifted a hand toward him as though she could physically stop the words. "Please."

He watched her. He had lived his life among the privileged, duchesses and heiresses and debs, but true nobility was a rarity. So rare, in fact, that he wasn't sure if he recognized it or was simply conjuring it in his own mind.

"He would not be so loyal to you," he said, but it was a struggle to keep his tone steady, to refrain from grinding his teeth and shouting that she was a fool to stay.

"Is that what you think I would want?" she asked. "Loyalty?"

"Doesn't every woman?"

The shadow of a scowl ripped across her face. "I am not every woman, Dancer."

No. Hardly that. And yet he knew so little. "Who are you?" he asked.

She glanced at her clasped hands. "I am Poke's woman."

The world went quiet, cushioned by the soft rhythm of hooves on the snow-packed streets.

"No," he said, though he knew he was a fool. "I don't believe you are."

There was something in her expression then. Almost a hopefulness, almost joy before she stashed it away. "That kind of thinking will get you killed."

He smiled. Obviously he'd lost his mind. "I thought perhaps we wouldn't have to tell him."

Her own lips quirked, but she glanced down at her hands again, as if loath to allow him to see her smile. "Don't underestimate him. 'Tis a fatal mistake."

"Leave him. Right now." The words spurted out, against his will, against his better judgment. "We could simply keep traveling."

"He would find me."

"The docks are not so far," he said, and felt excitement surge like a thunderstorm inside him, though he knew better than to let it break. "You have a carriage."

"Paid for by Poke. You think the driver is not loyal to him? You think he would not stop me? Even if I managed to escape, he would surely hasten back to the Den." She paused. "Unless you killed him before he spoke to his master." The world went silent. "Is that your plan?"

He watched her, remembering so easily how she had tricked him in the past, had made him believe she was asking for his help.

"I tire of your ploys," he said easily. "Just as I tire of your belief that Poke is all-powerful. He is man just like any other—"

"No. He is not just like any other man." She squeezed her eyes closed. "I cannot believe that. I won't let myself."

He scowled, trying to decipher, to understand.

She drew a careful breath and raised her chin as if silently finding her balance. "I'll not leave him. Don't speak of it again."

Frustration ground through him, cranking bile into his system like poison. "Then you're a fool," he said.

She exhaled heavily. " 'Twas a short-lived truce."

"My apologies," he snapped.

She shrugged as if uncaring, but there was something in her eyes. Was it pain? Had he caused it?

Unwanted regret rippled through him.

"I'm sorry," he said, and it was sincere now. "I am in no position to judge."

She smiled, but there was no honest happiness. Not anymore. "I'm sure you are."

"I was married, before . . ." He paused, searching for strength to say the things he'd never said.

She remained silent, but scowled as she brought her gaze rapidly back to his.

"I had a child," he added. "They needed . . . In truth, I never understood their needs. I only knew I couldn't fulfill them." He glanced out the window, unseeing, before realizing his cowardice and forcing himself to catch her gaze again. "But no. That's not quite the case. 'Tis not that I could not, but that I chose not to."

The carriage rumbled steadily along beneath them. "So you starved them?" she asked.

He started at her ridiculous assumption. "Of course not. Even my father . . ." He paused, gathering his wits.

"So your father was cruel."

Memories crowded in. Secrets, sins, Caroline's haunted eyes. "Worse to some than others," he said.

"But he fed you. Just as you fed your family."

"Yes, but—"

She shrugged. "Then you must have beaten them?"

He saw her ploy now and scowled. "Cruelty comes in many forms, lass."

"So you humiliated them. Degraded them. Hated them."

"I—"

"She probably cried herself to sleep each night."

He said nothing.

"Did she cry, Dancer?"

He glanced out the window again.

"Did she?"

"No," he admitted.

Their gazes clashed. "If I did not know better, I would think you know little of pain," she said.

He tensed. "What do you know?

Silence crept in, tightening the tension, but finally she lowered her gaze to her hands. "Only what I see in your eyes."

He had to force himself to speak, to dare ask. "What do you see?"

She seemed to struggle with the answer, but finally she raised her mercurial gaze again. "Not cruelty."

He gritted his teeth, thinking back. "What of cowar—"

"I've seen cowards," she snapped, then lowered her voice and her eyes. "You aren't one."

Something swelled in his chest, but he dared not acknowledge it. She was a thief, after all, and a liar. But she was beautiful. And phenomenally strong. He watched her. She had always seemed so distant, so cool, but what of her heart? *What risks had she taken? What danger had she withstood?* he wondered, and despite her words, he was certain she would not have failed in his place.

"Leave him," he said, managing, just barely, to keep his voice steady. "I'll pay for your passage. Anywhere you wish to go."

Her nostrils flared, as if she had caught the scent of freedom, but then she smiled. "There lies the trouble," she said and tilted her head slightly, as if she herself were baffled. "I don't wish to go anywhere."

"I don't believe you." Or perhaps he didn't want to. Perhaps, after all his years of flagrant worthlessness, he needed to help someone and refused to believe his damsel in distress didn't wish to be saved.

"Believe what you like," she said, and looked away.

"Shandria." He grabbed her arm. She turned with an expression of utter disdain, and he drew his hand slowly away, forcing himself to release her.

"Perhaps we'd best work alone this day," she suggested.

Something akin to panic flared in his gut. Something he could neither understand nor condone. She had survived her entire life without him, after all, and yet the idea of sending her off alone . . . "Forgive me."

"I have. I merely think—"

"Just . . ." He paused, blindly searching for words. "This once let us pretend we are naught but an average pair out to enjoy the day."

She smiled a little. "But I am not average," she reminded him. "I am a thief, and if I return to Poke without—"

"Don't mention him."

Was she holding her breath? Was she looking at him as if he'd gone mad?

"Let us make a pact," he said. "We shall not refer to him this day. We shall pretend."

"And what are we pretending?"

"That we are wealthy. That we are privileged."

She stared at him for several breathless seconds, then, " 'Tis easier for some than others."

And watching her, he had to laugh, for though he knew she suspected he was of noble blood, it was she who exuded breeding and refinement.

"Something amuses you?" she asked.

"Do this for me," he said. "This one favor, and I will make certain you don't return to the Den empty-handed."

Their gazes melded. "Are you such an accomplished thief then, Dancer?"

No, but he was wealthy, and he could not tell her. What a strange twist of fate. "Trust me," he said. "Just this once."

"Why?"

"Because sometimes days slip away. Opportunities . . ." He fought the emotions that welled up in his throat. "Opportunities are missed. Chances to be happy."

She merely stared at him, and he shrugged.

"Perhaps it's a sin, maybe the worst sin of all."

"To fail to be happy?"

Or to make another happy. To see her smile. The thought made his heart ache.

Silence stretched into eternity. Beneath them, the carriage slowed to a halt.

"Just this once," he said, "we could be something different."

"What?"

"Kind," he suggested, and smiled at her raised brows. "To each other."

"Rather a radical means of searching for happiness, isn't it?"

"Aye," he agreed. "But we could pretend we're not ourselves."

"We would be kind people."

"Just so."

"Very well," she agreed, and shrugged. "But just this once."

Chapter 17

She was a fool. And fools died young. But when he reached for her hand, Shandria followed him out of the landau and onto the half-frozen mud of the street.

"This once," he said again, and she nodded.

They dismissed the driver.

The cobbled walkway that ran parallel to the shops had been swept clean of snow, but a couple squeezed past, avoiding a frosty puddle as they laughed together. The man carried a bundle of parcels wrapped in paper and tied with twine. The woman held his arm. She was looking up into his face, and he was smiling. There was something between them, a contentment, a joy even. Shandria's heart twisted.

"What first, my lady?" he asked, his voice quiet.

She tilted her head up toward him. Was he mocking her? she wondered, but his expression was somber, his eyes intent.

"My lady?" he said again, and cocked his arm. She slid her hand beneath his elbow with a thousand misgivings.

" 'Tis entirely your decision."

He waiting, watching her.

"My lord," she added, and he smiled with his eyes.

215

One could not trust his lips, for they were wont to lie, but his eyes were hopelessly honest.

"Very well then," he said. Squeezing her arm gently against his side, he steered her round a corner. "I think we shall have a chocolate."

She stopped him, dragging self-consciously on his arm. "I have no money."

"Don't be silly," he said, and canted his head down toward her. "The gentleman always pays."

She stared at him, feeling breathlessly foolish. It was all naught but a game to him. But it was a dangerous one. "In truth," she said, fighting the web, "I know no gentlemen."

His face was sober, his eyes dark and sincere. "Call me Benjamin," he said, and gave her a truncated bow, never loosing her arm.

"Benjamin," she repeated.

"And what shall I call you, my lady?"

She was almost drawn in, almost pulled under, but she shook her head and slipped her hand away. He caught it at the last moment.

"This once," he murmured. " 'Tis all I ask."

Fears and uncertainties warred within her, "Rosalind," she said.

His eyes smote hers, and then he smiled. "Have you ever had a chocolate, Lady Rosalind?"

It was difficult to breathe when he looked at her that way. As if she mattered to him, as if she were something of import. "No . . . my lord, I don't believe I have."

"Well then," he said and settled her hand back in the crook of his arm. " 'Tis well past time."

A bell jangled merrily as they stepped inside the coffee-house. The bustling proprietor glanced up, giving them a brief smile as he waved them to a table. It was small and

round and accompanied by a half dozen of its identical
mates. There were several unoccupied, though more were
spoken for. Near the door, an impeccably groomed ma-
tron glanced at Shandria's shoes, then leaned toward her
contemporaries. The trio shared a few hissed words and
murmured behind their cups.

Shandria felt her face warm, though she knew far better
than to care. God's truth, her entire world was drowning
in danger. Every breath might be her last. Every step
might be fatal, and yet, her heart took the blow. Will
handed her into a chair. That's how she thought of him—
Will—not Slate, not Dancer, though she insisted on call-
ing him that, of reminding them both of the absurdity of
his presence there. But in her heart he was Will—educated
and kind, with a life far from Darktowne. A life filled
with laughter and peace and warmth. A life where he
would be perfectly comfortable visiting a shop exactly
like the one where they now sat. But not with her.

Taking the chair across from her, he studied her face.
Too closely. She dropped her gaze to the linen cloth and
tried not to listen to the women behind her.

"Tell me . . ." William leaned forward with casual
grace. His hands, she noticed, were perfectly clean despite the days he'd spent at the Den, and his fingers were
long and well sculpted. "Do you cause such a stir everywhere you go, my lady?"

Their gazes smote and held, then he nodded toward the
women gossiping behind her. "It's difficult for them I
suppose."

She stilled the restless rustling of her hands with an effort. "Difficult?"

"They're no longer young. Perhaps they were never
beautiful. Certainly . . ." He paused. "They were never
you."

She scowled, far out of her league, and he smiled as he reached for her hand.

"Jealousy," he said, "is a cruel master."

She almost laughed, but her face felt flushed and her stomach oddly twisted. "I am certain they are not jealous."

"Are you?" His expression was absolutely serious. "Shall I ask them?"

She did laugh now, but the sound was nervous. "Don't be absurd," she said, but he was already rising.

"Dancer!"

He raised a brow.

"Sit down. Please," she hissed, flitting a glance toward the trio and tugging him back down. "Don't create a spectacle."

"I didn't create it," he said, and settled reluctantly into his chair. "I am but accompanying it."

She stared at him. Something quivered in her chest, and she felt odd, short of breath, strangely weak.

"So . . . Benjamin, is it?" she said, nervously changing the subject and flicking her gaze to the tabletop. "Charm must come with the name."

When she glanced back up she saw his surprise. She couldn't help but wonder if he were such a phenomenal actor or if it were honest emotion.

"Am I being charming?" he asked.

She refused to allow herself to wriggle in her chair, but kept perfectly erect. "Yes, I believe you are."

"Really?" His eyes had a faraway look. "I am never charming."

"You are a hideous liar."

He held her gaze in a gentle grasp. "Ask anyone," he challenged, and the room felt strangely breathless.

"I don't know anyone," she said.

"I think perhaps . . ." He scowled a little, as if surprised by the truth of his words. "I could say the same."

What did he mean? Secrets were hidden here, just below the surface, but she dare not delve into them, for with the secrets came emotions. She could feel them tingle beneath her skin. Best to keep it light, keep it careful, under the control of flippancy. "But if you did know . . . somebody . . . they would most likely find you crass?" she asked.

"And moody. Generally drunk. And not pleasantly so."

"Most uncharming."

"Decidedly," he said, and glanced up as a waiter approached. He was short, plump, and apple-cheeked, with a white apron and a yellow waistcoat. "We shall have two chocolates," Will said, "and some biscuits."

"Very good, sir," said the other, and after one quick, round-eyed glance at Shandria, hurried away.

And strangely, she found that she'd been holding her breath. Had it been that long since she had done something so mundane as place an order? So long since she had lived like a human being?

"Is something amiss?"

"No." She shifted her attention back to the table. "Nothing."

"Good. I'd hate for your ladyship's first chocolate experience to be marred by any dark thoughts."

Something sparked in his eyes. Was it mischief? "After all, nothing's too good for the duchess of Blackfeld."

There was a noticeable pause in the conversation behind her. Shandria shifted her eyes to the rear, but didn't turn her head. William raised one curious brow as if wondering what she would do next.

"The duchess," she said softly.

He smiled the slightest degree. "Of Blackfeld."

She shuffled her feet, reminding him of her shoes. "My poor estate must be in dire straits indeed."

"Not at all," he said. "Not when it is governed by a lady who cares more for her people than for her footwear. 'Tis not always the case," he said, and despite her cautious need to remind herself of the foolishness of this venture, she found herself drowning in his eyes, slipping below the surface. But she fought the suffocation just in time and straightened abruptly.

"I fear you've formed the wrong impression, my lord."

"Have I, Your Grace?"

The waiter stumbled slightly, then bowed, nearly sloshing their drinks onto the table. "I am sorry, Your Grace," he rasped, as wide-eyed as ever. "I didn't realize . . . I . . ." He glanced at the tray. "Let me hurry back to make certain your biscuits are fresh. I feel foolish, after all, not knowing—"

"No." She cleared her throat and strictly kept herself from glancing at the ladies behind. "I am certain they are fine."

"But—"

"They look quite lovely. Really."

"You're certain?"

By the time she had convinced him to leave their order, the women had hustled out the door. Will smiled. She straightened her napkin and pursed her lips at the inoffensive spoon before raising her eyes to his. "Are you enjoying yourself?"

"Immensely. And what of you?"

She wanted to say no. She should have said no. But it would have been a lie. Curling her bare hands around the chocolate mug, she took her first sip.

* * *

Nearly an hour had passed before they tripped back outside.

"What now?" he asked, hugging her arm to his side and looking into her eyes.

"More chocolate?" she suggested, and he laughed.

"I doubt there's any left in the entirety of Skilan."

"Wouldn't you know it? Just when I have developed a taste for it."

"A taste! You drank mine and yours and two more. 'Tis fortunate I stopped you before you grabbed the poor child's at the next table."

She laughed, and his steps faltered as he pulled her to a halt.

"What is it?" She glanced to the right, instantly cautious, but his gaze never left her face.

"Laugh again."

She gazed around her. A pair of gentlemen watched from the doorstep of a milliner's shop. She glanced down, nervous at their scrutiny, but more so by William's steady attention. "You're causing a stir."

"'Tis not my fault," he assured her. "Perhaps they've not heard beauty before."

"I don't know what you're talking about." The gentlemen had turned away, but seemed still to be listening.

"Your laughter," he said, "is like champagne."

"I've not tasted champagne."

"Some would consider that a crime." There was a sadness in his face, sadness and regret, deep-seated and scarring. "I fear I may have imbibed too much to feel the same."

And suddenly she wanted to hold him, to wrap him in her arms and make the world better, but she was not such a fool. So she played the game. "Tell me, my lord, is this how you charm all your conquests?"

"Believe this, my lady," he said. "I would be hard-pressed to charm a turnip."

"Which makes me what?" she asked, though she knew she should keep her mouth shut. "A parsnip?"

"A duchess," he corrected, and his eyes smiled again. Her heart hitched up tight, but she dare not pay it heed.

"Come then," she said, her voice carefully flippant, "I shall allow you to buy me diamonds."

Thus they strolled down the cobbled walkways, peering in shop windows and watching people watch them.

"Do I have my gown turned about?" she asked finally, for it seemed that every person they passed was staring at her.

"It wouldn't matter," William said. "if Your Grace did so today, on the morrow the entirety of Skilan would copy the effect."

She stared at him. "You don't really believe they think me a duchess?"

But at that moment a costermonger stopped his cart and dropped the shafts into the snow. Dipping into his rickety vehicle, he rummaged about in a basket, then approached Shandria with a bow and a flourish.

"Your Grace," he said, and handed her a perfectly symmetrical orange.

"I . . ." Flustered and stunned, she reached for the reticule that hung from her wrist. "I'm not certain I have adequate—"

But the little man bowed again. "Please, my lady, consider it my privilege," he said, and, smiling, tottered away, dragging his rickety vehicle behind him.

Will watched her in amused silence.

She stared after the man. " 'Twas a fluke," she said. "Surely the others would not believe such a thing."

He canted his head at her, challenge in his eyes. "Shall we find out?"

"I don't—"

"Come," he said.

And so the afternoon passed as they went from shop to shop. The clothier draped her with a dozen rich fabrics, cooing over her trim figure and elegant lines. The cobbler all but cried when he saw the sorry state of her shoes, especially when William assured him, she'd given her best slippers to a poor street waif who needed them more.

As for the milliner, she rapidly trotted out a young woman with a vast array of silly hats, only allowing them to leave after they'd assured her they would return at a later date.

When they finally stepped back outside, the sun was a golden orb balanced between the slanted blades of the distant mill. Like a dollop of molten gold, it shone like the day just past.

Down the street, a lamplighter bobbled on his stilts as he touched a flame to a stubborn wick.

Shandria glanced down at the tiny silk flower the milliner had given her as a parting gift.

"Are you hungry?" William asked.

Dreams slipped quietly into the ensuing darkness. But perhaps reality could be held off a moment longer. "Do you suppose they've secured any more chocolate yet?" she asked.

Will tucked her hand under his arm. A pair of young maids passed to their right, glancing shyly at them before hurrying away, heads bent close together.

"I sincerely think you have consumed every drop in Christendom."

She forced a smile. The sun had almost set. The day

was behind them. Reality loomed dark on the horizon. "If I can't have chocolate, there is little reason to eat. We might just as well be about our business," she said, glancing at the inn beside them. The thick, warbled panes of the windows glowed from the lights within. The mouth-watering scents of fresh bread and roast mutton wafted on the crisp air.

"Our business?" he asked.

She could feel him glance down at her, but found she could not meet his eyes, for he had carefully erected a dream, and she found it hideously painful to awaken. But she was nothing if not practical.

" 'Tis late," she said, "and I've achieved naught."

"The day's not over, lass." Was there desperation in his tone or just sadness?

"Aye," she said, gripping the tiny rose harder. " 'Tis. Over and done."

"Not till we step back into his house."

She noticed that he didn't speak Poke's name aloud. As if the spell would be broken if he did. And perhaps it would, but she shook her head, remembering hard-learned lessons. "I must—"

"No." Turning slightly, he gripped her hands in his. "You mustn't do anything. Not today. Just this once . . ." His expression was earnest, his eyes irresistible. "Let me take care of you." And she was drowning.

"You don't understand." Her voice was barely audible to her own ears. Panic burned like poison in her gut. She could not let herself care for him, not on pain of death. His or hers. "If we return empty-handed—"

He lifted her gloved fingers. The rose blossomed sweetly between them. "But they're not empty."

" 'Tis not a jest," she whispered. " 'Tis deadly serious."

"I know," he said and his expression concurred. "But all will be well. You needn't worry."

"But . . ." She skimmed the faces of the people around her, then hurried her gaze back to his. "You're a horrible thief," she whispered, and his eyes smiled.

"Yes," he agreed, and kissed her.

Chapter 18

Gemini jerked, roused from her restless sleep. Had he awakened? She glanced at the Viking. That's what she called him, for she dare not use his real name, not even in her own head. For it wasn't safe.

He moaned and she lurched forward to touch his brow. Was he feverish? Was he worsening? But no, his skin felt cool to the touch. Too cool? Was he cold? She shifted the blankets higher on his chest and scanned his face for signs of awareness. But there were none.

He was wounded. Pierced. Her eyes stung with the thought, but she hurried her gaze busily to her handiwork. She'd torn his sleeve from his tunic and used it as a bandage for his arm. Fresh blood had seeped into the cloth, so she eased out the knot, washed the wound, then wrapped it in a swath of fabric she'd torn from an old gown.

Lying quietly on his back, he looked peaceful, despite the angry wounds. Ox had called him ugly, and maybe he was, but she had spent a fortnight under his guard at Westheath Castle on Teleere. She had listened to his stories of his wee sisters while he brushed the tangles from her hair, though his only appointed task was to keep her from escaping. Aye, he was Laird MacTavish's master guard, a fighting man, a warrior, but his hands . . . She skimmed her gaze to where they lay on the bed and felt her eyes fill with tears, for even they were torn. She touched his scraped knuckles with her fingertips, but he didn't stir. Not a flicker of awareness crossed his peaceful features. He looked almost boyish in his quiet slumber. But he was not a boy. Reaching up, she gingerly traced an aged scar that bisected his eyebrow. Gone was the scowl he so often wore, leaving his face relaxed, but the years of battle had left a host of old wounds to blend uncomfortably with the new. No, he was not a boy, full of silly thoughts and arrogant ways. He was a man full-grown, wise with years and well-worn experience.

"Trussing up the turkey, lass?"

Gem twisted about, swiping at her cheek as she did so. Oxford stood in the doorway, his face etched with a perpetual jeer.

"Going to serve 'im for the Yuletide feast, are you, Gemini?"

He stepped into the room. Danger crowded in with him. She narrowed her eyes. She had dealt with a hundred men of his ilk. If she couldn't sidestep them, she could generally outwit them; but things were different now, for she had another's life to consider. She stood up slowly, shielding her patient behind her.

"Done torturing kittens are you, Ox?"

"Aye." He sneered at her. "Come to torture something a bit larger, I 'ave." He glanced at the Viking's face. "If 'e's still alive, that is."

"Oh, 'e's alive," she said. "But you'd best leave 'im be."

"And why's that?" he asked, stepping up close. She refrained from backing away. Though evil washed off him in waves, there was nowhere to go.

"Didn't your mother ever warn you not to poke the sleeping bear?"

He smiled at her. "'Ere's the thing," he said, and crowded closer still so that she could smell the stench of him. "I poke 'ooever I wish."

She clenched her fists and stood her ground. "Oh that's right," she said, "you didn't 'ave no mother. Seems you was spawned by the devil 'isself."

Ox jerked his fist up, but she had her knife at the ready, and pressed it against his belly.

"Let fly, Ox, and you'll be rotting in 'ell afore you know what stuck ye."

He snorted his disdain, but lowered his fist. "You think you can kill me, girl?"

Her hand was shaking. She pressed the blade more firmly into his gut. "Could be I can't, Ox," she said. "But I can sure make you wish you was dead."

"It's time someone's put you in your place," he snarled, but in that instant, Poke entered the room.

"Well, there you are then, my little ones."

Ox held her gaze. Gem held her breath.

"Not quarreling again, are we?" Poke tsked.

"Call 'im off," Gem gritted.

Poke raised a genteel brow. "What's that, Gemini?"

Caution rushed in on her. "'E's 'elpless," she corrected, nodding numbly toward the Viking behind her. "It wouldn't 'ardly be fair."

Poke smiled. "Are you threatening our guest again, Mr. Oxford?"

Ox leered. "I only said I think 'e'd make a fine Yuletide feast, the way 'e's trussed up all tidy like."

Poke chuckled. "Cannibalism, Mr. Oxford? Surely not."

The Ox pressed closer. "And *you* would make a tasty bit for dessert," he gritted into her face.

She felt herself go pale, but braced against the weakness, for it surely spelt death. "Go to 'ell, Ox."

"Not afore—"

"Mr. Oxford," Poke crooned. He was right beside her now, so close she could touch him, if she were ever so foolishly bold. "I think it time you took a walk outside."

"Fuck—" Oxford snarled, but when he glanced up, Poke met his gaze straight on. He had not a weapon to hand, and his smile seemed almost angelic, but there was something in the air—the smell of death, as clear as day.

"What were you about to say?"

The room fell silent. Tension cranked up tight, like an ancient crossbow, too long unused.

"It stinks like 'ell in 'ere," Ox snarled, and stepped back a pace. "I need me some air."

Gem's knees almost buckled when he turned away. Indeed, it took all her strength to keep her upright.

"Gemini."

She turned toward Poke, and he reached out to stroke her hair.

"Whatever shall I do with you?"

The knife was shaking like a windblown thistle. She pressed her arm against her thigh, hiding her weakness in the folds of her skirts. " 'E ain't right in the 'ead, Master Poke," she said.

He raised his brows as if surprised, but nothing surprised Poke, surely not his henchman's derangement. "You think Mr. Oxford is addled?"

"Aye. 'Tis certain," she said.

He skimmed his knuckles down her throat, watching her with eyes of angelic blue. If she didn't know better, if she hadn't seen what he was capable of, she would think him quite sane. "How old are you now, Gemini?"

Her throat had closed up again and breathing was difficult. "I don't know just exact," she said. "Six-and-ten, mayhap."

He smiled. "You've grown quite bonny under my tutelage."

She licked her lips and kept herself from moving beyond his reach to safety.

"And talented." He skimmed his fingers along her bodice.

She stared at him, her heart wild in her chest.

And then he kissed her. She stood frozen in place, terror and dread mixed to lethal doses in her pounding veins.

He drew slowly back, his eyes lazy and knowing. "Put the knife away now, lass. Your hand is shaking," he said, and, turning, left the room. His footsteps echoed down the hallway. A door opened and closed.

She exhaled sharply and dropped to the chair, feeling dizzy and deathly sick to her stomach.

"So that's it then?"

She jumped, jerking about to face her patient. He lay perfectly still, but his eyes were open and glaring.

"Jesus!" She said it like a prayer, though she was certain God had forgotten her long ago. Or at least she *had* been certain. Until this moment. "You're . . ." She reached out, then drew her hand shakily back. "You're awake."

His eyes never flickered from her face. "He's the reason ye left."

She shot a glance at the door, but there was no one there. No one within hearing. Still, she dare not say what was in her heart. "I thought you was going to die."

He drew a heavy breath, flaring his nostrils. "Did ye?"

She lowered her gaze and restrained all the feelings that jumped like silvery fishes inside her. "You've been unconscious for days."

"And why is that, lass?"

"Don't you remember?" She could barely get the words out. Could barely force herself to think of the night he'd arrived, stepping through the doorway, already bloody, already wounded, but still on his feet, still determined to . . . To do what?

"I remember a good deal," he rumbled.

"They stabbed you." Her hands were shaking in earnest now. "I couldn't stop them."

"Why?" he gritted.

Her face twitched with the agony of struggling for strength that had abandoned her long ago. "I wasn't strong enough. I—"

"Why?"

She sobbed once, but that was all she allowed herself "I tried to stop them. But—"

"The devil with *them*," he growled. "Why did ye leave?"

She blinked, trying to clear her eyes, trying to think. "Leave?" She almost laughed. "What are you talkin' about? I been 'ere since the first—"

"I would have let ye go," he rasped. "Would have seen ye safely on your way. Ye needn't have snuck off while me back was turned."

"I don't know what you're talkin' about."

"Aye, ye do, lass. Ye do."

She stared at him. "They all but killed you, Viking. They all but crushed your skull, and all you babble on about is my leaving!" Anger roared up inside her. "What the devil is wrong with you? Why did you come 'ere?"

His eyes flashed, and his jaw flexed with rigid emotion, but when he spoke, his tone was level. "I came for answers, lass. I think I deserve that much."

Unwanted memories crowded in. Memories of laughter and peace and hope. She stared at him, trying to push them aside. Dreaming was dangerous. Hoping was deadly.

"Why did ye go, Gem?"

"Why?" She laughed, feeling breathless and lost and panicky. "What else was I supposed to do?"

"Stay put. Stay safe."

"Safe!" She laughed. "At Westheath Castle? Where they 'ang folks like me?"

"I vowed to protect ye. Gave ye me word of—"

"You weren't there, Viking. Remember?" she hissed.

His scowl deepened, darkening the angry wound on his high-boned cheek. "You had guards. Men who—"

"Men who'd just as soon kill me as look at me. I'm a thief, Viking, in case you forgot."

"I haven't forgot," he rumbled. "I believe you took me horse when you left."

She cleared her throat, shifting her eyes away. It had been a spiteful thing to do. She might be a thief. She might be a liar. But she wasn't spiteful. Usually. "Aye, well, I 'ad to leave," she said. "I didn't belong there." Not without him. "The guards was lookin' at me funny."

Something glowed in his eyes as he leaned toward her and tightened a fist in his blanket. "Did they touch you?"

She could only hold his gaze for a moment. "No," she admitted. "But I didn't trust 'em."

"They would have kept ye safe," he said, relaxing marginally. "Until me own return."

But when would that have been? It had been agony without—God's bones! What was wrong with her? She was no sniveling milkmaid. She was independent. Strong.

Tears burned her eyes. She fought them back.

"Well they didn't," she snapped. "They didn't keep me safe, cuz Poke come for me, didn't 'e?"

Understanding flashed in his eyes, but he narrowed

them, hiding his thoughts as he glanced toward the door. "The one that came to Westheath whilst I was gone?"

"Aye."

"Poke, you call him?"

What was he thinking? To look at him some might believe him slow witted. Some would be dangerously wrong. "Round 'ere 'e's known as lord and master."

He stared at her and it took all her strength to keep from collapsing under his glare. "Ye had but to yell for help."

But what then? Who would have suffered if she had defied him? Poke hated MacTavish with mind-numbing potency. Indeed, none dared speak the laird's name in his presence, but he knew little of the Viking guard called Burr, and damned if she wouldn't do everything in her power to keep it that way. "Yell." She shook her head, laughing at him. "It was my own idea to go."

Silence fell like death into the room.

"Was me own company so hideous then, lass?"

She stared at him. He had a face like a belligerent gargoyle, but even now, battered and beaten, she wanted nothing more than to reach out and touch it. Damn her and her foolish weaknesses. Would she never learn that she was meant to fend for herself? There were no knights in shining silver. Not for her.

"If you remember," she said. "You were no company a'tall."

"I vowed to return."

"When?" she whispered. "After you had saved MacTavish a thousand times more?"

"He's me laird. 'Tis me place to look out for him."

"Aye," she agreed, and nodded slowly. "And 'tis mine to look out for none but myself."

"Then get yourself gone," he snarled, and nodded toward the door where Poke had retreated. "Afore 'tis too late."

There was such passion in his face, such intensity. Why? Was it for her? But it didn't matter. It couldn't.

"It's already too late," she murmured.

"Nay." He gritted, his brows beetled. " 'Tis not. Not if ye wish to go. I'll see you safely away."

She snorted. "And how, Viking, do you think you'd manage that?"

"The same way I come in."

She almost cried at the harsh sting of the memory, of seeing him beaten and bloodied. "Look at yourself, Viking," she hissed. "The way in all but got you killed."

"But it didn't, lass."

"Because I stopped them." Her eyes were burning and her throat felt tight. "But I won't do it again, old man. Not for the likes of you."

"Ye think I'm asking for your help?"

"No. I think you far too foolish for that. I think you too damned proud. You believe there is naught that can stop you. Not broken bones or gaping wounds or battered . . ." Her voice cracked. He was watching her, his swollen face stern, his icy eyes solemn. She stared back, barely able to draw a breath. Only a fool would fall in love with this man. Only a damned fool.

"I'm not so weak as ye think, lass," he rumbled, and despite everything, his hand felt strong when he reached out and took hold of her arm. "Neither am I deluded. If I say I can do a thing, I can do it."

She watched his earnest face, and against her wishes, hope raised its dark head. Maybe he was right. He was no callow youth, no dreamy-headed lad imagining his own strength. He'd been through hell and back again.

She glanced rapidly toward the door, and he must have

guessed her thoughts, for he spoke immediately, his tone deep and harsh.

"I'll see ye far from here, lass. That I promise."

Safe. The two of them, far away. The hope was almost painful in its intensity. "But . . . there are guards."

He narrowed his eyes. A muscle jumped in his jaw. "That I noticed."

"And Poke's no fool." She could barely hear her own voice as she leaned against his mammoth chest.

"I'll see ye safe from Darktowne," he growled, and beneath her hand, his muscles tightened like cords. "Then ye've but to hie yourself back to Teleere. Once on the isle, ye shall be safe."

"Hie myself . . ." Reality shifted back in, steeped in loneliness, heavy with fear. "You won't be with me?"

He shifted his gaze, sideways and back. "I may be delayed a spell, but it matters naught." He gripped her arm harder. "Get yourself safe to the castle. Demand to speak to the lad. He'll hear ye—"

"A spell?" she whispered.

"I'm still strong, lass," he said. "Do not doubt that. But it might take me a bit to catch up to ye."

She scowled, as though she couldn't quite understand his meaning, as though she didn't know he planned to die, to see her safe and fall like a martyr in her bloody trail. Her throat tightened and burned, but she wouldn't let him know. "So I'll be going without you," she whispered.

"Aye, but ye needn't worry, lass." His face was intense, and his hand shook as it circled her arm. She felt the weakness now. The weakness and the desperation. "I'll keep them well occupied. That I vow."

"Aye." She nodded. It seemed almost as if she were in some horrid dream. In that odd place just before waking when there was almost hope. But not quite. "I am certain you could keep them busy, Viking." In her mind, she saw him in a pool of his own blood. But whether it was the future or the past was impossible to say. It would all end up the same. "But Poke . . ." She shook her head and maybe she smiled, for she felt eerily out of her mind. " 'E 'as awful power. And 'e's clever." She shook her head. "Don't forget 'ow—"

"So ye . . ." The muscle in his jaw jumped violently this time, and his fingers, blunt and powerful, dug into her arm. "You harbor feelings for him?"

"Poke?" she asked, her voice strangely dreamy.

"Aye," he growled.

" 'E keeps me fed."

"And safe? Does he keep you safe, lass?" He glared at her from his battered face.

"I keep myself safe."

"You're naught but a child!" he gritted. "Without enough sense to—"

"I'm not a child."

He shook her with a snarl. "You're little more than a bairn, without the sense to stay where you're protected."

"And what about you?" She was breathing hard, and her heart ached in her chest as she leaned forward to hiss into his face. "You were safe. Why the 'ell did you 'ave to come 'ere?"

The room fell silent but for their panting breath. His eyes bore into hers like angry agates. "Because every wee bairn needs looking after."

"I'm no bairn," she spat. "I'm a woman well grown, and I can look after myself."

"Oh aye," he snarled. "And I can see you're doing a fine job of it thus far."

"I was," she said, "until you stumbled in here, wreaking 'avoc." She nodded violently, almost weeping at the memory. Almost breaking down, but she lifted her chin and strengthened her resolve. He would leave and he would leave whole, regardless of the consequences. "Poke trusted me. Valued my talents. But now, since you come—"

"What talents?" His tone had been dark before, but now it growled like a feral beast from his chest.

She knew what he meant immediately, and something inside her sparked and flared, but she narrowed her eyes and held her ground. "My talents are my own, Viking, and have naught to do with the likes of you."

"What talents did you share with him, lass?" he asked again.

"You're not me da!"

"And thank the gods for that!" he snarled. "But until the bastard shows his face, it looks as if the task is left to me."

She actually laughed. "So that's it then. You see yourself as me dear old da?"

His face reddened, almost as if he were embarrassed, almost as if he were thinking things that shamed him, but he held her gaze for several seconds, then shifted his fretfully toward the wall. "Aye," he said. "And as such I'll see you safely gone from here."

Her heart crunched in her chest. "Will you now?" she asked.

"Ye have me solemn vow."

She leaned closer until their faces were only inches apart. Was he holding his breath. "But Da," she whispered, "Poke is so very strong. So clever." Reaching out with her free hand, she laid her palm against his brawny chest. "So alluring. Indeed—"

"Lass," he growled, and beneath her hand, his muscles strained like leashed tigers.

"Yes, Viking?" she murmured, breathing the words against his skin.

His breath was coming hard, his heart beating fast beneath her fingertips. Beating. Still beating. Tears gathered behind her lids, but they would not fall.

"I . . ." He paused, gritting his teeth and closing his eyes against some internal struggle. "I failed ye before. But I'll not do so again. Ye have me word."

Her heart cried even as her resolve hardened. He would not die. Not here. Not now, and God damn it, not for her.

"You don't wish to fail me?" she asked.

He raised his gaze from her lips and nodded. She smiled.

"Good," she said, and, straightening quickly, ripped her arm from his grasp. "Then get the 'ell out of my 'ome."

Chapter 19

∽◦◦◦∽

"Wine?"

The maid who held the bottle was buxom and comely, but Will barely noticed. Wine. How long had it been? And what would it hurt? One drink. Surely he deserved that much. Needed that much.

But he felt Shandria's gaze on him. Felt the heat of it. The question in it. He moistened his lips, then, unable to avoid her gaze a moment longer, turned toward her.

Her eyes were the color of Sedonian mists, slanted and intense and as deep as eternity. He jerked his gaze away.

"No," he said, addressing the maid, though he couldn't quite look at her. "Thank you." He gritted his teeth. "None for me."

"Your Grace?"

She didn't answer, and he turned to find her attention locked on his face. Questions were there, yes, but there was more.

Something stirred violently in his soul.

"Your Grace," the maid repeated. "Wine?"

"Oh." She turned away, flustered. "No." Glancing at her hands, she fiddled with a fold in her skirt. "Not this evening," she said and skimmed her gaze back to his.

"Just a meal then."

She was beauty itself, but what was she thinking? There was something in her face, something he couldn't quite identify. It almost looked like . . . admiration.

The maid cleared her throat. "The . . . ahhh cook has prepared an excellent gooseberry capon."

Could it be that she cared for him? That despite all his hideous shortcomings she . . . But no. Why would she? She could hardly afford to be so foolish. He was there for his own reasons after all. But he hadn't planned to meet her, had he? He hadn't been prepared for her at all. Who could be? She was like sunlight on raindrops, like music in the dark. So melancholy that when she smiled you thought you would surely die to feel that joy just a moment longer.

The maid shifted uncomfortably.

"My apologies," Shandria murmured, snapping her gaze from his.

"The capon," Will said, though for one cockeyed moment he couldn't quite remember what the words meant. "The fowl will be fine. And soup, if you have it."

"Very good, my lord," she said, and, with one last glance, hurried away.

Shandria cleared her throat. It was a beautiful throat, smooth and pale and as elegant as a swan's.

He felt his body tighten with desire. When, he wondered, had he become fixated on throats?

"I—"

"I hope," he began simultaneously, then shook his head and waved toward her. "My apologies. Please, speak."

"I just . . ." She glanced at her lap again. "As I said earlier, I've not enough funds for such a meal."

She thought him a pauper. A thief. And that was as it should be, of course, for that was what he needed her to believe, and yet that knowledge grated at the very core of his being.

There was nothing he could do but make light of it.

"Are you thinking I will tell you to grab the chicken and make a dash for the door?"

She smiled just a little. "I admit I was rather hoping you might have a more sophisticated plan in mind."

"I thought I might simply pay for it." He shrugged. "Not terribly exciting, I know, but effective . . . I'm told."

She scowled a little. "Is that why you think I do it?" Her tone was sober, her expression the same. Honesty hovered like magic, threatening to break the mood. But knowledge loomed there too, as seductive as old Scotch. "Do you believe I steal for the thrill?"

"I was hoping it wasn't simply to please your master." His tone revealed feelings unspoken, but she merely nodded.

"Poke," she said. "He will know we ate here."

"Is that a concern? Surely we must eat."

She raised her elegant chin. "He doesn't like men to"—she shifted her mercurial gaze off to the side—"to toy with his possessions."

His muscles cramped up tight. "Is that what you are to him?" he asked, though he had already warned himself not to. "A possession? A thing?"

She met his eyes with level intensity but said nothing. And there was nothing he could guess, for she was an eternal enigma. A will-o'-the-wisp. A dream.

"If that's the case . . ." He carefully unclenched his fists. "If he doesn't want others with you, why would he send us out together?"

Worry twitched her irresistible lips. "Is it the truth you want . . . William?"

There was something about the way she said his Chris-

tian name that made him feel all turned about. Disoriented. Giddy.

"I think it's the truth I need," he said.

Her nod was shallow, her lips pursed. "I believe Poke
wants us to . . . share a bed."

"God yes." The words sprinted out before he could
stop them. He dropped his eyes closed and cleared his
throat. "My apologies. I never—" When had he become
so idiotically loose-lipped. He'd been a more predictable
drunk. He was like a fucking cannon, loosed on the
quarterdeck of life.

Her eyes were lowered again but the glimmer of a
smile flitted around her lips. "You never what?"

He didn't answer for a moment. Couldn't. For she was
there, so close he could reach out and touch her if he so
chose, or if he could no longer resist. And in the light of
his newfound lack of control, that could very well happen. And now he was staring at her like a daft half-wit
when he should be answering . . .

"I never lose control," he said.

She flitted her silvery gaze to his.

"With women," he added, and winced when she raised
a brow at him. "Not that I do with men either. I'm not
that sort. But women haven't moved me . . . I didn't
mean that as it sounded. I'm moved, physically. It's
just . . . Emotionally . . ." He closed his eyes and exhaled
carefully, lest he spew out any more idiocy. "I'm sorry."

She was staring at him when he opened his eyes, but
she dropped her gaze in a moment, her expression an
impish meld of perplexity and humor. "You needn't apologize," she said. "Not to me."

Why? Because she was a thief? Because she didn't deserve it or . . . Oh God, could it be because she felt the
same baffling emotions he did? His heart slapped against

his ribs and his hands trembled anew. Fuck wine. This was far more intoxicating, far more deadly, but he steadied himself. "Why shouldn't I apologize?"

"I've heard far worse," she said. "From men." She cleared her throat again and fiddled quietly with something in her lap. "And far less charming."

"I'm not charming. I'm cold and reserved. Always have been."

"Cold," she said, then laughed a little. "Perhaps I've been associating with the wrong sort."

Poke. The conversation kept returning to him regardless of Will's better intentions. But there it was again. "Almost certainly," he said, then shifted the topic, made fretful by his own weaknesses. "Why would he want us to sleep together?"

"I believe he always half hopes for treason."

"Treason. You make him sound like royalty."

Her gaze held his, then flickered away, but it was too late. He had seen something inscrutable in her eyes.

"Who is he?" he asked.

But she was already gone, emotionally, honestly. "It doesn't matter who he is," she said. "Only who he thinks he is, and he will see any disloyalty as treason . . . against him."

"Then why—"

"He doesn't need a reason to kill," she said quickly. "But sometimes it entertains him to have one."

Even the murmur of the other patrons seemed to dim in the ensuing quiet. "Why are you with him?" he asked finally.

She stared. " 'Twould be a difficult thing to explain."

"Perhaps I could understand it, if you speak slowly."

She smiled a little but remained silent.

He shrugged. "I've been sober for some time."

She lifted that ghost of a smile to him, and his heart twisted in agony. But he soothed it as best he could, binding it with banter.

"How did you meet him?"

"I was an orphan," she said, then laughed at his stricken expression. "It wasn't like that. I was just a wee thing. Too young to remember when I was taken in. They were Rom. A young man and his wife. Gypsies, you might call them. They traveled, entertained, taught me . . ." She shrugged. "Many skills."

"Theft?'

"No." Her answer was fire-rapid. "No," she repeated, and lowered her gaze. "They were . . . are . . . good people. Honest. Though others are loath to believe it. After all, they are nomads, well out of the circle of what is acceptable."

He nodded as if he understood, though, of course, he did not. Just a fortnight ago he would have been one of those who were unable to accept. "We were in London, performing." She looked away, across the inn, though he doubted if she saw the other patrons, for her expression was distant and wistful. "I was young. And wild, I suppose. It seems, now, like a thousand years ago."

He let the pause lengthen, not bothering to remind her that she was still young, and so beautiful it hurt to look at her.

She glanced down. "I met a man."

He crunched his hands in his lap and refused to let the feelings show in his face. How could any man think of her with another and not feel this aching jealousy. If for no other reason, he was certain Poke was mad.

"He was wealthy. Handsome. Charming I suppose. My father didn't approve. We were Rom. Shouldn't mix with his sort. There could only be trouble. But . . ." She smiled. His heart was becoming accustomed to the pain. "We met secretly. It was terribly exciting. We planned to marry."

Dammit to hell.

"But . . ." She cleared her throat. "He needed his inheritance. His stepfather held it for him. Jonathan knew just where it was kept, and the old man knew little of me. In fact, he was growing feebleminded and hardly recognized his own kin anymore. He had a score of maids, none of whom he knew by name. It would be so simple for me to slip into the house and get what was rightfully my betrothed's."

Will felt sick, defiled and disgusted by his own kind. "And was it?"

"What?"

"Simple."

She laughed, but it sounded brittle. "Hardly that. I was apprehended, but . . ." She paused.

The server approached, carrying a wooden tray. The food was distributed quickly and efficiently, and they were left alone.

"But?" he asked.

She shrugged. "I was imprisoned for a time," she said simply, and tasted her soup. Barley in a dark broth.

He watched her. "And the young man?"

She smiled. "As it turns out, he was more interested in his inheritance than in a Rom lass with little funds and no title."

"But you were released."

"Eventually," she said.

"Did you return to your family?"

She skirted her gaze away. "They had moved on."

"You couldn't find them?"

"He . . ." She paused and shrugged, but it was stiff and ill at ease. "Things had changed."

"What things?"

"Perhaps I was too ashamed to go back."

"Perhaps?"

"I was foolish and weak." She studied her soup. "Mistakes I don't mean to repeat."

"So you do not steal because of weakness?"

"What do you think?"

"I believe everyone deserves to have one weakness."

"Not I. Not anymore."

"Why do you continue to steal?"

"Your soup is cooling."

"Why?" he asked.

"What else would I do?"

Marry me. The thought blazed in his head, stunning him. He doused it with icy reality. With facts. With logic. Was he mad?

"What of your family?"

"They are gone. Far away."

A thousand arguments slammed through his brain, but he stilled them, for there was something missing, something amiss. Something almost there. He forced himself to take a bite of capon smothered in sauce, but he failed to taste it.

"Perhaps they miss you," he said finally.

She didn't answer.

"Do they know where you are?"

"No."

"Don't they deserve that much?"

Her eyes flared at him. "No!"

"Were they cruel to you, then?"

Her mouth tightened the smallest amount. "They

called me *Yonnen*. It means 'kitten' in the ancient tongue."

He stared at her, mesmerized. "Because of your eyes?" he asked, and realized they seemed strangely bright.

She cleared her throat and shrugged. "It's long past now."

"It doesn't have to be."

"Yes." Her tone was sharp. A man glanced up from a nearby table, but who could resist looking at her. She was like the sun. "It does," she added. "Let it be."

"I don't understand."

She broke a piece from her bread. "I don't believe I asked you to."

"Were they cruel?" he asked again.

"No," she said and though the answer sounded final, she continued eventually. " 'Twas I who betrayed their trust."

"People have been known to forgive."

"Have they?"

"So I'm told."

She shrugged. "They have other children. Other daughters to take my place."

He tried to hold back the words, but it couldn't be done. Truth will out. "No one could take your place," he said.

Her eyes lifted. They were as bright as midnight stars. With tears? If she cried, he would die. "You don't know me," she whispered.

"I'd like to."

"Why?"

"Don't you know?"

She swallowed. "You must leave," she said. "Go back to where you came from. Before it's too late."

"I have nothing to go back to," he said, and suddenly

it seemed so true. The manse, the parties, the snobbish elite. None of it could match her ragged charm.

"You lie," she said. "You have a great deal, but not here. You don't belong here."

"Where then?"

She studied him in silence. "In a country house some-where. With servants." Her voice was ultrasoft. "Perhaps a wife?"

His heart cranked up tight. "Are you asking if I am wed, lass?"

"No. I've no wish to know about you. I can't afford to. I just—" She halted, seeming lost.

"I'm not. Married. Not anymore."

Her expression crumbled into relief for the briefest second. Or did he imagine it? "I was," he said. "once, as I told you. But no longer."

She drew a careful breath through her perfect nose. "She was lucky."

"No." It hurt to say the truth out loud, but maybe it was not so difficult as keeping silent. "I made a poor hus-band, and a worse father." He hadn't even managed to make a decent brother.

"I'm sure you're wrong."

"I'm not."

Her eyes were steady and sure. Not a flicker of doubt showed there. "I'm sorry I can't convince you."

"I was sorry I ran out of Scotch. At the funeral."

"Everyone needs to forget at times."

"Perhaps some need to forget more often than others. Constantly, even."

"Perhaps," she said. "But some find they no longer need that crutch. If they're strong."

Emotions curled up hard in his gut. "You think me strong?"

She shrugged and dropped her gaze to her lap. "I only know what I've seen."

What had she seen in him?

"I think most might be convinced to give up drink rather than die of poison," he said.

"On the contrary," she argued mildly. "Many don't."

"I didn't taste it in the Scotch," he said. "Where'd you come by the potion?"

"Don't be ridiculous. I did no—"

"I admit that I rather resented it when I was spewing up my intestines, but now . . ." He watched her. "Now I find I can't bear to miss a moment."

Her eyes caught his.

"With you."

Her cheeks went pale, her eyes wide and silver. "Don't do this," she whispered.

"I can't resist," he admitted simply. "And it's strange, amazing really. I can always resist."

"Please—"

"The thought of him touching you—"

"Don't—"

"My lord."

They jerked their attention to their server. She gave a tentative smile.

"I was but wondering if we would have the pleasure of your company this night."

Their gazes met across the table. Neither breathed.

"We have a lovely room," she continued. "Private, discreet. Clean as—"

"Yes," Shandria said, not turning her eyes away for an instant. "We shall stay."

Chapter 20

Perhaps it was a fine room, but Will failed to notice, for she was there, in front of him, within reach. Like a light in a dark place.

"Why?" he breathed. "Why would—"

But in that moment she kissed him. He tried to resist, to find some sense, to understand, but there was no hope. Her lips felt like heaven against his, her hand like a dream against his cheek.

She drew back slowly, her silver eyes gilded by the light of the fire behind him. "Because you've a good soul," she whispered.

He shook his head with painful honesty, but she pressed her palm more firmly against his cheek, as if to stop the movement.

"Do you know how long it's been since I've been touched by a man with a kind soul?"

"What about Poke?" Will murmured. "If he finds out—"

"I shall make certain he doesn't," she said, and kissed him again.

And he ached, throbbed to pull her tight against him and ease the pain. But there was so much at risk. "How?"

he asked, but the word sounded more like a moan and she smiled.

"I'll think of a way, Dancer. I'm no innocent."

He watched her eyes, alive with a thousand emotions. "Aren't you?"

"Would I be here if I were?"

"I don't know, lass," he said, and it was true. "I'll be the first to admit I'm confused. Why are you doing this? Why me?"

Her smile was almost whimsical. "Perhaps there have been scores of others."

He watched her in the flickering light, watched the shadows dance across her delicate features. "There haven't."

"I meant for me."

"I know."

Her eyes were incredibly bright, and he wondered again, foolishly, he was sure, if she would cry.

"Surely I deserve a bit of pleasure," she whispered.

But did he? Could he ever deserve this woman who lived with evil yet managed, somehow, to rise above it, to live outside it. "Aye, you do," he murmured. "But, with me?"

She chuckled. "You do seem to be the only man in the room at present."

"I don't know what you think, lass. But . . ." She kissed his neck. "I'm no great . . ." She was unbuttoning his shirt, and there was something about that simple movement, the feel of her fingers against his chest, as if every nerve ending was buzzing with life, right there, beneath the humming surface of his skin. "I can't remember the last time I did this . . . sober."

She glanced up. "You'll remember this time," she said, and kissed his chest. "I promise."

He laughed, but the sound was tortured. "I just . . ." He grabbed her arms. "Why here? Why now?"

She shrugged. "Memories maybe, of better times. Better people. I need . . ." She paused. "Please. Touch me."

There were tears. In her eyes. Good God, there were tears. One glistened on her lower lashes, and there was nothing he could do but reach out and catch it on his thumb.

"Don't cry, lass. I beg of you. I'll do whatever you wish."

"Even make love to me?" she whispered.

He laughed. Or maybe it was a sob. Who could tell? Everything was turned about, twisted into a strange parody of reality. "Yes. Even . . . Yes."

She reached out, undoing more buttons and slipping his shirt from his chest. Her hands skimmed like velvet across the bandage and over his nipples, jolting him with glassy shards of desire.

"I like the way you look." Her eyes lifted back to his. "Honest." She touched his shoulders. Her hands were firm and warm as they slid down his arms, sweeping his shirt to the floor. "Noble almost."

"I'm not . . ."

She kissed his nipple. A nerve snapped somewhere in his gut, yanking him up hard.

"Noble," he said and gritted his teeth.

"There are different kinds," she murmured. Her breath whispered against his damp nipple. "Of nobility."

"I'm no kind."

She held his wrists in a light grasp. "You're a horrid liar."

"Only when I'm sober."

"You're always sober," she said, and lapped his nipple with her tongue.

He gritted his teeth against the assault. "You seem to have that effect on me."

"My apologies," she said, and, easing upward, kissed the corner of his mouth. Her tongue touched his skin.

"Holy hell!" He jerked back. "Why are you doing this?" His voice sounded angry to his own ears. "Is this a trap?" Perhaps he had misjudged her. Perhaps he wanted to believe she was good. Perhaps he needed to believe she was good. "Do you wish to know who I am? Is that the way of it?"

She stepped toward him, shaking her head.

"Because I'll tell you."

She stopped, her expression somber.

"I'll tell you whatever you wish to know."

The room went deadly silent. "And what if I share that news with Poke?" she whispered.

Their eyes held.

"My full name is William Enton. I'm the third—"

But she had already pressed her fingers to his lips. "Hush. Please," she said and closed her eyes to the harsh reality of the moment. "I don't want to know. I can't know."

"Why?"

"It's better this way."

"Better?"

"Mysterious."

He scowled at her. "Lass—" he said, but now her hands were on his trouser buttons. Easing them open. He tried to stop her, but he couldn't seem to reach down. The feel of her knuckles against his erection was a sharp bite of ecstasy.

"Just this once," she whispered. "Let me do something for myself."

"For—" Holy damn, his pants were dropping to the floor.

"Look at you." She sighed and smiled as she stepped back a pace. "You want me."

"Dammit, lass, a damned block of salt would—"

"Then take me," she said and suddenly her garments slipped down, baring her breasts, framing her waist.

He didn't know how she had done it. It was probably magic, a sacred incantation. The firelight gleamed on her skin like sunlight on ivory. Her breasts were high and firm, capped with taut, dusky peaks. Her waist was tight, narrow, curved like a priceless statuette. And her navel. There was something ridiculously, painfully, arousing about her navel.

He stepped forward, not because he had planned to, but because he had no choice. She shivered as he brushed his knuckles across her breast.

"I'll not hurt you," he vowed.

She licked her lips, eyes closed, head tilted back. "I know."

"How?" he asked, and skimmed his fingers up the elegant sweep of her throat. Her hair felt as soft as satin beneath his fingers. The pins came away effortlessly. Like one would dream. Her coif loosened, slipped and fell like golden shadows about his hands. Bending down, he held her face and kissed her lips. A thousand emotions struck him like fire. A thousand needs screamed. But he knew so little and there was so much to learn. "How?" he whispered again.

"I trust you."

"Why?"

Perhaps the question was rasped, for she laughed. The sound was throaty and soft, like the irresistible stroke of her hand.

"I don't need to know your heritage to know your character."

"I have none."

"You're wrong," she said, and kissed him.

There were no more choices then, no thoughts. He kissed her back. She wrapped her arms about his waist and retreated toward the bed. Her gown fell to the floor with fantastic ease. His fingers skimmed down the sweet firm curves of her buttocks, and she moaned, arching into him and sliding her own hands down his backside. His undergarment retreated happily, then became bound on his erection, scraping against the aching sensitivity of its head.

He sucked air between his teeth, and she rounded his body, slipping the fabric free and brushing him with aching gentleness. He gritted his teeth against her touch, and she skimmed her hand lower, down his shaft, cupping his balls. He jerked against the silken assault. Need slammed into him, and he grabbed her arms, but when he looked into her face, the world seemed to slow to a halt, for her eyes were as wide as eternity, as lost as a child's.

"Lass, I don't pretend to be in control here." He shuddered again and tensed against the aching pleasure before lifting her hand away and desperately trying to decipher her mood, her needs. "But I'll not have you regret this."

"I'll not regret—"

"Then tell me what you want." Her lips parted silently. He kissed them. "What do you want me to do?"

"I thought I made that clear." She tried to reach between their bodies, but he pressed up against her, and even that simple gesture was almost too much. He swallowed hard and held on to his control by a ragged thread.

"You've made nothing clear. Not who you are. Not

why you're here." He drew a careful breath. "Not why you've chosen me."

"I told you," she whispered. "I like the way you look." She skimmed her hand down his spine, easing lower, between his buttocks.

Sweat beaded his forehead.

"Isn't that enough?" she asked.

God yes. But he watched her face in the flickering light and found that he could almost read her emotions. "Is it, lass? Truly?"

Quiet stole in for the briefest heartbeat, then, "I may die tomorrow, Dancer. Why not take pleasure where we can?"

"You might die?"

"And so might you," she added quickly. "Life is short. Unpredictable. Lie down."

"I—"

But she kissed him full on the mouth. A kiss filled with passion and lust and bursting, aching life. "Lie down," she breathed.

He did, without volition, without thought. He lay on his back, propped on his elbows to watch her, his feet draped down the side of the floor, still bound in his clothing.

She lifted them onto the bed, and he turned obligingly to stretch out along the mattress. Her breasts gleamed as she shifted in the firelight, then she mounted the bed so that her knees straddled his and she faced away. Firelight danced along her back, glowing on her buttocks.

She unlaced his shoes. Her bottom nestled against his thigh, wet and warm and achingly seductive.

He dropped his head back in abject agony, but not so far that he couldn't watch her. Not so far that he couldn't see the timeless hourglass shape of her as she gripped his legs between hers as though she couldn't wait to feel him slip inside. As though she wanted him as desperately as he wanted her.

His second shoe dropped to the floor. His clothing followed. She leaned forward, raising her bottom from his leg and baring her moist, glistening core.

His throat felt hopelessly dry. His mind utterly empty. Only one part of his anatomy was functioning properly, and that part ached with impatience.

Turning, she glanced over her shoulder. Her hair brushed his thigh, tightening it on contact, and he growled, throbbing with need. He curled his hands around her legs, and she arched her back, open and ready. He could mount her, take her, but not before he felt the curve of her buttocks against his palms.

Drawing up his legs, he rose to his hands and knees and slipped his hand over her thigh. There was a scar there. He kissed it, then moved sideways, to lick the hot, damp cleft of her. She straightened with a gasp and twisted about, but he captured her breasts and drew her back up against his chest. Sliding his hand upward, he skimmed her endless throat and tilted her face toward him. Their lips brushed, slow now with heat and anticipation. Her nipple peeked out between his fingers, cherry red and erect as a palace guard. He teased it with his thumb, and she tightened her buttocks around the throbbing length of his erection.

He bit back a groan and slid his hand over the hollow of her belly. Tilting her head back beside his, she arched her back, opening her stunning beauty to him. He slipped his fingers into the tangled triangle of her hair. She was wet and warm, soft and inviting, and he could wait no longer. Turning her in his arms, he kissed her. Her breath was quick and shallow. Her lips trembled. With desire? Or was it fear? The idea struck him like a blow.

"Lass?" he whispered, but she was already pushing him down. Her hand felt small but irrepressible against his chest and he fell back with her atop him, straddling him, controlling him, and though her lips may tremble, her eyes were steady. She reached between them and captured him. He gritted an aching moan and pressed his head into the pillow. He felt her shift lower, but nothing could have prepared him for the jolt of her lips against his erection. He grasped the blanket in clawing fingers and gripped his control with the same ferocity, but her tongue flicked along his shaft, and for a moment he thought he might explode like a cannon.

He swore as he grabbed her arms and dragged her up his body.

"Lass!" Was he panting? Surely the baron of Landow did not pant. But what of Slate? "You're driving me mad . . ." She was straddling him again, shifting his attention from his words. "But if you're not ready . . ."

Her eyes were huge. She tilted her body slightly, canting her heat against his shaft. He sucked air between his teeth and let his eyes fall closed for a moment.

"I am ready," she whispered, and leaned forward to lick his nipple. "I but ask one favor."

His body jerked of its own accord. "Yes!" he rasped.

"What?" She whispered the word against his damp skin, glancing up.

"Yes," he repeated.

She wriggled slightly. He felt restless and tight and moments from utopia. "You don't yet know what I would ask."

He held himself absolutely still. "I fear it may not matter," he said, but she didn't smile. Instead, she raised her hips and gently slid around him. He entered the moist gates of ecstasy the tiniest amount.

He groaned at the silky paradise, but remained perfectly still, letting her play.

"I would have your vow," she said, tilting up and down so that the bursting head of his desire was whetted and extracted with excruciating slowness, "before we—"

"Holy hell!" he rasped. "Ask then!"

She went perfectly still, hovering just out of reach. "You must leave," she whispered.

The world went absolutely silent. He found her eyes. "What?"

"You will leave this place," she murmured, "and never return to Darktowne."

His body trembled, but he kept himself focused, balanced on the knife-edge of desire. He drew a careful breath, steadying his nerves. "That's your stipulation?" he asked.

She felt as tense as a tightrope above him. "Yes."

"You would trade your virtue for my disappearance."

"Virtue." She laughed, but the sound was not musical. "I fear you overestimate—"

"You would trade your body to see me gone?" he rephrased.

She tilted her bottom against his length. " 'Tis no great hardship, Dancer. You are—"

"You would—" He tightened his fingers on her arms and fought for a dozen kinds of control. "You would fuck me to be rid of me?"

She stared at him, her eyes swallowing her face. "Yes."

"Why?"

"Don't you—" She paused, seeming to struggle for control, for words. "You're trouble," she whispered, and eased around him again.

He grasped her hips, trying to stop the silken torture. "Trouble for whom?"

"For me! If Poke realizes I'm attracted to you . . ." She shook her head. Silky strands of gossamer hair danced across his chest.

He squeezed his eyes closed. "So you will fuck me so that Poke doesn't know you are drawn to me."

She flicked her eyes away and back. "Yes."

"You lie," he said, and watched her in the flickering silence.

"I've no reason to lie. Surely you can understand." She could still move her hips, could still torment him with her lush, wet heat. "I'm only looking out for myself. You can hardly blame—"

He cut her off, afraid if he waited, if he didn't immediately learn the truth, it would be too late. "Is it because of Jack? Is he the one you hope to protect from my horrid influence?"

She was holding her breath. Even in the darkness, he could tell that much.

"What do you know of him?" she asked.

"Is that why you're doing this? To get me away from him?"

"You'll only cause him grief," she said.

"Am I such a bastard as that?"

"Leave," she rasped, and pushed herself around him.

It took all his control to remain still beneath her. "You think him safer with Poke than he was at Landow?"

"Landow?"

He had given away more than he'd intended. But who could blame him? She was perched atop him like a vision of heaven, and hell had already broken loose. "Landow," he growled. "My home."

"He was there with you?" Her words were raspy, her face pale. "Safe?" The single word was almost a sob. "And you let him go?"

"I didn't mean to. He—" Guilt crowded in, fogging the issue. He gritted his teeth, trying to focus, to think. "You want him there with me," he murmured. "It's not Jack you protect."

"No. It's me," she hissed. "As I said, I'm not safe so long as you—"

But he could tolerate no more. Twisting, he tossed her onto the mattress and knelt beside her. His erection rose like Poseidon between them.

"And you're sure as hell not trying to protect yourself."

She gritted a laugh. "You know nothing, Dancer."

"Why do you want me gone?"

"I already—"

"What's worth sacrificing your own . . ." He motioned toward her. She lay on her back, propped on her elbows, her body bare and smooth and so achingly tempting that he felt himself spasm at the sight of her. "What would make you lie with me? Are you so bored? Are you daft? Do you hope to make Poke jealous?"

The sound she made was indiscernible, something between pain and ridicule. Between laughter and lunacy. And suddenly he knew.

"No." He whispered the word, for suddenly everything was blindingly clear. "No," he said again, and stumbled onto the floor.

She scrambled to her hands and knees, staring at him with wide, desperate eyes. Her hair swept over her shoulders in silken waves, almost able to hide the beauty of her peaked breasts. He winced at the sight and forced himself back a pace. "Tell me."

"I don't know what you're talking about," she whispered.

"Damn you," he said, and, snatching a blanket from the bed, whipped it around his waist. "Damn you."

"So that's it, is it . . . William?" she said and stepped closer. He crowded back. "William of Landow. What are you? A viscount? An earl? Or are you really a duke? This entire day were you laughing at me, pretending I was your duchess?" She chuckled, crowding up close. Her breasts jiggled slightly. His mouth felt dry. "All the time knowing you were too good for me. Oh, you'd lie with me, but only if it was on your terms." She leaned close. "On your—"

He grabbed her shoulders, holding her back. "I may be a cowardly bastard," he gritted, "but I'm not yet that low."

"What the devil are you talking about?"

He stared at her. "It's me," he said. "You're trading your virtue for my protection."

She froze. Terror flashed through her eyes, but in a moment she laughed. "You're mad."

"Maybe," he agreed and pushed her away, afraid that if she stayed so close there would be no hope, no refusals, no control. "But I'm not mad enough to make you my shield. To let you . . ." He motioned wildly, feeling as crazed as she suggested. "To let you lie with me, then march back to Poke and take the consequences while I . . . Christ!" he swore and grabbing her, shook hard. "Do you think me that weak? That pathetic?"

Her expression was inscrutable, her eyes half-closed. "I wasn't doing it for you, Dancer."

"Truly?" he said, and snorted. "Then I must simply be irresistible. I must just make you randy as hell."

She shrugged, but she felt stiff. "You *did*."

His body jerked spasmodically, but he managed to

push her back out of his reach as he swore and paced past her, trailing the blanket. "Damn you," he cursed. "Damn you. I'll not have your death on my conscience. Not yours too. But I've a bargain for *you*." He stopped abruptly. His heart jumped against his ribs. "I'll lie with you if *you* leave." For a moment he actually felt hopeful. Her eyes were gigantic. Her body was tense, then she laughed.

"Why would I wish to leave the most powerful man in Sedonia?" she asked, whisking her clothing from the floor and scraping it over her head.

He watched her narrowly, trying to decipher the mystery, but it was far too deep for his shallow mind. "Why would you want to cuckold him?"

She shrugged as she fastened her gown. "A lass needs a bit of variety."

Lies. All lies and nothing else. But what had he expected?

"Go back to him then," he said, "before he suspects something."

"I told you," she said, snatching up her shoes, "he already suspects something."

His stomach pitched violently. "What will he do to you?"

She stared at him, saying nothing, and he could not help but snatch her to him again.

"What'll he do?" he rasped, but she jerked out of his grasp and yanked the door open.

"Nothing you can prevent," she said, and stepped into the night.

Chapter 21

Will rushed through the darkness. His heart rapped like a hammer against his ribs. Once sanity had settled back into his lust-flushed brain, he'd tried to catch her. Tried to stop her. But she was like the shadows, disappearing into the night. Where had she gone? Back to Poke? What would he suspect? What would he do? Questions roared with gale force through him as he raced down the alleys, his lungs straining and his muscles screaming with agony.

He pushed open the Den's front door. Nothing happened. No hurled accusations. No threats. Perhaps she hadn't returned. Striding inside, he rushed into the parlor. The Scotsman slept on, but the girl named Gem roused from her chair.

"Where's Shandria?" Will asked.

She scowled.

"Princess," he corrected. "Where is she?"

She nodded toward the hallway. "Poke's chamber, I think."

He turned like a puppet on wobbly strings, but there was nothing else to do, nothing but to stride down the hall, to lay his hand on the latch, to push the door open.

And she was there. Safe. Whole. She stood before the

fireplace like a princess amongst her countless trinkets. Gone was any sign of passion or emotion. Her face was set like a cameo, but she was well. Will's knees felt weak at the sight of her, but he kept himself carefully where he was, lest he spurt across the floor and drag her into his arms. Lest he berate her for her carelessness, beg her for her forgiveness. Plead for her touch. Jesus, God. She was safe. Thus far.

"Mr. Slate," Poke crooned, and for the first time Will noticed the master. He sat in an upholstered chair to the right of the fireplace, his expression almost amused. "How . . . unusual to find you here . . . in my private chambers."

Will was still lucid enough to feel fear, but he stepped inside and closed the door behind him. What had she told Poke? What story should he spew?

"My apologies," he said, and allowed himself the briefest glance at her regal face. Just to make sure, to be perfectly certain she was well. "But I thought it best to speak with you straightaway."

"Oh?" Poke sat back slightly. Firelight played across his pretty features. "And what did you wish to speak to me about, Mr. Slate?"

Will turned toward her then, giving himself one quick instant to decipher what he could from her face, but he should have known better. There were no clues there, only cool distance. Unless, perhaps . . . Was there a spark of anger? And if so, was it honest emotion shining through the perfect mask? But no, she had survived too long, had learned too much to make such a mistake.

He turned back, his mind hammering desperately away.

"You can hardly blame me for trying," he said, and formed a careful grin.

Poke canted his head and twined his fingers in his lap. "Certainly not," he agreed.

So had she actually admitted some indiscretion, or was Poke only playing along?

"Ice princess or not," Will continued, "she's a fine piece of work."

"Indeed."

"But I didn't force her."

Death crept about the room on careful feet, peering into corners, searching for the unwary.

"Are you saying my lady lay with you of her own accord, Mr. Slate?"

Is that what she had said? Panic spewed through him, but he steadied his nerves. Poke liked nothing better than toying with people's minds, unless it was destroying them. So he forced a laugh. "Do you think I'd come back here if I'd lain with her?"

" 'Tis difficult to guess what you would do, Mr. Slate," Poke said, and rose with catlike grace to his feet. " 'Tis difficult to guess much about you. So perhaps you'd best tell me in your own charming words." Pacing to his desk, he skimmed his fingers across the edge of an ornamental letter opener. It had been sharpened to a fine point and glistened lustily in the firelight.

"She didn't tell you I tried to . . ." Will paused as if confused. "She didn't tell you?"

Poke smiled. "My princess can be quite tight-lipped."

"Your princess," Will said, allowing a small spark of his own emotion, "is damned deadly."

True interest shone in the villain's face. "Do tell."

"I only asked for a kiss." He waved an open hand rapidly, as if fending off a blow. "Nothing more."

Poke turned, his eyes gleaming in the firelight. "Did I

give you some reason to believe I wished to share her charms?"

Will straightened slightly, meeting the other's eyes steadily. "You sent us out together."

Death crept closer, grinning. "And you thought it a perfect opportunity."

Will tilted his head and rubbed his wounded arm. "I only wanted a kiss."

Poke watched him, his eyes bright.

Will turned his gaze to Shandria and back. "She keeps that little knife well hidden."

Crossing the room, Poke brushed a stray tendril from Shandria's neck. "Until it's needed," he said.

Will snorted. "I think it best if I work alone henceforth."

"No luck then, Mr. Slate?"

"On the contrary," Will said, and drew forth the black pearls he'd purchased after the sale of Lord Perceval's steeds. They gleamed with dark elegance in the firelight. "I did quite well . . . after she left."

"Ahh." Poke sighed, and glanced at Shandria. "Pretty baubles."

"I can get more," Will assured him. "If left to my own devices."

They watched each other. "On the contrary," Poke said. "I think my lady inspires you."

"She—"

"Indeed . . ." he interrupted, skimming his fingers down her arm, "I've another mission for the two of you."

"Truly, I'm more effective alone."

"Perhaps," he said. "But you're more trustworthy with her. And more entertaining. And, too, this next little test will require a pair of thieves. Clever thieves. Do you think yourself up to the task, Mr. Slate?"

"What task is that?"

"There are documents I have a need for."

"Documents? Why—"

"Mr. Slate." Poke's expression was falsely pleasant. "Do not think that I am always so patient as I have been this day. I only forgive you your transgressions with my bonny lady because I know the effect she has on men. Indeed, 'tis why she is so valuable to me. So I shall excuse you this once. But you might think twice before crossing me again."

Will nodded. "When do we go for the documents?"

"Soon enough. But for now we'd like to be left alone. We have things to"—He slipped his palm over the curve of her buttocks—"discuss."

Will tried to move, to exit with some grace, but she was there, alone, with him. He flitted his eyes to hers, but they were as cold as crafted steel. He turned away finally, for he had little choice. Indeed, he had no choice at all. For the decision was hers. He closed the door behind him. His muscles were cramped. He felt sick to his stomach. From the far side of the door, he heard Poke's voice, heard her soft reply, but he couldn't make out the words.

It was a private conversation. In their bedchamber. With the fire crackling in the hearth. Memories of her tortured him. Of firelight on her skin, of the soft sigh of her breath against his chest. Turning woodenly, he reached for the door handle, but in that instant he heard the magical sound of her laughter. It sliced through him, cutting him to shreds. He jerked his hand away and pushed himself down the hall.

In the parlor, the Highlander was sitting up. He rumbled something, and Gem answered, but their voices were muted and in that instant the Scot noticed Will. He raised his gaze. Gem followed suit. There was anger in her face. Anger and secrets. They were everywhere in this house, as thick as cobwebs. But Will wanted none of them. Let her mend her giant, and let Shandria lie with the beast.

Grinding his fists, Will strode from the house.

Behind him, Gem dipped a spoon back into the stew.

"Who is he?" Burroun's voice was little more than a rumble.

" 'Tis none of your concern, Viking," she said.

She could feel his hard gaze on her face and kept her eyes carefully lowered.

"Is he Poke's man, then?"

"Truth to tell . . ." she began and raised the spoon to his mouth. "I don't know 'oo 'e is. 'E come 'ere some days afore you. Seems like the thing to do this Yuletide, aye? Visit the rubbish down to Darktowne."

She held the spoon for him, but he remained unmoving, his hard gaze locked on her face until she could no longer avoid it.

"I didn't come for a visit," he rumbled.

Dammit all! He drew at her, pulled her in. It wasn't right. Wasn't smart, for she did not belong in his world. Could not survive there. She was a thief! He was the pirate lord's most trusted guard. But there was such intensity in him. Such warrior magnetism. And despite all good sense, it *seemed* that she would be safe so long as she was with him. Safe and cherished. The idea twisted her heart. And he was still watching her with those fierce, unwavering eyes.

"Why did you come then?" she whispered.

A muscle twitched in his granite jaw. "Do ye really need to ask, lass?" His midnight voice quivered like an arrow in her heart, but what was he feeling?

Did they share the same terrifying emotions? Was he

shaking inside and refused to admit it? "Yes!" she said, frustration burgeoning as she studied his battered face. "I do. You're a fool to come. A fool to risk your life. Why the 'ell are you 'ere?"

"I'm here because ye stole me h—" Anger and passion burned in his eyes, but he stopped his words abruptly, breathing hard and glaring. "You stole me horse," he said with grinding calmness.

She straightened her back. "You come all this way from Teleere, tracked me down, braved Darktowne . . . for an animal?"

He shifted his eyes away with a brooding scowl. Was he blushing? "It was me favorite horse."

His voice was sulky, and she laughed out loud, emotions warring like soldiers in her soul. "Well then, you can just march on back where you come from, old man, cuz I left the beast back on the isle."

A muscle jumped in his jaw again. "Then you'll have to return to Teleere. Show me where he is."

She snorted at the idea. "Listen," she rasped. "I'm 'ere cuz I want to be 'ere. So you'd best just get your tattered arse gone afore it's too late."

He shook his head, stubborn to the grave. "I can't do that, lass, for I fear your Poke's a bad influence on ye."

"What the 'ell you talkin' about? I was a thief before I met 'im, and I'll be a thief—"

"Your language," he said. "You're cursing again. Thought we'd taught you better at Westheath."

"Well you didn't. You didn't do nothing for me at Westheath. Nothing but make me dream of—" She stopped short, out of breath and panicked, but his eyes had already narrowed.

She had learned long ago not to trust that narrowed stare. She'd outwitted a good many in her years on the streets, but this was different, still deadly, but not in the usual way.

"Dream of what, lass?" he rasped.

She licked her lips. "Nightmares more like," she said. "Couldn't sleep a wink inside them castle walls. Couldn't breathe neither."

"So you're happy to be here then, are ye?"

" 'Tis better than being smothered by the likes of you. I make my own rules 'ere. Do what I wish."

He gritted his teeth. A vein swelled like an angry river in his massive throat. "So you wish to sell yourself to men like Poke?"

She drew in a sharp breath. "I never said I sold myself."

"You spread your legs for free then?"

"Damn you, Viking," she swore, and jerked away, but he'd caught her wrist. She turned slowly back. " 'Tis none of your affair where I make my bed."

Anger danced like lightning across his battered face. "I have wounds what say different."

Her eyes burned suddenly, stung like ashes. "I didn't ask you to come 'ere."

"No," he murmured, "but I'm asking you to leave, lass."

"Why?" She leaned closer. Her hair, loosed for the night, fell across his arm. He watched it caress his skin and almost seemed to wince, but when he raised his gaze back to hers, it was steady once more. "Why do you care?" she whispered.

"I told you long ago, I don't like to see lassies hurt. When me own sister—"

"I'm not your sister."

"No." He shook his head. "You're more the age of a daughter to the likes o' me."

"And I'm sure as 'ell not your daughter," she hissed, and leaned closer still, so that her hair brushed his chest.

His breath hitched, and he trembled, but in a moment he raised his attention back to her face.

"Don't go doing nothing foolish, lass," he rumbled.

"Foolish?" She shook her head. Her hair danced onto the bulging muscles of his injured arm. She watched him swallow. "I wasn't the one what broke into the Den. I wasn't the one what was nearly killed."

"I'm not easy to kill," he vowed, but his tone was shaky.

"You're flesh and blood, ain't ye?" she asked, and placed a hand against his chest, feeling the rise of his nipple beneath the rough tunic. Through the warmth of his skin, she could feel the battering ram of his heart, but he had once again ceased to breathe. Why? "Bone and muscle."

"Lass—" His voice sounded tortured.

"Why did you come?" she whispered. "Truly."

He winced as if tortured. " 'Twas me own job to protect you."

"I was naught but a thief brought in for questioning," she said, and slid her hand down his ribs. He twitched under her ministrations, muscles bulging. "Why protect me?"

" 'Twas me laird's wish."

She bumped her fingers over the taut expanse of his abdomen, then onto bare skin, and watched him grit his teeth against the assault. "Did he wish for you to come here?" she asked and slid her hand under his shirt.

His muscles quivered beneath her tingling fingers. She raised her eyes to his.

"Was it his idea?" she asked.

"He's"—Burr inhaled sharply, flaring his nostrils—"been distracted these days."

"So you came of your own accord," she deduced and slipped her hand along the track of his ribs. "You—"

"Lass!" He caught her other arm, though it was obvious he did not mean to keep her from leaving, but to hold her at bay. "This is not right."

"What isn't?"

"This . . ." He glanced down, and in that moment she realized his face was red, with the color running madly down toward his spectacular chest. It made her want to touch it again, to lay her head against the strength of it. To pretend, if just for a moment, that his strength was for her. "I did not mean to give ye a false impression."

"And what impression is that?"

"That I came because I could not forget how you felt in me . . ." He paused, breathing hard and scowling. "That I had feelings for ye."

She watched him. He was a warrior of the old world, stubborn to the bone, loyal to the marrow. But he had standards, limits.

"So you don't care for me, Viking?"

His cheek twitched. "I've no wish to see any wee lass hurt. 'Tis me duty to—"

"So you would have risked your life to find any maid who left your care?"

He tightened his lips and glared at her. "Don't make this something 'tis not."

"And what is it?" she whispered.

He stared at her lips, then tightened his jaw and closed his eyes for a moment. " 'Tis naught but duty," he said.

"Duty."

"Aye. I've come to see you safely back to Teleere."

"And if I agree? What then, Viking?"

His scowl darkened, though she would have doubted that it could. "Then you'll be safe."

"And I'll live as what? Your laird's servant? I'm a thief. You think 'e'll trust me?"

"The lad'll trust whom I tell him to trust."

She almost laughed. "The lad," she said, "being the lord of the isle."

He nodded.

"The sovereign ruler of Teleere."

"Aye."

"And the 'usband of the queen of Sedonia."

"The lad's getting a wee bit big for his britches, granted," he said. "But if I say you stay, you stay."

Despite everything, his offer was almost irresistible. Almost, but not quite. She forced a laugh. "I go where I will, Viking."

His face was absolutely somber, and when he next spoke, his words were little more than a rasped whisper. "Even if I wish for you to stay?"

Her throat closed up tight. "Why would you?" she murmured.

His eyes were as intense as a hawk's, as deep and impenetrable as forever. "Ye're not safe here, lass," he rumbled.

"Neither are you."

He shrugged. His heavy shoulders lifted and fell. " 'Tis not for you to worry on."

"No, of course not," she said. "After all, you're the man, the warrior."

"Aye, lass," he agreed. "I am that."

"You've lived your life."

He drew a deep breath, flaring his nostrils. "Long and hard," he said. "And I'd have it no other way."

"So why not sacrifice it for me?"

He stared at her. "'Tis me own task," he said, "as a warrior, and a man."

Tears stung her eyes, but she shook her head and blinked them back. "I don't need your 'elp, Viking."

He gritted his teeth and tightened his grip. "Course not," he rasped. "You're doing grand here, ye are. But I tell ye this, you'll die young if ye stay. You'll die young, and you'll die bloody."

"And I tell you this," she hissed, and leaned down so that her face was inches from his. "'Tis not yours to say how I die."

Worry skittered across his face. "Get out, lass," he rasped. "Get out while I can assist ye."

She let silence settle in. Let his hands tighten on her arms.

"Please," he said, and the word seemed to grate against his very being.

But she shook her head, and because she could no longer resist, because she was far too weak, she leaned down and kissed him.

Sanity settled into her soul, and for a moment, for a brief flicker of time, all was right, safe, proper.

She drew slowly away. His eyes were tortured, and his hands trembled on her wrists.

"Leave," he whispered, but she shook her head and drew slowly away.

"Not without you, old man. Never without you."

Chapter 22

Will's dreams were dark and confusing that night, shadowy half memories of Elli. But the images shifted, and in the end it was Shandria who lay still and broken beside a fiery carriage.

He woke in a cold sweat, swung his feet to the floor, and wandered silently about the Den. Every aching instinct insisted that he go to her, take her in his arms, protect her. But despite pretenses, he was not Slate. Nay, he was only William Enton. And she had chosen another.

Padding restlessly past the parlor, he saw that the giant was resting peacefully. Both Oxford and Gem seemed to be gone. Peter was in the kitchen, eating a loaf of bread and drinking from a battered clay cup. He glanced up as Will wandered past.

Not a sound issued from Poke's bedchamber. Will gritted his teeth and strode into the parlor.

The Highlander opened his eyes. "She's alone," he said, his voice as dark and deep as the night just passing.

Will turned. "What?"

"The lass you look for is alone."

A noise sounded in the doorway. William turned, muscles tensed.

"What's this then?" Oxford shifted, skimming the

room restlessly. "The corpse speaks." He grinned and stepped inside. "But not much longer, aye?"

The Scot said nothing, but lifted his gaze with slow deliberation to his adversary. Sandy-colored stubble covered his anvil jaw, and his eyes were as steady as a stone as he watched the other approach.

"What you lookin' at?" Oxford asked.

"Tobhair mu marc-shluagh."

"What's that?" Ox rasped, surprised by the ancient Gaelic, but in that moment Peter strode into the room, effectively separating them.

"You're talkin' gibberish again, old man," he said. His tone was casual, but Ox was not so easily mollified.

"What'd 'e say?"

Peter shrugged and handed over half his loaf. The Highlander raised an arm the size of an oaken bough. Muscles rippled through his shoulders in bunched waves. "He don't make no sense."

Ox grinned. "Not since 'e crossed my path leastways."

"Aye," Peter agreed. "You're fierce indeed. You and Black." He took a bite of his simple fare. "And Dag . . . and the bloke what got to him afore he reached the Den."

Ox narrowed his eyes. "You tryin' to say something, lad?"

"Me? No. Too bad he was already wounded though, aye, Ox, elseways you coulda showed your mettle?"

"It wouldn't a made no difference."

"Not against you," Peter agreed, and waved his bread mildly. "Your . . . skills . . . is known far and abroad."

"And don't you forget it, laddie."

"Couldn't. Not even if I wanted to. After all, you brought the giant here down."

"And I'll fuckin' well do it again if 'e gets mouthy."

"I'm certain you will," agreed Pete, and passed over his

cup. The Scotsman took it without shifting his gaze from the Ox. "I just hope I'm here to see it, is all."

Ox slipped a long curved blade from his trousers. "Well, you're 'ere now."

"What's 'appenin'?" Jack appeared in the doorway like a wraith. His eyes were as round as agates, his skinny body tense as a bowstring.

Will swore in silence, but Peter smiled, though there was something flinty in his eyes.

"Nim," he said, sounding jovial. "Go tell the others Ox is plannin' to finish off the old man."

The boy shifted his eyes from Peter to Oxford.

"Only they might not care to watch," Pete added, "seein's as how the old fellow there can't hardly lift his head yet."

Jack skipped his gaze from Pete to the giant and loosened his fists cautiously. "You need 'elp gettin' to the privy again, Uncle?"

"Uncle?" Peter said, as jolly as ever.

Jack crossed the floor, passing Oxford's wicked blade without a glance. Will held his breath, muscles cranked tight. "Used ta know a daft cripple down ta Berrywood," the lad said. "Everyone knowed 'im as Uncle."

Peter retrieved the battered cup and handed it to Jack, who raised it to his lips, but didn't quite seem to drink. Their gazes met and caught.

" 'Ow do we know 'e's a cripple?" Ox said. "Could be 'e's fakin' it. 'iding under little Gemini's skirts." He stepped forward, knife raised. Evil wafted with him, thick and cloying.

The giant raised his eyes, gray as the northern sea in the somber light of the morning. Not a flicker of emotion showed in his face. Not a breath of fear. Just steely steadiness. Holy hell, who was this man?

Tension rode the room like an Irish horseman.

"What else you doin' under 'er skirts, old man?" Ox asked, and stepped forward. "Nothing I ain't done long afore you got 'ere, I'll warrant."

A muscle twisted in the big man's jaw.

It almost sounded as if Peter swore, but he was already smiling as he yanked a flask from his waistcoat and offered it to the other. "Heard you had a big haul last night, Oxford."

Ox straightened and took the proffered whisky. He drank, wiped his mouth, and squinted over top his grubby hand. "Fuckin' coachman never knew what 'it 'im."

"No one like you for out-and-out brutality," Peter agreed.

Ox narrowed his eyes. "Nothin' like me for nothin'," he said, and lowered his gaze back to the Scotsman, but Jack had inadvertently stepped between them, showing the Irishman his back.

"Go ahead and sleep, gaffer," he said, but from his vantage point, Will could see the boy's eyes. There was pleading there. Pleading and abject desperation.

The Highlander drew his attention deliberately from Ox to hold the boy in a steady stare. Their gazes held and melded, new steel on battered iron, then, like a kindly bear, the Scotsman closed his eyes.

Jack eased back a step. "Well, guess it's my turn to make breakfast, then."

Peter delayed only a breathless second before he groaned. "God's balls, I'd rather eat dirt. What say you, Ox? Shall we step out and see what we can scare up at the market?"

Oxford stared at the slumbering giant for a moment

longer, then snorted and finished off the flask before shoving it back into Peter's hands.

"I 'ad me a full night's work," he said, "and there ain't nothing like a little blood to get me dicker up. I'm off to find me a bit of company."

The room echoed with Oxford's jaunty footfalls.

"You do that, then," Peter said, all congeniality as he wiped off the mouthpiece of the flask with a grimace.

The front door opened and closed.

Peter's exhalation was audible. "God's nuts!" he said, not turning toward the Scot behind him. "You want to live out the day, old man, you'd damned well better be smarter than the Ox."

A soft snort issued from the giant. "Me wick is smarter than the Ox."

Peter glanced toward him in some surprise, then laughed out loud.

"What's wrong?" Gem rasped, sprinting breathlessly into the doorway. "What 'appened?"

"Ox was 'ere," Jack said.

" 'E was walking jaunty." Her face was as pale as death, her voice breathless. "What'd 'e do?"

" 'E robbed a coachman," Jack said. "Last night afore—"

"What'd 'e do to the Viking?"

Jack scowled and stepped aside. The Highlander's gaze lifted to the girl's, and there was a difference in his eyes, a fierce emotion so potent not a soul dared speak.

Gem's knees seemed to buckle. For a moment she rested her shoulder against the rough timber of the doorjamb. Every man there watched her with bated breath, but she found her balance soon enough. Clearing her throat, she shifted from the doorway before skimming

the faces around her. "I was afeared all my tender minis-
tration 'ad gone to 'ell, is all," she explained.

No one spoke.

"I invested a good deal of time into that big bloke."

So little Gem was in love. Something twisted in Will's
chest. It might have been his heart.

"Don't want it goin' to waste." She crossed the floor
with careful steps, as if just managing to keep from dash-
ing to him. "I figure 'e could pull down a castle bare
'anded, once 'e's mended. Fella like that could be worth
somethin'." For a moment, Will thought she would reach
out to touch her patient's face, but she curled her fingers
into his blanket instead, holding fast, as if she would top-
ple over without the support. Their gazes met and held,
green and gray. Hillock and sea.

Peter cleared his throat. "Well, Gemini, since you're up
and about, maybe you could see to breakfast. Save us
from Nim here."

No one spoke.

Peter flicked his gaze nervously toward the door.
"Saint's stones, Gem, come out of it."

She didn't even manage to shift her gaze, but the giant
pulled his from hers with an effort.

"He's gone," he said, his voice as low as ever.

"What?"

All eyes turned to him.

"The man you call Poke," he intoned. "He left some
hours ago."

"Yeah?" Peter grinned, then nodded toward the Scotsman. "Well then hell, Gemini, you might as well have at
him."

She was still transfixed, staring at the massive Highlander as if he might disappear at any moment.

"Gem?" Peter said, still grinning.

She came to with a jerk. "What?"

"I was wonderin' if you'd make breakfast, but I see you got other things to do."

She turned with wooden slowness, putting her back regretfully to her patient. Her cheeks had flushed a sunrise pink. "I don't know what you're talking about."

Peter laughed, the Viking glowered, and Jack shifted his gaze carefully from one to the other as if silently searching for clues.

"I'll prepare breakfast."

Will jerked his attention to the doorway, and she was there, as silent as a wraith, as beautiful as a winter blossom.

Her face was pale, but she appeared to be unharmed. He remained perfectly still by dint of control he was certain he didn't possess. She shifted her gaze from Peter to Gem, seeming completely unaware of him, as if she hadn't moaned in his arms, as if she hadn't offered herself. As if she hadn't begged him to take her.

"Is your patient well enough for a meal, Gemini?"

The girl didn't turn, but kept her back perfectly aligned as she faced away from the mattress. "Aye, I think 'e could take a bit."

"Good then. Nim, fetch a bucket of water, will you, lad? Peter, we've only one egg left. If you'll give me the ones you filched yesterday, we'll have us a feast."

He grinned. "I didn't tell you I filched eggs, Princess."

"No. You didn't," she said, and smiled before disappearing into the hallway.

The young men hurried from the room. Gem cleared her throat, half-turning but not quite meeting the Scotsman's eyes. "I'll bring your meal as soon as it's ready. Rest until—"

"Nay." His refusal was almost inaudible in its deep response. "I'll dine at table."

Will left them to their argument. He wondered who this man was. He wondered why he was there, but another mystery intrigued him more. He found her in the kitchen. She'd tied a folded towel about her waist and was already mixing ingredients in a wooden bowl. The picture was strangely domestic and curled dizzily into his mind like a forbidden herb.

She cracked a brown egg and whisked it into a froth with a bundle of tightly tied twigs.

He crossed the room. Floorboards creaked beneath his feet as they did for none other in this den of thieves. "What would you have *me* do?" he asked.

She glanced up, her eyes sparking. "I believe I made that clear last night."

Memories smote him like hot embers, burning his mind—her breasts, pale and luscious in the firelight, her legs entwining his own, pulling him into the heat of her body. He fought the sharp edge of desire and curled his hand around nothing.

"Why did you want me to leave?"

"I believe I made that clear also," she said, and brushed past him to scoop flour from a cloth bag.

"And what would Poke have done? If he'd found me gone?" Will rasped, grabbing her arm.

Their gazes fused. "That's none of your concern."

Anger sprinted through him. "So you will protect me," he hissed. "Coddle me like a damned child, while I—"

"Nim," she said, freeing her arm and pushing past him to address the lad who stood sloshing water over the side of a wooden bucket. "Place half of it over the fire, if you will, and use the rest for washing up."

"Washing up?"

"I'm sure you've heard of it," she said. " 'Tis when you use water to cleanse yourself."

He made his eyes go round. "You put the actual water on your skin?"

"Aye," she said, giving him a wry glance, and he grinned impishly.

"Could be I 'ave 'eard of such a thing," he said, and shifted his gaze rapidly to Will. "Though it was sometime ago."

"Try to remember," she said, and shooed him out of the kitchen before pulling a small, potbellied crock out of the pantry. Removing the cover, she peered inside, then slipped the dish into the pot of water that hung above the fire.

Peter entered with a rag bulging with eggs the color of dark onions. "I'd planned to hoard them for myself."

"Then you should have been more clever," she informed him. "Put them in the water straightaway," she ordered, and he did, then grinned as he straightened and glanced toward the wooden bowl.

"Puffs?" he asked hopefully.

"Aye, if you get yourself cleaned up."

"Yes, my lady," he said, and hurried from the room.

William watched her. A new side, another facet, but he should hardly be surprised, for he knew so little about her. Nothing really, except what she let him see, what she trotted out for bumblers like him to witness.

"How did you learn to cook?"

She didn't glance up but kept her attention focused on the batter she spooned onto a black, metal pan. "Even Rom eat," she said.

"Your mother taught you?"

Her clever fingers fumbled, but in an instant, she was back on track. "Had I had my current skills, we could have eaten better."

"What skills are those?"

"Thievery," she said, turning away and slipping the pan into the squat, black oven.

"And what of your other skills?"

She turned to stare at him, her face expressionless. "If you've something to say, Dancer, say it and have done."

He stepped up close, unable to bear the strain any longer. "How do you know he'll not force you?"

"I don't," she admitted, then forced a smile. "But judging by your actions, I have little to worry about."

He caught her arm. "What the devil does that mean?"

"Peter." She glanced up. Will released her arm with a hard effort. "Set out the crockery. We shall dine shortly."

Peter bumbled noisily through the kitchen, but if he had noticed anything untoward, he made no comment. Instead, he whistled between his teeth, balancing an ungainly load of dishes on his way to the dining area.

Will watched Shandria, aching to loose his questions, to hear the answers, but Jack's reappearance distracted her, then she checked the puffs and removed the fat crock from the pot with a rag and hustled Peter off to fetch the cider, until finally the meal was placed on the table and the "family" was gathered around. She surveyed the steaming dishes as she took her own seat.

Jack reached for the basket of puffs, but Shandria cleared her throat, and the boy drew his hand slowly back. A glimmer of amusement passed between them. "We have a guest," she said, and glanced at the Scotsman, who'd just eased himself into a chair. Gem had found him a clean shirt, but the sleeves had been made for a lesser man and ended several inches short of his broadboned wrists. His knuckles were scraped, and his face was still swollen and distorted.

But the lady of the house seemed oblivious to every disconcerting element, as if she'd carved out this precious moment and would not let it be ruined. "What shall we call you, sir?" she asked.

The giant turned to her, his eyes as steady as the earth. "The lad called me Uncle," he said finally.

"Uncle it is then." She nodded, still meeting his gaze full on. "Jack, pass the eggs, if you please."

And so the breakfast began. There were no threats, no bullying. Indeed, there was not so much as belligerent silence or poor manners.

Peter sighed as he opened the potbellied crock and spread warmed honey onto his steaming puff. He tasted the first bite, closed his eyes ecstatically, and said, "Thank you, Gemini."

"I didn't do nothin'."

"And that's why I'm thankin' ya," he admitted, and took another blissful bite.

"I can cook if I 'ave to," she said, skimmed her eyes restlessly to the Scot, then tasted her buttered eggs and brightened. "Just thank God I didn't 'ave to."

There were snickers and sighs. Will watched Jack dig into his eggs. The boy felt his gaze and lifted his eyes, then fell back to his meal.

Will thoughtfully tasted the puffy biscuit. It melted dreamily in his mouth as he skimmed those who surrounded the table. A gray-bandaged stranger who was not what he seemed. A fox-faced girl with quicksilver hands. A lad he himself had tried and failed to tame. A young thief who provoked trouble but protected all. And himself—perhaps the biggest fraud of all. He shifted his attention to the woman at the head of the table and felt his breath bind in his chest.

The princess thief. She was leaning toward Peter,

speaking softly. The young man laughed and glanced at Gemini.

"I asked her to see to it," he said. "but she seemed mightily distracted this morn."

The girl pulled her gaze from the Scot and scowled. "I weren't distracted." But her face was flushed again. "I 'ad a busy morning is all."

"And it would have been busier still if she'd a had her way," Peter murmured, and twitched his brows at his own lascivious meaning.

"What's that?" Gem asked.

"Nothing. 'Tis naught." He grinned as he helped himself to another biscuit. "I just never seen you so . . . busy," he said, and shifted his gaze from one person to the next. Jack's eyes gleamed, and Shandria almost smiled, but the Highlander glowered, his head slightly bent, his huge hands curled like mallets upon the table.

Peter's visual trip around the table came to a jolting halt. "No offense, Uncle," he said.

The narrow eyes held Peter like a vise. "I'm not forgetting what you've done for me with the Ox, laddie. But you'll be showing the lady your respect, or we'll be speaking more about it out-of-doors."

"Lady?" Peter's brows were hidden somewhere in his hairline. "You mean Gemini?"

The big man's brows lowered another quarter inch. "I owe her me life."

Pete flicked his gaze to the girl and back. "Aye aye. That you do," he agreed, then, keeping a perfectly straight face, added, "and I'm thinking she's ready to collect your gratitude."

Jack snickered, but the Scotsman straightened with careful slowness. Peter tensed. Jack's eyes grew wide, and Shandria spoke.

"Poke's gone." Her voice broke the freezing tension. "Ox is otherwise occupied." She speared Peter with her silvery gaze, then shifted her attention to their guest. "There will be peace at this table."

Their gazes met and held. The Highlander nodded solemnly, and Peter fell to his meal, happy as a pup.

"Pass round the cider," Jack requested.

Peter quipped, the others laughed, and Will watched.

So this was it then. This was what it was like to have a family. Squabbles, teasing, friendship, peace. How had she managed it, when, never in his life had he found that same harmony even with his own kin? How was it that she could forget the bad, sift out the evil, and find this little corner of happiness?

He looked across the table at her. If he tried, if he really worked at it, he could almost pretend they were together. She was the lady of the house. He was her husband. Their brood sat between them. And tonight, when all was quiet, they would retire together. He would take her to his bed and touch her skin. Her gown would fall away . . .

"You look a bit flushed, Slate," Gem said. "Everything right with you?"

Yanking himself from his dreams, Will twisted his head toward Gem. The table had gone quiet. Every face was turned toward him.

"Aye," he said, but everything wasn't right and wouldn't be so long as Shandria was in danger.

She was light and hope and happiness. And she needed him. His heart ached with the thought. She was his redemption. Aye, she was strong, but so was he. Now. Because of her. And he would take her away, keep her safe, make her smile, for nothing would be right until she was happy. Indeed, nothing would be right until she was his—in his life, his arms, his bed, with her silvery eyes closed and her ivory breasts—

Someone cleared his throat.

Will glanced about the table. Five pairs of eyes still watched him.

Dammit, he thought. Family life was hell.

Chapter 23

❧

The house was quiet. William cataloged the occupants in his mind. He knew where each one was. Except Poke. Where the devil had he gone? He hadn't yet returned to the Den. Had he? It was difficult to be sure, for each thief seemed quieter than the last, and only the foxy ears of Darktowne's own denizens seemed able to detect the movements of the others. Still, Will was certain Princess was alone in her bedchamber. But of course he couldn't go there. He would have to be insane. Poke could return at any moment, and there were guards. Though the place seemed quiet, peaceful almost, he knew the house was surrounded. The neighborhood was watched. Indeed all of Darktowne was under close scrutiny. Perhaps the same could be said about the entirety of Skilan.

If Poke's men heard of Will's treason, if they even suspected, Poke would soon know, too.

And yet Will found himself in the middle of the hall. He had to talk to her, for he was losing his mind. He could think of nothing else, not his reason for coming, not his own safety. She burned in his thoughts like a beacon of hope, but what did he know of her really? Had he become one of those doe-eyed, passionate fools he had always detested? Yes, he burned for her, but was there any reason to believe she shared his feelings? Perhaps she was truly in love with Poke. She stayed with him, after all, which could only mean that Will was insane even to consider what he was considering.

Disgusted and grindingly frustrated, Will determined to return to his bed, but he found, with some surprise, that he had already arrived at her door.

A floorboard creaked quietly under his bare feet. Will's heart thrummed heavy in his chest. Maybe he was wrong. Maybe Poke was with her even now, and yet he reached for the latch. His arms felt strangely wooden. The ancient house groaned somewhere far off, bumping up his heart rate. But no one spoke. No ogres materialized from beneath the carpet, no demons slipped from the shadows.

A prayer sighed through Will's mind as he turned the latch. It ground beneath his hand. He gritted his teeth against the sound and stepped inside. The room was dark. The fire had burned to embers and cast dwarfed, flickering shadows across the foot of the bed, but granted little light upon the mattress. William squinted into the darkness, trying to see. One person or two? It was impossible to tell. The blankets were scattered and pulled over the pillows.

"Amazing," a voice said.

Will twisted about. An apparition stood beside the door. He almost jerked back, but in that instant he recognized her. Shandria, slim as a reed and absolutely serene as she stepped away from the wall. The stark whiteness of her nightrail seemed to mock him suddenly.

"I didn't believe you could become more foolish," she said, "or louder. You've surprised me yet again."

He steadied his heart and forced a shrug. "Life can be

so dull. It's nice to be surprised from time to time, don't you agree?"

"No. I don't," she said, and crossed the floor to the hearth. He noticed that she held a poker in her hand and prodded the glowing faggots with the sharp, black metal. "Why are you sneaking about the house?"

What the devil *was* he doing there? he wondered wildly, but he kept his tone flippant. "Are you saying you heard me coming?"

"I heard you think about getting out of bed. Why are you here, Dancer?"

A half dozen clever answers zipped through his mind, but in that moment she straightened and with the fire behind her, each irresistible curve was thrown into glowing, breathtaking relief.

"Do you want to lie with him?" he rasped.

She turned with the poker still in her hand and her perfect face set. No uncertainty showed there. No fear. Did she even comprehend that emotion?

" 'Tis a bit late for conversation, isn't it, Dancer?"

He took a step forward, drawn against his will. She raised the poker and canted her head, reminding him of the blood on her hands. She had killed before. But she had cried, too. Who was she? Truly. Inside.

"Isn't it?" she asked again.

Anger melded with frustration, scorching his insides. "I'll not hurt you, lass," he gritted.

"Hurt me?" she repeated, and laughed as she lowered the poker. "No, I daresay you won't. Sometimes I wonder how you've lived this long with the skills you lack."

"The fact that I cannot walk like a wraith doesn't mean I'm without skills."

"No." She set the poker aside. "Not everyone can be as clever as my protector."

Acid churned in his gut.

Through the fragile cotton gown, he could see the graceful sweep of her legs and remembered how they had looked bare. How they had felt, long and firm against his own. "Don't toy with me," he said, and loosened his fists. "I'm not in the mood."

"Truly?" She seated herself on the bed and pulled her knees up to her chin. Only her toes were visible now, bare and tiny and ridiculously alluring. They were only toes, after all. It wasn't as though her breasts were gleaming pale and bare in the firelight. It wasn't as though she was offering herself to him. But she tilted her head, looking up through the lush forest of her lashes, and he felt himself tighten and swell. "And what are you in the mood for, Mr. Slate?"

He was the lord of Landow. The baron of boring, the king of calm.

She slipped her feet to the floor, baring her legs nearly to the knee. He swallowed hard and did his best to think.

"Mr. Slate?" she repeated.

"I'll have answers, lass," he said, snatching his gaze from the graceful strength of her calves.

She took a step toward him. "And what are the questions?"

"Do you want him or nay?"

"I'm not certain what you mean, Dancer. Indeed—"

"Do you want to fuck him?"

She raised her brows the slightest degree. "I dislike that word," she said. "It's so crass."

"Dammit!" he swore, and jerked toward her. She didn't draw away but raised her chin in defiant challenge.

"Who the devil are you to ask?" she demanded.

"I'm—" he began, but stopped himself short and shook his head as he turned away. "I'm possessed," he said, and ran his fingers dismally through his hair. "I'm out of control."

"Are you certain? For it seemed as if your control was exemplary last night when I asked you . . . begged you to—"

"Ask me again!" he demanded, swinging back. "I was insane then. But I'm better now."

She stared at him for several seconds, then laughed and settled back onto the bed. "You're insane now, Dancer."

He tried to deny it, but his life was in mortal danger. Just being in this chamber compromised his continued existence, yet he was here, demanding answers to questions he had no right to ask. "But it's your fault," he said.

She smiled a little. Her teeth flashed like pearls in the revived firelight. "I don't think so."

He blew out a careful breath, searching for solid footing. "I used to be quite sane. Ask anyone."

"I don't know anyone."

He smiled at his own words returned to him and let a fragment of truth slip into the room. "I'm out of my depth, lass."

"Aye. You're buggered as a thief," she agreed. "You breathe like a racehorse, and you've the stomach of a milk-fed maid. But I'm told you're a fine dancer."

He held out his hands. "Do you wish for a demonstration?"

"I fear I must decline," she said, and smiled.

His breath caught in his throat. And he had been doing so well. Had gone entire seconds without feeling faint in her presence. "Lass—"

"Don't say it," she said, her voice firm and quiet.

And she was right of course. It mustn't be said. "I think of nothing but you."

"Don't," she whispered.

"I lie awake."

"Quit it."

"I can't bear to think of him in your arms." He paused, fighting for control where there was none. "In your bed. In your—"

"Stop it!" she hissed.

"You think I want this? Dammit!" He tried to jerk away but found he couldn't pull his gaze from her face. "This isn't me. I'm . . ." He shook his head. "Sane."

"Prove it," she whispered, her voice urgent. "Go away. Go home."

He stared at her. "I have no home. Not anymore. Not without . . ." He stopped himself just in time, just before the worst of the traitorous words were loosed. Before he remembered how she had looked at the head of the table, with the ragamuffin clan sitting about her, adoring her, obeying her. "I have no home," he repeated.

"You'll die here, Dancer. There is no hope in Darktowne."

"Then leave," he said.

"I cannot."

"Because you love him?"

She stared at him point blank for several seconds. "My feelings for him matter not at all." Her voice was painfully soft in the flickering darkness.

"I just . . ." His soul ached. He ground his teeth and tried to remain lucid. "I would know. Before I lose what little senses I have left. Please."

"I am his," she said simply.

Will drew a careful breath and tightened his fists, holding them hard against his thighs lest he lose control. "Tell me this then." He gritted his teeth against the agony of his own words. "Has he taken you against your will?"

"My will," she murmured. Her eyes glowed like quick-silver in a burst of firelight, then faded to misty gray. " 'Tis difficult to remember what my will is."

"Lass—"

"No," she said. "He has not."

He exhaled carefully, lest the world explode into a thousand piercing shards. "Then you enjoy—"

"Cease!" she hissed, and suddenly, like magic, like the flick of a thought, there was a blade at his throat. Her gritted teeth gleamed in the firelight. Her breath came hard. "I do not care to discuss this."

A droplet of blood slipped warm and slow down his throat and into his shirt. He would be a fool to speak, for the ice princess had melted, and he had no idea what the repercussions might be. "I would know," he said.

"You've no right to ask." She pressed harder. Their eyes held, but her hand trembled, jiggling the blade against his neck. "Leave it be, Dancer."

Calm her. Compliment her. Agree with her. A dozen soothing rejoinders prodded his mind, but she was so close, her breasts all but pressed to his chest, and he couldn't think. "Has he taken you, lass?"

She pressed harder. Blood ran in earnest. But in a moment, she yanked the blade from his neck.

His head felt light, but other parts were heavy. "Lass—"

"No," she said. "He hasn't."

He shook his head, unable to comprehend. "Why?"

She watched him, her mercurial eyes narrowed.

He raised a hand. "Surely, he must have tried. He must . . ." He felt breathless and foolish. "Who would not? And if he's as powerful as you say . . ."

"Are you suggesting that I lie?" Her voice was quiet, carefully back under control.

He watched her in silence, then, because he could no longer stop himself, he reached out and touched her face. "I am asking how he can resist."

"You did."

He forced a shrug, trying to keep from pulling her into his arms, trying to keep from committing suicide. "Is he . . . does he prefer men?"

"I believe he prefers power."

"What?"

She drew a slow breath. He could hear it in the darkness and felt strangely tempted to step closer still just to feel her breath against his skin. "Owning me is power. Keeping me guessing when he will . . . if he will . . ." She lifted her chin and turned regally away. But she trembled. He was sure of it, and there was nothing he could do but go to her.

"Lass," he whispered, and reached out to grasp her arms. He would allow himself this one touch. Just this one. "I can get you out of here. I can keep you safe."

For a moment she remained absolutely still, then she shook her head. "You don't know what you're dealing with, Dancer."

"Then tell me," he gritted and turned her in his arms. "What am I dealing with?"

"Powers greater than you can—"

He tightened his grip, shaking her gently. "He is just a man. Not even a man. A—"

"A duke?"

"What?" he hissed.

"Have you never heard of Lord Wheaton?" He stared at her, lost and bemused. "Lord Penworth's nephew?"

She said nothing.

"The laird of Teleere's nephew?" he repeated, speaking slower.

"The old laird is dead," she intoned. "Another took his place, I believe. A bastard son."

"Cairn MacTavish rules the isle," he said. Teleere's turbulent history was well-known to all who befriended Sedonia's young queen, and he was just beginning to understand Shandria's meaning. Yet he refused to believe.

"Yes. MacTavish, a pirate bastard rules instead of the old lord's acknowledged kin."

"What are you saying?" he whispered, but she didn't answer. "What do you know of Teleerian politics?"

"MacTavish is the acknowledged laird. The beloved ruler. But Lord Wheaton continues to bedevil him." Her eyes were wide and bright, her face solemn. "'Tis said 'twas he who killed the laird's first wife," she whispered. "Seduced her and killed her."

Will dropped his hands and stepped abruptly back. "You can't mean . . ."

She didn't speak.

"Poke is not . . ." He shook his head as if to disavow his very thoughts. She watched him in silence. "But he would need a fortune to fund a campaign against Mac-Tavish, wouldn't he? He would need . . . an army. But that's ridiculous. It's . . . How would you know this?"

"It drives him mad. Having MacTavish in his seat of power. Hearing the people sing his praises. Knowing the bastard has wed the celebrated queen of Sedonia. She should have been his. It all should have been his. Had he not been banned from his native land. Had he not been unjustly dishonored, he would have wed the queen himself."

"He said that?" Will hissed.

"None other will do," she intoned. "Not until she is his."

"So he's impotent? Because of the queen?"

She shrugged. "Perhaps I simply don't move him."

He laughed at the thought, but his mind was spinning. "So he holds you but does not take you. Amasses a fortune he does not spend. Builds an army . . . Holy hell."

"Absolute power is all," she said. "Torturing his underlings is merely a diversion."

Will drew a slow breath and studied her exquisite features. No man could know her and not be moved. Of that he was certain. "His defeat has driven him mad," he reasoned, "and he blames his inadequacies on Tatiana's marriage to his enemy."

The room echoed in silence.

"Tatiana," she whispered. "The queen. Who calls our sovereign ruler by her given name?"

"He leaves you unmolested," he repeated, stunned by the realization, "because you are not MacTavish's?"

"Who sent you?"

"All his efforts are directed toward the pirate lord," he murmured. "God Almighty."

"He won't help you here, Dancer," she whispered. "God has abandoned Darktowne. You must help yourself."

"And leave you?" He reached out against all good sense and touched her face. "With him?"

"Get out," she said again. "Take Jack."

"I can't."

"Why?" she rasped. Anguish and horror seemed to rip at her throat. "Why?"

He knew he should drown the feelings. But he didn't want to. Not anymore. "Because I love you."

"No." She shook her head and stumbled back a step, and now there was fear. It filled her eyes like a dark tide, swallowing her face. "Don't say that."

"I love you," he said, "and I'll not leave without you."

"Are you crazy?" She gripped his shirt in both hands suddenly, her eyes wild. "Don't say that!"

He almost laughed. For it was ludicrous really. Laughable. He had come for revenge. He would stay for love. It was as simple as that.

"I'll not leave until I know you are safe."

"Then I'll go." She was breathing hard, but he had ceased.

"What?"

"I'll go. I'll leave the Den."

"When? How?"

"I'm not certain yet. But we cannot go together. 'Twould be too risky. You must leave. Before he returns."

"But what of—" he began, then stopped and watched her closely. "You lie," he said. "You don't plan to go. You hope to send me away. To protect me. Again. When—"

But she'd stepped back and was pressing the tip of her blade to her throat.

"Shandria!" He lurched forward, but she was already drawing the knife away. A plump drop of midnight blood rolled down her alabaster neck. He swore, but she put her fingers calmly to the open wound, then stepped forward to press it to the nick she'd made in his throat.

"I vow on my blood," she whispered. "to leave this place. To leave Poke forever if you will go."

"But—When?"

"Within the week. No more. So long as you promise never to return."

He shook his head. "You don't plan to leave."

"You're wrong," she murmured. "I will leave this place for a better one. That I promise you. But we cannot go together."

"I can't abandon you here."

"Abandon?" she whispered, and smiled, that whimsical, fairylike expression of hope. "No. You have rescued me. Given me the strength to leave. But you must promise not to return and look for me. Not to ever come back."

"Then how will I find you?"

"I'll find you."

"You don't—" he began, but in that moment she kissed him with such sweet longing that he felt dizzy with it.

He groaned but managed to back away. "Not again," he warned. "I'll not be tricked this time. You cannot distract me with your body."

Shandria laughed out loud, knowing it was foolish, knowing she should not be flattered. Life hung by a gossamer thread, and yet she was happy, for this moment. "Then perhaps you'd best leave," she said.

"Tonight?"

"Immediately."

He drew her into his arms, and it felt like magic. There was no longer pain in his eyes, no shame. Dare she hope that was because of her?

"But if I go now, Poke will think I left out of fear," he said. "Perhaps he will believe I lay with you."

"He won't," she said, and because she could not resist, she kissed him again. He slipped his hand behind her neck, drew her close, and groaned against her lips, but in a moment he pulled away.

His expression was intense, his desire hard and obvious against her belly. "How do you know?"

"I've lived with evil for a long while."

"When will he return?"

He desired her. This man with the poet's soul and the warrior's heart, wanted her, and somehow that knowledge made her feel like laughing, though she knew it was foolish. "He'll not be back before the dawn."

"You know this?" His tone was breathy, urgently hopeful. "You're certain?"

"He has a home apart from here. A place where he is not called Poke."

"Then we have tonight."

She knew she should deny it, should send him away before she realized what she was missing, but just this once, she would allow herself to be weak.

"I'll not risk you, lass," he murmured. "But if you think it safe—"

"It is safe," she whispered, and kissed him.

Wrapping her in his arms, he dragged her against him. His lips crushed hers with hot passion, then blazed a trail down her throat to her breasts. His arousal throbbed between them, promising, tempting. He moved lower, cupping her breast, then finding her tingling nipple with his teeth.

She cried out, shocked by the urgent burst of desire.

"I'm sorry."

It took her a shattered moment to realize he had released her. Had, in fact, backed away a few horrific inches. He was breathing hard, and his teeth were gritted, but he spoke again, which seemed, suddenly, to be a terrible waste of her time, and his lips. She watched them move.

"I would make this good for you, lass. Take it slow."

"Slow?" she whispered. She was wet and empty. He was hard.

"Aye." He reached out, but drew his hand carefully back, as though he didn't quite trust himself. "I'll not rush you if—"

Reaching down, she pulled her nightrail over her head.

His lips stopped their foolish talking, and suddenly they were on her again, kissing her breasts, suckling. She closed her eyes to the ecstasy, letting herself drown in the feelings. His hands replaced his mouth, moving lower, slipping kisses down her belly. She felt flushed, hot, needy like never before. Never imagined.

His fingers skimmed down her waist and around, cupping her buttocks, bearing her closer. She moaned when he kissed her hair, then he was lower still. Perhaps she should be embarrassed, but the feelings were so potent, so overpowering, that she could do nothing but spread her legs, welcome him in.

And then he licked her.

She stifled a scream, but she could not control her knees, and they buckled, sending her tumbling into his arms. He caught her, holding her as if she were a precious flower, cradling her against the heat of his body. His clothed body. She found his shirt, needing to be closer, to feel the warmth of his skin against hers. His shirt opened. She slipped her palm inside, felt his muscles tighten and shift. Pushing the garment aside, she slid her hand down his ribs, then moving closer, she kissed his shoulder, his chest, trailing downward until she found his nipple with her teeth. He jerked his head back with a growl, and she felt a shaft of hot desire burn through her. She pushed him back, and he gave way, but in a moment he was on his feet, moving away.

Frustrated and achy, she reached for him, but he only snatched the blankets from the bed and spread them before the hearth. Firelight gleamed in his eyes as he turned to her, and when he pressed her onto the floor, she went willingly, wanting him atop her, inside her.

But he merely settled onto an elbow and stared at her,

dragging his gaze with slow heat down the length of her naked body.

She shivered under his perusal and reached for the corner of the blanket, but he caught her hand and lifted it to his lips. His lips felt hot against her palm.

"Please . . ." His voice was soft with longing, whispering against her tingling skin before he released her. "Don't cover yourself."

She curled her fingers against his kiss and let her fist drop restlessly to her side. And he smiled with his eyes, watching her.

"You are beauty itself, Shandria," he whispered, and touched her face.

She closed her eyes to the tender caress, and he slipped his hand over her body with reverent slowness, down her throat, over her breast. She quivered and arched beneath his touch.

"Beautiful and strong." His hand bumped over her ribs, onto the hollow of her stomach, where it rested just above her most private parts. "Elegant. Practical. Too good for the likes of me." He found her gaze with his, and there was a shadow of sadness again. Sadness that broke her heart.

She reached up to touch his face. "True goodness is a rare thing, Dancer," she whispered. "But I know it when I see it." Firelight danced in his soulful eyes. "And I see it in you."

"Truly?" The word was whispered, but not without hope, not without gladness.

"Aye. There is nothing wrong with you," she said, and shifted so that his fingers brushed her thigh. "Except that you are slow."

"My apologies," he said, and kissed her.

She did not stop the caress to rid him of his shirt, and

soon his chest was bare. She slid her hands over his shoulders, down the bunched, lean muscles of his back, drawing him closer, skin against skin, heart against heart. But there was an impediment.

She slipped her hands between their bodies and he rolled onto his side, allowing her access to his trousers. Her knuckles brushed his erection, and he drew a sharp breath, muscles quaking at her touch.

And it was that shiver of feeling that made her kiss him again, slow and deep. For though many men desired her, there were none whose soul she could see in their eyes. None who owned the goodness she could feel when he touched her.

His buttons opened beneath her fingers, and she eased his clothing down, over the hard mounds of his buttocks and away until they were both naked. His skin gleamed like dusky gold in the firelight, and when he kissed her she felt strangely molten. She pushed him onto his back, and he went easily, pulling her with him until she was stretched atop him, her core damp and open against his hot shaft.

Their gazes met with smoldering heat. Then he reached up to run the flat of his nails along the side of her breast and down to caress her thigh, to draw it near until she was straddling him.

It was as natural as breathing to rock against him, to feel those first breathless strains of impending fullfill-ment, to feel his testicles press firm and hot between her cheeks.

Grasping her waist, he lifted her. She arched, moaning, and he slid inside. They exhaled together, and she settled against him, knees gripping, hands clutching his arms as she drew him into her.

There was no time for thought now, no need to contemplate. They had begun the dance as old as time. And though, in the back of her mind, she knew his desire to move slowly, there was nothing she could do but increase the tempo. No way to fight the burning demands of her body. And perhaps he did not mind. His hands gripped her thighs with ferocious need. His muscles rippled and bunched as he rocked to her rhythmn, faster and faster. Desire, hungry and insistent, pushed her on, pulled him in. His face was intense, his eyes closed as they strained desperately together, wildly climbing to the peak until she reached the crashing crescendo.

She gasped and stiffened, arching back, welcoming the savage release on a shuddering breath, before letting her muscles go limp and loose.

He opened his eyes with a feral growl, and lifting her from him, set her upon his swollen cock. She lay atop him, sated and weak, feeling him pulse against her belly and knowing with sated certainty that she had been right.

There was nothing in the world wrong with him. Body or soul.

Their breathing was harsh and fast. Their hearts beat together, quick and hard, then slower. Steadier. She slipped onto her side, and he cuddled her against his chest, her leg sprawled across his, her arm against the quieting tempo of his heart. Contentment crept in, more alluring even than satiation, more consuming, more ravaging, for happiness was not her lot. But it would be his. She would make sure of it.

He brushed the hair from her face and kissed her shoulder. And somehow it was that simple caress that brought hot tears stinging to her eyes. She turned her face away. Now was not the time for weakness.

He exhaled shakily and let his fingers bump along her spine. "Sorry," he murmured.

An apology. And she didn't know whether to laugh or cry. But she supposed she must respond. Somehow. "Sorry?" she asked, still turned carefully away, lest he know the truth; she was weak to the core. Weak and shaken.

He smoothed his palm over the rise of her buttocks. "They could probably hear me breathing all the way to Berrywood."

She forced a chuckle, but it was weak, shaky.

"Lass?" he said, twisting to see her face. "Are you well?"

"Yes. Of course. I am fine."

But he was no fool. "What's wrong?"

"Nothing. I'll . . ." She paused and raised the back of her hand quickly to her cheek. "Maybe I'll miss you."

"When I'm gone."

"Yes."

"But it won't be for long."

She said nothing. Couldn't.

"It won't be long," he repeated, but there was already suspicion in his tone. "Before you join me."

"No. Of course. Not long," she said, and glanced at him.

She knew the moment he realized the truth.

"You're not planning to meet me." His tone was flat and low.

"I said—"

"You said you'd leave here for a better place."

She was a fool. Too weak, too much in lov— She stopped the thought before it dared fully form. Trounced it into oblivion. "And I will," she said, struggling for flippancy. For control.

"Heaven," he said.

She almost winced, but kept her chin up, her gaze steady.

"You're hoping for heaven. Because you're sacrificing yourself for me."

"Don't be ridiculous," she scoffed, but she could no longer hold his gaze and turned away.

He shoved his hand behind her neck. She cringed at the scrape of pain, and he swore, for he had found the truth—behind her neck, beneath her hair, hidden like the ugly secret it was.

"Lass," he breathed, but she refused to look at him. Humiliation ground into her soul.

He grasped her shoulder and turned her away, exposing her back and she went willingly, for she dared not meet his eyes. She felt his hand tremble as he brushed her hair away, heard his hiss of outrage when he saw the wounds—the burns, just the size of a cheroot.

"I'll kill him." His voice was as steady as a stone, now, as if there were no alternatives. No choices, and with that cool announcement, terror stormed through her.

She jerked away, twisting as she did so. "Don't say that," she demanded, but not a flicker of emotion showed on his set features. The goodness was gone from his eyes, replaced by deadly determination.

Her heart lurched.

"Where is he?" he asked.

She scrambled to her feet, naked and shaken. She'd wanted these few moments, just this tiny span of time for happiness, but horror had stolen back in with sly insistence. "I'll not tell you."

He followed slowly, watching her. "Then I'll wait here for him."

"No!" She was on him in a moment, her fingers like

claws against his arms. "Damn you! You promised! You said you'd leave."

"And you said you'd follow."

"I never—" she began, but he pried her hands away.

"I will kill him," he repeated quietly, and turned to collect his clothes.

"No." Her voice sounded flat and lifeless in the failing firelight. "He'll kill you."

He turned to watch her. There was something in his eyes now. Sorrow perhaps, but no regret. Limned by the firelight, with the ragged bandage crossing his beautiful chest, he looked like an angel of death, of vengeance.

"So be it then," he said and pulled on his pants.

Her throat ached. "You don't care?"

He smiled as he tugged on his shirt. "That used to be the case," he said, as if mildly fascinated by some internal debate. "Now I find I care too much. Life is strange."

"So you'll die. For me?"

"Yes," he said, and touching her face, gave her a wistful smile.

Fear shivered through her like an icy lance. Fear and hate and love so strong it nearly knocked her to her knees.

"Then he will kill me," she intoned. "For betraying him."

His fingers froze on his buttons. Their gazes clashed.

"You know it's true," she said. "When you are gone, there will be no one to stop his hand."

"He won't know about this." Will's eyes were narrowed and steady on hers. "He'll have no reason to believe I had anything to do with you. How could he?"

"I'll tell him." Her voice was low and flat and deadly in the flickering dimness.

"No," he said.

She felt the single tear track hot and silent down her cheek and onto her breast. "Yes," she argued, "if you die, I die."

"Damn you," he swore.

"Too late," she murmured. "I've already been damned."

Chapter 24

She had been gone for days, not even returning at night. Will paced and prayed and found himself lying awake, listening for the slightest sound. But of course, in the end, he never heard her return. She was simply there in the morning. It was all he could do to keep from pulling her into his arms, from shaking her, and cursing her, and kissing her.

Instead, he said nothing. She looked gaunt and pale, but so far as he could tell she was unhurt. So his prayers had been answered. So there was a God. Still, after all these years there was a God, waiting through the oblivion he had made of his life.

Gem, too, was back. Though she still spent a good deal of time beside the Highlander's sickbed, she was often gone during the evenings, and the Scotsman waited, watching, though he seemed to be asleep. Except when the girl was there, then his eyes would follow her, deep-set and brooding. It was clear that when all hell broke loose Gem, at least, would have a protector.

The thought surprised Will, but perhaps it should not have. He was waiting, though he didn't know what he waited for. But something was about to happen. He knew it suddenly, as surely as he knew Shandria had returned.

And he was already scheming how to see her alone. He closed his eyes against the idiocy and tried to discourage himself, but in the end there was no need, for Poke returned that same evening.

"My cubs," he said, standing in the doorway like a returning hero, "I hope all has gone well in my absence."

Will quieted the hate, calmed his breathing, waited.

Poke turned to face Shandria. Her nonexpression was perfectly in place.

"All is well enough," she said.

He raised a brow. "Was there trouble?"

"Nim was nearly caught near Overstreet," she said. "I think he should not return there for a spell."

Poke spread his hands, palms up. "Of course, as you wish, my love. Are there other problems I should be informed of?" he asked, and skimmed the faces around him, but when he arrived at Will, he stopped and raised his brows slightly. The glimmer of a smile played across his plump lips. "What of you, Mr. Slate? Any . . . frustrations on your part?"

Frustrations? Rage roared through Will like a hurricane. Every screaming instinct demanded revenge. But this was not the time. Not now, he told himself, and remained as he was. "The weather has made our tasks difficult," he said. "Not many care to venture out to have their pockets picked, what with the rain and cold."

Poke stared for several seconds. Muscles bunched with anticipatory need in Will's back, but he waited, breath held, and finally the bastard turned away.

"And what of you, wee Gemini? How is your ward faring? Any improvement?"

" 'E's stronger," she said, and skimmed a dark glance at Oxford, who leaned against a nearby wall. "But 'is mind don't seem very sharp."

"Ahh," Poke tsked. "Well, perhaps it never was, aye?"

"Oxford's been baiting him."

"Has he now?"

Gem shuffled restlessly. "I think Uncle might be of some assistance to us should 'e mend proper."

Ox straightened. "That fucking turnip ain't got no place 'ere in Darktowne. I shoulda put an end to 'im first thing. But I guess I'm too kind'earted."

"Kind'earted." Gem's face was pale. "You ain't got no 'eart."

"And 'e ain't gonna either when I get through with 'im," Ox snarled.

But Poke laughed. "Ahh, 'tis good to be home. Truly, I missed you all. So much in fact, that I brought gifts."

They stared.

He laughed again. " 'Tis the Yuletide season, my dears," he said. "Time for merriment and peace. Princess, my love, would you fetch the parcels I left in the hall?"

She nodded blithely and turned away, returning a moment later with a cloth sack.

"Thank you, my dear," he said, taking the bag from her and setting it upon the nearby table. "Who shall be first?"

No one spoke. "Well then, I shall simply distribute them myself."

He did so, digging into the bag and dragging out one gift at a time. Each item was wrapped in brown paper, tied with twisted hemp, and passed down the line to the appropriate recipient.

"Very well then," he said, rubbing his hands together when the bag was empty. "You may open them."

It was like a parody of Christmas, like a surreal mockery of the same. Will unwrapped his gift to reveal a silver flask.

"As good as any fine baron might possess," Poke said, his eyes gleaming. "We must share a drink this night."

Will nodded and loosened his grip, remembering to breathe.

Ox received a knife, long and curved and deadly. He grinned as he tested the blade. Shandria watched, her expression unreadable, her eyes flat.

"Princess," Poke said, "you've not opened yours."

She did so now, bowing her head slightly and revealing a small medallion on a golden chain.

"For my lady. Here, let me see it on you," Poke said. He took the necklace from her fingers, stepped around her and clasped it behind her neck . . . over her wounds. The wounds he had caused. Will tightened his fists. "There." He kissed her neck and turned her toward him with a smile, as if he weren't a soulless monster, as though he didn't deserve to die slow and ugly. "It looks lovely on you, my dear. Don't you think so, Mr. Slate?" Poke's dark eyes were sly as they turned to Will. Their gazes met and caught.

Hate burned like acid in Will's soul. The other silently raised a brow.

"Mr. Slate?"

"She looks like a princess," Will said, and though he tried to keep emotion out of his voice, he fear he failed.

Nevertheless, Poke laughed. "Aye, she does that. Well, my wee cubs . . ." He clapped his hand happily. "What do you think of your gifts?"

There were murmurs of thanks.

"Good then." He clapped his hands. "Time to go about your business, aye."

The occupants scattered like late-autumn leaves, all but Gem, who hurried off to where the Scotsman slept in the corner.

Will turned away.

"Mr. Slate." Poke's voice was matter-of-fact, but when Will looked back, he saw the predatory gleam in the other's eyes. "I'd have a word with you if I may."

Will tried to think of an excuse, but finally he nodded, loosened his aching grip on the flask, and followed the other out of the room.

Walking to a battered sideboard, Poke uncorked a bottle and smiled. "'Tis what I appreciate most about my wee cubs," he said, pouring out a glassful. "Loyalty. I can leave my Scotch in plain view." He raised the bottle. "And not a drop disappears."

Will said nothing.

"Come here, Mr. Slate. Come here."

He had little choice and no excuse. Taking the flask from Will's frozen hand, he carefully filled it from the bottle.

"Happy Christmas," Poke said, and, lifting his own drink, nodded for Will to do the same.

And despite his hatred, despite his blinding rage, he wanted nothing more than to drink. But his hand was steady even if his mind was not.

"Cheers," Poke said, and lifted his glass.

How long had it been? Weeks certainly. Weeks of agony and deception and danger. One drink would not hurt. One drink. But Shandria's face glowed in his mind.

"I'd best not," Will said, and lowered the flask with a hard effort.

Poke raised a brow. "You're refusing to drink with me?"

"If you'll remember, I had something of a bad experience the last time I indulged."

"Ahhh yes," Poke said, and laughed. "But you are whole and hale now. Indeed, you look quite marvelous. I think life at the Den has agreed with you." Motioning to an upholstered chair, he sat down in the other.

Will took the seat indicated, holding the flask tight in a white-knuckled hand.

Poke drank again, still watching. "Aye, marvelous," he repeated. "There is nothing like larceny to put color in your face and muscle in your arm, aye." He sipped elegantly at the amber swirl of Scotch. "Unless it is love."

Will lifted his gaze to Poke's. The flask trembled in his hand.

Poke raised his brows. "Which is it, Mr. Slate, love or larceny?"

Will shrugged. The movement all but cracked the frozen muscles of his shoulders. "It must be larceny. Since love is hard to come by."

"Is it?" Poke asked. "Even for a handsome bloke like yourself?"

He said nothing. The Scotch called to him. He refused to look. Refused to answer.

"But what of my princess?"

He caught his breath, but kept his tone steady. "What of her?"

Poke waved a graceful hand and smiled. "Surely 'tis a bit late to pretend you're not drawn to her."

Far too late.

"After all, I believe we had a discussion on the topic not so long ago."

"I've learned a great deal since then."

"Have you?" Poke asked. "Enlighten me."

"She's not interested," Will said, then canted his head as if mildly amused. "And . . . you'd kill me."

Poke stared for several seconds, then threw back his head and laughed. "Very good, Mr. Slate. Very good indeed. I like you." He drank, still smiling. "I hope you're happy here at the Den." He seemed to wait for a response.

"Happy enough."

"Good. Good, for 'tis time for me to call in that favor."

He watched Poke raise his cup. Watched him swallow.

"Favor?" He could barely force out the word.

"The documents I spoke of."

"The ones you want me to retrieve."

"Just so."

"Where are these documents?"

"A place called Shirlmire Court. Perhaps you've heard of it."

"I'm afraid I'm not welcome in those circles."

"Aren't you?"

"Would I be here if I were?"

Poke laughed. "So Tambrook won't recognize you should you be seen."

"Tambrook? He's the lord of the estate?"

"Yes."

"I don't usually filch documents."

"This is a special occasion."

"What would I gain for my troubles?"

Poke rose slowly to his feet, his gaze not leaving Will's. "So bold, Mr. Slate. So bold. But that's what I like about you, aye? Let me just say I will make it well worth your time."

Nothing was worth his time, nothing but watching Poke die, slow and painful, with fear in his eyes. "Very well then," he said. "When would you like me to go?"

"As it happens, Tambrook is hosting a masked ball on the morrow. 'Twill be the perfect time. My friend is becoming impatient."

"Your friend?"

"You didn't think I wanted the papers for myself, did you?"

"I hadn't considered."

"And yet you agree to take on the task. 'Tis very commendable of you, Mr. Slate. Your loyalty is much appreciated."

Will rose to his feet, the flask still gripped hard and fast.

Poke raised his glass. "To larceny," he said. "And love."

Will clicked his container against the cut crystal. Poke drank, then eyed him over his rim.

"I don't like to drink alone, Mr. Slate."

And there was the threat. Though thinly veiled, it was easily recognizable. And yet nothing mattered—not the pistol that bulged beneath Poke's jacket, not the memory of the blank look in Black's eyes as he died. The only reality was the sight of the scars that marred Shandria's neck. The jagged feel of the burn beneath his fingertips. The fear in her eyes.

"Drink, Mr. Slate," Poke said.

There was nothing else to do, not if he hoped to see her safe. He raised the flask to his lips and drew in the slightest amount. It seemed, almost, as if he had never tasted it before. As if, in all the years he had spent intoxicated, he had only guzzled it and never truly appreciated the exquisite amber glory of it.

His hand trembled only slightly when he lowered the flask.

Poke smiled. "Very good, Mr. Slate. Get some rest why don't you. I go to spend some much-needed time with my lady." Refilling his glass, he set the bottle on the sideboard and left the room.

William watched him go, but in his mind's eye he saw

Shandria. She lay on Poke's bed, her breasts bare, her eyes half-closed.

He strode to the door, stopped, paced back. The flask shook in his hand. Oblivion. It was right there. So close. So damned—He drank. It felt like bliss going down. Like life and death, heaven and hell. And suddenly the flask was empty. He turned and found the bottle.

"Was it all a lie then?"

He started back. Jack stood only inches away, his eyes narrow and somber.

"What are you doing here?" Will's voice sounded odd to his own ears.

"I live 'ere," Jack said.

"Why?" He had offered the lad much. Had given him a room, meals.

"I been wonderin' the same 'bout you."

The Scotch called to him. He glanced at it. Holding it at bay one ragged second at a time.

"You come to enlighten me again?" the boy asked. "To teach me letters and honor and all them things the old man tried to beat into me?"

"I apologized for him." Will tightened his grip on the flask. He should have beaten the damned schoolmaster to within an inch of his life. But Will had been oblivious then, well above the mundane pain of a tattered street urchin. And the old bastard had come with sterling credentials. He'd tutored Sedonia's royal heirs, after all. Surely that was enough said. Or so Will had told himself. But it was all foolishness, of course, for he knew evil came with noble titles. Had learned that as a child.

The boy shrugged. "It don't matter none. 'E didn't even leave no scars." He shuffled his feet, eyes narrowed. "But I been wondering about 'er."

Will knew immediately who the boy referred to.

"Princess Tatiana." She had saved the lad when he'd been caught red-handed with a fat jewel tucked into the ragged lining of his coat. She had stood up to her blood-thirsty advisors. Had, in fact, forced Will to take the boy in. He almost smiled at the memory. But the whisky called, rankling his concentration.

"No." Nim said. "The other one."

Will shifted his gaze restlessly back to the lad. Those had been turbulent times for Sedonia. Turbulent and dangerous. The princess was young and new to the hard responsibility of the throne. Few knew her well, except Nicol, the viscount of Newburn, of course. And yet, even Will had seen a change in her that spring. A change he suspected had something to do with the journey Newburn had made to Teleere. Something to do with the maid he had met there. Had the viscount actually set an impostor on the throne? he wondered suddenly. Will should have suspected such a thing before, of course, but hard drink had a way of fogging one's perception. And it was all but impossible to believe—until he looked into the boy's eyes. The lad knew the truth, had guessed it long ago, though Will couldn't imagine how. But then, the lad hadn't been dulled by liquor and raging self-pity, had he?

"Was it all a lie?" he asked again, his voice barely audible in the waiting silence.

Princess Tatiana, sovereign ruler of Sedonia, had found love with Teleere's notorious pirate lord. An unknown little minx had won the jaded heart of Lord Nicol of Newburn. But Will was yet alone, and even now Shandria lay with another.

"Yes," he said, and grasping the smooth neck of the bottle, raised it to his lips. "It was all a lie."

"Put it down, lad," someone rumbled.

Will turned. Scotch sloshed against the bottle's smooth sides. The Highlander stood but a few short paces away and reached out now to steady himself on a nearby wall. They'd given up on finding a suitable shirt for him, and the cords in his bulging forearms danced with muscle. But his legs trembled at the same time.

"You'd best lie down," Will said. "Lest you crack the damned floor when you fall."

"Ye've had enough, lad," he rumbled, his voice deep as the night.

Will tightened his grip on the bottle. It felt smooth and solid against his fingers. A solace. A balm. If they'd just leave him to it.

"And why the devil would you care how much I had?" he asked.

"I don't," said the Highlander. "But the lassie does."

William glanced toward the doorway, aching to see her, to feel her, to hear the dulcet sound of her voice. But she wasn't there. She was with another. With a man she should detest but refused to leave.

"She cares, does she?" Will asked, and swirled the enticing drink. "Truly?" Then why did she stay with the bastard? Why did she not at least try to fight? he wondered. But in his tattered heart he was certain he knew the truth, had seen it a dozen times. She loved him. Despite his acidic cruelty, or maybe because of it. "And how would you know that, Uncle?"

"I'm sober," he said.

Will nodded steadily, but his hand shook. "I tried that."

"Not long enough."

He squeezed his eyes closed, and though he attempted to hold back the words, he could not. "She's with him."

"Aye," agreed the Scot, and drew a few steps closer.

"And she'll stay with him, lad, if you can't so much as control your own hand."

Will glanced at the bottle. Power was there. Strength. "Damn him," he gritted.

But the Scotsman shook his head. "You're not ready yet, boy," he said, and shuddered.

"I'm steadier than you, old man. And I'll be steadier still. After a drink."

The giant shrugged. Muscles rippled through his shoulders like windswept waves. "I've heard that before, lad," he rumbled. "Said it meself, in fact."

"You make your choice, Scotsman. I'll make mine."

Gem appeared in the doorway and crossed the floor on silent feet. Standing beside the giant, she looked as slim and fragile as a spring blossom. But it was all an illusion. Life was a sham. Little Gemini was as tough as hammered steel. She would be fine on her own. They all would. And yet, she reached out, and seemingly without thought, took hold of the giant's arm. His muscles bunched like sailor's knots beneath her hand, and he bent his broad neck to scowl down at her. She raised her worried gaze to his. Something passed between them. Something indefinable, then the Scot looked up again, his battered face set in new signs of determination.

"Aye," he rumbled, and sighed as he braced his gigantic feet. " 'Tis your choice, laddie. You can set the bottle aside or you can wish to hell you had."

Will raised his brows and didn't bother to stifle his laughter. "Are you threatening me, old man?"

"Naught but stating the truth, lad."

"I've not claimed to be a fighter," Will admitted. "But I might point out that you can barely stand."

" 'Tis true," agreed the other. "But this I tell ye, me

young buck, the day I can't best a drunken sot, is the day they'll put me in the ground." The room went silent for a moment. " 'Tis not that day, lad, and you're not that sot."

But he wished he were. Wished to God for the oblivion he used to know, but somehow he feared that he would never experience that dark solace again. It would never be the same, for he had learned too much. Had felt too deeply. He tightened his grip and stared into the yawning neck of the bottle. If the answers lay there, they were lost beneath the surface of the amber liquor.

He could feel Jack's gaze on him, could feel the boy's troubled thoughts, but he had no answers, no solace, no hope.

"I've a task to perform tomorrow," he said, avoiding all eyes, but not quite able to lose the weight of the souls around him. "I'll be gone some while . . ." He couldn't quite seem to force out the rest of the words.

"I'll be here, lad. As will they." The Highlander nodded to indicate the youngsters who stood beside him. "Whole and hale unless I've breathed me last."

Will glanced at the bottle. It still called, but its allure was weakening, drowning in the need to protect. "Very well then," he said, and set the Scotch ever so carefully upon the sideboard before turning his gaze to the giant. He looked old and tired, like a weary lion. "I believe I'll spare you the pleasure of thrashing me."

The Highlander nodded. " 'Tis just as well, lad. I was hoping for a wee nap," he said, and turned toward the door. But in that moment his legs buckled. Gem grabbed him about the waist. Her hands slipped against his bare skin, and the giant closed his eyes and gritted his teeth as if her touch were an irresistible torture. "I can make it on me own, child," he gritted.

She was pressed against him, her bosom crushed to his bare skin, her narrow fingers splayed across his abdomen. "I'm not a child, old man," she rasped, and William nearly laughed out loud.

Holy hell. And he thought he had troubles.

Chapter 25

She was dressed in a high-collared ivory gown with her hair swept up and her hands clothed in sky-blue kid gloves. She wore a cloak of sapphire velvet with a hood that covered her soft wheaten curls.

Will's heart stopped at the first sight of her. "What are you doing here?" he asked.

She gave him a curt nod and turned toward the landau. "Poke insisted that I accompany you."

So she would be in danger. Again. As would his heart. "Why?"

She glanced over her shoulder at him, her etched ivory face perfectly serene in profile. " 'Tis impossible to tell my master's wishes."

He almost swore, almost snatched her to him, insisting that she was no man's slave, that she was free to do as she pleased, but he did not, for he knew better. He had made love to her, after all, had held her in his arms, had felt her quiver with passion and more—at least for him. For him it had been so much more, an eternity of emotion, a wealth of brimming need. And yet she stayed with a man who would abuse her. Why, but for love, or a dark facsimile of the same?

He watched her mount the single step, and he could do

little but follow suit. The carriage jostled into motion. He carefully kept himself from touching her.

Evening descended. They rolled along the streets, through the ruts that finally made way for cobblestones, and on, into open countryside. But Will saw little, for she was there, stealing his breath, jumbling his thought. Feeling her gaze on his, he turned finally. Their eyes met with a jolt.

"What if they recognize you?" she asked.

Poke had given him a charcoal tailcoat to be worn over a ruffled white shirt. His black trousers were a bit loose around the waist and a tad too short, but he had worn much worse when he was acknowledging his title, the shabby lord of Landow. Who was he now? Who but a fool?

"I don't know what you're talking about," he said, and watched her.

She didn't turn away. "I can do this job better without you."

He shrugged. It was difficult to breathe when she sat so close. Impossible to think of anything but the feel of her skin against his. "As can I."

Denial crossed her face, though she didn't voice it. Glancing out the window, she watched the world roll away for a moment. "Tell me what it is you want." She fell into silence, then turned to him again, her glorious face solemn. "Tell me why you came."

But they were two entirely different things. He had come for answers, for revenge, for foolishness. He wanted her. As simple as that. And yet impossible.

"I imagine I want the same things you want."

Something shone in her eyes, before she switched them back to the window. "Did I take something from you, Dancer? Did I wrong you in some way?"

Aye, she had stolen his heart, and she would not give it

back. He stared at her, as regal as a princess, as sad as eternity.

"Is it revenge you've come for?" she asked. Raw emotion shone in her eyes for one flashing second, bewildering in its intensity, but she blinked it away, found her cool equilibrium, and guessed again. "Perhaps it was Poke. Did he take something you cherished?"

Was that it then? When she had protected him, when she had kept him safe, was it really only a ploy to spare Poke? Did she think, perhaps, that Will might have some power to harm him?

" 'Twill be a bit before we reach Shirlmire," he said. "You'd best rest."

"You know the way to Lord Tambrook's."

He almost smiled. He would be daft to think he could fool her.

"We'll arrive late. 'Twill be dark." He paused, thinking. Was there any reason to believe they wouldn't recognize her? Any reason to think she wasn't of noble blood?

"And what of you?" he asked. "Will they know you?"

"As I've said, Dancer, I am naught but the daughter of the Rom."

"And yet they call you Princess."

She glanced out the window again. " 'Tis simply what Poke calls me," she said, "to help him forget what he cannot have."

He knew he should keep quiet, gritted his teeth in an attempt to do just that, but he failed. " 'Tis difficult to believe that even a bastard like Poke could refuse to see your quality."

She skimmed her eyes to his. "Leave it be, Dancer."

Aye, he would say no more. "He treats you like a beast," he said, his gut wrenching tight. "Worse than a beast."

"Shut up," she said.

He smiled. "And yet you cherish him."

"I've a knife," she hissed.

"Aye, you do," he admitted. "But you'll not use it. Not on him. For despite everything, you cannot live without—"

"I would kill him!" she hissed.

Will rasped a sharp breath, trying to formulate a question, but she was already speaking.

"I would kill him if I could," she said, calming herself.

"Then why—"

"Because I can't," she said, and continued smoothly on as if she'd never spoken. "I suspect you will refuse to leave, even if I promise to do the same after the documents are delivered."

He almost laughed out loud at the ridiculous idea that he might be foolish enough to believe her again.

She pursed her lips and glanced away. "Nevertheless, I will leave if I can. If you choose to tell Poke . . ." She shrugged. "So be it."

"You think I will betray you?" he rasped.

She shrugged. "I would suggest you leave first," she said.

"Before you."

"Yes."

He chuckled as he shook his head and fought down the churning emotions. "You keep me guessing, lass. I'll give you that."

She didn't respond, but turned to gaze out the window again. And his mind spun away. Might she be telling the truth? Did she have a reason to lie?

"Why now?" he asked again.

"This document . . . 'tis of the utmost importance to him. He will be well distracted."

"Distracted." He glared at her, trying to reason. "He

was gone for days. You could have left a dozen times during his absence."

"No," she said, "I could not."

"Why?"

"I cannot say."

"Cannot—" He snorted a laugh. "And yet you ask me to trust you?"

"No," she said, "I don't. I ask you to leave."

There was no sense. No understanding. But maybe she was telling the truth. Maybe she would leave. The idea made him feel all but giddy. "So . . ." he said, forcing his tone to be light and desperately needing time to think, to work things out in his mind, to find a moment of normalcy. He exhaled carefully, trying to relax, watching her. "You are the duchess of Blackfeld again?"

She glanced up at him. "Is there such a place as Blackfeld?"

"If you live there and still don't know . . ." He shrugged. Why now? Why would she leave now? "How will others?"

"I don't live there."

He studied her in the failing light. Her dialect suggested English bloodlines, but the delicate height of her cheekbones and autumn wheat hair gave her a look of Scandinavia. "Blackfeld," he said, "of Finland."

She tilted her head at him. "I've not been to Finland."

"Who has?"

"The Finns, I suspect."

He must keep his wits, give himself time to think. Keep the tone casual, lest he fall on his knees and beg her to leave immediately. Before it was too late. "But how many Finns have you met at a masked ball?"

She glanced out the window again, lost in thoughts she would not share. "None recently."

"There you have it then."

"So I am—"

"Lady Rosalind, the young, recently widowed duchess of Blackfeld, of course."

"And you?" She said the words almost breathlessly. "What are you? My brother?"

"No!" He said the word too quickly, but did not try to retract it.

She watched him in silence, and he finally spoke, for there was nothing else to do.

"You can surely make them believe you're a duchess. Hell, if you wish it, you could convince them you're a witch or a street urchin or a foreign heiress. But they'll not believe you're my sister."

She didn't ask why, for the answer was certainly as clear to her as to anyone who might see them.

"Who then?" she asked, her voice soft in the falling darkness.

"Your lover." He didn't try to stop the words, though he knew he should.

"Dancer—"

"A baron," he said, striving for insouciance again.

"Far beneath my own esteemed status," she countered. "Why would I consort with such a lowly gentleman?"

"Because I'm a fabulous lover."

She almost smiled. "Are you?"

"I'm penniless."

"So poverty improves your skills?"

"Naturally. And I'm a poet."

"Ahhh. Of course. Do you have a name?"

"My intimate friends call me Ben."

"How many intimate friends do you have?"

"One," he said, and though he tried to draw his gaze from her face, he could not.

"I'm honored."

The carriage pulled to a halt. The footman opened the door. Will handed Shandria down. If she was nervous, he couldn't tell it, unless there was the slightest bit of tension when she took his arm.

But in the end it was ridiculously simple to gain access to the house. She was the duchess. The word circulated quickly, though it was hardly necessary, for it was obviously true, despite the fact that she wore a simple catlike mask to hide her beauty. He was her companion, dressed in charcoal tails and a mask like a dark swan. It was laughable really. But he didn't laugh.

The ballroom was filled to overflowing. Will escorted her to the refreshment tables, crowded with silly foods and expensive wine. He caught her a cup and declined any for himself.

"A poet who doesn't drink?" she asked.

"I'm intoxicated by your beauty," he said.

"Of course," she answered wryly, though his words were true.

"Your Grace."

They turned in unison. She said nothing, but stood as straight and slender as a willow.

"Your Grace." The speaker was a squat little man with a balding pate and a mustache that sat slightly askew on his whisky-flushed face. "I am Lord Donnett. I have been told you are from Finland. I spent some time in Turku while conducting business there."

She merely stared, her brows arched regally above the silly mask.

"Does . . . ahhh . . . the duke wait there for you?"

"My apologies," Will said, "my lady does not speak Sedonian."

"Ahhh," said Donnett, switching smoothly to French

and keeping his gaze on her. "I understand. I but wonder if your husband—"

"Or French," Will added.

The little man scowled, then rallied before turning to her again. "May I—"

"Or English." Will bowed. "If you'll excuse me. This is our special song." Lifting her hand, he led her onto the dance floor.

"We have a song?" she murmured.

"I'm a poet, remember?" He was a fool. He knew it for a fact, and yet his heart felt light. Maybe it was true. Maybe she would leave Poke. Maybe the document was some sort of catalyst he couldn't understand. "Certainly we have a song."

"And you dance."

"I believe I told you that from the start."

"I assumed you lied."

His heart clenched as he turned her to face him, as he took her hand in his and felt the slim, tight curve of her waist.

"And as I told you before," she said, her voice low, her gaze askance, "*I* cannot dance."

"I assumed you lied," he said and drew her close. She felt so right there, so slim and strong and carefully carved, if a bit stiff.

"Relax," he suggested, and whispered a brief explanation of the waltz as they swayed across the floor. But it did no good. Her legs tangled with his. She hissed an apology, and though it intrigued him, he refused it. "What are you thinking, lass? You can fool a host of thieves, but you can't best the gentry?" She straightened immediately, and though he would have sworn it couldn't be done, she forced herself to relax, to move with him, to sweep across the floor as if she'd done so a thousand

times. When the waltz ended, he led her back to the refreshment table and leaned close to whisper his congratulations.

She gave him a sidelong glance, then looked about the
darkened room. A gentleman with a beard and curling
side whiskers said something to a companion and turned
as though to approach them. Will had little choice but to
lean in and kiss her.

She drew in her breath and he smiled. "There are few
things that discourage conversation more than seeing another man kiss the woman with whom you'd hoped to
converse."

She stared at him blankly and he turned his eyes to indicate the man behind him. She raised a brow. "The fellow who's taking drinks back to his wife?" she guessed.

He waited a few seconds then turned. The gentleman
did indeed seem to be well occupied. "One can't be too
careful," he hedged. "I'm fast running out of languages
you don't speak."

"I can't dance either, but that didn't seem to deter
you."

He brushed her chin with his knuckles, needing that
simple touch. "No, you can't," he said, "but the duchess
did tolerably well."

"Perhaps I'd be insulted," she said, "if Mr. Slate
weren't such a pathetic burglar."

"Touché," he said, and though everything about her
stole his breath, he did his best to appear nonchalant, unmoved, sane. She would leave the Den. He believed it in
his soul. He must. It was that or return to the man he
used to be. The man without hope.

"Well," she said, "we'd best be about our task."

"One more dance," he insisted, struggling to delay the
night.

"I must not," she said. "Where do you think we'll find the—"

But he kissed her, for life was short and deadly dangerous. She drew away with a soft hiss.

"I'm merely attempting to blend in," he explained, but it took all his strength not to drag her into his arms and beg for the truth, for assurance. She would leave Poke. She must. Instead, he nodded casually toward a couple cozied up behind a potted fern. "But I'm more likely to get arrested if you look at me with such panic."

"And how should I look at you?"

"As if you care for me."

Something sparked in her eyes, but she doused it in a moment. What did it mean?

"Perhaps they will merely think I have some decorum," she suggested.

" 'Twill never work," he said, and slipped his hand up her back, assuring himself she was still safe, that there was yet hope.

"That charming, are you?" she asked, but there was a breathlessness to her tone.

"Well that, of course," he said, and kissed her neck. "And the fact that you're of royal blood."

"An immodest lot?"

He kissed the corner of her mouth, needing that contact. "Decidedly scandalous."

"Dancer," she said, but her voice was breathy.

"Ben," he corrected, and pulled her fully against him.

Her breath came in soft rasps against his face. "You're drawing attention to us."

"Shandria." He remembered how her legs felt around him. How she'd pulled him in, almost desperately, almost lovingly. "You cannot walk into a room and fail to draw attention. To make men dream. To make them hope." He slipped his hand lower, over the sweet curve of her bottom.

"Quit that," she breathed. "Before you get us tossed out."

"We're amongst the gentry," he argued, and kissed her, slow and long. "We are more likely to garner applause."

She drew back, looking disoriented, but found her voice in a moment. "We dare not be so conspicuous."

"But what would be more conspicuous?" he asked, and pulled her gently back into his arms. "Cowering in a corner, or proving we've nothing to hide?"

She opened her mouth to speak, but her lips were too enticing. He kissed them again.

"No one would believe I could resist you," he whispered.

"What has come over you?" she asked, her voice breathless.

Beauty. Hope. Life, and the knowledge that it could all end in a flash. That one must hold on to it whenever possible. "Perhaps it's the music," he said and reveled in the feel of her breasts pressed against him.

"I wasn't aware it was so dangerous," she whispered.

He tried not to be drawn into her eyes, tried to be strong, but he was not. "Shandria," he murmured.

But she turned away. "No. Don't say it. Please. I must see this done."

But he loved her, and surely it was a sin not to admit it. A crime not to tell the world. But fear was back in her eyes, shining like a beacon.

"Then promise me," he said.

Her lips were parted, her eyes huge behind the feline mask.

"Swear you'll leave him, and I'll not forestall you."

Her lips moved, but no sound came.

"On your mother's life, lass. Swear it."

"I swear," she vowed and he dragged her into his arms and kissed her, drinking her in, devouring her.

When he drew back, she felt limp in his arms, soft and awed and vulnerable. He couldn't resist kissing her again, but she stopped him with a hand to his chest. Her eyes skimmed sideways. It wasn't until then that he remembered they were not alone. Not until then that he realized they were being watched. But it failed to matter.

"Please," she whispered. "The papers."

He scowled, trying to focus. "Where will they be?"

"Upstairs," she breathed, and he needed no more excuse. Sweeping her into his arms, he carried her up the carpeted steps.

And true to his word, applause broke out behind them. He ignored it completely, as he did the bluestockings who glared as they hurried past.

"Which way?" he asked, when they'd reached the top.

Perhaps she planned to answer, but her parted lips were too alluring, so he kissed her again, and when he drew back, she seemed to have forgotten how to speak. He turned right.

"Which one?" he asked.

She shook her head.

He stopped at the first door and found her lips with his own. She kissed him back, her mouth open, her tongue soft and imploring.

"Lass," he breathed, and reached for the door handle. It opened beneath his fingers.

"It'll be locked," she said.

"What?"

"The room. 'Twill be locked."

It still took him a moment to understand, but finally he did. She could be his. But not then. He had but to wait, to finish this mission, to see her safely away.

They hurried down the hall. Three more doors opened beneath his hand. The fourth resisted.

Their eyes met, then she slipped her hand behind his neck and kissed him. He let her slide her feet to the floor, but once there, he found he could not loose her. Instead, he pressed her back against the wall. Her breasts felt high and firm in the palms of his hands.

Someone hurried down the hall, but Will failed to notice, for her fingers were twisted in his hair, pulling his head lower. Her flesh was soft and yielding above the ivory bodice. His cock throbbed with pounding impatience. But suddenly she was backing away, through the magically opened door. For a fraction of an instant he was aware that she held a slim piece of metal in her hand, but then she was kissing him again. The door closed, shutting them into the darkness.

"Is this the right room?"

"Yes," she murmured, and pulled his head back down.

Holy hell, he must be crazed. "How do you know?"

"I know," she said, and suddenly her hand was inside his pants, slipping along the hard length of his erection. He gritted his teeth and tried to stop her, but he failed to do more than rasp out a throaty groan.

Was there something they were supposed to do? Something . . .

"Lass," he said, but she squeezed and suddenly he was pulling up her gown. And underneath . . . Underneath there was nothing. Her buttocks felt firm and smooth, her legs strong. He grasped her thighs, pulling them up. She wrapped her arms around his neck and kissed him with explosive passion. He lifted her onto his erection. She arched back. He groaned at the rasp of torturous pleasure and dipped his mouth to her breasts. They were warm and high and well exposed above the smooth ivory gown. She squeezed around him, drawing him deeper inside, drowning him in surging need.

He bucked against her and she answered back, straining against his desire, riding hard. It was all he could do to keep up. He matched her pace and she held on to his hair, grating, pushing, gasping for breath, until she spasmed wildly. It was too much to bear. He pumped into her, heard her rasp of pleasure, felt her legs loosen, let her slide away from him. Bracing his back against the door, Will closed his eyes and struggled to remain on his feet.

The hiss of a striking match made him open his eyes. Footsteps in the hall made his breath stop, but he grasped the latch at the same time. The footfalls stopped. The door latch wriggled, but he held it tight.

From below, a waltz drifted into the room, overrun by the sound of his pounding heart. And then the footsteps rapped away.

He let his eyes drop closed.

"We can't stay," he whispered, but she was already beside him, a scroll in her hand.

"Is that it?"

She merely nodded, and it disappeared. Her gown fell back into place. Glancing up at him, she reached for the door latch. He barely managed to step aside and then she was through. He followed her, and she took his arm, not a hair out of place, not a wrinkle in her skirt.

It was the simplest thing in the world to escape Shirlmire Court even though it seemed that every person there turned to watch their exit.

They were settled into the carriage in a matter of minutes. The night streamed past them.

She'd only removed her mask a few minutes before, but she looked no less exotic. No easier to understand.

"Were you just trying to distract me?" he asked, and found her eyes. "Not that I'm complaining, mind." The muscles of his thighs were still twitching. "But I would know. Was it an act to keep me from causing you trouble? Or will you leave him?"

She drew a careful breath. "I still have my knife, Dancer, had I simply wanted to distract you."

"As I said, I wasn't complaining."

She smiled and, slipping across the carriage, sat beside him. Her lips were as soft as a dream against his. And it was strange, for even now, with his muscles screaming and his life in mortal danger, there was nothing he could do but lay her back against the seat and drown in her beauty.

The sun was just rising when the carriage slowed.

Will touched Shandria's shoulder, rousing her from sleep. She woke, instantly alert as she straightened from his lap. It was the first time he had ever watched her sleep, and it was entirely possible that his heart would never be the same.

But there was no time to dwell on that. He had to be sharp, be ready, for he would not fail her, no matter the circumstances, no matter the cost. This once, he would do what was right.

The carriage rolled to a halt. She retrieved the scroll from the opposite seat, then lifted her gaze to his.

"If I asked you to leave—"

"No," he said.

The journey up the broken walkway to the Den seemed to last a lifetime.

Voices sounded from the sitting room as they entered the moldering old house. Shandria's back was absolutely straight as she followed the sound of the conversation.

Poke rose from a chair near the fire when she stepped into the room. "Ahh." His voice was as melodious as a chant, his eyes as bewitching as a serpent's. Will remained perfectly still, ready, praying. "My little cubs have returned. And how did you fare?"

She held the scroll in her palm. "I believe this might be it," she said, and handed it over.

Will watched his face. Watched him smile. Watched him beam.

"Well done," he said. "Well done indeed. Wouldn't you say, Bentor?"

"Indeed," another agreed from the far side of the room, and Will's blood froze.

He knew that voice. He knew that name. Lord Bentor. Cask! His old drinking companion. Will turned slowly, and the baron was there, tall and paunchy, his expression affable, his fist wrapped around a pewter mug.

"Well done indeed," Cask said. "I would never have thought you had it in you, Will."

Chapter 26

Will's mind seemed to swing in a slow, lethargic circle. Lord Bentor. There. In the Thieves' Den. Why? He had no answers. Indeed, he feared to voice the questions, for even the most innocuous action might be a deadly mistake. And he could not die. Not yet.

"You know our friend here?" Poke asked, surprise in his tone.

Cask's gaze never left Will's. "Indeed I do," he said, and drank.

"Truly?" Poke said. "Then you must enlighten us."

Silence spilled into the room, then, "Might you remember a certain lady?" Cask began and narrowed his eyes as if in thought. "The incident took place sometime ago. She was in a carriage. You were to stop her conveyance and retrieve certain documents in her possession."

Though Will kept his gaze on Bentor, he could feel Poke's eyes on him, cunning as a serpent.

"Ahh yes, the lady of Landow, I believe she was. A spirited woman if I remember correctly. She refused to yield. Told her driver to ply the whip."

Cask sighed. "That does indeed sound like our dear Elli."

Going to the sideboard, Poke poured himself a drink. "But what has this to do with our own Mr. Slate?"

Bentor smiled. "Slate?" he said, and laughed. "Is that what you call yourself these days, William?"

Will remained quiet, silently calculating. Why was the baron there? Why would he come?

"I fear I misjudged you, Will. I wouldn't have thought you had that much imagination," Bentor continued. "Or backbone. Whatever are you doing here?"

"A fine question," said Poke, and glanced toward Ox, who loomed nearer. "Why have you blessed us with your company, Mr. Slate. Or, my apologies, William, is it?"

"We knew there was a traitor," Will said.

The room fell into silence. "What's that?" Cask's expression tensed marginally.

So he'd struck a nerve, had guessed right. Excitement sizzled in Will's veins.

"Sedonia's intelligence has grown considerably since its union with Teleere," he said. "Queen Tatiana knew someone was spilling our best-kept secrets."

"Are you saying you're a spy, Will?" The baron's tone was disbelieving, mocking, but his eyes . . .

Will remained silent. He could feel his heart pounding against his ribs, but he forced a shrug and paced to the left, away from Shandria, away from her escape. "They approached me after Elli's death. Said she'd been killed because of experiments she was conducting for the crown."

Cask tsked, seeming to relax. "She was killed," he said, "because of her own foolishness. She had concocted an interesting little formula and was ready to turn it over to king and country. But I had other buyers who were willing to pay a good deal for it. She had but to hand it over, and all would have been well. My friend, Lord

Wheaton here, is a professional, after all. Unfortunately, your wife had a good deal more spunk than you did, William," he said, and, smiling, lifted his gaze to Shandria. "Perhaps 'tis a trend. Who is this lovely maid?"

Fear and rage twisted like brambles through Will, but he kept himself perfectly still. "They know, Cask," he said.

The other tipped up his mug, drinking. "And what is it they know, my friend?"

"They know where I am. They know about the document. They planted it at Shirlmire, in fact, to determine the traitor's true identity."

"What an interesting theory."

"Darktowne is surrounded."

Cask's eyes narrowed, but in a moment he threw back his head and laughed. "Truly, I owe you my sincerest apologies. I had no idea you were so imaginative."

"The truth takes little imagination."

"Lord Wheaton," Cask said, not turning away, "is Darktowne surrounded?"

"Indeed it is," Poke said, taking an elegant sip of aged Scotch. "And I pay my men well for their services."

Desperation brewed frantic schemes, bubbling them into Will's system like wine. He turned his gaze with deliberate slowness to the Den's master. "Queen Tatiana pays them better," he said.

Poke's rage was immediate and palpable, spewing into the room like venom. "You lie!" he rasped. "MacTavish's bitch knows nothing of Darktowne!" Rage spilled from him like boiling tar, turning his hands to claws, his face to a murderous mask.

"As it turns out, you were quite unimportant, Poke," Will continued. "Tatiana only wanted the man who was financing you."

"You expect me to believe that our precious little

princess has concocted such an elaborate plan to catch me?" Cask asked.

"It doesn't matter what you believe," Will said. "Her troops are closing in even as we speak."

Poke snarled something inaudible, but the baron of Bentor laughed.

"You needn't worry," he said. "William is lying. Fairly convincingly, but lying, nevertheless. The queen is naught more than a silly girl. She knows nothing."

"Perhaps that was true once," Will agreed. "But things have changed. She has learned a good deal, as much from her advisors as from her husband." He turned his gaze casually back to Poke. "The laird of Teleere."

"That bastard," Poke snarled, "is not the laird of the isle." And suddenly there was a knife in his hand. Beside him, Shandria hissed a gasp, but Will dared not glance her way.

"Let him kill me, Cask, and you're as good as dead," Will said. "That I promise you."

Cask held out a restraining hand, stopping Wheaton in his tracks. "If what you say is true, I'm dead anyway. I fear Sedonia frowns on traitors."

" 'Tis true," Will agreed. "But as you said, Tatiana is little more than a girl, with a girl's softness. You are her favored advisor's friend, or once were. Leave Darktowne with me now. Admit your part in this, and she will have—"

"What of you, Princess?" Poke interrupted, and Will's heart jolted in his chest. His mind froze, and his hand trembled.

"She has nothing to do with this." He tried to sound casual, but his muscles were petrified, his mind panicked.

Poke smiled and slipped back under control. "Is that true, love?"

"I'd never met her before Peter hauled me in," Will insisted. "She suspected me from the first."

"Aye," Poke agreed, and held out his hand. "Come here, Princess. We'll let these two fine gentlemen work out their differences. There's no need for us to become involved."

She stared at him, eyes wide, face immobile.

"Come," he repeated, then smiled and nodded toward Ox, "and I'll make certain no one harms our Mr. Slate."

"No," Will rasped, but she was already stepping forward, already sacrificing herself.

Will leapt forward, but Poke snatched her against him, spinning her about so that her back was pressed to his chest and a knife pricked her throat.

Will slammed to a halt. The world ground to a stop. Hope ceased to live, spilling him into darkness.

"Don't harm her." The words were Will's, though he hadn't consciously spoken. "Please."

Cask glanced from him to Shandria and raised a fascinated brow.

Poke smiled and flicked the blade across her throat. She didn't move, didn't whimper, but a narrow rivulet of blood was already flowing down the satiny whiteness of her neck, nauseating with its stark contrast. But she was still alive, still breathing, still watching him.

"William." Her voice whispered in the room. "Go," she begged.

"Let her go." His soul shook, but his voice was steady. He turned his gaze to Cask. "Take me hostage. We'll leave Sedonia. I'm a lord of the realm, the viscount of Newburn's good friend. They'll not risk me."

"William," Cask tsked, his tone shocked, as he canted his head in vague fascination. "You've fallen in love."

"I swear to you." Will could barely hear his own voice.

Could barely breathe past the agony of fear. "She knows nothing of this."

Cask laughed. "The lord of aloof," he said. "The cold baron."

"Let her go," he said, "and I'll not spill the truth. I'll swear you're innocent." He brew a careful breath. "I'll tell them I'm the traitor."

But Cask shook his head. "My God, Will, what has happened to you? There was a time you had some pride."

Will shot his gaze to Shandria. There was still hope. Reason to live, if only for a little while.

"I beg you," he said, his voice steady in the pulsing tension.

"So you've betrayed me." Poke's voice was soft as he shifted his weight to look into Shandria's face. "You've betrayed me . . . for him."

She turned her eyes toward his face. Gone was the mask. In its place was a swirl of haunted emotions. "He's lying," she hissed, teeth gritted. "I'm the spy. Let him go, and you might yet survive the day."

"Two spies," Poke said, and, smiling, leaned forward to kiss the corner of her mouth. "Such a pity," he whispered and tightened his grip on his knife. "For both of you—"

Something flashed into her hand. She struck. Poke screamed and loosened his grip. She leapt away, but he was already reaching out, snatching at her.

Will lurched forward. Something exploded. Heat burned his arm. He staggered back, but Poke was close, knife in hand. He lunged again, and suddenly Poke was beneath him. Pain sliced his chest, but Will was already closing his hands around the other's neck.

"Ox!" Poke rasped.

A movement behind him. Will shifted, rolling sideways. A knife slashed along his arm.

Ox snarled into his face, but suddenly there was a roar, and the Irishman was tossed aside.

The walls shook around him, but Poke twisted, gained his feet, and leapt away.

A pistol exploded. Someone screamed. From the corner of his eye, Will saw the Scotsman retrieve Ox and toss him into a trio of men who crowded the doorway, but Poke crouched only a few feet away, a knife uplifted.

"Traitor," he rasped, and lunged. The blade hissed like a serpent past Will's face, but he was already diving under the blade, slamming into Poke. He plowed forward. The wall stopped him. Poke grunted and jerked his knee up.

Will staggered sideways. His shoulder struck the wall. Poke lunged. Will caught his arm, but the knife hovered an inch from his face.

"I'll butcher you like a steer!" he snarled. Drool dribbled from his gritted teeth. "Then I'll kill her. Slow. Till she begs—"

Rage exploded like gunpowder. Will slammed Poke sideways. The thief's head struck the oaken doorframe. His eyes widened in shock, then he dropped to his knees. He opened his mouth. Blood trickled from his lips, and he slumped slowly onto the floor, eyes wide and staring.

Will staggered about. The room was in chaos. The Highlander stood, besieged by a swarm of thieves. Cask was gone.

Shandria! He skimmed the room, and found her. Still alive, her arm bleeding. She held a knife in one hand, a chair leg in the other. He staggered toward her.

Someone lurched at him from the right. But she was there. So close. Nearly in his arms. It was all he could think. All he could do. "Shandria," he whispered.

She screamed his name.

He watched her raise her arm. Saw a flash of silver arc

from her hand. A gun exploded near his ear. Pain erupted in his skull. He turned slowly. Someone crumpled at his feet, throwing his arms wide. The pistol fell from twitching fingers. Shandria's knife quivered in his chest. Will watched it shiver like a silvery fish, like a mackerel running up a dark red stream. Almost pretty. Almost, he thought and dropped to his knees. His shoulder struck the floor, making his head reel.

"Will!" She rushed toward him, but from the corner of his eye he saw Poke roll to his side, saw him reach into his jacket. "Will." She dropped down beside him, reaching for him. He couldn't see past her. Couldn't see Poke! Death swooped in. Her death. He roared a warning, tearing aside the oblivion and slamming her to the floor.

A gun exploded. He felt the impact in his side, felt the bullet burrow in even as he snatched up the fallen pistol. A spark pistoned from its muzzle. Poke jerked, slammed against the wall behind, and drifted languidly to the floor, blood smearing down the plaster.

Quiet settled into the room. Or was it just in his mind? But it didn't matter, for she was safe. Whole. Will looked into her eyes and knew the truth. She would leave. She would live, because of him.

He heard footsteps echo against the floor, jarring him with the impact. But it felt like a distant dream. Almost pleasant. She was safe. She was well, and he was sleepy. He felt his eyes fall closed.

"No," she whispered, touching his face. Her fingers were magic against his skin.

"I love you," he whispered.

"No." There were tears on her cheeks, but he could only smile, for she was safe.

Chapter 27

❦❦**I**'m told she is mending well." Lord Nicol Argyle cleared his throat. "She sends her regards."

"Where is she?" Will asked, and stared down at the courtyard beneath his window. Nearly ten weeks had passed since his return to Landow Manor. But still the place seemed strange to him. Quiet and empty, but almost peaceful. Perhaps the ghosts had given up, had gone away.

"At her home. Though they won't tell us the location."

Will turned. Nicol glanced down and swirled the Scotch in his glass. How strange that it was no longer tempting.

"Us?" Will asked.

"Anna is trying to learn her whereabouts. But the English have given us little information. Only the . . ." He winced. "Only the few facts we were able to pry out of them. It seems they're extremely protective of their . . ." He paused.

"Spies?" Will said, and found he was still stunned by the idea. She wasn't a thief. Not in the proper sense at any rate. She was a spy, an agent of the English government. "I had no idea. 'Twas clear she was more than . . ." He drew a careful breath and reminded himself that the

353

world was not crumbling around him. All was well. His life was not in danger. There was no need to worry where his next meal would come from. And yet . . . He turned his mind aside. "So even Tatiana can't find her."

"We'll keep trying, Will. The English have been cooperating with our troops. We worked well together in Darktowne."

Will nodded, slowly, still trying to assimilate the facts. "Cask . . . a traitor."

"It was a surprise to all of us. I never even considered it, didn't imagine he'd . . ." The viscount winced. "I can't believe he took his own life."

There was a great deal that was difficult to believe. "No sign of Jack yet?"

"No. He's a clever lad. I fear we'll be hard-pressed to find him if he wishes to remain hidden, but the search goes on."

"Peter?"

"He's safe. Comfortable." Nicol almost smiled. "An interesting chap. He sails for Teleere in a few weeks' time. Laird MacTavish thought it best for him to leave Sedonia for a spell, after all the information he's shared."

"He's been helpful then."

"Extremely."

"But nothing about Shandria's whereabouts."

"I don't think he knows much, Will. Once she was returned to her own country . . . There's been no trace of her. I'm sorry. Truly. More than you know."

"No," Will said, and shrugged. Pain skittered down his arm, but it hardly mattered. She was gone. "You needn't be. I shouldn't have asked for your help so soon after your wedding. 'Twas selfish of me." He tried a smile and wished for a drink, not to drown reality necessarily, but to have something to do with his hands. "How is your bride, by the by?" He reached into his coat pocket for a cheroot. No point in giving up all vices at once, after all.

Nicol produced a match. "She has a name, Will."

"Of course," he said, feeling a sliver of guilt. It seemed he'd been rather rude at their wedding. Rude, even before he'd stumbled idiotically out of the palace and into mortal danger. "I know she does. I didn't mean—"

"I'm just not sure what it is," Nicol admitted.

Will smiled at the viscount's obvious discomfiture, then exhaled a waft of sweet smoke and allowed a bit of tension to drain away. " 'Tis strange, isn't it?" he asked. "You and I, noblemen, peers of the realm, attracted to . . ." He paused and took a seat by the fire. It danced with merry disregard. "Well, they aren't exactly princesses, are they?" Though he was quite sure Nicol's had once pretended to be.

There was a slight but intriguing pause. "Not exactly," admitted Nicol.

Someday, perhaps, Will would investigate that pause, but not just now. He would allow his grief. See what came after. "But at least your lass wasn't married, aye?"

"I'm sorry, Will. I—"

"No. My apologies," he said, and, shaking his head, rose again, restless and foolish. " 'Twas a shock is all. I never considered she might be wed. I always thought of Poke as the enemy. Her master. If I could just see her free . . ." His words crumpled to a halt.

"I'm sorry," Nicol said, and Will managed to smile at his own pathos.

"Self-pity," he said, and shook his head. "I should have given that up with the drink."

"You've been through hell. No one could blame you if you're a bit morose."

He smiled. "She would."

Nicol cleared his throat. "From what I heard, she's an amazing woman."

And gone. Out of his reach forever. Another man's wife, according to English sources.

"Will—"

He started from his reverie. "I'm sorry. Yes. Of course. You should return to your bride."

Nicol was frowning. Perhaps, Will realized, he was being rude yet again, but a rap sounded at the door, distracting him.

"My lord?"

He turned toward his housekeeper. She was a short, plump woman with a ready smile and a good soul. One that had taken Jack's disappearance hard. Why hadn't he realized that at the time? Why hadn't he recognized the good as readily as the bad? "Yes, Mrs. Angler."

"I've no wish to bother you, my lord, but a letter just arrived."

"Thank you. I'll be with you shortly," he said, and forced a smile as he glanced back at Nicol. "I seem to be the height of fashion since my adventures. A few wounds and tales of derring-do and voilà, every deb from here to Londonderry is begging for a waltz."

Nicol didn't return the smile but extended a hand, then stepped up close to slap Will's back. "I'll stop by tomorrow," he said.

"There's no need for you to waste every day with me, Cole," Will said, stepping back. "Truly. I'm well on the mend."

"It's been but a few weeks." Nicol's voice sounded troubled.

And the future loomed like a black mountain, but surely Will could still muster a modicum of backbone. "Buck up,

Cole," he said, doing his best to sound cheery. "Or I'll be forced to tell your wife you're as soft as pastry filling."

"Too late," Nicol said, and in a moment he was gone. The house echoed with loneliness. Will turned into the silence, challenging it.

"My lord," Mrs. Angler said, not two feet from where he stood and already handing over a sheaf of crumpled paper.

He took it with some misgivings. It was nothing more than a tattered scrap, stained and wrinkled and folded in two.

"I don't mean to pester," she said, looking worried. Had he always caused others so much concern? "But it seemed strange, being delivered so late and all."

"Of course. Thank you," he said, pacing back into the morning room and closing the doors behind him.

For reasons unknown, his hands shook when he unfolded the note. The letters scratched upon the parchment were spidery and irregular. The message was short. The signature shaky.

Need elp. Dusc tamorow. Saint Andrues.

Jack

Will's stomach knotted up tight. He read the missive again, then once more, before pacing the room. Finally, he closed his eyes and rested his head against the windowpane. The glass felt cold and smooth.

So she hadn't abandoned just him. She had left Jack, too. In the back of his mind, he had wondered if she had somehow managed to take the boy with her. But no. She was alone with her husband, he thought, and couldn't even guess if that should make him feel better or worse.

Or perhaps . . . He straightened slightly, staring down
at the courtyard below. Perhaps it was a new twist. Perhaps someone was trying to lure him back to what remained of Darktowne. Perhaps there were scores to
settle. Perhaps it was a trap. And perhaps, beneath his
well-tutored smile and fetchingly brave stoicism, he
didn't give a damn.

Saint Andrews was silent when Will stepped beneath
the ancient stone archway. The dark-stained pews marched
away, empty and solemn. A candle flickered on the altar,
blown sidelong by some unseen draft, like a ghost long
past but still disgruntled.

His footfalls echoed on the hardwood floor. A scratch
of sound hissed from the narthex, but when he turned
there was no one to be seen.

"Jack?" He said the name quietly, and found that once
again, despite everything, fear rode up his spine. How
many of Wheaton's men had survived Tatiana's scourge
of Darktowne?

Something creaked. Premonition crept along his skin.
He turned with slow wariness. His muscles felt stiff, his
lungs tight. He shifted his gaze—and caught his breath,
for she was there, not forty feet away.

"Shandria." He whispered her name like a prayer, like
a sacred incantation, and though she said nothing, he knew
it was she, for his heart was no longer dead in his chest
but beat in hopeless longing to the rhythm of her breath.

She took two faltering steps toward him and stopped.
Silence stretched like darkness between them. Emotions
warred like storm clouds in his soul, but he tamped them
carefully down, remembering. He was a baron again, after all, and she another man's wife.

"So you are well?" he asked, and was surprised that

the words would come, so mundane, so matter-of-fact, when his life was nothing without her.

She nodded. Even with the hood, her face looked pale, her cheeks hollow. Was she in pain? Hungry? The thoughts ached through him, almost pushing him toward her, almost breaking his resistance. "And you?"

"Certainly," he said. "Of course."

She cleared her throat and glanced about. "I received a missive from Jack. I thought . . . He made it sound as if I were needed."

Her voice was the same as ever. Dulcet, heartbreaking in its beauty. "I received the same letter," he said, his tone sounding gritty against hers.

She dropped her gaze to her hands. They were gloved in soft, ivory suede. "I suspect he wished for us to speak," she said. "Perhaps he thought we could . . ." She paused, and it almost seemed for a moment that her voice quavered. And it was that tiny weakness that drew him forward. But just one step. Just one before he caught himself. "Perhaps he wished for us to mend our differences." She glanced up again, her eyes haunting from the shadow of the russet hood. She looked thin and fragile, fostering a host of unacceptable emotions. She was not his to coddle or even to contemplate, but he could remember how she'd felt in his arms. How she'd made his life worth living. "Where is he now? Do you know?"

"No," Will said, and tightened his fist with his shuddering resolve. "I tried to hold him before, as you know."

"No." Her eyes felt like sunlight against his soul, but she lowered them in a moment. "I suspected there was a history between the two of you, of course. But he never said."

She was wed, he reminded himself again. But did she love him? And what of her husband? Did he know the truth? Did he realize she was everything, all that was good, all that was right with the world?

But Will had no right even to contemplate such things. No right to her at all. He forced his mind away. "He was caught stealing and was about to lose his hand," he said, returning resolutely to the story. "Princess Tatiana stayed the punishment and insisted that I take him in. I fed him, had him tutored, took him here," he said. "To this very church. But I could not make him stay."

Silence again.

"Or wouldn't," he corrected. "Perhaps I didn't want him to. Not really. He was a thief, and my wife had been killed by . . ." He cleared his throat.

"I'm sorry." She glanced toward the door, then down at her hands where they worried each other. "Well . . . I'd best be gone," she said, and turned away.

His heart ripped in his chest. He tried to speak, but she had already stopped, had twisted slightly toward him, though she didn't catch his gaze.

"I want you to know . . ." Her voice was whisper soft, almost inaudible. "That I understand."

He clenched his fists. "Understand what?" He could no longer control his tone, pretend all was well. For all was damnably wrong. He took one rapid step forward, then stopped himself. "Understand what?" he repeated, his voice low in the echoing darkness.

She gave him a hint of a twisted smile. Her eyes shone like silver in the candlelight. Bright as hope. But there was none. "If the situation were reversed . . . perhaps . . . perhaps I would feel the same."

His throat was burning, his heart bleeding. Damn her for making him love her! "Oh?" he said, and breathed a painful laugh. "And how do I feel, Shandria? As if you lied! As if you tore the very heart from my—" He was breathing hard, clenching his fists, struggling for control.

Her face was as pale as winter. "I won't bother you again," she whispered, and turned toward the door.

He caught her before she'd reached it. Caught her without intending to, without conscious thought. But his hand was tight around her arm, and his breath came in hard pants.

Her lips were trembling, her eyes wide, her cheeks wet with tears.

Will's heart jolted to a halt.

"I didn't know about your wife," she whispered. "I would never have . . ." Her words faltered. "But still . . ." She raised her chin. "I understand why you've no wish to see me."

The sanctuary fell into sacred silence. Will stood absolutely still, barely breathing, waiting for the world to make sense.

"You could have told me you are married," he said.

She frowned, her mercurial eyes tortured, her bright mouth twisted. "What?" she whispered.

Anger flooded him. Anger and frustration and raw hopelessness. "Damn you!" he swore, and tightened his grip. "How dare you make me love you?"

They were inches apart. Her eyes were as wide as the heavens. She shook her head. "What?" she whispered again.

He rasped a harsh laugh and jerked his hand away, but God knew the things he wished to do to her.

"They told me you were a spy," he said. "Told me why you were there, in the Den." He longed to turn away, but he couldn't help but look at her. Despite everything, he wanted nothing more than to drink her in, to kiss away her tears, her hurts. "Told me you were married." He laughed. "I shouldn't have been—"

"They lied," she said.

The world crumbled around the edges. Breath refused to come. Silence stretched out tense and quivering between them. "Lied?"

"I'm not wed, Dancer. How could I be . . ." she began, and laughed mirthlessly. "I'm rarely in one place for more than a few months. They send me—"

"You're not wed?" He could barely hear himself over the pounding of his own heart.

"What I told you was true," she said. "About my parents. About Jonathan. I attempted to get his inheritance for him. His father apprehended me." She closed her eyes for a moment. "Since then I've been . . . They could imprison me again," she said. "For my crimes." She shrugged, the movement shallow and quick. "And there's my family."

"They're blackmailing you," he said, but she shook her head.

"Not blackmail. Not anymore. After what I've done . . . what I've seen, what else could I do? I'm not fit . . ." Her face crumbled for an instant, but she straightened. "They tell me I'm needed."

She was. Desperately. And there was hope now, when he thought there was none. "They?" He barely managed the word.

"Jonathan's father is a member of the House of Lords. 'Twas he who first suggested that I . . . assist them."

"Jonathan," he said. "The man you loved. The man you risked your life for . . . he let them use you?"

"He—"

"Tell me, lass," he said, and felt his stomach twist with the question. "Do you plan to spend your entire life protecting those who don't care whether you live or die?"

She lowered her gaze for a fraction of a second. "This last mission was . . ." For a moment the terror escaped her soul and shone like fire in her mercurial eyes. "They are not usually so dangerous."

He watched her, unable to look away, unable to resist the merciful spear of hope.

"Indeed," she continued. "They have promised—"

"I care." The words came unbidden, bursting from his soul, but she shook her head and lowered her gaze to her clasped hands.

"You don't know who I am."

"Maybe not. But I know who I am."

Her eyes snapped to his, surprise and uncertainty making them as wide as the midnight sky.

"I'm selfish," he said. "Cold."

She shook her head, but he hurried on.

"I had a sister. Caroline. She was six years my senior. She was . . ." He drew a deep breath, struggling. "Beautiful. Fragile. My parents . . . The lord and lady of Landow." He drew a deep breath. "They detested each other. Barely spoke. But Father . . ." Oh God. To say it out loud. To say it and know it was true. "Father loved Caroline. Doted on her. Found her. . . . irresistible, I guess." He let the words lie there between them, let the horror sink into her soul as well as his own. "I knew," he said. "I knew something was wrong. She kept growing paler, thinner. I found them together . . . in her bedchamber." It was hard to hold her gaze, harder still to go on, to voice the truth of his sins. "But I was terrified to confront him." He cleared his throat. "Thus I went to Mother."

Her eyes were gigantic. The silence felt heavy and hard.

"Surely she stopped him," she whispered.

He almost smiled at the hope in her voice. "Mother

was very proper. Very . . . strong. I didn't realize how strong. She could throw me across the room. Against the wall. I thought . . . I was a boy, remember, and overly imaginative I suspect, but I truly thought she meant to kill me. She assured me I would suffer worse if I ever spewed such lies again."

"Will—"

He held up a hand. "I told myself there was nothing I could do. And then Caroline became ill. When she died some weeks later it no longer mattered. I told myself it—"

"It wasn't your fault," she said, and her face twisted with pity. "You were just a child yourself. You tried—"

"I failed," he corrected. "She needed me. Needed someone, and I failed. Just as I failed my wife. And my son."

"People die, Will. You can't—"

"But I didn't fail you."

The world settled into silence.

She shook her head. "No," she said, and a tear slipped with sacred slowness down the alabaster beauty of her cheek. "You didn't. You saved my life. I owe you—"

"And you saved my soul." He said the words simply, succinctly. It was so clear now, as ever bright as her eyes. "Marry me," he said.

Her lips parted, but no words came. She shook her head once.

"I don't deserve you," he said. "But I ask nonetheless. Save me again, lass."

She shook her head, her expression still tortured. "I cannot—"

"Please," he whispered.

Her lips moved soundlessly for a moment, then she breathed a laugh. "Have you heard nothing I've said? I've spent most of five years as a thief. My parents are Rom. Yours are nobility."

"Don't say that to me," he said. "Not after what I've told you."

Compassion touched her lovely face, but she went on. "My father whittles wooden toys for children," she said. "My mother sells them for a few sentrons at the villages where they stop. Don't you understand? We're not in your—"

"We'll find them," he said. "Invite them to the wedding."

She huffed a laugh and shook her head. "I don't even know—"

"Will you marry me?"

"Yes," she whispered, and suddenly she was crying. He pulled her into his arms, cradling her against his heart, feeling joy erupt like sunlight in his soul.

"Don't cry," he murmured, though his own cheeks were damp as he stroked her hair. "Don't cry, love. I'm not as bad as all that."

Maybe she chuckled, but he was never sure, for in that moment she lifted her lips to his. They trembled as he kissed her, and the world was right.

But a sniggle of noise sounded from the pews, and in a moment she had jerked a knife from its hidden spot. She would have moved away, but he held her close against him, not daring to let her go.

"Who's there?" he asked.

Silence spilled around them, but finally someone rose from between the benches.

"Nim." Shandria's voice was little more than a hiss.

"'Tis good to see you, Princess." Jack's face was gaunt, but a smile lurked around his mobile mouth.

The boy looked taller, though no broader. Will stroked Shandria's arm. She was real. She was safe. But she was worried for another.

"Where have you been sleeping, lad?" he asked.

"Wherever I wish." Their gazes met. "Well . . ." The boy paused momentarily. "I'd best be getting along," he said, and, turning quickly, hurried between the pews.

Shandria jerked frantic eyes to Will. He felt her angst like a spear in his soul and almost laughed aloud at the poignant opportunity to make her happy.

"Want a job?" he asked, raising his voice.

The boy stopped, turned slowly. "What's that?"

Will shrugged. "The queen's own army couldn't find her," he said, and nodded toward Shandria. She was safe. She was here, in his life, in his arms. "You did."

"The queen?" The boy canted his head. "You mean Princess Anna."

"Yes."

"Is that the maid I knew or the one what came behind her?"

"The second one."

Jack's brows lowered, and he turned away.

"But I see the other regularly."

The boy kept walking.

"I believe she was a thief."

Jack stopped and turned. A smile glimmered in his eyes. "I figured as much. She cheats at dice, you know."

"No," he said, and laughed for the sheer joy of living. "I didn't."

"You sure got yourself in a rough crowd fer such a fancy bloke."

"It's worse than you know, lad. She married a friend of mine. Lord Argyle. Perhaps you remember him."

The boy scowled. "The one what convinced you to take me in?"

"Aye."

Jack nodded, his expression solemn, his eyes intense.

"Is she 'appy?" he asked, and Will smiled at the tenderness in his tone. When Jack loved, it was forever. What a man he could be if there was someone to care. Why hadn't Will recognized such potential before? But the answer was there beside him, in his arms, in his life. "Is she safe?"

"Your Anna?"

The boy seemed nonplussed by the reference and nodded again.

"You could ask her yourself."

The lad's eyes were narrowed, his brow wrinkled.

"Make sure he's treating her well," Will added.

" 'E's wealthy?"

"Yes. A viscount."

"Then I suspect she's in good 'ands," Jack said, and swiveled away.

"She wouldn't turn her back on you, lad," Will said.

The boy glanced around.

"Surely she deserves a visit at least, after searching for you these long months."

"Searching?" His voice was soft. Love was a hard master, breaking down the most belligerent barriers.

"You could visit her," Will repeated. Quiet settled restlessly around them. "Of course, you'd have to live at Landow Manor."

"With you?" he whispered.

Will turned to gaze into Shandria's eyes, then touched her face, because he could, because there was no way to resist. "With us," he said.

"Two princesses," Jack mused and worried his lips. "Sounds confusin'. But I 'spect I could give it a try."

Chapter 28

The palace was filled to brimming. Bouquets of bright blossoms adorned every table. Wedding guests milled about, gossiping and drinking and laughing.

But Will remained silent. He'd always hated weddings, he thought and laughed out loud. Shandria turned toward him, eyes smiling, and he couldn't help but pull her against him, to find her lips with his own, for she was happiness itself.

"Lord Enton."

He turned toward the intruder. "Your Majesty," he said, addressing the young queen. She was both beautiful and kind, but surely she had better things to do than disturb him just then. "And my lord," he said, shifting his gaze to Laird Cairn MacTavish and bowing again. "You honor us."

"We wished to congratulate you," Tatiana said.

"Thank you, Your Majesty."

"And to thank your bonny bride," MacTavish added. "Wheaton has bedeviled Teleere and her allies for a score of years. We suspected one of Sedonia's lords was funding him, but we had no way of knowing Lord Bentor was that man. Not until he took the bait your people had planted."

"I didn't expect him to come to the Den. I assumed Wheaton would take the papers to him," Shandria said.

"As did we. Thus the late arrival," Tatiana admitted. "Had our troops been a few minutes later, your bridegroom would not have had the luxury of swooning."

"Begging your pardon, Your Majesty," Will said, skimming his gaze ruefully to his bride. "I was badly wounded, and—"

"He is fortunate to have had you to save him. Our thanks," MacTavish said, and, taking Shandria's hand, kissed her knuckles.

Will scowled. He had heard somewhere that MacTavish was thought to be the most handsome man in all of Teleere. Of course, they were in Sedonia, but that didn't make his attentions any more welcome.

"I do not deserve your gratitude, my laird," Shandria was saying. "Indeed, it is I who am grateful. We are eternally in your debt. For your forgiveness as well as your timely intervention." She skimmed her eyes to Will. The mental nudge was as sharp as an elbow to the ribs.

"Yes," he agreed, still glaring at their joined hands. "Our deepest thanks."

The royal couple stared at him. "His mouth gives thanks," MacTavish mused, "but his eyes seem to be cursing like a one-legged sea dog."

"Me thinks you're likely to lose a hand if you don't release his bride, lad," someone rumbled.

Raising his gaze, Will watched the giant Highlander shoulder his way through the crowd. Burr, he was called—MacTavish's mentor and well-seasoned guard.

"Truly?" MacTavish said, sounding surprised, though he loosed Shandria's hand as he turned from Burr to his queen. "I thought your William was known to be somewhat restrained?"

"Sometimes people soften under the right influence," Tatiana said.

"Aye," Burr agreed, and chuckled, "though the lad here was already plenty soft afore you come along, lass."

MacTavish turned. Trouble showed in his eyes, replacing the modicum of decorum he'd first exhibited. He had scars aplenty. Rumor had it that more than a few had been caused by his good friend and mentor.

"Are you finally admitting the truth then, old man?" he asked.

Burr's brows lowered. "And what truth is that, laddie?"

"That your weakling tutelage left something to be desired."

The Scotsman smiled. "Are you challenging me, boy?"

"I would," MacTavish said, "but I think I'll let the wee lass take care of that."

"What lass?" Bur rumbled, but his face was already flushed.

"The red-haired one what leads you around by the . . ." The laird paused, skimmed his attention from his wife's high-browed gaze to Shandria. "Nose," he finished.

"I don't know what the devil you're yipping about, but if you hope to leave these festivities afoot, you'd best—"

"Even *your* memory can't have grown that weak, gaffer," MacTavish said.

The Scotsman spread his legs. Beneath his tartan, muscles strained like oaken boughs. "I'd hate to cause bloodshed during the merriment. I've worn me best plaid."

"And I'd hate to bleed," Cairn admitted happily. "Luckily, the lass will protect me."

" 'Twould be a mistake to believe you can hide behind your lady's title," Burr said, and MacTavish laughed.

"Not a'tall," he argued. "I was speaking of *her*."

"Viking," Gem said, and, slipping through the crush, took Burr's arm in both hands. "I've been lookin' for ye."

Burr paled like an untried boy as he glanced down at her. She'd pulled her fire-bright hair up atop her head, and her gown was made of spring green muslin. It hugged her tidy little body like a lover's touch, pressing her pert bosom toward the smiling heavens. The indomitable Highlander looked as if he were about to swoon.

MacTavish beamed. "She's been looking for ye," he reiterated, and Burr rallied weakly, pulling back his gargantuan shoulders with a glare.

"My apologies, lass," he rumbled. "I fear I have important affairs to see to."

Gem scowled and shifted her hand restlessly to his chest. Burr stiffened as if shot. "Can't they wait?" she asked, turning hopefully to MacTavish. "I was 'opin' 'e could teach me to waltz."

The laird of Teleere couldn't have looked happier if he'd been declared God, but he doused the smile and forged a scowl. "I'd like to allow it, lass, but ol' Burroun has been severely injured, and what with his advancing years, I think it best if we coddle him a bit longer."

"Coddle—" Burr growled.

"Aye," MacTavish continued, ignoring him. "Wee bonnie lassies like yourself tend to get old men overexcited, and while even Will here is well past his prime, he'll most likely be able to withstand the rigors of—"

"You watch your mouth around the maids, lad," Burr warned.

"You see," MacTavish said, shaking his head sadly. "He's no longer able even to talk of such things. 'Twould be best if you'd find some young buck to satisfy . . ."

"Shut your trap, boy." Muscles bulged like pythons in

Burr's arms, and his face was red. "I raised you better than to spew such talk."

"Aye, you did," he admitted. "Raised me from a wee bairn. But ye know yourself you're too old to raise up a daughter. True, you won't need to be changin' her swaddling," he said, and grinned. "Though you might want—"

William never saw the Highlander swing. One minute he was standing quietly, the next he was doing the same, only the laird of Teleere had flown into the crowd behind him. He ricocheted off a young gent, who rebounded into another.

MacTavish staggered, found his balance, and grinned.

Gem's eyes were as wide as goblets as she shifted them from the laird to the giant. Burr's eyes were narrow, his face solemn. "Lass," he said, his voice a bear rumble as he turned to face her. A muscle ticked in his jaw, and his face was the color of an autumn apple as he cleared his throat. "Lass," he began again, then, "I'd marry you if you'll have me."

Gem's round mouth opened. She blinked, then leapt into his arms. He caught her with a growl, dragging her to his chest and kissing her with ferocious ardor.

The crowd stared in wide-eyed, speechless shock.

"Triton's ball," MacTavish said, his eyes sparkling with glee. "You'd best save your strength, old man. You already hit like a maid."

The couple didn't seem to notice. Indeed, judging by their actions, it was entirely possible they'd forgotten where they were.

MacTavish cleared his throat, and, finally, Burr drew back his head and allowed Gem to slide to the floor, though he still held her tightly against his chest. "You looking for more trouble, lad?"

"I'd like to," MacTavish admitted, and shook his head

as if deathly disappointed, "but I think the lass here has other plans for you just now."

Burr turned his gaze to Gem, and his eyes softened. Gone was the warrior who had hewn a throne for his chosen laird. In his place was a man humbled by love.

Rising on her toes, Gem whispered something in the Scotsman's ear. Will would have sworn Burr's face couldn't flush any darker. He would have been wrong again.

Rumbling a good-bye, Burr bent, lifted Gemini into his arms, and plowed a path through the crowd.

MacTavish waited until he was well out of sight to cradle his chin. "Triton's balls! I think he broke me jaw."

Queen Tatiana sighed. "One shouldn't bait the bear if one doesn't wish to be eaten," she said, and turned briefly toward the newlyweds. "If you'll excuse us, I think we'd best leave before my clever husband falls on his face."

MacTavish smiled blearily. "I had little choice," he explained. "He's been miserable since the lass left Westheath."

"Aye, you're a wonderful friend," Tatiana said wryly, and touched his face with tender fingertips.

He grinned as he caught her hand. "Let me prove it," he murmured.

She blushed, and her words were too soft to hear, but their exodus spoke volumes.

Shandria blinked. "Interesting friends you have."

Will turned toward her, feeling the warmth of her presence, the beauty that was her. "Do you think so?"

She raised a brow, and he laughed in that hopelessly euphoric manner he'd always detested in others. "I suspect you're right," he said. "I simply didn't notice before I met you." He found her hand and drew her close. "Before I was alive."

Her eyes met his, then she kissed him, slow and warm

and promising. Feelings swirled like magic, tingling his nerve endings, tightening his body.

"You're alive now," she murmured.

"Aye," he agreed, "I believe I am," he said, and, lifting her into his arms, followed the Highlander through the crowd and into happiness.

Roses are red, violets are blue,
but these books are much more fun than flowers!
Coming to you in February from Avon Romance . . .

Something About Emmaline by Elizabeth Boyle

An Avon Romantic Treasure

Alexander Denford, Baron Sedgwick is a gentleman much envied for his indulgent and oft-absent wife, Emmaline—who is in fact a mere figment meant to keep the *ton* mamas at bay. But one day Alexander starts receiving bills from London for ball gowns in his imaginary bride's name, and he realizes a real Emmaline is about to present herself, whether he likes it or not!

Hidden Secrets by Cait London

An Avon Contemporary Romance

A missing boy, an unsolved murder, the feeling of impending danger. Marlo cannot figure out how they are connected—until she finds and develops an old roll of film that unlocks the past. But as she gets closer to the truth of the missing boy, she must choose between two men for protection. And if she makes one wrong move, it will be her last . . .

In the Night by Kathryn Smith

An Avon Romance

A life of crime is not what Wynthrope Ryland wanted for himself, but he will do what he must—if only to protect his dearest brother, North. Moira Tyndale, a stately viscountess, is to be the victim of this ill-timed theft, but she is also the one woman who can tempt him . . . or perhaps, somehow, set his wrongs to rights.

Stealing Sophie by Sarah Gabriel

An Avon Romance

Connor MacPherson, a Highland laird turned outlaw, must find a bride—or steal one. Intending to snatch infamously wanton Kate MacCarran, he mistakenly abducts her sister, Sophie—recently returned from a French convent. Quickly wedded, passionately bedded, Sophie cannot escape, and cannot be rescued—but perhaps this is not such a bad thing after all!

REL 0105